Saving the Winchester Inn

Sofia Sawyer

Champagne Book Group

Saving the Winchester Inn

This is a work of fiction. The characters, incidents and dialogues in this book are of the author's imagination and are not to be construed as real. Any resemblance to actual events or persons, living or dead, is completely coincidental.

Published by Champagne Book Group
2373 NE Evergreen Avenue, Albany OR 97321 U.S.A.

~~~

First Edition 2020

pISBN: 979-8-578659-56-0

Copyright © 2020 Sofia Sawyer All rights reserved.

Cover Art by Robyn Hart

Champagne Book Group supports copyright which encourages creativity and diverse voices, creates a rich culture, and promotes free speech. Thank you by complying by not scanning, uploading, and distributing this book via any means without the permission of the publisher. Your purchase of an authorized edition supports the author's rights and hard work and allows Champagne Book Group to continue to bring readers fiction at its finest.

www.champagnebooks.com

Version_1

*For those who are still searching for
a place where they feel they belong.
I hope you find it.*

Chapter One

Cordelia Winchester's phone vibrated across the glass top of her desk, disrupting her from her work. She dragged her gaze from her computer and glared at her cell, noting the area code from her quaint hometown in North Carolina.

"Not today, robocaller," she muttered, hitting the ignore button.

Anyone she needed to talk to from Fraser Hills was programmed into her contacts. If it was important, they'd leave a message. As the director of one of Boston's premier event planning companies, she was too busy for unsolicited calls, real or telemarketing.

Turning back to her laptop, she scanned her endless to-do list, her eyebrows pulling together as she focused on the overwhelming tasks left. Christmas was always crunch time for her company. Holiday parties. Galas. Fundraisers. All extravagant events for clients with deep pockets. They wanted the best of the best, and she was expected to move mountains to give it to them.

More importantly, in less than a month, Cordelia will have pulled off the most prestigious event she'd ever been tasked with. Elizabeth Sinclair's holiday fundraiser was an opportunity of a lifetime, and if all went well, it would seal the deal for the promotion to vice president Cordelia had tirelessly worked for.

Eight years of long days, compromised weekends, and sacrificed free time would actually mean something.

Everything was riding on this.

She couldn't afford to be distracted. Not even for a minute.

I just have to survive these next five weeks.

Her phone vibrated again. It seemed louder and more annoying than last time, grating on her nerves. She closed her eyes, sucked in some air, and let out a controlled breath before picking it up and checking the display.

A photo of her younger brother appeared on the screen. As much as she loved him, he didn't have a clue as to what was appropriate conversation during business hours. Cordelia had been caught on one too many calls with him babbling about God only knew what. That was the benefit of living at home and working part-time at her family's tree farm. He had all the time in the world to chat.

She, however, did not.

Her boss, Melody Kensie, owner of Kensie Affairs, breezed through the doorway, startling Cordelia. Fumbling with her phone, she quickly hit the ignore button before placing it face down on her desk.

I hate when she does that.

"Melody. H-hi. H-how was your Thanksgiving?"

"Adequate," Melody responded without a hint of emotion. Her skin was wrinkle-free thanks to her permanent Scarlett O'Hara face—not a smile in sight. Ever.

Cordelia straightened and folded her hands on her desk to convey she was the capable and competent professional Melody relied on. "How can I help you?" she asked, forcing her voice to sound confident.

"I want a status update on the Sinclair event. Now." Cutting and direct as always.

Melody was one of Boston's elite, having started her business at the ripe age of twenty. Now in her forties—not that she'd ever admitted it—her high standards and unrelenting expectations could strike fear in even the thickest-skinned person.

Cordelia grabbed her planner from the desk and flipped it open, resisting the urge to wipe her sweaty palms on her slacks. "Absolutely."

If there was one thing she learned from working with Melody, it was to always be prepared. She'd seen colleagues get fired for merely hesitating. Cordelia wasn't about to lose that promotion now, not for something so stupid.

"Cordelia," the sweet voice of the young office manager sounded on her desk phone intercom. "Your brother's on line one."

Cordelia tried not to let her agitation flare at his poor timing and punched the button to respond. "Thank you, Talia, but I'm in a meeting. Can I call him back?" She eyed Melody and noted her slight look of annoyance.

"He says it's urgent," Talia responded.

Melody arched an eyebrow, a simple gesture that always made Cordelia feel small. "My office. Fifteen minutes." She left the room without waiting for a response.

Cordelia clicked a button next to the blinking red light and lifted the receiver to her ear. Cocking her head to peer through the glass door of her office, she spotted Melody speaking to another colleague just outside. Cordelia spun away from the door and ducked behind her desk as if that position would prevent Melody from overhearing.

"Mike, this isn't a good time," she whispered into the phone.

"Lia!"

She winced at her childhood nickname. No matter how many times she told her brother she went by Cordelia now, he still insisted on using it. As much as she wanted to correct him again, she'd have to pick her battles. Right now, she needed to get him off the phone ASAP.

She peeked over her shoulder and let out a breath when Melody disappeared into her office. She straightened. "What do you need, Mike?" she asked in a clipped voice.

"It's Mom and Dad," he started, causing her pulse to spike.

Her parents were getting older. It was only a matter of time before health issues kicked in. Although her family's inn kept them young and spry, as her father would say, there was only so much a person could do to pause Father Time.

"What about them?"

"There's been an accident at the inn." His phone crackled, making the news more ominous.

She stood from her chair and placed a shaky hand on her desk for balance. "Are they okay?"

"They're in rough shape, but the doctor says they'll recover." He sighed. "The inn took a beating too."

"What do you mean?"

"There was a freak storm last night. Mom and Dad were in the upstairs room toward the back. You know, the one that overlooks the big Fraser?"

"Yeah, I remember." Her breath caught in her throat as she waited for Mike to get to the point.

"Well, they were prepping for guests coming the following day, and I guess some rough wind caused the tree to snap. That thing was old, it was going to happen eventually. The top fell onto the roof, and it collapsed. It all came down on them."

Cordelia gasped, hand to heart. "My God. How bad are their injuries?"

"Took a bit to pull them out from the debris. Dad has a collapsed lung and a broken rib. Mom has some bruising around the face and a fractured wrist. All in all, they didn't make out too bad, considering."

She lowered herself into her chair as she processed the news. "That's horrible."

"Yeah. I tried calling from the hospital a few minutes ago to let you know what the doctor said." If Mike was agitated with her, he didn't sound it. If anything, his voice hinted of exhaustion and stress.

Guilt for ignoring the call hit her hard. Cell service was spotty in that part of town, which explained the poor connection now. He likely had to drive a few miles just to get a couple of bars. "Sorry, Mike. I had no idea."

"That's not the only reason why I'm calling." He paused for a minute, his tone more serious than she'd ever heard. "With Mom and Dad out of commission for the next few weeks, we need your help."

"Sure, whatever you need. I'll transfer funds later today. Just tell me how much."

"No, Lia," he said with exasperation. "We need you. Here. To run the Winchester Inn."

"No way." She took a breath and checked her harsh tone. "This is my busy season. I can't leave Boston right now."

"Yeah. We're well aware. You've missed the last couple of Thanksgivings and Christmases because of it."

Was that attitude?

His words only intensified the tightness in her chest. "I have an enormous event to deal with. Coming home isn't an option."

"You know Christmas is our prime season for tourism. With the Winchester Inn needing repairs, we're losing reservations. Things have been tight for the last few years, sis. Mom never told you because she didn't want you to worry, but if we can't pull through this year, the inn's done for. Our family legacy will be gone." There was another pregnant pause. "It will affect the town too."

She had made it a point to walk away from that life years ago, giving them a clear message she didn't want the family legacy to be *her* legacy. She wanted something of her own, and she had stuck to that.

Now, she was getting sucked back in.

Cordelia was lodged between a rock and a hard place, but how could she consider *not* going? Her poor parents were in the hospital, and their inn was struggling.

And the quiet desperation in Mike's voice chilled her. It was rare to see her little brother so serious about anything, which only made the situation that much more alarming.

Sighing, she said, "Let me figure out some things and get back to you."

"Tonight?"

"Yes."

Cordelia hung up, closed her eyes, and rubbed her temples, trying to relieve the tension headache threatening to ruin her day.

It didn't work.

Opening her eyes again, she turned to her computer and scrolled through her jam-packed schedule. Flying home seemed impossible, that was obvious. Her boss had given her the opportunity to prove herself, and although she'd been an exceptional employee, she didn't have the leverage to take time off to go to North Carolina. Not with this high-profile event in the works on top of the other five she was planning simultaneously.

Melody was, in a word, tough. She had high expectations and a low tolerance for "slackers." And it didn't take much for someone to be placed in the slacker camp. Cordelia worried that even broaching the subject would knock her out of the running for the promotion.

But then there was Mike. He seemed…distressed. Her usually affable, easygoing brother was actually concerned. If he was concerned, then she should be tenfold.

Cordelia stood from her desk and walked to the oversized windows that overlooked the city streets of Boston. Even with the overcast day, enough light filtered in so she didn't need to turn on the harsh fluorescents. She preferred the natural light. It was nice to have a bit of nature streaming in when she spent her days surrounded by skyscrapers and concrete.

She caught her reflection in the glass. Her tailored slacks, silk blouse, and sleek brown hair made her appear poised and sophisticated. Inside, however, she was anything but. If she thought she was stressed before, her levels were now well off the charts.

Looking down from the tenth story window to Congress Street, she watched a steady stream of people walked below on a purposeful mission to wherever they needed to be. Even though it was the day after Thanksgiving, Bostonians were still hard at work, as was she. Most people would argue they were workaholics, but she respectfully disagreed. This was a city of the doers, the innovators, and the ambitious. Things happened in Boston, which was what drew her there for college. It was a far cry from her sleepy hometown, nestled in the mountains. Fraser Hills was quiet, predictable, and boring.

When she decided to leave home, she knew she wanted to be working alongside these brilliant, determined New Englanders with their big ideas and endless energy. It was also one of the reasons she stayed after graduation. The constant buzz of exciting things on the horizon was addictive.

Beyond the bustling sidewalk, families cheered as their children gleefully threw what they pretended was tea overboard the Boston Tea Party Museum ship's railings. Although tourism was lighter in the colder months, Cordelia assumed they were here to catch the last of the autumn leaves or to spend the holidays with family who lived nearby.

Family.

She couldn't turn a blind eye and let them fend for themselves. She loved her parents and brother, and respected all they did to keep the Winchester Inn running as the heart of Fraser Hills.

This couldn't have happened at a worse time.

The Sinclair event was for a vocal woman who challenged everything she did. Cordelia often ended her day in bed with a splitting headache, a side effect of her clenching her teeth in a pleasant smile as she tried not to let Elizabeth's constant criticisms get under her skin. It wouldn't be easy to move up to the VP role, but she could have done without the snide remarks. Or those damned pursed lips Elizabeth made whenever she was disappointed.

Which was always, it seemed.

Cordelia straightened and composed herself, smoothing the nonexistent wrinkles from her slacks. She lifted her head in determination.

One week to go home and get things sorted out. Maybe less.

If there was one thing Cordelia possessed, it was impeccable work ethic. She'd proven time and time again she could manage a lot, flawlessly handling the curveballs often lobbed at her. Melody couldn't deny that.

Cordelia'd jump on a flight, check on her parents, find them temporary help, and come back to Boston. She'd convince her boss nothing would fall through the cracks. After all, it was a digital world these days. She'd be accessible 24/7 by email, phone call, text message, or video. Her clients would be none the wiser she was out of town.

One week, that was all. Cordelia would assure Melody that despite the circumstances, she had everything under control.

Dear God, I hope so.

Chapter Two

Two days later, Cordelia stood outside the Asheville Regional Airport. Slipping on her sunglasses to battle the glare of the sunrise, she scanned the area for the car rental stand.

A gust of wind whipped around her, giving her cheeks a healthy sting and offering a not-so-subtle reminder to zip up her jacket. Despite being in the South, it was cold. Not the same cold as in Boston, which seeped deep into your bones and made you think you'd never know what warmth felt like again. Instead, the mountain air here was reinvigorating and intoxicating, inspiring one to get outside and take a hike through the woods or hit the slopes.

Taking a deep breath, she filled her lungs, easing the tension she'd held on to for far too long.

What would it be like to have time to do those things again?

She sighed. This was no time for nostalgia or comparisons. Time was ticking. She needed to get the car, drive the forty-five minutes west to Fraser Hills, check on her parents, meet with the contractors she'd thankfully strong-armed into coming on short notice, ensure the inn was in good hands, and get out.

Based on her schedule, it would take four days, tops. Maybe three if she didn't tap into the contingency time she scheduled for the unexpected.

She prayed she wouldn't need it. Although Melody had allowed her to take the short trip, it was obvious Cordelia was on thin ice. As the lead event planner, the only way she'd been able to convince Melody was by promising she'd be back in time to run point for the Sinclair event at the State Room, a breathtaking venue in Boston.

Craning her head to the right, Cordelia spotted a tiny sign with an arrow directing people to the otherwise hidden rental booth. Beelining for it, she opened the glass door and was greeted by a smiling face.

"Well hello there, ma'am," the young boy said. "How may I help you today?"

It took her a moment to process his accent. Did the people here really have that strong of a twang? No wonder her college roommates poked fun at her, so much so that she tried to tone it down to fit in with the Northerners. Doing it for as long as she had, her Southern accent was now practically nonexistent.

"I have a reservation for Cordelia Winchester." Placing her stylish carry-on on the laminate-tiled floor, she folded her manicured hands on the counter as she waited for the teen to access her information.

"Alrighty. Here we go, ma'am. I see a Hyundai sedan reserved for four days with a drop off at this location." He looked up from the screen and shot her another cheery smile. "Is that correct?"

She nodded and suppressed the urge to tap her foot, her patience already wearing thin. She forgot how slow everything moved here. "Yes, thanks."

"Great." He swiveled the screen to face her. "I'll need you to review this information and sign at the bottom. I'll pull the car out front in the meantime."

"Perfect." She scrolled through the endless forms, opting out of unnecessary add-ons, and signed at the bottom. By the time she was done, the employee was back and handing her the keys.

"Drive safe." He shook her hand enthusiastically.

She gave a tight smile in return. In Boston, you were lucky to get eye contact, let alone a grunt of acknowledgment. All this chatting and grinning was throwing her off.

She grabbed her bag and exited the rental store. Placing her carry-on in the trunk, she slipped into the driver's seat and got situated. Pulling up her map app, she plugged in the address for the Winchester Inn to see which route would get her there the fastest. Every option lit up green.

Hmm, I guess there's not much traffic this early in the morning.

It was a rare occurrence to find traffic moving freely in Boston this close to rush hour. The smooth ride would be a treat.

The drive to Fraser Hills was uneventful, if not productive. As Cordelia navigated the empty roads through small towns and farmlands, she made calls to the office and her vendors, and gave an update to her most important client, Elizabeth Sinclair. By the time she ended the call, she had turned off the highway and taken the exit ramp that led to Fraser Hills Road, the main street that went through downtown.

Her breath hitched as the town came into view. The impeccably clean streets were lined with cute shops, restaurants, cafes, and stores. The center of the main road had a roundabout with a small park. A picturesque gazebo sat square in the middle. But it wasn't the small-town America feel that was appealing, it was seeing it with the Great Smoky

Mountains backdrop. The distant mountain range looked like it was outlined in blue, and the infinite trees lining the hills were now speckled with yellows, oranges, and reds as if someone painted them just that morning. The mountains protected the town, cocooning it in a valley of impenetrable walls.

Maybe that was part of the reason Cordelia left in the first place. She felt safe in Fraser Hills and sheltered in the valley. *Too* safe. If you hiked up far enough, you could see the town, a small speck in an otherwise rural area of North Carolina. Whereas other people thought the open lands were freeing, to her, the nothingness was suffocating, closing in on her each day that passed. The disconnectedness from the world made it hard to envision a fulfilling future.

She wanted more for her life than what would be passed down to her, which is why she purposely traded in mountains for skyscrapers. A future could lie in any one of those tall, shiny buildings. And if not, she could easily hop on one of the many flights around the world to find a new calling. The world was at her fingertips in Boston.

Staying in Fraser Hills would have been too easy. Wasn't life about handling challenges head on to see what you were made of? About discovering you could do more and be more than whatever you'd been pigeonholed into?

Taking the roundabout, she passed by Evergreen Avenue and continued on Fraser Hills Road. She loved this section of the main strip, with the manicured Fraser firs lining the median and the rushing stream that ran under the small bridge, leading to the heart of the town: the Winchester Inn. Her home.

Despite being the largest building in town, it was homey. Off-white cypress siding covered the two-story structure, complete with black shutters that lined large windows. An ornate wrap-around porch dominated the first floor, with a wide staircase leading up to two windowed wooden doors. Rocking chairs painted deep blue and window boxes filled with seasonal flowers gave the inn a pop of color. Smoke floated lazily from the chimney.

Cordelia remembered sitting on those rocking chairs in the fall when she was growing up, wrapped in a throw blanket, a mug of hot chocolate keeping her hands warm. She enjoyed watching the leaves change and the town slow down right before the holiday rush started.

Aside from Christmas, fall was her favorite time of year. Although Boston didn't provide the same serenity as a rocking chair on the veranda did, she embraced the vibrant colors of the trees through the crisp autumn months. During the rare free time she found, she'd visit one of the local parks when the colors were at their peak. Those days, she could breathe.

In the fast-paced life she lived, it was hard to remember to do that sometimes.

She pulled into the circular driveway and parked. Stepping out of the sedan, she made her way to the back of the inn to see the damaged roof, following a stone pathway around the side of the inn, which stopped before it reached where she needed to be. She eyed the soggy ground and then down at the pumps she was wearing.

Not exactly made for off-roading.

Leaning around the corner of the house, she noticed the remainder of the giant Fraser fir towering precariously over the inn. The top had broken off and was now lying on the ground, chopped into pieces. She tilted her head for a better view of the collapsed roof but couldn't get the right angle.

Assessing the muddy ground again, she identified a few dryer spots along the way. If she could make it to those, she would be fine. Kind of like playing the lava game when she was a kid.

She took a giant step, reaching the first dry area successfully, and then a small leap to the next. More confident with her decision, she hopped along to the section she needed to inspect. She was mid-hop to the next spot, but before she could land, something flashed in her peripheral vision and slammed into her knees, causing her to pinwheel her arms to keep her balance. But it didn't work. The next thing she knew, she was flat on her back.

In the mud.

She laid in the cold slop, stunned by what happened, and tried to catch her breath. A moment later, a face hovered over her and gave her a sloppy, wet kiss.

"Willow," a voice commanded from a distance. The dog stopped its frantic kissing and ran to the man who was calling.

Cordelia pushed onto her elbows and took stock of the damage to her body and clothes. Her back was sore and the cold seeped through her slacks and jacket, causing a chill to run up her spine. Her pants were caked in mud—they would be impossible to clean—and one of her pumps stuck out from the mud, doing its best reenactment of the Titanic in its final moments.

A hand thrust in front of her face. She grabbed it without looking up, but couldn't help noticing the owner of said hand lifted her with ease. She bent to pull her shoe out of the ground, and her gaze trailed up the length of the man who had helped her.

Work boots. Long, solid legs in dark jeans. Broad shoulders and athletic build. All very nice, but it was his face that had her heart beating uncontrollably. His strong jaw was covered with dirty-blond scruff, and his olive complexion complemented his light brown hair, which still held hints of being sun-kissed from the summer. Blue-gray eyes popped under his thick eyebrows, and full lips hitched up on one side in a boyish smile.

He was ruggedly handsome, not at all like the clean-cut, well-manicured men from the city.

"Looks like you're a long way from home," he noted in a playful tone. His deep voice had a hint of Southern to it, but not from the Carolinas. Cowboy, maybe.

Next to him sat the dog who knocked her over, a shaggy golden retriever mix with random tufts of hair spiking out awkwardly. Her ears were covered in crinkled hair like they were styled after an eighties icon, personifying a bad hair day.

The dog gave a big lopsided smile, its tongue lolling.

"She yours?" Cordelia asked as she tried to shake the clumps of mud off her pants.

"Yup. Sorry about that. She gets excited sometimes. She saw you hopping around and thought you were playing." He patted the dog on the head and pure adoration filled her goofy face. "This your first time here?" Another attractive grin crossed his features as he nodded at the shoe in her hand.

She bristled at the realization he was mocking her. Patronizing her. She dealt with that type of "humor" while building her career in Boston. She battled it and won.

She'd be damned if he thought he could get away with it.

~ * ~

Logan MacDermot appraised the woman and her sudden change in demeanor. She went from adorably embarrassed to prickly and cold. Straightening her back, she raised her chin as if to assert dominance and prepare to battle.

For what? He didn't know.

But it was clear she wasn't about to back down, even if she looked ridiculous, all full of mud with her one heeled foot slowly sinking into the ground.

Her light brown eyes turned to honey as the sun broke from a cloud and shined down on them. They were beautiful, even if they were tiny slits staring him down.

"For your information," she said in a steely tone, "this *is* my home."

Logan cocked his head in confusion. "I'm sorry?"

She huffed a breath. Her tight smile was meant to intimidate. "I'm Cordelia Winchester. This is my family's home."

He recalled the photos scattered around the main lobby of the inn. Mariam and Ron had many pictures of their family, with Mike and his sister, Lia, in various stages of their childhood. They often featured a lanky, freckle-faced girl with wild curls who was always up to something. Hiking, working with animals, steering the Christmas sleigh. Every picture showed her with the biggest smile.

He took in the woman in front of him with her straight brown hair, unblemished skin, and curves he could tell were hidden under her jacket. Not a smile or freckle in sight. This couldn't be the same person, could it? Yet, out of all the stories Mariam had shared with him, she'd never once mentioned another daughter, so it had to be.

She held her head high as if she were royalty, and he supposed in a town like this, she was.

Although, for one wavering moment, uncertainty flashed across her face, but in an instant, it was gone.

"Cordelia." He let the name roll over his tongue. "You mean Lia? Little Lia Winchester? The prodigal daughter has returned." He hoped his light teasing would get her to loosen up a bit.

She scowled at him. He rewarded it with a smile that only seemed to irritate her more. "It's Cordelia. And you are?"

"Logan MacDermot. I'm the superintendent. I make sure everything's in working order at the inn." They both turned to the roof's gaping hole. "Well, almost everything. That'll be fixed in no time though." He held out his hand and she eyed it like he was handing her a dead fish, refusing to take it.

Okay then.

"Mac's our superintendent."

He dropped his hand and stuffed it into his pocket. Clearly, he wouldn't be getting a warm welcome from this ice queen. Lia may have grown up in the South, but her Southern hospitality was long gone. "Mac *was* your superintendent. He retired four months ago and moved down to Tybee Island. Wanted to enjoy the island life for his retirement."

She crossed her arms. "Why wasn't I told about this?"

He shrugged. "From what I understand, you don't want much to do with the inn." At least that's what Mike said when Ron urged him to call her after the accident.

If his statement bothered her, she didn't appear ruffled by it. "Well, I'm here now."

"That you are."

Chapter Three

Cordelia stomped through the grass—no longer caring about the mud—toward the cabins located behind the inn used for housing her family and the superintendent. After she moved away and her brother had gotten older, her parents converted the large cabin they grew up in into two smaller one-bedroom cabins so Mike could have his own private space.

She pounded on his door.

Swinging it open, he beamed when he saw her. "Lia." He went in for a hug, arms outstretched to embrace her, but stopped and stepped back when he saw her muddy clothes. "Come in."

"What happened to Mac?" she demanded as she pushed by him and into the kitchen.

"Whoa, whoa. Easy now. It's a little too early to be this worked up." He ran a hand through his thick, disheveled hair.

She shot him a pointed look and turned on the kitchen sink, scrubbing at her filthy hands. "Who's managing the inn if you're still in bed?" She didn't want to sound judgy, but this was typical Mike. Unreliable. If her parents could trust him to step up, she wouldn't have had to adjust her whole week to come down here.

"I just came from there. Everything's taken care of for now." He flopped onto the small couch like his schedule was wide open for the day. "Plus, reservations are down, like I told you on the phone. Word got out about the damage and now people are cancelling. There aren't too many guests to deal with for the breakfast rush, and I have calls forwarding to my cell."

"How down is 'down?'" This was the town's busiest time of year. The inn was *always* full.

"It's not looking good."

She stood in front of him in her power stance and folded her arms across her chest. "Stop stalling. Spill it."

"Ten rooms are currently booked."

"Ten?" Her voice raised in disbelief. "That's half capacity."

Mike grimaced. "I know. And the reservations don't pick up again until closer to Christmas. That's only if more people don't pull out between now and then. Yelp and TripAdvisor reviews are killing us."

Bewildered, Cordelia shook her head. "I thought the roof issue only affected two rooms."

"Technically, yes. The tree damaged the roof above two rooms. But…" He paused.

"What?" She gritted her teeth.

"Donnelly Matthews is our inspector. He wants us to fix the roof for the whole back section of the inn, plus the right side. Something about it not being up to code." Mike made air quotes.

Donnelly was from the neighboring town, Mountain Village, fifteen minutes up the road. Fraser Hills and Mountain Village have been rivals for decades. As the story went, the towns' tree acreages ran alongside each other, and although both towns were lucrative in their businesses and worked in harmony by agreeing to sell to different regions, a forest fire broke out and destroyed the majority of Mountain Village's trees.

Fraser Hills had been somehow left unscathed, causing Mountain Villagers to accuse them of sabotage. There were no witnesses or leads as to how the fire started, even to this day. The two towns have had bad blood since.

Without the tree trade, Mountain Village had fallen into disarray. People left, businesses closed, and upkeep was hard. It wasn't until another ten years after the fire had passed that their Fraser trees grew back. By then, many of their customers were now working with Fraser Hills. Their neighborly peace had been destroyed in that fire and never recovered.

"Donnelly Matthews." Her voice rose so high, she was almost surprised it didn't shatter the windows. "Of course. Those people have it out for us."

"Well, maybe," Mike agreed. "But let's be real. The inn's two hundred years old. And, sure, we've made updates and renovated throughout those years, but we haven't touched the roof since before Mom and Dad took it over. Tree aside, the roof could have collapsed on any one of our guests if we had a big blizzard or something."

Cordelia bit her bottom lip. "But it hit them instead," she whispered to herself. Digging a towel out of the hallway linen closet, she tossed it on the couch and took a seat next to him, weary from the chaos of this morning. "How are they? I was going to stop by their cabin now."

"Dad's gonna take longer to recover, but they think he'll be up and about in a week. Mom has a splint on her wrist and is in pain but will be mobile much sooner. The doc has them on some heavy-duty pain medication. They're probably knocked out still."

"Maybe I shouldn't bother them yet."

He bumped shoulders with her. "Yeah. Give them a couple more hours of rest. In the meantime, let's look at Logan's proposal for the roof repairs."

"What's his deal anyway? What happened to Mac?"

"Mac was getting up there, Lia. It was time for him to retire, so he referred his nephew. Said he wanted us to be left in good hands."

"Nephew?"

"Yeah," he said it as if she were slow. "Logan *Mac*Dermot is Mac's nephew who relocated here from Charleston." She still wasn't following. He sighed and rolled his eyes. "Mac's name is Murphy MacDermot. How did you not know this?"

She shrugged. "He was always Mac to me. I never heard anything different."

"Christ. He's not Madonna. Of course he has a full name."

She scowled at him. "Okay, you don't have to treat me like an idiot."

"This is one of those rare occasions when I can, so please let me just have this moment." He laughed as she swatted at him. Mike dodged her blow and dug his phone out of his pocket, opened up an email, and passed it to her. "Here are the numbers."

She scanned through them, her blood pressure rising and temple throbbing as she read. "These prices are ridiculous. This guy is taking advantage of our situation."

Her distrust for Logan grew even more. She stood, ready to hunt him down and give him a piece of her mind.

Mike jumped to his feet and blocked the door. "Don't you think you're acting kinda unreasonable? We have two-thirds of a roof to repair and replace. It wasn't going to be chump change."

"I've been dealing with vendors long enough to know the typical markup. These prices make me suspect he's trying to skim some extra money for himself."

Early in her career, she'd learned that lesson the hard way. People saw a young woman new in her field and took advantage, making her believe she got the best deal so she didn't bother to negotiate.

Contractors had always been the worst offenders, mansplaining things to confuse her so much she'd blindly trust their word.

She wouldn't fall for that again.

"Lia," Mike warned, "I think you've got him all wrong."

"You haven't been out in the real world, so you don't get that

19

people like him and Donnelly exploit those who are too trusting or uninformed. This guy is going to swindle us."

"Ouch. That was uncalled for, don't you think? Maybe I didn't jet off to Boston, but I still can spot a snake when I see one. Why would he try to bankrupt the inn when we're the ones who pay his salary?"

Pushing him aside, she ignored his good point. The pressure to get things done in four days might be making her a touch irrational, but Cordelia wouldn't get results by pussyfooting around. "I'll take care of this."

~ * ~

From the inn's second story window, Logan watched Lia storm across the grounds from Mike's cabin. She managed to make good time to the inn's back entrance even with her heels sticking every step of the way.

From a distance, he could see her jaw set in that angry, determined way of hers and wondered what pissed her off this time.

Who knew that a kind, loving, and easygoing couple like Ron and Mariam could produce such a little firecracker?

Logan turned from the window and started to clean the collapsed roof. The sheetrock from the ceiling covered the guest bed. One of the windows had been boarded up after being shattered by a branch. Wooden rafters lie broken on the floor. The tarp covering the roof's substantial hole shifted as a light breeze passed over it. From the looks of the debris, he had his work cut out for him.

Thankfully, Jim Smith at the nearby mill had extra time on his hands, so Logan was able to contract him at a fair price. With Jim on board, Logan expected to get the work done in half the time and for significantly cheaper than the local contractors, which was a relief. Christmas meant everything to the town, and he wanted to do right by Mariam and Ron. They'd been nothing but welcoming since he arrived nearly four months ago.

After moving fallen sheetrock out of the way, he turned to grab a rafter, finding Lia standing behind him.

"Jesus!" How she managed to get to him so fast and so quietly was baffling. She seethed, still in her mud-covered clothes. "Don't you want to get changed? You look like you lost a wrestling match with a pig. You'll scare the guests like that."

She waved his comment off. "There are more important things to discuss first, like the ridiculous cost to replace the roof."

"It needs structural repairs too. Donnelly—"

"I know all about Donnelly. Regardless of the added construction needed, the price is inflated."

He crossed his arms and her gaze flicked to his biceps before looking back at him. "What are you implying, Lia?"

There was something refreshing about her brazen personality. Her accusations were uncalled for, but it only made him want to rile her up more. And judging by earlier, he'd already figured out which of her hot buttons to push.

There was that scowl again. "It's Cordelia. And what I'm implying is you're overcharging us." Her voice was strong and commanding. Mariam always gushed about how quickly Lia had moved up in her career, and he understood why. She was terrifying.

About as terrifying as a growling puppy.

"I've met people like you in my line of work," she continued. "You take advantage of others when they don't have any other options. I know you're a stranger here—"

"I may not have grown up here like most of you, but I'm no stranger." Logan dropped his arms and closed the distance between them. Her eyes went wide, and she sucked in a breath, but didn't move. "Look around you. Maybe things seem the same on the surface, but a lot has changed since you last took any interest in this town. You had no clue Mac left or that the inn and town were having trouble for years. If there's a stranger here, it's *you*."

She clamped her mouth shut, her lips forming a tight line, seemingly stunned speechless.

He wondered how long it had been since someone challenged her like this.

"What's more," he added, "I'm aware of what's at stake here. My uncle loved this place and your family. I knew what I was getting into when I came here and have no intention of taking advantage of your family, one that my uncle thought of as his own."

Silence hung between them as they stared each other down.

"Don't touch a thing until I get comparable quotes from other companies. Got it?"

He ran his hand through his shaggy hair and exhaled. "Do what you have to, but my quote is the best you'll get. I've been in this business since I was old enough to hold a hammer. I grew up fixing and building things on my family's ranch in Texas, and I've worked within the constraints of historic architectural refurbishing in Charleston. I know how to repair this inn the best and most cost-effective way I can. You won't find better. Mark my words."

"We'll see." She turned on her heel to go.

"One more thing, Lia," he said, making her pause at the door, her back still turned to him. "You may run the show up in Boston, but you'll soon learn I'm not one to shy away or back down."

She stood there for a moment longer, and he was sure she was ramping up for another snarky remark.

Instead, she left the room just as silently as she had come.

Chapter Four

Cordelia's determination was something she prided herself on. But what she called determination, others would call stubbornness. In this case, she agreed with them.

After cleaning up and changing at Mike's, she met with three local construction companies she'd previously scheduled to come out and give a quote. A couple of frustrating hours later, she concluded Logan was right. Not only was he the cheapest by a long shot, but he was the only one who could complete the work before well before Christmas.

Not quite ready to admit she was wrong, she put a pin in that conversation to check on her parents.

Now that it was late enough in the morning, she finally made her way to their cabin and knocked on the front door, cracking it open.

"Anyone awake?" she called out into the open living space.

"Lia, honey," her mom's voice sounded in the distance. "Is that really you?"

"It's me."

"Well come on in. Let me get a look at you."

She smiled to herself and entered the cabin, finding her mother, Mariam, on the couch. Even with her swollen eye and bruises and cuts across her cheek, her mom's face lit up in that special way of hers that made everything feel like it was going to be okay.

"Where's Dad?" Cordelia asked.

"He's in the bedroom. It's going to be another few days before he can move around." A warm smile softened her features. "My goodness, it's been so long since I've seen your beautiful face. Come here and give me a hug."

Cordelia took a seat on the couch and pulled her mom into a tight embrace. Her mom was always the best hugger. She forgot how nice it was to receive one that was so full of love and openness. That was just Mariam. She put every ounce of love into everything she did.

"When did you get in?" her mom asked.

"Early this morning. Mike said you guys were still resting, so I looked into the roof repairs before coming by."

Her mother nodded. "Good thing. The medication the doctor gave us is a doozy. It would have been like waking the dead if you came earlier." She tilted her head and inspected Cordelia. "Roof repairs, huh? Then you've met Mac's nephew? Isn't he so handsome? And sweet too. It's nice having him here." Her eyes twinkled as she gushed over Cordelia's nemesis.

"Sure, Mom," she replied halfheartedly. "I don't want to bug you right away, but we have to go over the details of the inn and what you need from a management perspective. I only have a few days here. I want to make sure you're taken care of while you and Dad recover."

Her mother's face was crestfallen. "A few days?"

"I'm sorry." She sighed, hating how quickly her mother's excited smile disappeared. "It's not a good time for me to take any longer. I have a lot on my plate at work. I was lucky to get down here at all."

"That simply won't do."

"I'll get you a great temporary manager who will keep everything running smoothly. It will be fine."

Her mother shook her head and grabbed Cordelia's hands tightly. "You don't understand. We need you here. I wouldn't ask if it wasn't important." She stroked Cordelia's hair in that calming way of hers. "I know you have a life in Boston and a job promotion on the horizon. I'm so proud of you, honey, but your family needs you. The town needs you."

Cordelia's eyebrows knitted in confusion. It wasn't like her mother to put the pressure on. "I don't understand. Mike said reservations were down. That should be resolved in no time once the roof is fixed."

"That's just one small part of a much larger issue."

"What do you mean?"

"We've been having issues the last few years." Mariam looked away and took in a deep breath. "The warmer winters mean shorter ski seasons. Also, less snow in December forced us to cut out some of the holiday activities that drive people here to begin with. Rainy summers led to fewer hikers and campers. Our Summerfest has been rained out two years in a row. Don't even get me started on how the weather affected our tree farm. In any case, reservations have been down even before the roof collapsed. Not as many tourists are passing through town. With events being cancelled and the weather putting a damper on outdoor activities, there's been little reason to. The Winchester Inn is the heart of Fraser Hills. As we fail, so do the surrounding businesses."

Cordelia's father was also the mayor of the town, which meant a lot of the town's success fell on the shoulders of the Winchesters.

"I had no idea. How could you not have told me?" A hint of betrayal laced her voice.

"Oh, honey. Parents like to protect their children, even if they're grown and hundreds of miles away. Your dream was to be a success in Boston, and you're doing that. How could I have ruined that for you? If I told you the truth, I ran the risk of you coming here. We tried our hardest to figure it out ourselves, but with the roof collapsing, we're in over our heads.

"If things don't turn around this Christmas season, the future of Fraser Hills and the Winchester Inn looks bleak. A few businesses have already shuttered up. The ones that are still open are hanging on by a thread. We need a boost in tourism, and fast. I've seen what you've done at your job, especially when you were in a crunch. If anyone can breathe new life into our Christmas events and help us get people coming back, it's you. You're a marketing and event planning whiz. That's why we need you here. We've put our heads together and tried everything. Now we're out of options. You're our only hope."

A quick bark of laughter escaped Cordelia's lips, her mind reeling from the news. "What?" she asked in disbelief. "*I'm* your only hope? *Me?*"

A guilty but hopeful look crossed her mother's face. She nodded.

"This is a pretty big ask. You know that. Right?" Her stomach dropped as she processed. She couldn't outright deny her mom's request without hearing the facts first. Cordelia was a natural problem-solver and had always found crafty solutions when the pressure was on. There had to be *something* she could do.

With so much at stake, she needed to determine what was feasible. She tapped the notes app on her phone to start making a checklist. "What do you need from me?"

"To stay here through the season and help out." Cordelia's stomach dropped even lower, but she said nothing. "Mike will temporarily move in with his girlfriend so you can live in his cabin for the next few weeks. I need you to use your marketing magic to make this the best Christmas the town has ever seen."

"That means…" She wasn't sure if she was ready to deal with what that meant. Her mom just dropped a bombshell.

"That means you'll take over the Christmas events and come up with a new spin to entice tourists to come back. You'll have to get the rest of the town on board with any adjustments or additions to our normal traditions."

Perfect. Just perfect.

"Christmas in Fraser Hills starts on December first. That only gives me two full days to plan." She shook her head. Her brain was about to explode. "Why didn't you tell me this when I called on Thanksgiving?"

"We thought we could figure it out. We planned as best as we could." Her mother worried her mouth. "I now realize that was a mistake. What we came up with isn't enough, especially with the rooms out of order at the inn."

Crafting a new marketing plan that quickly didn't seem feasible, but it wasn't impossible. Cordelia had been dealt some tough high-touch situations that required a quick turnaround. She figured it out every time.

"Anything else?" She was almost too scared to ask.

Her mom's gaze landed her for a second before darting away. "Well..."

"Mom. C'mon."

"You'll also need to work with Logan to sort out the roof repairs and handle the day-to-day at the inn until the doctor says it's okay for me and your father to work again," she rattled off.

Cordelia's fingers stopped typing, and she raised her gaze to look at her mom. "Why can't Mike handle the inn?" She couldn't hide her resentment.

Mike basically did nothing. It wasn't fair to have all of this dropped on her while he was off doing God only knew what. Probably binge-watching Netflix.

"Your brother's been managing the tree farm. We're a little short-handed this year, so he's taken on extra hours, and that was before Dad got hurt. He's running it all on his own now."

"And you trust him not to mess it up?" Cordelia asked with dry sarcasm.

"Oh, you hush." Her mom swatted at her and winced from the movement, likely aggravating sore muscles caused by the accident. "Michael will help whenever he can until we're back on our feet."

Cordelia placed her phone on her lap, freeing her hands to rub her temples. Her skin itched at the thought of staying in Fraser Hills longer than expected. She needed to get back home, to Boston. She had too much going on to be put in this position. She obviously didn't want to leave her family in a bind, but it wasn't right for them to just expect her to drop everything to fix a problem she could have helped them with remotely had they come to her sooner. She had a life too. Didn't that matter?

How would she pull this off anyway? And more importantly,

how would she tell her boss about her extended trip to North Carolina? If she didn't stay, her family ran the risk of losing the inn. If she did, she'd likely lose her job. Melody hadn't been happy when she asked for a few days. Cordelia hardly believed that asking for a full month during their busy event season would go over well.

What would happen if all her effort to save her family's inn didn't work? They'd still lose the inn and she'd be jobless.

This was a mess. She had to figure out a way to make this work, for all their sakes.

Her mother offered an encouraging smile, seemingly unaware of Lia's internal conflict and anger, and patted her leg. "It's a lot to put on you and I feel horrible for even asking, but we need a miracle. I believe you can do this, Lia. You always find a way."

Cordelia conceded. "So now what?"

"Now it's time to get to work." Her mother nudged the phone on Cordelia's lap. "You might want to write down what I'm about to say."

Cordelia lifted her phone, needing to think of how she could make this work for everyone and, hopefully, get back to Boston ASAP.

~ * ~

They spent the next hour going over the calendar of Christmas events, who oversaw what, and which events seemed to generate the most interest and which were duds. This was followed by a breakdown of the day-to-day handling of the inn. By the end of it all, Cordelia had several pages of notes and cramped hands. Her mother, who was still exhausted from the accident, was fading fast.

As Cordelia saved the notes, worry crept through her, making her doubt she could juggle it all, even if her boss allowed her to stick around for the month.

And that was a big if.

"You're going to have to take over leading the town meeting about the Christmas activities in a couple of hours. You can share the updates then," her mom instructed. "I just don't have it in me to attend." She struggled to get off the couch, waving off Cordelia's help, and shuffled toward the bedrooms. Before disappearing into her room, she added, "One last thing, honey. If we want to pull this off, you're going to have to rely on Logan. He's been a big help around here, and I have faith he'll do whatever he can to get the inn in working order as soon as possible."

"Trusting strangers isn't my thing."

Of course, keeping people at arm's length wasn't healthy, but it worked for her.

However, her mom was right. She needed Logan to get the roof sorted so they could log more reservations. That is, if he could stick to his proposed timeline of ten days until the construction was completed. It would still give them at least a couple solid weeks to book at full capacity during their busy season. Not ideal, but it would help a lot.

She already had a few ideas floating through her head to boost the buzz, bring in tourism dollars, and hopefully squash the negative reviews caused by the damage to make up the difference the inn would lose during the days of construction.

But first, she needed to face Logan.

She left her parents' cabin, passed by Mike's—her new temporary home—and walked straight to Logan's place. She took a deep breath and knocked hard, hating that she had to admit she was wrong. But she needed to put her pride aside for the sake of her family and this town.

He appeared at the door and rested his arm above his head on the doorframe. A stray lock of hair fell carelessly across his forehead, making her wonder how a man like him had such effortlessly flawless hair. Did he go to the same barber as all the Disney princes?

"To what do I owe this pleasure?" He flashed his signature boyish grin. The way his mouth rose higher on one side caused her insides to flutter. The round muscles in his shoulders and pectorals strained against his Henley shirt while he leaned against the door frame, making her forget her words.

She mentally scolded her body for betraying her. Yes, Logan was breathtaking in a way that was one hundred percent masculine. And, yes, she loved the way he seemed so unguarded. Casual. Attainable.

For a moment, his presence defied her ability to keep people at arm's length. He was pulling her in, and she wasn't sure how or why.

Get it together.

"Listen, about earlier…," she started.

"Uh huh." His blue-gray eyes shined with a playful gleam.

"I want to apologize for how I acted. Coming back home threw me off, and knowing my parents were hurt put me a little on edge. So…sorry."

He pushed off the door and crossed his arms, his grin still firmly planted on his face. "A little?"

"Okay. A lot. I'm used to having to show confidence and leadership. As a woman, people tend to take advantage of us, especially in business. I need to make it clear I don't take any shit early on."

"Don't worry about it. I understand."

"You do?" She didn't expect his quick acceptance. After their interactions earlier in the day, she assumed he'd make her work for it.

She deserved it, after all.

His smile faded slightly. "I do. But you also have to understand that not everyone is out to get you. Some of us are honest people."

She looked down at her feet. "I know."

He placed a calloused finger under her chin, and tilted her head up, forcing her to look at him. His gaze searched hers. "Do you?"

She flushed at his touch. Usually, she wouldn't let a stranger touch her intimately like this, but everything in her body refused to pull back.

When it was clear she wasn't going to turn away, he lowered his hand. She cleared her throat. "Okay. I know it in theory. I just have a hard time believing it."

"I guess I'll have to earn your trust."

She gave a small, genuine smile. "It'll be a challenge," she half-joked. "But you're off to a good start."

"I assume you're referring to my estimate. I saw the contractors on-site."

"You would assume correctly." She bit her lip. "You were right. You were the most cost-efficient and fastest. By a long shot," she admitted.

Logan's dog, Willow, poked her head out with a happy smile. "Well, since we're all about apologies and starting over, I guess Willow's sorry for knocking you into the mud."

Cordelia bent and scratched the dog behind the ears. "Mistakes happen. All's forgiven."

"Hey, Lia," Mike called out as he walked the path to Logan's cabin. He adjusted a duffle bag on his shoulder and tossed her a set of keys. "Cabin's all yours. I'll see you at the meeting later."

"Thanks."

He jumped in his truck and headed off. Logan eyed the keys in her hand. "Looks like we're neighbors now."

"For at least a few days."

"You're not staying the month?" He cocked an eyebrow.

She fiddled with the keys. "I'm not sure. I'm torn. I have responsibilities back in Boston, and now I have this dropped on me. I'm worried about letting everyone down, but I need a minute to think about how I can make it work. I also need to talk to my boss about my potentially extended stay."

She clamped her mouth shut. She wanted to trust him but wasn't quite ready to spill her guts so freely.

"I'm sure your boss will understand. You're helping your parents recover."

If only it were that easy.
"You don't know Melody."

He studied her for a moment. She almost expected him to make another comment about her being a stranger and not caring about the town. Or accuse her of using her job to make excuses not to stay. Couldn't he and her family understand the position she was in? By staying, she'd likely lose her shot at the promotion or her job all together. It was hard to think about losing that opportunity. She'd worked hard to make a career she was proud of.

Then again, so did her parents. They put their whole lives into the inn and their town.

Rather than judging, he simply said, "You'll figure it out. I believe it."

~ * ~

At a quarter to seven, Cordelia parked outside the town's favorite bar, The Lodge. Catering to the visitors enjoying winter sports on the surrounding mountains, the bar was outfitted to provide a log cabin feel, complete with plush couches and coffee tables perfect for mingling, a roaring fire, and some of the best cocktails to warm guests up on frigid nights.

She slid out a stool and took a seat at the solid wood bar, tapping her nails on the surface as she waited to get the bartender's attention. If she was going to handle being thrust into her hometown again, she needed something to calm her nerves before the meeting.

Recognition flashed through her mind as the bartender appeared to greet her. "You didn't tell me you were coming back home," Cordelia exclaimed as Sarah Connors winked and smiled at her.

Sarah was one of Cordelia's best friends growing up, and although they lived drastically different lives, they still managed to stay in touch. Cordelia's complete opposite, Sarah embraced a punk rock vibe with a growing number of tattoos and colorful hair.

But the differences didn't stop there. Whereas Cordelia focused on building a stable career and taking the traditional path, Sarah was a free spirit. Ever since college, she'd often jet off to some remote place or foreign country for months at a time. She hadn't slowed that pace of life since.

Sarah put down the cocktail shaker and jumped over the bar to give her old friend a hug. "Hey, dude. Of course I'm here. It's almost December in Fraser Hills. I'd never miss it. I just got in yesterday myself."

In between trips, she'd come back to Fraser Hills and work at The Lodge. One of Sarah's long-time childhood friends, Tommy Nunes, owned the place and was used to her breezing in and out at a moment's notice. Sarah once told Cordelia all she had to do was shoot him a quick text a couple days before rolling into town and he'd always squeeze her in on the schedule. With Christmas being the town's busiest time of year, he was likely grateful for the extra help.

Sarah was known for her unique craft cocktails, typically inspired by her adventures. Cordelia never understood how she could live the vagabond life, with no set path or plan, but she also found herself envious of the amazing experiences her friend had.

Cordelia wrapped her in a tight hug, just then realizing how much she missed Sarah. The last time she saw her was three years ago when Sarah had a stopover in Boston on her way to some remote village in Switzerland.

"I heard about the inn. That's a bummer. I hope your parents are doing okay." Sarah made her way back behind the bar. "Want a drink?"

She groaned. "Yes, please. Christmas event planning aside, I don't think I'm ready to face everyone."

Sarah slugged her in the arm and picked up a clean shaker. "You'll be fine. I'll make you my special. It's called Fireside Night. It's got bourbon, a tobacco smoked ice cube, and a few other secret ingredients. It'll give you the strength to handle the onslaught of questions you'll no doubt get." She winked again.

"Sure. Whatever. I'll take it," Cordelia said as she rubbed her shoulder.

As Sarah whipped up the drink, Mike and his girlfriend—Sarah's younger sister—walked in. Where Sarah was punk rock, Bee was more retro. She had the style of a fifties pin-up girl, with her checkered shirt tied at the waist, high-waist jeans, curled hair, and dark red lips.

"Hey, Bee. Long time, no see. How have you been?"

"Great! Opened a restaurant in town a couple years ago. It's been challenging but fun."

"Mike mentioned that. I'll have to stop in while I'm here."

"Awesome. It's New American so I'm sure you'll find something you'll enjoy."

Sarah slid the drink across the bar to Cordelia. "Tell her about your secret sushi menu."

"It's not a secret if you keep telling everyone." Bee's face flamed red.

Sarah rolled her eyes.

Bee glowered at her sister before turning back to Cordelia. "Well, since she can't keep her mouth shut, if you're looking for good sushi, just say the code word 'zen' to whoever's taking care of you. We source some of the best ingredients from the coast, so supplies are limited. Once the daily specials are done for the day, it could be a while before we have those specific options back on the list."

Cordelia laughed to herself, remembering the younger Bee's crazy obsession with sushi. After all these years, her obsession clearly hadn't lessened, and she'd somehow found a way to incorporate that passion into her restaurant in her own fun, exclusive way.

As they caught up, more of the key players for the Christmas events filtered in. Cordelia was overwhelmed with hugs, and questions about what she'd been up to and whether she'd be staying for long.

It was a lot to process, being back in a place where so many people knew her life story. In Boston, she'd rarely run into someone she was acquainted with unless at a work function. To be surrounded by so many people she'd known since childhood was surreal.

"Hey, girl," a man's voice as smooth as honey said from behind her.

She spun in her stool and found a tall man with flawless tanned skin, dark brown eyes, and an infectious grin. "Daniel, I thought you were living in New York."

Daniel Fernandez was another one of Cordelia's good friends from a lifetime ago. Although they didn't stay in touch after college, she often kept up with him through social media.

He waved a hand and pursed his lips. "It was fun while it lasted. I learned a lot about the music biz, but there's too much competition up there and way too many distractions. Not to mention the cost of living is outrageous, so working odd jobs to pay the bills didn't exactly give me time to work on my music career. Plus, the guys up there are such whores. I got tired of the hookup scene."

She laughed at his frankness. "So what are you doing back here?"

"I manage the music shop and give lessons while I'm working on my album. Me and Walt from the gallery and Savannah from the cafe are in a band too." He nudged her with his elbow. "Hoping you can find a way to squeeze us in some of the events this season."

"I'd love to hear you play."

He smiled and clapped. "Great. We play tonight. Here, actually. We'll be setting up after the meeting."

"I'll stick around."

Seeing her friends again warmed her insides even more than Sarah's *very* strong drink. She didn't realize how isolated she was in Boston and how much she missed simple human interaction until this moment. How did she think she could come here and not be affected? Did she really believe Fraser Hills wouldn't lure her back by dangling all the good things she'd left behind?

Cordelia exhaled a slow breath. She couldn't let those thoughts get to her. Even if Melody allowed her stay the month and she'd have a job to return to, she couldn't run the risk of letting the nostalgic feelings make her think she might have been missing something. If she did, she might never leave Fraser Hills again.

The thought terrified her.

Coming here was temporary. Her real life was back in Boston. Fraser Hills was her past. She left for a reason and needed to remember that.

Her phone buzzed, alerting her to start the meeting. Making her way to the fireplace—the focal point of the room—she got ready to address the crowd, a ragtag group of about thirty people all focused on her.

She swallowed hard. "Hi, everyone. It's great to see you all again. As you're aware, my parents and the inn have had a setback this week. Mom's brought me up to speed so I can help you plan the next few weeks accordingly. For the most part, it appears most of the events will go on without a hitch. There are a couple we may need to adjust based on the repairs to the Winchester Inn."

"What I'm concerned about is whether people will actually show up," Amber Florence from the sports outfitter commented. "Ski gear rentals have been down thanks to the crappy weather. I don't want to spend all this effort to put on these events if no one's even here to attend them."

"Yeah," Jeff Jones from the diner quipped. "We purchased a ton of food in anticipation and ended up tossing half away. It was costly waste."

Cordelia froze like a deer in headlights. She took a long sip of her drink and swallowed hard.

"I don't mind the quiet," Kathleen Lane from the florist shop said before Cordelia could speak. "But this time of year is what we rely on. I wouldn't have opened my shop a couple of years ago if I knew things were going downhill."

A few more people grunted in agreement, causing Cordelia's anxiety to rise. She'd never seen such negativity from these people, which only made her realize how dire the situation was.

"All right, hold on. I only recently learned about the problems you're all experiencing too. That's why I'm proposing a few additions, tweaks, and changes."

Jeff scratched his head. "You of all people should know we're a town of traditions." His tone was defensive.

She threw her free hand up in the air as if to surrender. "Of course. And the traditions will be there. But I understand some traditions were compromised due to the weather, and that really hurt you."

A few members of the crowd nodded. Good, she had their attention.

"That's why I want to incorporate new things into the mix. We need to get positive buzz. We want to create a sense of FOMO even if the weather isn't working in our favor."

"FOMO?" Kathleen questioned. "What the hell is that?"

"'Fear of Missing Out.' It's about creating a sense of urgency. We want people to worry they'll miss out on a unique experience. It creates a perception of exclusivity. We use this tactic in event planning and always see attendance spike significantly."

"So what's the plan, Lia?" Sarah asked from her place behind the bar.

Cordelia smiled at the audience. "I have a few ideas but want to flesh them out tonight. I'll stop by your businesses tomorrow and loop you all in."

For the first time since arriving, she was excited about the possibilities. She just hoped they could pull it off.

Chapter Five

"Morning, neighbor." Logan held up his thermos of coffee in greeting when he saw Lia leaving her cabin the next morning. Dawn had barely broken, so he was surprised to see her out and about.

Even from yards away, her perfume's subtle scent of jasmine and citrus drifted over him, awakening his senses the way coffee never could. It reminded him of the rare good moments when he lived in Charleston and spring started to bloom. The intoxicating fragrance from the confederate jasmine bushes filled the city, and he often found himself stopping to literally smell the flowers.

The urge to do the same to her filled his thoughts.

He shook his head, trying to break the spell of Lia Winchester.

He couldn't deny she was beautiful and capable. She had a way of pulling him in, but it was never a good look to hit on your boss's daughter, especially one who had little to no trust for him. Not to mention, she was only there temporarily.

The last thing he needed was a romantic entanglement, even though a casual fling would be the best option to fulfill his needs of female companionship.

A fling was the only thing he could offer anyone, not that she seemed remotely interested.

Truthfully, Logan wasn't ready to put his heart on the line. It had been half a year since he finally let go of the idea of his almost-fiancée, Jolene Calhoun. He'd worked hard to be everything she could ever want and need in a man, and more. But, somehow, that hadn't been enough. *He* hadn't been enough. It took him a while to get over her betrayal. He bristled at the memory.

With a fresh start in Fraser Hills, he didn't want to do anything that would jeopardize his second chance. And certainly not with a woman who was bound to be a dead-end relationship.

Sure, he told Lia he'd work to gain her trust. In hindsight, with what he'd been through with Jolene, that was an unhealthy choice. Whatever he did needed to be for him. No one else.

However, there was something about Lia that made him want to be someone she could count on. Someone who could help lighten the load of everything she'd been forced to take on.

Maybe it was the ballsy way about her. While many Southerners would find her backbone and her vocal way of expressing herself off-putting, he found them exciting.

He'd dated many Southern women in his lifetime, Jolene included. They were mostly about manners, tact, and keeping up appearances. For some, it was only on the surface. Through Jolene, he learned the hard way that their focus on reputation and pleasantness could hide the truth of their actions.

With Lia, though, you knew exactly what you were getting. No surprises. He liked that.

"Early start for you, Lia?" he asked as they left their front porches and walked side by side along the path that led to the inn.

"It's Cor—" She paused and shook her head. "Forget it. What's the point? I'm always going to be Lia here," she muttered the last under her breath.

"This is normal for me," she continued. "Plus, I have a lot to accomplish before the tree lighting tomorrow."

"A woman on a mission," he commented with admiration. "Where are you headed?"

"Making rounds to the key committee members for the town's Christmas events. First stop will be Lovie's bakery."

"Need a lift? I'm headed down there anyway to get supplies before Jim delivers the wood later today."

As she bit her bottom lip before responding, Logan couldn't help but wonder what her lips would feel like pressed against his. He paused at that unexpected thought.

"I could be a while," she answered.

"Don't worry about it. Delivery isn't until noon. I have some time."

She smiled the first genuine smile he'd seen from her yet. Albeit, it was small, but it was a start. "Okay. Thanks."

She followed him to his Ford F-150 Super Duty truck parked on the side of his cabin. Logan offered a hand and helped her in. He tried not to let the tingling sensation from her touch affect him.

Much.

No entanglements. His mind was being smart about it, but his body had a different agenda apparently.

"Quite a truck you have here," she noted when he slipped into the driver's seat.

He patted the dashboard affectionately. "Couldn't do my job without it. It's served me well these last few years. This truck can haul anything." He cranked the engine, the truck rumbling to life, and started on the short trip downtown.

"So," Lia said, breaking the silence. "Why'd you decide to come to Fraser Hills anyway?"

Logan glanced at her, noticing the calm, almost aloof demeanor. For most people, the question was seemingly innocent. Small talk. But he knew there was more to it when it came to her.

"It was time for me to move on from Charleston. Although it's a great city, the circumstances weren't right. I wasn't in it for the long haul, but wanted to make sure my next move offered something worthwhile."

She studied his profile. He forced himself not to meet her captivating honey-brown eyes. "And what would that be?"

He shrugged. "A sense of belonging, I guess."

He had never told anyone that and was surprised he shared it with someone who likely had ulterior motives for asking the question. Her ice queen personality may be melting, and they may have agreed to an unspoken truce, but she still had her guard up. He was certain of that.

"Long story short, I moved to Charleston to follow my girlfriend at the time who was in grad school there," he continued. "Things didn't turn out as expected. And although Fraser Hills is much smaller, Charleston can also feel small. I couldn't settle in and make it a place of my own when I had constant reminders of why I went and failed. I needed to move on."

The truth was, he wanted stability too. Somewhere he could lay down roots. In the first few months he'd been in Fraser Hills, he believed the move was the right choice. Sure, the town had hit a rough patch with tourism lately, but he was hopeful they'd turn it around. With all the stories his uncle shared, he was confident they would.

Logan liked the quiet town and the people who called it their home. It was almost as if he was a permanent fixture of Fraser Hills already by the way they welcomed him and made him feel like one of them.

He'd given himself a year to decide if this would be long-term or not. In his gut, he felt it was. But when Lia came into town with her skepticism and her not-so-gentle reminder that he was a stranger here with zero history, his world got shaky. His desire to prove to Lia he belonged was just as much for him as it was for her.

Within twenty-four hours, she made him question himself. Maybe his conviction was an effect of the honeymoon period. After the newness wore off, would they still stay the same?

And if not here, where?

Her gaze bored into him. He was prepared for her to ask more intrusive questions about Charleston, but to his relief, she pivoted. "It can take a while to make somewhere feel like home."

Her voice sounded far away, as if lost in her own memories. The sincere comment revealed a little more than he suspected she meant to. It only made him want to chip away at that chilly exterior more.

He gave a self-deprecating grin. "Was three years not long enough?" He looked over, taking in her shocked expression.

"Why wait so long?"

He raked a hand through his hair, not in the mood to reopen old wounds, but he had to build a rapport to make the next few weeks as easy as possible. He gave her as much of an answer as he could without allowing her to press for more.

"The move to Charleston required a lot of change and some sacrifice. I liked it—don't get me wrong—but it wasn't my choice. When it was time to move on, I wanted to make sure I was doing it for myself. No other reason. I wanted to be somewhere I could be part of the community. A new home." He shrugged. "I'm thinking maybe Fraser Hills could be that place."

Lia nodded. "The people here are great. Impossible to replace."

He wasn't sure what to make of the emotion behind her quiet statement. From the outside, it seemed like she wanted nothing to do with this town, but her admission hinted at something deeper.

She pointed at a parking spot on Evergreen Avenue just in front of Lovie's bakery, a quaint storefront with large glass windows proudly showcasing delectable treats. "Pull over there."

Their moment was over.

"Perfect. Mind if I stop in too? I'm starving."

"Sure."

"Her breakfast biscuit sandwiches are to die for," they said in unison.

She laughed, her eyes twinkling in the morning sunlight. The easy smile was a stark contrast from her typical serious expression. The beauty of it struck him, and he thought his heart might damn well beat out of his chest.

She tucked a strand of hair behind her ear, sending her intoxicating flowery scent in his direction, making his brain turn to mush.

"Glad to know that some things don't change," she said.

When they stepped onto the sidewalk, Logan took a deep breath of fresh mountain air to try to shake himself from the allure of Lia's perfume. He needed to get a grip.

They walked into Lovie's inviting bakery. Although the decor mainly included pastel pinks and blues—definitely not a palette Logan would choose—something about the space was homey. He could imagine his own mother coming out of the kitchen with gooey cookies straight from the oven.

"Hi, Lovie." Lia greeted the tiny woman who was placing fresh bread in the large glass display case.

Lovie was a sweet woman in her early sixties, one of the many people in this town who gave Logan a warm welcome when he first arrived.

"Lia, darling." Her delicate well-worn hands rested the remaining bread on the counter with care. She gracefully made her way around the counter to give Lia a tight embrace. Pulling back, she looked at Lia with adoration. "It's been so long since I've seen you. It's nice to have you back."

Lia's kind smile eased the hard edges of her face. For a second, Logan saw the tension leave her shoulders. She seemed approachable. Soft. "It's great to see you. I'm popping in to talk about the events planned for this month."

Lovie let go of Lia and led her to one of the handful of bistro tables nearby. Not wanting to intrude on their discussion, Logan went to the counter to read the breakfast specials to give them some privacy, which was nearly impossible to do in the small space.

"I'm sorry I missed the meeting last night. Emmett came to town unexpectedly." He overheard Lovie say.

"Emmett's here?" The interest in Lia's voice tempted Logan to eavesdrop.

"He stopped by before his meeting in Charlotte. Don't worry, you'll be able to catch him. He'll be back in a few days. He was so pleased when I told him you were here too."

"It's been a while since I've seen him."

Lovie patted Lia's hand. "I always thought you two made such a perfect pair."

Logan could see Lia's gaze land on him out of his peripheral vision. He felt bad for listening, but he was too curious to learn about the history between her and this Emmett guy to stop.

"I really cared for him, but I think we were too similar," she responded, her voice a touch softer than before. "Both passionate about our careers."

"You were young then. Time has a way of putting people right where they belong eventually. Maybe now is the right time."

"Maybe." Lia's unconvincing tone made it sound like she was uncomfortable with the conversation but was trying to be polite.

"Seems like fate that the two of you—both of whom rarely come to Fraser Hills—are here at the same time. Don't you think?"

Lia laughed and shook her head. "I'm here to help the town and fix my family's inn, not fall in love."

The older woman gave a serene smile. "Love doesn't give you much of a choice. When you fall, you fall. One day, you'll learn you won't have much say in the matter."

"If and when it happens, I'll be sure to let you know."

~ * ~

It was only noon, and Lia was already exhausted. She spent the entire morning making rounds to get people up to speed on the new outline for the December events. Despite some last-minute changes and additions, everyone was on board and eager to help.

If only all her clients were this agreeable and flexible.

Logan had tagged along most of the time, and she couldn't help but notice his calming presence and the way the townspeople greeted him as if he were already one of their own. Having him there took the pressure off when people begged her to come back home permanently. He'd been a shockingly good buffer. However, she was still a tiny bit jealous of everyone's instant adoration of him.

Maybe he wasn't such a stranger after all.

"They really miss you." Logan's deep Texan accent disrupted her thoughts.

They sat at a two-top table near the front windows of Bee's restaurant, a cute place with about fifteen tables and a small bar. The retro vibe boasted vibrant reds that contrasted with blacks and whites, totally matching Bee's style. Even the jukebox in the far corner added the perfect detail to pull the place together.

Mulling over what to have for lunch, Lia was impressed with Bee's menu. The choices weren't overwhelming, but the options available were completely gourmet.

She rolled her eyes. "They say that to all us Fraser Hillers who come back for a visit. Not that many of us ever leave. I'm nothing special."

She continued to stare at the menu, barely processing the words on the page. Between the town, the inn, and her job, there was too much to think about. It was hard to focus on something as insignificant as what to have for lunch when so much was riding on her.

"The club sandwich is good," Logan suggested, breaking the silence again.

She looked over the top of the menu and took stock of his earnest face. After their rocky start, he was trying. His hopeful smile and offer to drive her to town made that clear.

"Thanks," she said while putting the menu down and folding her hands on top. "So, I know I was focused on the events today, but I want to talk to you about the roof. What's the game plan?"

He leaned back in his chair and crossed his hands behind his head, putting his broad body on display.

Wow. That's a body of a man who's worked hard his whole life. Lia's face flushed.

"I had the permits expedited, so we're good to go there," Logan said, interrupting her highly inappropriate thoughts. "I'll stop by the hardware store when we leave here. The wood should've been delivered by the time we get back. With the amount of roof we need to repair, I think we'll be on track to finish in seven to ten days like I'd initially planned. That includes fixing the damaged rooms."

Lia's eyebrows shot up. "How did you get the permits approved so fast?"

"Donnelly pushed them through."

She shook her head, her shoulders rising to her ears. "That's not like him. Something's up."

His forehead crinkled as he stared her down. "Are you always this suspicious of people? Or is it just something about Donnelly that gets you this riled up?"

Before she could give him a snide remark, Bee strutted up to the table in all her retro glory. Her curly hair was pulled half up with some teasing, and her lips were as red as ever.

"Hey, guys. So glad you came in." The tension between Logan and Lia eased with her there.

"How's rooming with my brother? I apologize for taking his cabin and sticking you with him."

Bee threw back her head and laughed, her dimples on full display. "He's not as bad as you think. I mean, it is Mike, though."

"Sure is."

Bee shrugged. "You'll probably always see him as your little brother, but he's grown up some. We stay over at each other's places from time to time, but this extended roommate situation might help us see if we're ready for the next step."

"Wow, that's exciting." Lia's words were one hundred percent genuine. A live-in girlfriend? If that worked out, she wondered how long it would be before they walked down the aisle.

"We'll see. Anyway, what can I get for you?"

Lia and Logan both ordered the club. Water for him and a coffee for her. She was running on fumes. Logan thought she got an early start. If he only knew she'd been up since four this morning handling her tasks for work before she hit the pavement today. Even after making good traction this morning, she still had a full day ahead of her.

When Bee left them, Lia eyed the patrons nearby. Scooting her seat in his direction, she rested her elbows on the table, and dipped her head closer to whisper. "Listen, being that you're new here, I'll get you caught up. Donnelly doesn't do things out of the goodness of his heart. His town and our town aren't on the best terms."

"Because of the whole thing about Fraser Hills allegedly sabotaging their tree trade?"

She hadn't expected him to be so dialed in to the town's history already. "You heard about that?"

"Yeah." He looked at her like she was an idiot. "And it's kinda hard to believe a guy would work against us because of some old rivalry that happened before he was even born."

She pursed her lips. "We're a very proud and loyal bunch in the South. People hold grudges."

"I can tell," he said under his breath. "It might have been a while since you've been past the Mason-Dixon Line, but people are genuinely nice here. And neighborly. Even people like Donnelly."

She snorted and turned her head.

"I'm surprised you weren't reminded of that today," he continued. "Didn't you see how those people welcomed you back? They were happy to see you. Even though you hightailed it out of here the first chance you got, they put their faith in you and your plan to make this an amazing Christmas season."

She turned back to him and narrowed her eyes, distrust washing over her again. And here she'd thought they were making progress at keeping things civil. "That's because they have to. This might be their last shot at keeping the town afloat."

"No." He leaned forward and held her gaze, his face now only inches from hers. "They're doing it because they love you and believe in you. Were you always this skeptical or did the North harden your heart?"

His enchanting steel-blue eyes pulled her in, distracting her from saying whatever retort that had been on the tip of her tongue. Shaking her head, she straightened, trying to recover. Lia needed to stand her ground, but as she tried to muster up a solid argument, she realized she had none, forcing her to consider what Logan was saying.

She knew these people. How could she consider them anything other than the wonderful people they were? Quirks and all.

"You're right," she admitted. "Fraser Hills was a great place to grow up. Not just because of the location, or the downtown, or the mountains. This place is what it is because of the people." She thought for a moment. "I want outsiders to see that."

"How do you mean?"

"I mean if we're going to pull off making this the best season yet, we can't just promote events. We need to make it a one-of-a-kind experience."

"And that can only be done by letting the town show their true spirit," Logan followed her train of thought. As her mental wheels turned, she couldn't contain her grin. "What is it?"

New enthusiasm breathed life back into her tired body. "I have an idea of how I can do that, starting with the tree lighting." Lia sprang from her seat and threw on her coat.

"Whoa. Where are you going?" he called after her retreating back. "You haven't eaten yet, and I drove."

She turned and peered over her shoulder. "Grab a to-go box for me, will you? Don't worry about the ride. I'll figure it out. Right now, I have an event to plan."

Chapter Six

Whatever new-found vigor Lia had the day before was long gone this morning. She deflated as she stood behind the reception desk at the Winchester Inn.

It was barely seven in the morning. The hint of first sunlight flooded through the large windows of the lobby, washing over the dark wood floors and ornate rugs. Not much had changed at the inn. The wainscoting and floral wallpaper stayed intact. The comfortable sitting area to the side of the front door still encouraged guests to take a seat and unwind.

Lia remembered thinking the decor was old and tired whenever she'd visit from college, and half-expected the couches to be wrapped in plastic and the scent of mothballs to linger in the air. As she got older, she appreciated the charm of it. Despite its age, no wear and tear were present. Her parents maintained it well, preserving a bit of history.

But it wasn't the decor that gave her a slight panic attack, it was what her mother was showing her.

"And this here is where we keep the reservations." Mariam used her splinted hand to point to a large scheduling book on the desk.

"Okay..." Lia sucked in a breath, her stomach gurgling with anxiety. "Do you transcribe this to the computer?" She eyed the large box monitor perched on the corner of the desk and wondered if it was a first-generation Macintosh. Everything else was vintage in this place, why not the computer too?

A blank look crossed her mother's face. "No, this is where all the reservations are held."

"You're saying all our customer information is stored here?" She picked up the thick book. "In this? This easy to ruin, hard to search, disorganized, archaic book."

"Yes," her mom said, ignoring Lia's outburst. "Up to two years out."

She flipped through, seeing customer names and phone numbers scribbled on the pages in pencil. "Do you also have their email addresses?"

Another puzzled look. "What for?"

Panic bubbled up again. Lia clutched her stomach and closed her eyes. There weren't enough antacids in the world to deal with this. "To email them. You can send newsletters about upcoming events, like the ones we're planning for this month, for example. Also, you can let them know about specials. Emails can re-engage them and make them repeat customers."

"We've been doing it this way forever." Her mother's tone was defensive and held a bit of hurt.

"That way doesn't seem to be working anymore. Wouldn't you agree?" Mariam's face fell at the snippy tone, making Lia feel bad instantly. "Listen," she said more delicately, "you need to trust me on this."

She turned to the computer, pulling off the various sticky notes stuck to it, and booted it up. The ancient machine groaned to life and, eventually, loaded the desktop. She opened the web browser and thanked God it didn't use dial-up, which she almost anticipated with the state of things.

"Okay. First things first. Let's log into your Facebook account and see if we can drum up some interest in tonight's event."

"Oh, great. I have that set up at least." Mariam took over to log in, hunting and pecking the keys with her good hand. With a proud flourish, she showed her the page.

Lia cringed.

Scanning through the profile timeline, she realized just how bad it was. There hadn't been any new posts in nearly a year. From a marketing perspective, the ones that had been posted were basically pointless.

"How long have you had this page?" she asked in way she hoped wouldn't put her mom on the defense again.

"About three years. Michael set it up for me."

"What have you been doing with it since then?" She didn't have to ask. She knew the answer.

Not much.

"I've posted here or there." Uncertainty laced her mom's voice.

"Your most recent post was from last year, wishing everyone a Merry Christmas. No pictures. No links. No call to action."

Her mom's cheeks turned pink. "That's what I do with my own Facebook account."

Lia kept her mouth shut after seeing how much her mom's enthusiasm deflated. She couldn't bear adding to her hopelessness.

Within the first few minutes of being there, it became clear Lia's parents weren't technically savvy, and it was hurting their business. Mike said there were negative reviews online because of the roof incident, and her mom and dad hadn't been able to change the narrative.

She'd have to fix that.

"Don't worry, Mom. I'll spruce it up. Let's talk about the other items on this list, like housekeeping and food."

"Normally I do it all, but now I can't." She lifted her bum wrist. "Savannah Knightly at the cafe has been helping with cleaning after her morning shift. She already told me she'd be willing to pick up the slack while I'm recovering, which shouldn't be too bad if half the rooms are out of commission."

"Logan thinks he'll have everything sorted in about a week."

"I'm afraid I'll still be no use. Savannah is wonderful, but I don't want to put that all on her."

"I'll reach out to other cleaning services to help. Next," she said while typing up a to-do list on her phone, "what about feeding the guests?"

"I still do all the cooking as I always have, but since that won't work, I've talked to Lovie. She said she'll bring things for the breakfast rush. Willey Griffon down at the butcher and deli said he'll cover lunch and dinner. It's going to be buffet style, which I'm not too keen on, but it will have to do. Bee offered coupons for her restaurant in case people want a sit-down. Sweet girl, that Bee."

Lia pinched the bridge of her nose as she processed the information. Two events this month would take place at the Winchester Inn, and dinner was expected to be served. Her mother always cooked, but that option was off the table. She'd have to find other alternatives and quick.

"Dear?" Her mother rubbed comforting circles on Lia's back. "I know this is a lot to ask of you. Your father and I love and appreciate anything you can do. We should have come to you sooner, when things were starting to take a turn," she admitted, her eyes downcast. "Now we're in a real pickle, and it's a lot of pressure. I'm sorry."

Lia wrapped her mom in a tight hug, guilty that she almost didn't come to begin with or that she thought she could save the day with her original four-day plan.

"I've handled a lot worse and in a lot less time. Don't worry."

Her mom's smile reached her eyes, easing the knot in Lia's stomach. "Thank you, honey. If you wouldn't mind, I'd like to rest. All these anti-inflammatories are draining. If you need me, just holler."

The next three hours went by in a blur as Lia learned the

processes of the inn, got Savannah squared away with the cleaning schedule, set up for breakfast and lunch, handled reservations and cancellations, and managed the current guests' questions and concerns. Lia could balance a lot, but her head was spinning.

It was just before noon by the time she got the inn's social media accounts looking halfway decent and posted the event calendar for the month. With a few cheap social media advertising campaigns, she hoped she could reach new prospective visitors.

Next up on her list was revamping the website. As she made calls to a web developer to build a new site with the ability to make online reservations and capture leads, her cell phone chirped. Her boss Melody Kensie's name appeared on the screen.

"I'll have to call you back," she told the developer and hung up the desk phone. Clicking the answer button, she mustered up the most cheerful greeting she could. "Melody. Hi. I was just about to call you."

After a very terse conversation the day before about Lia's request to stay longer, she needed to be even more available than she'd been before to restore Melody's faith in her. Melody had been clear that the only reason why she'd allow it was because she didn't have time to find someone to replace her during their busy season. Although Lia's job—and apparently her chances of getting the promotion—were safe for now, Melody emphasized her performance in the days she'd be gone would be harshly evaluated.

The pressure was enough to make her crack, but she didn't. She needed this job, so she'd do whatever it took to put Melody's mind at ease.

"Cordelia." The woman's tone was cold and clipped. "I sent you an email nearly a half hour ago."

Lia groaned inwardly. No matter what you were doing—whether it was having an anniversary dinner with your loved one, at a doctor's appointment, or even sleeping—Melody expected you to answer immediately.

"Yes. Sorry I didn't respond. I was checking into it," she lied. "I didn't want to clog up your inbox until I had an answer." She turned to the laptop sitting next to her, found Melody's email, and scanned it. "I put a call in to the caterers to see if they can accommodate the vegan/gluten-free/low-carb items Elizabeth Sinclair's guest requires. I'm sure they'll have no issue."

What did this person eat? Air?

"If they can't, we'll have to find a new caterer. One that's more inclusive," she insisted without emotion.

"It's Christmas. All the best caterers are booked for other

holiday events."

"Make it work, Cordelia. Need I remind you that Elizabeth is not only a close family friend, but she has deep pockets and a lot of connections? This event is going to be well publicized. Everything needs to be perfect. Do you understand?"

"Yes, Melody."

"You assured me yesterday you could handle this from down there. You're my best employee, so I allowed it despite my reservations. Is this going to be an issue? There can't be any distractions."

"I've got this taken care of. I'll report back to you in a bit."

The phone disconnected without a goodbye. Typical Melody.

Lia leaned against the desk, trying to slow her racing heart and rising blood pressure. She could pull this off, but the micromanagement didn't help. When she wasn't dealing with the inn or town's events, she'd work late into the evening, early in the morning, and any spare moment she had midday to handle her work tasks.

To say she was exhausted would be an understatement.

The desk phone rang, and she snatched it up. "Thank you for calling the Winchester Inn. Lia speaking. How may I help you?"

"Lia, honey," her mom greeted. "How are things going?"

"Everything's fine. I'm getting up to speed."

"Okay." She paused. "There have been a couple of complaints." Her mom tiptoed around the statement as if to soften the criticism.

"What kind of complaints?" Lia asked through gritted teeth. She didn't have time for this.

"Some guests felt like they didn't have the true Winchester experience when dealing with you. They said you seemed eager to rush them off."

"That's insane. I was efficient. They have questions or needs, I get it taken care of. Quickly. How can people be upset about that?"

"Have you asked them about their stay so far? What they've done in Fraser Hills? Did you remember their names? Make suggestions?"

Lia pinched the bridge of her nose. "No."

"Those things matter to people here. They want to feel connected. Heard. They want the small-town charm. Not just to be taken care of like a pesky task on one of your to-do lists. Please try to be more personable with the guests."

"Okay, Mom. I'll do my best."

"I love you, honey. I'll be by later."

"Love you too."

Lia hung up the phone and placed her face in her hands, trying her best not to scream out of frustration. No matter how hard and long she worked, it was never good enough.

"Howdy, ma'am." She heard a thick Texan drawl say. Lifting her head, she found Logan approaching her in that slow, casual walk of his.

"Hi, Logan." She made a face.

"Don't be so happy to see me. I can't handle the flattery." He leaned his elbows on the counter and winked. "What's got you so flustered?"

She straightened, not wanting him to see her in a moment of weakness. "I'm not flustered. I'm fine."

"The fact your bright red face was buried in your hands makes me believe otherwise."

"Don't worry about me. What can I do for you?"

He pulled out blueprints and carefully smoothed them out on the desk. "Jim and I are starting on the roof today. I wanted to show you some of the changes." He pointed to the section on the back. "We're going to change the pitch slightly on this side to better handle the winter conditions blown down from the mountains. This is a sturdier design and will make the roof last a lot longer through the wear and tear from the wind and snow."

Lia inspected the map. "Will it be noticeable from the front?"

"Yes. It won't be overly dramatic, but the look of the building will change just slightly."

She shook her head. "No."

He raised an eyebrow. "What do you mean 'no'?"

"I can't accept this plan. The inn has been this way for nearly two centuries. We can't change it."

"Lia." Her name was firm on his lips. "These things happen all the time. Historic buildings need to be brought up to code, and sometimes that means structural or cosmetic changes. Compared to what I've dealt with in Charleston, this is minor."

"I don't feel right making this change. This isn't just a building; it's the whole reason Fraser Hills even exists. How can we change the start of a town?"

He touched her shoulder in a way that would calm most people, but instead caused a shiver to run up her spine. "I promise what I'm doing is not only required of us, as per Donnelly's instructions, but it's for the best. This small change will protect the inn in the long run."

Annoyance coursed through her at the mention of Donnelly. She tried to give him the benefit of the doubt, especially after what Logan said at Bee's, but the suspicion deeply ingrained in her was hard to shake.

Lia came around the reception desk, needing the moment of separation to get her wits back after his innocent touch, and stood in front of him. "Do you know the history of this place?"

"I know some."

"My great-great-great-great grandparents, Cordelia and Edmund Winchester, founded this town in 1825. They got married in the 1820s and were gifted the land. They spent years building their home—which they called the Winchester Manor—putting in long days and painstaking detail to make this place what it is."

"I suppose that's who you were named after?"

"Yes. Cordelia loved Christmas and always tried to spread holiday cheer during that time of year. With the lands covered in Fraser firs, she and Edmund started the Christmas tree and lumber trade. To encourage people to come here for work, the house was used as a place for people to stay as they got situated. For years, this house brought people from all over, offering them a safe place for a fresh start. It was filled with people who were passionate about making this town a success. They put everything into making something from nothing, just like Cordelia and Edmund.

"As the years went on, the main street was developed to support the town residents. Those who originally came here built their homes nearby and started families. Their relatives moved to the town too. The tiny town continued to thrive and flourish, despite things like the fires and the Civil War.

"Soon, the manor didn't need to house workers because they had established their own roots. So, they turned the manor into the Winchester Inn, giving families and friends of the people of Fraser Hills a place to stay when visiting."

"That's impressive," Logan commented.

"That's not all."

"Oh?" He seemed amused by Lia's passionate storytelling.

"The town grew because of the tree trade, which was sparked because of Cordelia's love for Christmas. So, every December, the town exploded with events that led up to Christmas. We kept a lot of those traditions alive, even to this day."

It had been so long since she'd told this story, maybe even since before she moved away. Looking back on it now as an adult, she was impressed with what her ancestors had done to grow this town from nothing. It pained her to think two hundred years of history might be lost if things didn't pull through.

"That's why I have a hard time stomaching this tiny change to the roof. Changing something that was so important to this town seems wrong."

It may be unreasonable to push back on this, but a nostalgic feeling of town pride got her worked up. She was scared the change would be the start of a ripple effect, potentially causing the end of the inn as she knew it. Glancing down at her heel-clad feet, Lia tried to process the emotions from the day. Was it possible to feel so many of them in one morning? It was exhausting.

"Hey." Logan bent to capture her gaze. "I understand what you're saying and I also understand what this inn means to your family and the town. Whatever we change is in the best interest of that. Can you trust me on this? I know it's hard for you. But I hope you can try."

He seemed so open and honest. It was hard to believe he had an ulterior motive, but her nature made her cautious. She needed to push past that for the sake of the inn. "Okay," she agreed. "Please don't make me regret this."

He crossed his heart.

~ * ~

It had been a long but productive day for Logan. After he got the green light from Lia, he and Jim had climbed to the roof and gone straight to work. The roof issue was affecting business at the inn, an already strained establishment for the last few years. He wanted to get things done as quickly as possible to alleviate that, but he had to get it right. He'd be damned if he did a shoddy job.

Not with the way Lia had put her trust in him.

She was cautious about accepting his promise. He wasn't sure what caused her to have so little faith in others, but he wasn't about to prove her right.

The day had been filled with back-breaking labor, but they'd made great progress. Ready to wrap it up for the evening, Logan made his way down the ladder and took a beat at the bottom to wipe the sweat from his forehead. Although the temperature had dipped into the mid-forties once the sun started to set, the exertion of framing the roof had him on fire.

Jim walked by as he put the last of the supplies away for the day. "You going to the tree lighting tonight?"

Logan checked his phone. He had about an hour before the festivities started. "Gonna grab a quick shower and let Willow out before I head over. See you there?"

"Sure, man."

Logan had never been to Fraser Hills for their Christmas events, but it was something his uncle talked about fondly. For an older man who was somewhat rough around the edges, it surprised Logan to hear

Uncle Mac talk about it with such enthusiasm. It was as if the town brought out his childlike spirit buried deep within his grumpy demeanor.

How well tonight went would was important for the success of the town, setting the tone for the entire season. Knowing Lia, she had something up her sleeve, especially with the way she darted out of Bee's the other day.

An hour later, Logan made his way to the town center, a circle in the middle of the main streets of downtown. The picturesque gazebo was adorned with twinkling lights, an abundance of poinsettias, and garland. He could picture snuggling up with someone on the interior benches, enjoying each other's warmth in the brisk mountain air, their skin highlighted by the white lights surrounding them.

Lia's face came to mind, causing him to pause.

He couldn't think of her. Not like that. Pursuing anything with her—even if she wanted to—would be trouble. Judging by how closed off she was to the world, he suspected she felt the same. But as soon as he pushed the thought out of his head, she manifested in front of him, making it impossible to forget her.

"Hi." Her words held a hint of excitement.

She was gorgeous in a black dress that accentuated her curves. Her dark red lipstick complemented her brown hair, which shined under the twinkling lights. He was stunned speechless by her beauty for a moment but recovered quickly.

"Hi. Looks great." He nodded to the large tree in the center of the park. "You've outdone yourself."

She smiled at the enormous tree, admiring the festive ornaments, grand star topper, and colorful garland. "Thanks. I had some help. I should get going though. The event starts soon, and I need to deal with some last-minute items. Enjoy the show."

There was a twinkle in her eyes, the one he saw the other day when inspiration struck her. He couldn't wait to see what she had in store.

She was in her element as she practically glided to the makeshift stage where Daniel and Walt were setting up their instruments. She pointed and directed, marking things on her clipboard, and fussing over decorations.

She was an elegant force of nature and he couldn't keep his eyes off her.

"Hey, man." Jim gave Logan a friendly slap on the back, pulling him from his trance.

"'Bout time you made it."

"This is your first Fraser Christmas, right?"

"Yeah. My uncle told me great things about it, and he doesn't get excited about much."

Jim laughed and handed Logan a cup of hot chocolate from the cafe's pop-up table. "That sounds like Mac all right."

"Figured I'd see what it was all about." He took a sip and groaned. "This is amazing."

"You think that's good? You should grab one of the Christmas churros from Lovie's table and dip it in the hot chocolate. It's practically a staple here."

They both turned at the sound of a mic clicking on and found Daniel's band had finished setting up. He tapped on the mic for a soundcheck and turned to give Savannah and Walt a thumbs up.

"Fraser Hills. How's everyone doing tonight?" Daniel's enthusiasm flowed from the mic and bounced through the crowd. The audience cheered in response. "As you all know, the tree lighting kicks off our season. We have a great lineup for you, so I hope you're as excited as I am."

The crowd cheered again. Logan noticed an abundance of people now filling out the park and beyond. He'd never seen the town so packed and hoped this was an indication of what was to come.

"After our performance, the Fraser Hills Elementary choir will come on stage to sing Christmas classics as we light the tree. Starting at eight, the tree farm will officially open for business. Be sure to stop in and grab yourself a bit of Christmas magic for your home. We'll kick things off in five minutes, so grab yourself a hot chocolate, a treat, or mulled wine—or in my case, all of it—from one of the vendors around the park and enjoy the show."

People dispersed to the different vendors, grabbing a last-minute bite or drink, marveling at the different crafts on display, and generally enjoying each other's company. The energy was palpable tonight, and the pride and love people had for the town made something stir inside him.

Something unfamiliar but not unwelcome.

Daniel, Savannah, and Walt came back on stage and started playing the first song of the night, *Rocking around the Christmas Tree*. They elevated the song, making it their own, but still respected the classic. Their stage presence had the crowd going wild, and Logan found himself enjoying the show along with them. They continued with upbeat versions of more Christmas classics for another half hour before they signed off, introducing the children's choir.

As the children took their places, Mariam walked on stage and stood at the mic, looking at the crowd with appreciation. "It's so nice to see so many familiar and few new faces here tonight. Unfortunately, my husband is still recovering, so he won't be here for the lighting this year. Hopefully, I can do it justice." She let out an endearing, girlish laugh.

"The tree lighting is a Fraser Hills favorite, and for good reason. It brings us all together and instills the holiday spirit in each of us. This Winchester tradition has been passed down from generation to generation for more than two hundred years, and I'm proud we've kept it alive.

"The tree lighting means many different things to different people. For me, as I look around, I realize it's an opportunity to bring us together. We're all here, in one place, for one unified reason. Our neighbors, our family." She stopped and gave Lia a smile full of love. "Friends, children, newcomers, and more. We're all here. And seeing this reminds me that everything will be okay. Our community makes it so.

"No matter what kind of year you've had—good, bad, unexpected, trying—it's because of those who we surround ourselves with who make sure we celebrate the good times and stay afloat during the hardships. Fraser Hills has seen a lot over the centuries, but we're still standing because of the wonderful people who live here. I'm so grateful for all of you.

"As we light this tree, I want each of us to be reminded of all we can accomplish if we come together, just as we are in this moment. We truly can overcome anything."

Mariam's hopeful face mirrored the crowd's. Logan was hit with the pang of something unfamiliar once again. It seeped into his bones and warmed him from the inside out. Her words struck him, but he wasn't sure why.

She turned to the children on stage, making sure they were ready to go, before addressing the crowd again. "Without further ado, the Fraser Hills Christmas season has officially begun!"

As the choir began to sing a beautiful rendition of *Noel*, the tree lights came to life, washing over everyone with a colorful glow. The collective "oohs" and "aahs" surrounded him, making him feel like he was part of a special moment, one he'd never experienced before.

Yet even with the beautiful display in front of him, he couldn't help seeking out Lia. She was standing off to the side, next to her mother, admiring the brilliant tree. In her eyes, he could see a sense of peace.

She turned, her gaze capturing his. In that moment, it was as if he was the only thing she could see. As if there was no one else in the entire world with whom she'd want to share this special moment.

His heart thudded against his ribcage. His knees went weak.

Logan would do anything to keep her looking at him just like that.

Had anyone ever looked at him that way?

All that raw emotion. The hope.

He wondered if the words Mariam had said resonated with Lia too. Did she feel the same? Did being there remind her she belonged?

If it did, was it enough to make her want to stay?

As the question came to him, he wondered why it mattered. Where did Lia Winchester fit into his life?

Chapter Seven

Lia floated on cloud nine the next morning. As she bustled through the daily duties of the inn, took deliveries, and started updating her parents' reservation system, her mind couldn't stop the memories seeping in from the night before.

The music, the joy-filled faces, her mother's story, the way the event brought the town to life. She had forgotten how wonderful the tree lighting was. Even with the new additions of Daniel's band and the food vendors, the tradition was still alive and well.

She thought back to the events she had planned over the years. Fundraisers, galas, grand openings, anniversaries, product launches, corporate holidays, and more. All of them with their own flavor and focus. But one thing was the same for all of them—the crowd couldn't come close to what she saw yesterday.

There had been genuine love and hope. Heritage. History. People looked forward to this event and were happy to see one another. Everything about their reactions had been rewarding. It made her proud.

Sure, at the events she'd organized for work there were always polite smiles as people mingled among one another, wearing top-of-the-line designer dresses and suits. They gave off an air of importance as they took dignified sips of their cocktails, barely touching the gourmet appetizers being passed around.

And yes, people came together over their thousand-dollar plates for a charity or non-profit, unified in the mission to make the world better.

They showed face. They rubbed elbows. But the heart of it was missing. They cared about the causes enough, but some of it was more about the optics of their support and less about what it meant to them.

It just made the reason for the event feel hollow.

Over the years, guests and clients had praised Lia's work, but despite the positive feedback and her many deserved promotions at Kensie Affairs, she realized people simply tolerated the events. They weren't enthralled by them. Captivated. Fascinated.

And their polite discussions seemed superficial compared to her mother's heartfelt speech. It was apparent her words not only resonated with the crowd, but bonded them all.

For a moment, her mother's words struck her too, giving her pause and tugging on heartstrings she didn't even know were there.

Her words mattered.

Then there was Logan. After the tree lights finally lit up the night sky like a beacon of hope, she had the urge to search for him in the crowd. When she did, their gazes locked. They shared a moment. Something new for him. Something nostalgic for her. But special for them both.

That quick interaction caused a spark in her belly, making time stand still. There had been a shift between them, one that sent warmth through her, awakening something inside that had been long forgotten. She didn't know what to make of it. Wasn't sure if she was ready to consider what it was. But she couldn't deny how good it felt.

She'd always remember the way his lips tugged upward in an attractive boyish grin as if to say this moment was theirs and theirs alone.

It was amazing how one simple look from him forged a sense of connection she hadn't experienced in far too long.

Her cellphone rang, pulling her from the memory, and she grumbled as Elizabeth's name flashed across the screen. Lia cleared her throat, getting herself ready for whatever Elizabeth was bound to throw at her. "Cordelia Winchester."

"Cordelia," Elizabeth responded in her dignified voice. She was upper crust through and through. "I want to meet tomorrow to go over the event. I understand I have to choose a new caterer due to the menu changes for my guest's dietary restrictions?"

Although she posed it as a polite question, Lia could hear the distrust and distaste in her voice.

"Yes. We had to make a last-minute change due to a conflict with the original caterer. I assure you the new one is just as well regarded as the former. In fact, I believe you went to an event they catered this past February. You remember the gala for the children's hospital?"

"I've been to so many of these fundraisers. They all blend together." Her reply was curt, dismissive. "I'd prefer to do a tasting before we officially sign off on this. We have people sacrificing holiday meals with their families. It needs to be worth it for them."

Lia bit her tongue. She was well aware of exactly who was coming to this event and what was expected. She had the details memorized for months now.

"Very well," she said as accommodatingly as she could. "I'll set up a tasting with the caterer for you, but I, unfortunately, won't be able to make it myself."

"You told me you'd be back in Boston, did you not?"

"I've run into a few complications and need to stay in North Carolina longer, but it doesn't change the fact that I'm committed to making your event a priority and success."

"Yet you can't be there for the tasting? That seems to contradict your statement, does it not?"

"Mrs. Sinclair, I promise things will go smoothly despite this small hiccup. In a few days, I'll be more mobile and can fly up there at a moment's notice. But for now, I simply can't."

She could almost feel the woman pursing her lips in dissatisfaction across the line. "Perhaps Melody would be better suited to handle the event."

"Mrs. Sinclair, you're in good hands with me. Trust me." Lia attempted to sound as confident as she could without straight-out telling the woman where she could stick it. Kensie Affairs' clientele was high maintenance, but sometimes it was a bit much.

Elizabeth was the worst offender of them all. If Melody seemed overbearing, she paled in comparison to Elizabeth. Nothing was ever good enough, even if Lia exceeded perfection and expectations.

However, she knew this going into it. Melody was testing Lia to see if she was ready for the promotion. If she could handle someone as bad as Elizabeth, then she was prepared to manage the most elite clients.

Just a few more weeks of dealing with Elizabeth. Lia tried to keep her cool.

"I guess we'll see, Cordelia. But understand that I expect your utmost attention. I expect the best. Melody put her faith in you. I'd hate for you to disappoint both of us." The threat was hardly disguised.

"I won't. I'll call you later today with the time and place for the tasting. Will you need me to arrange a car for you?"

"No, I'll have my driver take me. I look forward to hearing from you, Cordelia."

A little worse for the wear, Lia ended the call. Was she really going to be able to save her town and the inn all while protecting her promotion?

"Lia," her brother's voice called from behind her.

She spun around to see Mike rolling her father in a wheelchair through the main entrance. She rushed to their side and planted a kiss on her dad's forehead.

He'd been holed up in his bedroom to recover the whole time she'd been back. And although she had poked her head in from time to time to see how he was doing, it was nice to finally see him out and about.

"Don't you have another few days of bed rest?" she lightly scolded even though she was delighted to see him moving around, confirming he wasn't as weak as he seemed when she'd checked on him.

Many people joked that Ron Winchester was Santa himself, and if she was honest, she believed it until she was about ten. With her father's tall frame, round stomach, and ruddy cheeks, he looked the part. Now as his dark hair had gone from salt and pepper to more salt, the resemblance was uncanny.

"And miss a chance to see my favorite daughter?" He laughed, causing himself to wheeze in the process.

His larger-than-life presence and commanding voice had become frail during his recovery. Despite that, he still found it in himself to make bad dad jokes.

"Your only daughter," she said with a smile.

"I heard last night was a hit. I was sorry I couldn't be there."

"You were missed." Mike patted him on the shoulder. "Everyone at the tree lot was asking about you. Said opening night wasn't the same without you there."

"You tell them I've left the lot in good hands."

Mike beamed at his praise. "Mom did a great job too."

"Thank goodness your mother was there to take one for the team."

"You would have loved it. She made the Winchester name proud."

"That's my girl." He chuckled, followed by another cough.

Lia crouched and studied him. "Are you okay? Do you need anything? Water? A doctor?"

He waved her off. "Don't be fussing over me. My bum lung is giving me some trouble, but I'll be fine." He rubbed his hands together with excitement, changing the subject. He always hated when people worried over him. "Your mother tells me you have some ideas to generate new visitors?"

"I do, Mr. Mayor. Hopefully, they're up to your standards." She grabbed a binder off the reservation desk, and Mike rolled him to the sitting area so they could both take a seat. She handed him the binder, and her dad flipped it open and nodded with occasional sounds of approval.

"This is very good, Lia. Very good, indeed." He pushed his reading glasses to the top of his head. "Do you think this could work?"

"Yes. Last night, I posted photos and a live stream on Facebook, and we already got three calls this morning to make reservations for this month. Those were all organic posts too."

He squinted in confusion. "Organic?"

"It just means I posted it normally. If we did a few cheap advertising campaigns, we could reach more people familiar with the inn and even build awareness with new ones. We wouldn't have to spend a lot of money to make a difference."

He frowned. "I don't think we have that sort of disposable income, with the roof and all."

"Don't worry about it, Dad. I'll use my own. Consider it a gift to make up for being an absentee daughter," she half-joked.

He squeezed her knee. "You aren't an absentee daughter, honey. Sure, your mother and I would love if you visited more often or even came back to stay, but we understand and respect your decisions. You're always going to be my baby girl—the one who was ready for adventures and getting her hands dirty—but I know you're a grown woman now."

A lump rose in Lia's throat. She remembered the adventures she'd get into with her dad and Mike. Always part of the "boys' club." Her mother would fret over the dirty clothes she'd come back in, often wishing Lia would take an interest in baking or something of the like.

But not Lia.

She was out there playing with the horses, chopping down Christmas trees, or building makeshift things for the inn. Daddy's little tomboy, they'd called her.

She couldn't even remember the last time she did anything remotely close. Adventures? Nope. Getting muddy and dirty? No way. Building things? Unless you consider the finishing touches for a high-class event, then maybe. It almost amazed her how different she'd become. Polished, refined, and on point. There was no room for mistakes.

"What's this?" Her father's question pulled her from her thoughts.

She glanced at the page he flipped to. "That's the calendar of events."

"I see that, but it appears there are new ones."

"That's right. We're adding more events. With new events filling our calendars, there's more opportunity to stay at the top of people's minds this holiday season."

Ron let out a low whistle. "This will be quite an undertaking. Are you sure you can handle it?"

"I have a few of the other townsfolk up to speed. They said they'd be ready and willing to help out."

"Maybe so, but it will be like herding cats."

Doubt seeped into her. "How do you mean? Things went well last night."

"Yes, because the tree lighting ceremony is a well-oiled machine at this point. You made a few changes with the band and vendors, but those wouldn't affect the overall event if they didn't go smoothly." He pointed to the new events. "This is uncharted territory for the town. I'm worried we're biting off more than we can chew. We need quick wins."

She chewed on her bottom lip. "I'm sure I could pull it off. Maybe I can work fewer hours at the inn to focus on it?"

She didn't want to mention she also needed the time to focus on her actual job. Trying to juggle all of this was a lot of pressure. She was starting to see the error of her ways for committing to so much.

Her father's comments made her worry she overpromised to everyone. "Mike, do you have any flexibility in your schedule to help cover the front desk while I take care of this?"

"Wish I could, but with the tree lot now being open on top of the general lumber orders, my days aren't super flexible." He rubbed the back of his neck with his hand. "I'll see what I can do."

"Okay. I get it. If not, maybe we can hire part-time help to run things here?"

Her dad shook his head. "We don't have the money."

"I can help pay."

"Even if you did, there's no one available. Not so close to the holidays. It would make more sense to cut the list down."

She looked at him with steady determination. "This list might be the only thing to get Fraser Hills on the map again. We need tourism dollars to support the town. Cutting any one of these could make a big difference in whether or not the town succeeds."

Just before Lia could silently start hyperventilating, Logan strolled in with Willow. The dog rushed to Ron and kissed his hands. He scratched her behind the ear, cooing at her like a parent over a newborn.

"Hey, Ron." Logan shook Ron's hand. "Glad to see you up and about."

"They tried to keep me down, but I wouldn't have it. It's Christmas, after all." He let out a hearty chuckle. "How's the roof coming along?"

"Great. Just taking a quick break to feed Willow and take her for a walk. Other than that, Jim and I have made progress. We're all framed out and making good time."

"That's wonderful news. Good job, son."

Lia captured Logan's gaze for the first time since he arrived. She flushed under his steel-blue eyes. His slow smile didn't help matters.

"What are you looking at?" He nodded at the binder resting on Ron's lap.

"Lia's plans for the inn and Christmas events. She's really going to 'modernize' things around here. I'll need a crash course on the Facebooks and this computer reservation system."

"It's Facebook, Dad," Mike corrected. "And I'll help you when she goes back to Boston."

Logan gave her a disappointed look, and for whatever reason, she couldn't stop the guilt from hitting her right in the gut. Not because she was going to leave her family again but because of Logan. It made no sense. She barely knew him.

"Did you see what she's proposing for events this season?" Ron raised his bushy eyebrows. "She's going to have her hands full."

"He thinks I might have issues rallying the townsfolk."

"I'd be happy to help if you need it," Logan offered.

"You would?" She tried to keep the breathlessness out of her voice. A few days ago, she couldn't stand the guy. Wouldn't trust him. Now she was thrilled about the prospect of working closely with him.

She mentally shook her head. It was that stupid tree lighting, that's all. A fleeting moment between them. It didn't change anything.

Right?

She couldn't let a silly fantasy get her all twisted in knots.

"Yeah. I really enjoyed the event last night. I'd be honored to help if you need it. Whatever you want, I'm your man."

You. I want you.

Lia shifted in her chair, wondering where the hell that thought came from. It wasn't like her to get googly and lusty over a man she met all of two seconds ago.

Being here was messing with her head. It must be all the fresh air. The sooner she got through this, the sooner she could get back to Boston where things were orderly, predictable, and made sense. There, she could control her life the way she wanted.

"Okay. Based on what Dad said, I'm sure I'll need extra hands. I'll keep you posted."

"Let me give you my phone number." Logan went to the reception desk and scribbled it down.

"It's fine." Lia followed him. "We're neighbors now. I can just knock if I need you, or I can find you on the roof." Having his number felt dangerous, like tempting fate.

"And if you're off the property and need help?"

He got her there. "I guess you're right."

"Great." He finished writing the last few numbers and handed

her the Post-it. "Looking forward to hearing from you, boss."
	He shot her a smoldering smile that made her insides liquefy.
	Good God, she was in trouble.

Chapter Eight

From dawn to sunset, Logan and Jim worked hard on the roof. The days were filled with intense labor and the added trickiness of keeping the noise to a minimum during the early hours so as to not disturb the guests.

It was just after noon. Thick gray clouds rolled in, stripping the sky of any sunlight and making the cold mountain air more bitter. Despite the exertion, Logan's face and fingers stung from the exposure. His hands burned from the vibration as he shot another nail into the frame with a nail gun. He needed a break. Needed to warm up and get something to eat.

He also wanted to see Lia.

Something changed between them the night of the tree lighting. Something in the way their gazes had caught and lingered for a moment had him curious about her. There were layers hidden underneath that standoffish, pushy, and reserved woman. He'd seen hints of it. In that moment, she'd let him in.

Not to mention, the stories her family shared made him question who she really was. At first meeting, he couldn't believe that girl and Lia were one and the same. Surely she couldn't have changed that much. Could she have?

But the way the light caught her brown eyes that night—making them look like magic danced in them—made him consider going against his better judgment. He wasn't looking for romantic entanglements, especially with a woman who would be gone before the new year and who was the daughter of his employer.

That would be a horrible decision.

He just wanted to see her and learn more about her…as friends.

Yeah, right.

Logan straightened from his hunched position, stretching his back and hamstrings. "Hey, Jim. Time for a break. I'm going to grab something from the kitchen. You wanna to come?"

"I have to run back to the mill for supplies. I'll get something there. Meet you back here in a half hour?"

"Works for me."

The two men eased their way down the ladder and went their separate ways. Logan banged his boots outside on the back stairs and shook off the remaining saw dust. A stupid grin was already on his face at the thought of seeing Lia.

He walked inside and down the short hallway that led to the reception area, only to be greeted by Mariam.

His smile faltered. "Hi, Mariam. Great to see you back behind the desk."

"Hi, dear. I'm afraid I'm not as useful as I used to be with this darn wrist." She held up the splint and looked at it with disdain. "I'm just helping out until Lia gets back."

Hope blossomed. "Oh? Where is she?" he asked as casually as he could.

Just making small talk. Nothing to read into.

She made a disapproving face. "Work calls. I know she has a job to do, and I'm so proud of her, but those calls always put her in a tizzy. She tries to hide it, but I can see it in her face and posture. There are some moments I swear I still see my sweet girl, but the phone calls seem to strip it away from her."

"I'm sure she's trying her best to manage Boston and here."

"Of course. I shouldn't complain. It's been two years since she visited last, so it's nice to have her here again. She's doing all she can to help. It's just," she trailed off, giving a half-hearted shrug. "I miss her."

Before Logan could respond, Lia strutted into the room like a woman on a mission. Miriam's sadness quickly disappeared, but Logan knew she was putting on a brave face.

Lia's stiff posture eased slightly when her gaze trailed along Logan's body leaning against the reception desk. He could have sworn a faint pink crept to her cheeks.

"Just the man I need," she said when she approached.

Is there a slight huskiness to her voice or am I dreaming?

"What can I help you with?"

Did my voice just crack like a pubescent teen?

Embarrassed, he cleared his throat. Lia's statement was simple, not a proposition. And even though he hadn't been in the dating scene for a while, he would like to believe he was smoother than that.

"You said you wanted to help with the events, so I'm cashing in that favor."

"Absolutely. Whatever you need."

"We're going to cut down a tree tonight."

He squinted at her. "Come again?"

"In two days, the inn has an event that includes decorating the tree that will stand in the lobby. Normally, we go as a family to pick out the tree but, clearly, my parents can't do it, and Mike has to manage the tree lot without Dad. We're short-handed."

"Can't Mike just bring a tree from the lot?"

She scowled. "If you haven't gathered, we're all about traditions here," she snipped. "Sure, the *easy* way would be to have Mike bring a tree, but we want to keep this as authentic as possible. That means trudging through the tree farm, finding the right tree, and cutting it down with a damn axe and handsaw."

Mariam wasn't kidding when she said Lia got into a tizzy after her work calls. She was fired up.

"A handsaw?" He scanned her tailored slacks and pumps before meeting her eyes. "You sure about that?"

She crossed her arms, apparently not liking how he doubted her abilities. "It may have been a few years since I've chopped down a tree, but I'm more than capable. All I need from you is to help me drag it back and load it into your truck."

"I haven't seen you wear anything but heels the entire time you've been here. Do you even have the right clothes to do this? It's snowy and slippery in those areas."

She scrutinized his work boots and light jacket. "Do you?" She waved her hand in his direction. "Don't worry about it. I'm meeting with Amber at the sports outfitters later to grab gear. Can you be ready at five?"

"Sure. I'll be wrapping up by then." He made a face.

"What?"

"It's going to be dark by the time we get out there. Could be dangerous. Wild animals. Trusting you to not chop me instead of the tree."

She squinted her eyes, the spark of friendly competition making them shine. "Can't handle a little adventure, Logan?"

This playful side piqued his interest. "I'm ready. Anytime. Anywhere."

Her mouth dropped open slightly as if understanding the hidden innuendo. He'd just found another button he could push with her.

With that small victory, he headed off to the kitchen for lunch, thoroughly warmed from their sparing.

~ * ~

Lia struggled up the walkway to her temporary cabin, breathing hard under the weight of the countless bags she was lugging. Her original four-day itinerary didn't include outdoor excursions, so she sorely lacked the proper clothes. After Amber had hooked her up with the essentials—snow boots, a winter jacket, thermals, thick socks, gloves, hat, and scarf—Lia had also made a few stops at the local boutiques for more appropriate clothes to wear around town.

After all, she couldn't go chopping down a tree in her slacks. Not with how expensive they were.

She loaded up on jeans, boots, sneakers, sweaters, and a few sportier clothes for laborious days. Some might balk at the amount she spent today, but if she was going to be here for another three weeks, she needed this. Even if she went up to Boston for a quick work trip, she wouldn't have mountain-appropriate clothes in her closet to bring back. All her shopping sprees had been focused on professional attire for the office or evening wear for her events. She couldn't remember the last time she bought a pair of jeans and a cute top for a casual night out.

She also couldn't remember the last time she had a casual night out. It was pathetic.

Her shaky legs carried her up the wooden steps that led to the small porch. Juggling the bags, she pulled the key from her purse and tried to push it into the slot.

"Need a hand?" A deep voice sounded from behind her, causing shivers to run down her spine. She peered over her shoulder to find Logan and Willow standing at the base of the stairs.

"If you wouldn't mind. Thanks." She handed him the keys. He turned the lock with ease, grabbing a few bags from her in the process. "You can put them on the table." She nodded in the direction of a small wooden table made for two in a nook near the kitchen.

Willow ambled in behind him, finding a small throw rug near the fireplace. She made three circles before curling up in a ball, her lopsided smile firmly in place.

"Willow, up. Don't be rude."

Willow nestled in more, making Lia laugh.

Logan rubbed his hand behind his neck and tilted his head. "I'm sorry. She's usually better behaved than this."

"She made herself right at home."

He smirked. "I guess she's dropping a hint that I need to get a rug for our fireplace." He eyed the mountain of bags on the table. "Somehow you made Fraser Hills look like Rodeo Drive. Are there even enough stores to produce that many bags?"

She grinned at him. "As a born and raised local, I know all the secrets of this town and where to find the best shopping."

"Secrets, huh?" He looked amused, that boyish grin making her insides flutter.

Lia shrugged. "Maybe if you're lucky, I'll let you in on one or two of them."

God, am I flirting? Horror coursed through her body. *When was the last time I flirted? Am I rusty? Am I embarrassing myself?*

"I'll hold you to that." He winked.

Okay, maybe I'm not as out of practice as I thought.

"I need to change into something more appropriate. Will you be ready to go in ten?"

"Sure. Let me feed Willow and grab the axe and handsaw. I'll meet you at my truck." He waved as he and Willow ventured off.

Lia tried not to let the strange sensation of excitement overwhelm her. She could have asked a handful of other people to help her tonight, but she wanted him with her. Alone time with Logan bordered on dangerous, but she couldn't figure out why. If she were smart, she should keep her distance, not giving into whatever sudden urges were stirring.

Delicious urges that made her feel insanely good.

I just invited him to make him feel like he's part of the community. I'll show him there's no hard feelings after our less than stellar start. That's all.

She couldn't stop herself from rolling her eyes at the crock of shit she was spewing. Whatever reason she'd decided to invite Logan tonight had nothing to do with being neighborly.

~ * ~

Logan leaned against his truck as he waited for Lia, using the time to dissect their most recent interactions. Was she flirting with him or was this her personality once the tough-as-nails facade wore off?

He shook his head. He didn't know her well enough yet to decipher if it was her being friendly or something more. He didn't want to be a fool and act on something that might not be anything.

Then again, he shouldn't be acting on it at all, even if something was there.

Before he had time to think deeper about it, Lia appeared.

Or who he thought was Lia.

There she was, completely transformed into a woman of the mountains. She wore tight jeans that showed off her shapely legs and thick wool socks that poked out the tops of her winter hiking boots. Although her new jacket wasn't formfitting, it only made him want to see what was hidden underneath. Her forest-green scarf and matching hat made her dark hair and brown eyes pop.

She was beautiful before, but something about the casual style made the statement ring truer.

"Hello. Earth to Logan." Her eyes sparkled with amusement. "Are you listening?"

"Sorry. Your transformation shocked me. I was stunned speechless." His kept his tone playful to hide the fact he was completely infatuated with her.

She rolled her eyes. "I asked if you had the supplies."

He patted the truck. "All here. Let's go."

He helped her into the truck, the feeling of her slender hand in his almost causing him to abandon all reason. He wanted to intertwine their fingers. Kiss the inside of her wrist. Anything that would allow him to touch her for a moment longer.

But he let her go. He needed to. Had to.

They drove in relative silence for most of the ride, with Lia occasionally providing directions. Otherwise, they sat lost in their thoughts. He wondered if she felt the heated tension between them too. Did she feel the spark when he took her hand or was it all in his head?

"Slow down," she instructed as she leaned forward to get a better vantage point. The sun was nearly set, reducing visibility. "There." She pointed to a gated dirt road a quarter mile ahead. He followed the road and pulled to a stop in front of a small sign that read, "Winchester Tree Farm."

Hopping out of the truck, she went to the gate. Withdrawing a key from her pocket, she unlocked the gate and pushed it open. The metal whined loudly, making it sound like she was opening the forbidden theme park gates in the movie, *Jurassic Park*. After he drove through, she promptly shut and locked it again before sliding back into the passenger side.

The dirt road was the only clear path in an otherwise overwhelming forest of Fraser firs. All around them, the lush green pines grew in various stages. Some were barely a foot tall while others rose more than ten feet. Although the truck windows were securely shut, the pine tree scent filled the cabin.

"I love that smell." She took a deep breath and sighed. "It's so fresh."

He made a noise of agreement. "Where to?"

"There's a dirt parking lot about a half a mile up on the right. Just keep going. You won't miss it."

The thick forest made the retreating sunlight even scarcer, forcing Logan to flick on his high beams as he followed the bumpy road to the lot. He spotted it a couple minutes later and slowed to park.

"We're the only ones here," he said.

"It's kinda late to be cutting down trees. It's dangerous when it's dark."

He cocked his head. "Remind me again why we're doing this."

"It should have been done days ago—in the daytime—but with the incident, we're behind schedule. I haven't even dug out the decorations from the storage room yet. I'll have to do that when we get back."

"Do you ever relax?" he joked.

"After the decorations, I have a bunch of emails from my work I need to respond to. So, no. Not while I'm down here, at least."

"That doesn't sound very healthy." He was concerned about her. Although she was a go-getter, there were moments when he could see the exhaustion setting in. Her careful makeup couldn't hide the dark circles under her eyes, and when she thought no one was paying attention, her shoulders slumped as if she didn't have the energy to hold them any longer. It had only been a week of her working like this. What would another three weeks do to her?

The desire to take care of her came on strong. When was the last time anyone had done that for her? She was the type to keep people at a distance, rarely asking for help. How would she feel if someone let her lean on them for once?

"Maybe not, but it's not forever. I'll survive."

Just like that, he was reminded of her short time here and the exact reason why he couldn't let ridiculous ideas like taking care of her infiltrate his mind.

They got out of the truck, zipped up their jackets, then put on their protective gloves. The temperature had dipped when the sun went down, and it was even colder this close to the mountains. He shivered under his light jacket as the wind kicked up.

The ground was covered with a thin layer of snow from the weekend, and Logan was certain patches of ice were hidden beneath. They'd have to be careful.

Lia handed him a flashlight, her breath coming out like smoke in front of her. "You ready?"

He removed the equipment from the back. "What's the game plan?"

"We find the perfect tree. We cut it down. Then bring it home."

"Find? As in, you don't know which tree you want yet?"

"That's part of the fun."

He gave her a sideways glance. "Maybe in the light when you don't have to worry about slipping on ice and cracking your skull open."

"Just trust me."

He was wary. "Okay. Lead the way."

They clicked on their flashlights and took a small path to the right of the lot. Lia stalked the trees, inspecting and evaluating their worthiness for the Winchester. He watched her process. Every time she came across a tree she liked she made a circle around it, felt the needles with her bare hands, smelled it, and checked its height.

He couldn't help but smile at her intensity. It was as if she was selecting a rare diamond.

Finally, after trekking around for nearly half an hour, she claimed she found the perfect one. They shined their lights on it, and from what Logan could tell, it was the quintessential Christmas tree. It had the perfect shape, the branches were full of vibrant green needles, and the scent was intoxicating. It brought him back to his own childhood Christmas memories. How this tree managed to do that when none of the other nearly identical ones had was beyond him. Lia had a gift.

"I think we can do this with the axe. Can you hand it to me?"

He shot her another concerned glance. Her confidence made him believe she knew what she was doing. She even told him so. However, when she gripped the axe, he realized they were both mistaken.

"Whoa. What are you doing?" He plucked the axe from her hands.

"Hey!"

"You said you could chop this thing down."

"I can." She reached for the axe again.

He held it away from her. "When exactly was the last time you held one of these or chopped down a tree?"

She considered it for a moment. "Um. Not sure. The Christmas before college?"

"So, twelve years ago," he said flatly. "I think you're a bit rusty on your axe-wielding skills. Thank God you asked me to come. You probably would've chopped someone in half."

She narrowed her eyes. "Well, don't let me stop you from mansplaining how to chop down a tree. It's not like my family owns a tree farm or anything."

"I won't get in your way. Just let me show you some pointers. A refresher, if you will."

He positioned himself behind her and hesitated for a minute, knowing the contact would be torture. But if he wanted to ensure neither of them lost a limb, it was necessary.

Wrapping his arms around either side of her, he brought the axe in front of them, careful not to have full body contact. He guided her hands one by one to the proper areas of the handle. "If you hold here, you'll have more control and leverage."

She scoffed. "What'd they do? Teach you that move in charm school? What's next? Are you going to show me how to hold a baseball bat? Maybe yawn and put your arm around me at a movie?"

"Are you asking me out on a date?" he teased. Lia nudged him with her elbow, knocking some air out of him. "Careful. We've got a weapon in our hands." He took a step out of her general range of reach. "You feel good?"

"Yeah, it's coming back to me now."

She pulled back the axe and swung it expertly, connecting to the trunk with a solid thud.

Nice. A businesswoman and a lumberjack. He was pleasantly surprised. Definitely nothing like his ex.

Not that he wanted to think about her right now.

Lia continued to chop away until the tree was nearly teetering on the last bit of trunk. She let out a breath and wiped sweat from her forehead.

"Care to do the honors?" she offered as she put the axe aside.

"As if you needed to ask." Logan walked up to the tree and got ready to kick it down, but his foot lost traction on hidden ice.

She gasped and reached out to catch him, causing her foot to skid on the ice too. Down they went together, falling into a tangled heap on the snow-covered ground. By the time they caught their breath, she was sprawled out on top of him. Despite the heavy winter gear, her curves were perfectly pressed against him.

It felt good. She felt good.

She pushed up onto her elbows, their bodies still connected. Logan's hands instinctively grabbed her hips to help steady her so she could get up.

Or so he could hold her there just for a second more.

His brain short-circuited with her lying on top of him, her face so close to his. The only clear thoughts he had were highly inappropriate.

"Sorry." Her voice sounded strained.

Lia's chest rose and fell rapidly, and Logan wondered if it was from cutting down the tree or if it was because she as aware of him as he was of her. She paused for a moment, looking deep into his eyes, and then rolled off and stood. Focused on brushing the snow from her clothes, she seemed as if she was busying herself so she wouldn't dare look back at him.

He rose to his feet and shook the snow off his back. "Are you okay?"

"I'm fine. You?"

"I'm good. Just put a damper on knocking down this tree."

"Let's get it down and go. I didn't realize how icy it was. I don't want us to have another accident while we're lugging this thing to your truck."

He wouldn't mind another accident like that if it meant Lia would be on top of him again.

He swallowed. *I'm in deep shit.*

~ * ~

The ride back to the inn was even quieter than the trip to the tree farm. Lia sat in the passenger seat, staring hard out the window, trying not to think of how it felt to fall on top of Logan. Or how his strong hands gripped her hips. Or how those hands would feel if...

No. No. No. No.

So what if she hadn't had a rush like that in forever? Or maybe ever? The sensation of his body pressed against hers, the roughness of his fingertips on her soft skin, the closeness of his face to hers. She had almost leaned down a couple more inches to close the distance.

Almost.

What was it about this man that had her acting like a lovesick teenager?

She bit her bottom lip. It'd been a while since she was alone with a man, especially in a non-professional setting. Her hormones saw an opportunity and were trying to take the reins. But her mind reminded her even a fling was a bad idea, especially with someone who worked for her family. How awkward would it be if he still worked there when she came to visit next? Even if they kept things light and casual, it would still be weird.

Why was she thinking about this? It was insane.

Just keep it professional. Create some distance.

"Thanks for helping with the tree today."

"No problem." His response was short. The tension in the car had shifted from sexual to civilly distant.

She didn't like it. "Can you help me bring it into the lobby when we get back?"

"Sure."

Another short answer. Logan didn't seem like the broody, silent type. Even when she tried to ruffle his feathers when they'd first met, he rolled with it, unperturbed.

She decided to let it go. Maybe the incident earlier made him uncomfortable. Maybe he hurt himself when he fell and didn't want to admit it.

Maybe he doesn't want you.

The thought gutted her. It was ridiculous to entertain the idea of being with him—even for a night—but she hated knowing that the special look they shared at the tree lighting might have been one-sided.

Logan pulled around the circular drive in the front of the inn and cut the engine. He got out without so much as a word.

She wasn't quite ready to dissect the feelings he had stirred within her, but she couldn't deny that she liked his company. There was something very real about him, and for the first time in a long time, she didn't have the overwhelming need to keep her walls up. Each moment with him knocked them down, brick by brick. She hadn't realized how exhausting it was keeping those barriers up all these years, and now she was scared to lose that sweet relief so soon.

She stepped out of the passenger side, slamming the door harder than she intended, and helped him unload the tree and bring it inside. Her mother had taken out the tree stand while she waited for them to return, making it a smooth transition from the car to the lobby.

Lia held the tree straight as Logan got down and disappeared under the thick branches to secure it in place. She snuck a glance at the small strip of bare skin poking out from the bottom of his shirt as he shimmied around the stand and worked the fasteners into the trunk.

Mariam came from behind the desk and stood next to Lia, marveling over the grand tree. The second floor of the inn opened to below, giving the lobby an airy feel and allowing them the option to get a much taller, fuller tree than the standard. The tree itself was probably twice the height of Lia and made a wonderful centerpiece for the lobby. Even without the decorations, it was beautiful.

"Is it straight?" Logan called out, his voice slightly muffled.

"It's good."

He slid himself out, stood, glanced at the women, and frowned.

"What's wrong?" he asked Mariam, who was wringing her hands. She winced when she remembered her sore wrist.

Lia turned to her mother and noted her anxiousness. "Is everything okay, Mom?"

"While you were gone, we had a few cancellations for later this month."

"Why? The roof will be fixed by then."

"I know, I know. But the people were nervous there would be complications that would delay the timeline. They said they'd rather go on a vacation that was a sure thing than find out last minute their trip is ruined." She shifted from one foot to another. "Some of them were families. I couldn't blame them. They didn't want to disappoint their children during Christmas."

"This is nuts." Lia was outraged. Things seemed to go well after the tree lighting, how did it turn so quickly?

"I even offered to have Logan call them back and explain where he was in the process for peace of mind. They didn't care."

Lia let out a sigh. "How many reservations were canceled?"

"Four."

She mentally crunched numbers. "Mom, we're going to be in real trouble if we don't get those rebooked. We're already taking a hit by giving the current guests discounts because of the construction and noise."

Her mother's eyes shined with unfallen tears, making a lump rise in Lia's throat. "Don't remind me."

Lia fished her phone out of her pocket and started scrolling through her contacts. If they were going to save the inn and the Christmas celebrations, she was going to have to step up her game.

"I've got an idea," she said. "I have to make a few calls. Logan, would you mind helping mom get out the decorations?"

His face softened. Whatever weirdness was going on in the car earlier subsided. "Absolutely. Come on, Mariam." They headed off to the storage area while Lia got to work.

She had a few contacts in Boston who owed her favors, and she knew just the person to call.

Chapter Nine

Lia sat bundled up on her porch early the next morning. Her laptop rested open next to her as she sipped her steaming cup of coffee. It was her second cup of the day, and probably not her last. She hadn't slept a wink last night between the incessant calls from Melody and managing the responses for the upcoming event at the inn.

Even though she pulled an all-nighter, she was proud of the progress she made with her web developer, Klare. She was sure Klare wasn't expecting a call for help late one evening, or to work through the night, but she'd been a good sport about it, particularly after she got the rundown on what was happening at the inn and in Fraser Hills.

It was rare for Lia to ask for help, but desperate times called for desperate measures. She would do anything to help her family and this town. Even if she didn't pull it off, it wouldn't be for lack of trying.

"Hey. You're up early." Logan strolled up to her cabin, his frame highlighted by the dim dawn sunlight.

Willow's wriggling body came running up behind him, and she gave Lia one of her signature lopsided grins. The dog was full of happiness, love, and energy. Lia couldn't help but smile in return. It was hard not to around her.

Or around him.

"I was trying to figure out how to fix the reservation issue. Want to see?" She held up her computer to offer him a peek.

"Only if I can steal a cup of coffee."

"There's still some in the pot. Cups are to the right of the sink."

Willow stayed by Lia's feet as Logan went inside. A moment later, he returned with a fresh cup in hand and sat next to her on the small wooden bench. The heat of his arm pressed against her, warming her all over.

She positioned the laptop so they could both see and refreshed the page.

"Is this the Winchester Inn website?" he asked as he scrolled through.

"It is."

Lia was impressed with how the new site turned out. The original one was so dated it could have passed as a spam site. With Klare's expertise, the site was now dynamic, welcoming, and user-friendly. Lia had dug out her mom's photo albums from the storage closet, plucking out old pictures of the inn, the town, and past holiday events.

Thanks to her mom's albums, they added a new tab to showcase the history of the inn and Fraser Hills, providing a story people could connect with. She added more details and photos about the current space, highlighting the different room options and the common areas, and linked their Facebook account and the town's tourism site so people knew what they could do while in the area. To bring the inn's reservation system to the 21st century, Lia created a contact page for email reservations and inquiries.

Lastly, she included an event calendar. People could click on the event name to get details about the event and any relevant pictures from years past.

"This is unbelievable, Lia," he finally said. "Your parents are going to be so happy."

"I also created the events' RSVP pages and ads on Facebook."

"You think this will work?"

"It's still early, but I've already seen responses come through for tomorrow's event."

Logan looked her in the eyes. His smile faltered. "Did you sleep at all last night?"

"No."

"Lia." He frowned, his displeasure evident.

"Don't try to lecture me right now, okay? I'm exhausted, but I had to do this. Maybe if I were around more, I would have known what was going on. I could have helped before it got to this point."

The admission surprised her. Lia's career aspirations created a wedge between her and her family, and now they were paying for it. She could have helped them revamp their website years ago. It was a small change she could have done remotely, but one that would have made an impact. Instead, she was too focused on herself. Too distant.

Too selfish.

She hung her head in shame. Whatever excitement she had about the website was overshadowed by the realization of how much she neglected her family.

Logan cupped her face with his free hand, lifting it up to meet his stare. The warmth from his palm contrasted with the cold air on her cheeks. His woodsy scent was calming, a smell that brought back old memories from growing up at the tree farm. She wanted to lean further into his hand, into him. She closed her eyes just for a moment to savor his comfort.

"Hey." His soft voice grabbed her attention, making her look back into his alluring eyes. "You can't blame yourself. You're here now. You're working hard to help everyone."

"It's not enough. I should have been doing more."

"The past is the past, Lia." His thumb traced the skin by her temple, down to her jaw. She loved his touch a little more than she should. "You need to focus on the present. Things are different. You're making a difference in their lives now."

Lia nodded, unable to find her words as his thumb continued to move along her bottom lip. They both stared at each other in silence, lost in the trance of the moment. The urge to kiss him was overwhelming. She could have sworn he started to lean in, or was she just hoping?

Willow barked and got to her feet, her tail and ears raised in high alert. They jumped away from each other, as if they'd been caught doing some horrible crime, and watched Jim's truck come up the driveway.

"Guess it's time for me to get to work." Logan's voice held a hint of disappointment.

"Yeah." Disappointment filled her too as he stood and whistled for Willow to follow him.

~ * ~

Logan stopped in at the inn on his lunch break again, eager to see Lia after their moment on her porch that morning. He couldn't help but comfort her when she showed her vulnerable side. For a second, he thought it would have been a mistake. That she'd recoil at his touch and rebuild those impenetrable walls from the first day she showed up. But instead, she leaned into him. Her eyes mirrored the same want and emotions that were raging inside of him.

He couldn't stop thinking about it.

His thoughts stopped short as he entered the lobby where chaos was unfolding. It appeared that the boxes of decorations had exploded. Tinsel was everywhere. Reindeer lawn ornaments surrounded the front desk. A string of Christmas lights nearly tripped him. Several of the townspeople were frantically running about and Lia was in the center of the circus, holding her clipboard and calling out orders like a ringleader.

She picked up a few strands of garland at her feet and handed them to a frazzled Kathleen. Amber and Sarah were unsuccessfully untangling the lights. Daniel and Walt were unloading a stuffed Santa and his sleigh.

Logan approached Lia. "What's going on?"

She turned to him, and he was struck by her beauty. For once, her hair wasn't sleek and straight, but full of silky loose waves. Not the wild mane he had seen in the pictures of her when she was growing up, but more of a "girl-next-door" vibe. Her makeup was minimal, only a swipe of mascara, blush, and some lip-gloss. He noticed a faint smattering of freckles across her nose and cheeks that were usually hidden. Her typical attire of expensive slacks, pumps, and blouses was replaced with jeans, a wool sweater, and boots.

She looked so real, like a woman from his dreams.

He grabbed one of her curls, watching it bounce when he let go. "This is new."

She tucked a strand of hair behind her ear and straightened her sweater. "Didn't exactly have time to do my usual routine."

"I like it. *A lot.*"

She blushed. "After you left, I got a call from Mom saying there were voicemails on the machine. She thought something was wrong. I came in and listened to them. They were calls about tomorrow's event."

"So what's wrong with that? That's good right?"

"Yes, but..." Her face contorted between happy and panicked. "But..."

"In my sleep-deprived state, I forgot to set a cap for RSVPs. We have well over the expected amount of people."

"That's great."

She smiled wearily. "Sure, if we had more time to prepare. We hadn't planned for this, so we had to improvise. We're throwing tents up in the back for added space and brought in a few other locals to provide food, drinks, and supplies." She exhaled a huge breath. "I never slip up. I always focus on the details. I can't believe I did that."

He threw his arm over her shoulder and gave her a quick squeeze. "Your mistake is our gain. Maybe it's not as organized and perfect as your other events, but the point was to make sure we got people here. Right? Now we have more than enough."

She didn't look convinced. "I suppose you're right."

Jeff, the gruff cook from the local diner, came barreling through the front door. "I got the tent. Where ya want it?"

"Set it up on the back patio." She pointed in the direction he should follow.

"Near the firepit?" He scratched his thick, dark beard.

"Yup."

"There gonna be enough room for me to make my dogs?"

Logan had never seen someone so serious about hot dogs.

"Jeff," Lia said, her voice calm and smooth, "why don't you look back there and find the best spot for you to set up. It's up to you as a thanks for helping me in a bind."

He grunted and headed to the back. Logan was thoroughly impressed by Lia's knack for easing even the grumpiest of people.

Mike came blowing through the inn next. "Hey, sis." He nodded to Logan in greeting. "I dug out the heat lamps. Only two of them work. Is that going to be an issue?"

"Between those, the firepit, and Jeff's grill, we should be fine with heat."

"Sounds good." He followed Jeff's lead to the back.

"Jeff's pretty passionate about hot dogs, huh?" Logan asked.

She shook her head in amusement. "You mean you haven't had Fraser Hills' world famous hot dogs?"

"I've heard rumors. What's the story behind it?"

"Jeff's been the diner cook forever. I guess the diner's owner had a food truck, but since he's getting older, he's retiring. Jeff's apparently going through some sort of midlife crisis and wants to take over the food truck. But first, he wanted to do a 'test kitchen' to see what people like."

"How could he get hot dogs wrong? What's there to test?"

Her lips twitched as she tried to hold back a laugh. "Oh, no, no, good sir. These aren't just any ol' hot dogs. These are *artisanal* hot dogs. He came up with all these unique, wacky, and fancy ways to make a hot dog. Apparently, he's started a trial run at the diner last year and they're a hit. I haven't had the pleasure myself, but it's all the rage."

"Was that a Southern accent I just heard?" Logan couldn't stop the grin spreading across his face. The sparkle in her eyes and playful banter was a welcome change. In moments like this, he could almost see the young Lia who appeared in the pictures at the inn.

"You must be mistaken," she drawled dramatically and winked.

Maybe it was wishful thinking, but her newfound investment in this town seemed to be good for her. She was having fun and was more comfortable in her skin than he'd seen since she'd arrived. Would she think so too? And if so, would it be enough for her to consider staying?

"This isn't doing it for me." Kathleen pointed at the lackluster garland wrapped around the banister and railings. "It's flat. I hate it."

Lia cringed. "It's not bad," she lied. "It's just...plain."

"I won't have people tying my name to this lifeless monstrosity. I'm going back to my shop to get more supplies. I'm going to freakin' dazzle people." And with that, she stalked off and out of the inn.

"Well, she's..." Lia tried to find the right word.

"Spunky?"

"Sure. Hey, while you're up on the roof, mind throwing Santa and his crew up there? Maybe string some lights, too?"

Logan looked around the room and eyed a massive wreath in the corner. "I'm assuming you want this hung on the front?"

She smiled at him sweetly. "If you wouldn't mind."

"I don't think this is right," Amber said.

They both turned around to see Sarah tangled up in the lights.

"I suppose this isn't typically how your swanky Boston events go, huh?" Logan quipped.

"Not quite."

He grinned at a frowning Lia. "Looks like you've got your work cut out for you. I'll leave you to it. See you later."

~ * ~

Somehow Lia survived the madness of the day. Setting up for the event hadn't gone smoothly, not by a long shot, but they had everything they needed to make it great. With the decor in place, a new layout to help the flow of people, Daniel's band to keep things festive, and an assortment of the town's best food and drinks available, it was bound to be a hit.

One could only hope.

Standing in front of the full-length mirror in her bedroom, she added the final touches to her evening's ensemble. Her black dress clung to her upper body, tastefully showing off her best assets, and cinched at her waist. It flared out to her knees, with hints of red tulle hidden underneath, only noticeable when she swished around. Her sparkly black stilettos shimmered in the light as she slipped them on before fastening a red jeweled necklace around her neck.

Leaving her hair naturally curly, she pulled it off to one side with a barrette that featured dazzling crystals. She lined her eyes and swiped on two coats on mascara, accentuating the smoky eyeshadow that made her otherwise plain brown irises seem mysterious and alluring. Finishing with a touch of red lipstick and a spritz of her favorite perfume, Lia was ready to go.

She felt sexy. Unstoppable. Although she might be overdressed, as the organizer and face of the Winchester Inn, she was confident about her selection.

And if she was honest with herself, she kind of wanted to impress Logan too.

Lia recalled their moment on the porch. She had let herself trust him just enough to tell him the truth about her insecurities, guilt, and worries. It had been so long since she opened up to someone. It was good to have an honest conversation. Maybe it was sleep deprivation. Maybe it was the nostalgia of being back here. She could try to rationalize it, but when he touched her face, all logic disappeared.

The way his rough fingers traced her skin with delicate care; she had never been touched like that. Not even when she and Emmett dated or with the few people she casually saw afterward. You'd think young love or new lust would involve all of that—the lingering looks, the tentative touches, the need to be closer, the wanting—but nothing and no one compared to the emotions Logan had dredged up in her.

For the last couple of years, she started to think those kinds of feelings didn't exist. At least not for someone like her. She assumed they were sensationalized in movies and books, or that her girlfriends had over-romanticized their own experiences.

But now she knew it was real, and it could happen to her. She just didn't know what to do about it.

Her phone's alarm went off. People would be arriving soon to set up, and guests would be coming in the next hour. Giving herself a last look, she grabbed her jacket, so she wouldn't freeze from the short walk from her cabin to the inn, and the clutch that held her phone—which Melody was sure to blow up all night—and made her way to the event.

Lia could hear the band tuning up as she walked down the back hall to the lobby. They were such a fun band to have for these events. She was thankful Daniel had come back.

The place looked amazing, especially with the string lights twinkling around. Although many of the decorations stayed true to the traditions, her helpers added something extra to the mix. It was as if they shared a piece of themselves, a real representation of the kind of people you'd find in Fraser Hills.

A winter wonderland filled the dining area, complete with fake snow and a mechanical motion-activated Frosty the Snowman that greeted people who walked by. Hand-cut snowflakes and green and red links made from construction paper crafted by the town's kids hung from the ceiling and doorways. Snow globes that played Christmas classics when you wound them up were scattered throughout the space.

She checked out the festive garland wrapped around the banister and smiled. Kathleen was right. Her updates would definitely "freakin' dazzle" people.

At that moment, Lia recognized the stark difference between here and Boston. Her events in Boston were precise and efficient. Here, they were anything but. However, these events outshined even the splashiest, most opulent one she'd done over the years, and it was all because of the love the people put into it. They were the biggest-hearted people she knew. No one could come close.

"Dogs comin' through," Jeff announced as he pushed by her with a large tray of hot dogs.

"Hey, Lia." Bee's dimples deepened with her wide smile. "We're all set in the kitchen. I have a couple of my staff ready to walk around with hors-d'oeuvres."

"And I'm ready to blow people's minds with my creations," Sarah called from the makeshift cash bar located in the dining area. "Oh man, wait 'til you see my special drink list. People are going to be feelin' good tonight."

Tommy placed the garnishes on the bar and gave Sarah a high five.

Lia poked her head into the dining room. "Good is great. Try not to get them too trashed. This is a family event, don't forget."

"Ha. Then the parents probably need this more than any of us."

A smile spread across Lia's lips as she shook her head and made her way to the opposite side of the dining room where Savannah was setting up the craft table to entertain the kids. "Hi. We're almost ready here," Savannah said as Lia checked the items laid out.

There was glitter, popsicle sticks, markers, felt, googly eyes, blank ornaments, and so on. "Looks like you've outdone yourself."

"The kids are going to have a blast making ornaments."

Decorating the inn's tree was part of the Winchester tradition. Every year, children and adults alike had the opportunity to craft a new ornament to hang. With such a large tree, Lia's parents also hung ornaments from years past to fill in the empty areas. They'd select different ones each year to make the discoveries interesting. It was a fun experience to find ornaments from decades ago.

As a teenager, she remembered how Ida Kaufman, an elderly woman who worked as a receptionist at the vet, found an ornament she made with her late husband when they first got married. She was a pip of a woman, but Lia couldn't deny how special of a moment it was for Ida to see that memory hanging there so many years later.

Lia wondered if she would find any of her old ornaments. Knowing how sentimental her mother was, she most likely would have hung one now that Lia was back.

Back for now, at least.

Within the hour, people flooded through the front doors. The calm before the storm ended abruptly and now the inn was filled with lively music, happy chatter, clinking glasses, and children's laughter. Her heart was full. Everything about it felt right.

How did she ever think she could find anything that could

compare to moments like this?

A young girl tugged on the hem of her dress. "Miss Lia, am I allowed to make an ornament?"

Lia bent to address the rosy-cheeked, blue-eyed girl. "Absolutely. If you go into the dining area, you'll see all the supplies there for you. I can't wait to see where you place it on the tree."

The girl looked at her with pure joy. Her mother came up behind her, placing her hands on the girl's shoulders. "Quite a party," the mother complimented her.

"I couldn't have done this without the rest of the town." Lia nodded toward the people mingling about. "And thank you for pushing through the permits we needed."

"My pleasure."

The woman, Justice Jane Millie, had been a few years ahead of Lia in school. She was always friendly, yet quiet and studious. Last Lia had heard, she went on to get her law degree at one of the Ivy League schools and practiced in New York before returning to Fraser Hills to start a family.

Lia was surprised a woman with so much ambition and experience would consider giving up a prestigious career for small-town life, especially at the height of her success. But seeing the girl, Lia couldn't picture Jane's daughter on the swings at a playground surrounded by beeping cars, tall buildings, and concrete. However, she could imagine her raven black hair—just like her mother's—whipping about her as she ran through the open fields in the valley.

Lia turned back to the entrance to greet more guests. Her heart stopped as Logan made his way up the front steps.

He traded in his usual rugged and manly attire for something more sophisticated. Tonight, he'd give Boston's most successful businessmen a run for their money. His light-gray slacks were paired with a navy button up, a color that made his eyes dark and inviting with a hint of mischief. He rolled up the sleeves to show off his muscular forearms. His hair, still damp from a shower, curled slightly behind his ears, and his scruff was cleaned up, showing off his strong jaw.

A slow smile spread across his face as his gaze locked on hers. Her stomach did a little flip.

"You're beautiful," he whispered in her ear as they embraced.

She laughed. "Well hello to you too."

He let her go and grinned. "Sorry. One track mind. Hello." He surveyed the room. "Looks a lot better than the disaster earlier today."

"Just better?" she teased.

"You're right. It's amazing, but you steal the show."

She blushed. "Flattery will get you everywhere."

He cocked his head, a smile still playing on his full lips. "Huh. I never noticed that."

Her face dropped. "What?"

"The little dimple on the apple of your cheek. When you smiled just now, it came out. It's cute."

"It only shows when I'm truly smiling." She touched her cheek, now embarrassed.

"Then I hope to make you smile like that more often."

The way he was looking at her made Lia wish they were back on her porch. Alone. Able to explore whatever was growing between them.

"Logan, my boy," her father called out as her mother wheeled him up, breaking their trance. "Happy to see you're able to enjoy another one of our classic events."

"Wouldn't miss it." Her heart fluttered at how kind he was to her parents, and how her parents seemed to have taken to him.

Ron let out a hearty chuckle. "I'm afraid I won't be able to stay the whole night—doctor's orders—but I wanted to make my rounds." He craned his head around and whistled. "Wow, Lia. This place has never looked better."

"I had some help."

"How were they?" he smiled knowingly.

"You were right about them needing a little extra guidance. But we pulled it off." She held her arms out wide, showing off the space.

"They always do." He turned to Logan. "I better see your ornament on that tree, son."

"Absolutely."

"Are you ready for our live stream?" Lia asked her parents.

Mariam shuffled back and forth on her feet. "I still don't understand all that stuff."

"We're going to stream the party on Facebook in real time so people can get a sense of what it's all about. Even if they don't watch the video live, they can still see it later. We can use it for some of the ads."

Her mom shook her head. "You kids. You have to share everything."

Lia furrowed her brows. "Do you want people to come to our events or not?" Her tone was a fraction too sharp.

"I suppose so." Mariam gave in.

Lia hugged her, trying to smooth out any negative feelings caused by her tone. She couldn't help it. She *needed* this to work. "Follow me." She pushed her father's wheelchair toward the tree as her mom trailed behind. Peering over her shoulder at Logan, Lia mouthed,

"See you soon."

As she found the perfect place for lighting, she asked the band to lower the music just a bit while they did the introduction. Daniel adjusted the amps.

"I'll give you a signal when it's time to turn it up again," she said.

She straightened her dad's tie and smoothed her mom's hair. "You ready for this? Just like we practiced."

"Ready when you are." Her father gave her a thumbs up.

Lia pulled her phone from her clutch, clicked on Facebook Live, and counted down to indicate when she'd start filming.

"Hello, everyone. This is Ron and Mariam Winchester at the Winchester Inn. We're thrilled to have you with us virtually tonight," her father began. "Christmas is our favorite time of year here in Fraser Hills, North Carolina. For as long as this town has been established—over two hundred years now—Christmas has been a cornerstone of the community."

"My family founded the Winchester Inn and the town of Fraser Hills," Ron shared. "Generation after generation of Winchesters have kept the Christmas traditions alive, making December a fun-filled time for the whole town."

Her mother smiled at the camera, her nerves seeming to disappear. "Tonight's event is one of our favorites. Here, the community is gathering for tree decorating, dancing, food, cocktails, and more. We'll take you around in just a minute so you can join in on the fun.

"Tonight is one of many events we'll have throughout the month. We have something for everyone. If you're ready to get into the Christmas spirit, stop by our website to see our calendar of events."

"And if one event isn't enough for you, you can stay here at the Winchester Inn for an extended visit. Spaces are limited, so be sure to book today," Ron added with a wink. "Let's party!"

Lia gave Daniel the signal. The music erupted, and people flooded the makeshift dance floor set in the open space of the lobby near the tree she and Logan secured. She weaved through the crowd of dancers, capturing the activity with her camera and showing off the decor before making it outside to where people lined up next to the grill where Jeff was cooking hot dogs. Others ventured out of the tented space and sat near the fire pit, making s'mores. Back inside, she zoomed in on the trays of Bee's delectable hors-d'oeuvres being passed around, and stopped to show off Sarah and Tommy animatedly making cocktails for people at the bar. Partygoers nearby laughed as they clinked their glasses in a jolly toast.

As Lia moved through the dining room to the arts and crafts area, she filmed Logan sitting at the table surrounded by a bunch of little girls. The girls fawned over him as they helped him beautify his ornament, handing him glitter, feathers, and jewels. He looked up and gave one of his toe-curling smiles before one of the girls grabbed his attention again.

Moving on, Lia made it back to the tree and showcased some of the ornaments. She worked hard to find ones with dates to show the history of the tree-trimming event. Panning out, she focused on her mother who was patiently helping a young boy hang his ornament, both laughing.

Mariam turned back to the camera and gave a warm, motherly smile that could make anyone feel loved. "Thanks for joining us. We hope to see you soon in Fraser Hills. From all of us at the Winchester Inn, we wish you a very merry Christmas."

Lia ended the live stream. "That was amazing." When she got back to her cabin, she planned to put together a paid campaign on Facebook to drum up new guests.

"How'd it go?" Logan asked as he walked up from behind, holding a very over-the-top ornament.

"I love your use of glitter and feathers." Her tone was teasing.

"It was Charlotte's idea. She had a creative vision. Who am I to argue with that?"

She found his good humor endearing. "Those girls seem to love you."

"I have two nieces. Three and five years old. I get to see them a few times a year when I go back to Texas."

It was sweet to see a rugged man like Logan be so gentle and patient with the children. It pulled on her heartstrings a bit. "Well, now it's time to pop your cherry and hang your masterpiece."

She clamped her lips tight, realizing how that came out. But when she saw his reaction, she was glad she said it.

Logan swallowed hard, his eyes hooded. He cleared his throat. "Where do I put it?" His voice was low and hoarse and slightly sexy.

"Wherever your little heart desires," she whispered close, letting her lips brush the tip of his ear. She couldn't help but flirt with him, especially when he looked at her like she was the most desirable woman in the world.

A group of children ran past them, reminding Lia where they were. She tried to shake away the sexual tension and bring them back to a safe subject. "Follow your gut. You'll know the perfect spot when you see it."

He dragged his gaze from her and focused on the tree. After a moment, he made his way to the right side and placed it above his head.

"Good choice," she said.

He scanned the other ornaments nearby. "Mine's right next to one of yours."

"What are the chances? Let me see that." She got on her tiptoes, reached for the ornament, and turned it around in her fingers to get a better look. "I made that when I was thirteen. It was probably one of my favorite years here."

"What made it so special?"

"I'm not sure. I think I was still caught up in the magic of this place." She took the ornament in her hand, the details reminding her of the night she'd made it. "I didn't think I'd ever leave Fraser Hills," she said to herself.

A slow song started. "Care to dance, Miss Winchester?" Logan's voice was thick with his Texan drawl.

She fanned herself dramatically, batted her eyelashes, and poured on her best Southern belle accent. "Why I thought you'd never ask."

She looped her arm through his and a shock of electricity coursed through her body. As he pulled her to the dance floor and placed his hands on her hips, she tingled everywhere. Her stomach twisted. The twinkling lights made his gorgeous eyes gleam, drawing her in, and all the tension in her body floated away.

Nothing but this moment mattered.

It had been a long time since she could let go enough to live in the moment. Her mind was always preoccupied with to-do lists, organizational needs, and daily worries. But here in Logan's arms, in the dim lighting of the Winchester Inn, she was free from all of that.

At this moment, all she could focus on was Logan's warmth. His strong hands holding her. His steady presence.

She didn't have to be anything more than who she was. Didn't have to prove herself.

Lia rested her head on his shoulder and closed her eyes. His cheek laid against her hair. It felt so right, so natural to be held in his arms like this as they swayed to the slow song filling the air around them.

She opened her eyes and saw her parents off to the side, smiling as they watched her and Logan dance together.

Lia was truly happy, and she didn't want that happiness to end.

Chapter Ten

"You're sure you'll be okay with me gone?" Lia asked for the thousandth time early the next morning.

"I can handle a day without you." Her mother ambled around, picking up stray cups and plates from the night before.

Lia plucked the plates from her uninjured hand. Her mother scowled. "You're supposed to be resting. I can't have you tiring yourself out cleaning if you need to cover the desk today."

Mariam snatched the plates back. "I'm fine. I'm going stir crazy in that cabin all day. I love your father, but too much idle time for both of us isn't going well."

"Is he pestering you?"

Her mother made a face. "You know all the wacky ideas he has to improve the town. I guess that's where you got your event planning genes from." She clucked her tongue. "My only saving grace is that he exhausts himself more quickly while he's recovering. His naps give me the peace and quiet I need. God love him."

Logan strolled in from the back. "Good. You're both here." His gaze traveled along Lia's professional attire and then settled on the small carry-on sitting near the desk. He frowned. "Going somewhere?"

"I have meetings with my clients in Boston. Just a day trip. I'll be back tonight."

Elizabeth had been insistent on Lia's presence during the tasting at the caterers. Although she told the woman she couldn't attend, Melody called last night to say she booked a ticket for first thing in the morning. It was non-negotiable.

He let out a low whistle. "You sure are a go-getter. I saw how late you stayed after the party."

Lia gave an exaggerated smile. "And don't forget the couple of hours I spent afterward setting up marketing campaigns."

"Workaholic," her mother mumbled under her breath.

Lia rolled her eyes. "This is how it is up North. You have to put in the time to get ahead."

Mariam put her hands on her round hips. "And that leaves exactly how much time for yourself?" she snipped. "When all's said and done, only your family and friends will be there for you. Your *job* isn't going to help you through hard times or be there when you're old and gray. Are you going to sit on your rocking chair with your *job* when you're eighty?"

The words stung, striking a nerve. Was her mother right? Had Lia's priorities been wrong? She'd been following in Melody's footsteps, putting her career first and setting relationships to simmer on the backburner as Lia fought her way to vice president. But as she considered the last few days, she was amazed by the ragtag team who came together to make the events a success.

People really did matter. She wouldn't have been able to pull off all these events without them. The sleepy town she had left behind was filled with self-starters, somehow even more reliable than her colleagues in Boston. It wasn't about being able to influence people to get things done. The people here got things done because they cared.

And then there were those moments with Logan.

Romance hadn't been on her radar for years, but he had awakened something inside of her. Stirrings of lust, longing, and maybe even…love?

Nothing like falling for someone she didn't have a future with, not with her going back home to Boston at the end of the month. She could barely make a relationship work when she lived in the same town as someone. How would something long distance work?

She rolled her eyes. Love? Relationships? She barely knew the guy. She was getting way ahead of herself.

Yet, her mother's words rang true, as much as she wasn't ready to admit it. It was no use. Things were the way they were, and that wasn't going to change.

Defensive, Lia crossed her arms. "If you're saying money can't buy happiness, then why bring me here to fix your mess? Because the town and the inn need tourism money to survive, right? If it wasn't for me being a workaholic, I would never have been able to pull together a plan to help you at the last minute." Her tone was cruel, but her mother's words had rubbed her the wrong way.

Logan stepped in. "Ladies, c'mon now." They both glared at him. He held up his hands in surrender. "Okay, you two can hash this out. But I came in to tell you the roof should be done tomorrow."

The tension between her and her mother disappeared.

"That's great news," Mariam said.

"What happens after that?" Lia asked.

"Then we'll fix the damaged rooms. That will probably be another couple of days after the roof. Otherwise, you can start reserving the non-damaged rooms as soon as we get the inspector in."

"Hopefully Donnelly won't give us any grief." She looked at her watch and turned to her mom. "Sorry I snapped. I think we're both under some stress."

"I'm sorry too, honey." They shared a quick hug.

The early morning flight back to Boston was uneventful, aside from a few cases of turbulence that rocked the plane here and there. Lia used the time on her short trip to catch up on emails and get herself prepared for the short, yet jam-packed day ahead. She had a ton of last-minute meetings set up to finalize her clients' events, especially Elizabeth's, which Lia was dreading.

She tried to shake off the knots in her stomach, convincing herself she was only worried about her mother needing help while she was gone.

As the plane taxied to the gate and she exited, her anxiousness returned. People poured in from the surrounding gates and walked purposefully through the terminals. Heads down. Unsmiling. Making their way to their destinations with the least amount of human interaction as possible.

Had it always been like this? Cold. Unfeeling. Disengaged.

After spending time in Fraser Hills with all those people constantly surrounding her, the difference was jarring.

Lia straightened and carried her bag, joining the stream of people. She felt the rhythm of it come back to her like second nature as her heels clacked against the tiled floor on the way to the taxi line.

She only had a few hours in Boston and had a lot to accomplish, so she switched gears to get laser focused. First, stop by the office to meet with Melody. Then, spend the afternoon meeting with Elizabeth and various vendors, and checking in on a couple other clients. Lastly, Lia planned to stop by her apartment to grab a few things and check her mail before rushing to the airport to fly home.

She shook her head. Boston was home. She was going *back* to Fraser Hills.

Funny how one week in North Carolina made her disoriented.

"Next," the woman managing the taxi line called out.

Lia walked in the direction of where the woman pointed. A short man took her bag, placed it in the trunk, then opened the back door for her before getting into the driver's seat.

"Where to?" he asked with a heavy Boston accent.

"Congress and Atlantic, please."

That was the extent of their conversation. Normally, she preferred the quiet. But today, the silence only made her feel awkward. After a week full of constant talking and people and parties, Boston should have been a nice break.

Being surrounded by all those people had been a lot to handle. Sure, Boston was significantly bigger than her tiny town, and people were definitely on top of one another here, but the people of Fraser Hills were different. There might not be millions of them, but the ones who were there made it a point to know you and include you.

It's been a weird week. It's all been weird.

Lia was a routine person, regimented by her calendar and to-do list. Fraser Hills wreaked havoc on her structured life. That's why she was out-of-sorts. Right? That, and sleep deprivation. She'd be better once she got back to the office and to her normal life.

And only had one job to deal with.

"Good?" the cabbie asked as he pulled up to the curb.

"This is fine. Thank you."

As she stepped out of the taxi, the wind whipped through the building-lined streets, blasting her with arctic air. It was as cold in North Carolina, but something about the air there made her bones ache. She wrapped her peacoat around her, though it was not nearly thick enough to stop the assault of the winter wind.

She hurried down the busy sidewalk, people bustling passed her without a second glance. Cars and buses zoomed by her with the occasional honk or siren in the distance.

Was it always this loud?

She pushed through the glass door of her company's building and approached the pristine elevator bank. The attendant asked to see her ID. She tried not to be annoyed that the guy asked for it despite having seen her for two straight years.

He pressed the button for the tenth floor on the elevator without a word or smile. As the elevator rose floor by floor, she mentally went through her to-do list, preparing for her discussion with Melody.

The elevator stopped and the doors opened, and for a brief second, she paused before getting off. It was a strange reaction that made no sense. She shook it off, took a breath, then continued down the hall. Lia made a right and walked down the bland corporate hallways until she reached the elegant glass doors to Kensie Affairs. Pushing through, she greeted Talia, the office manager, who was sitting at the front desk.

"Good afternoon, Cordelia." The young girl's smile was cordial but didn't quite reach her eyes. "Would you like a drink? Water? Coffee? Tea?"

"No, thanks."

"Very well. Melody will be available to speak with you in her office. She asked you be there in fifteen minutes."

"Great. Thank you."

Lia received a small nod and another one of those polite smiles in response. Talia returned to her computer screen, clicking at the keyboard without another word. Lia had been gone for a week, which was highly unusual. She waited for Talia to make small talk about where she'd been, but as the office manager continued to multitask, Lia realized small talk was a waste when it came to being as organized as they'd all been trained by Melody to be.

It was just as well. Lia didn't have a moment to spare on idle chat.

She considered how many hours were wasted each week at the inn with the constant chatter. All that time could have been put toward something more productive. Maybe if it had, they would have been in a much different situation.

She walked through the short hall to her office, the same sleek space where she'd spent endless hours planning extravagant, buzzworthy events. She remembered selecting the furniture and minimalist decor. All clean lines, muted colors, new fittings, and no clutter.

She laughed inwardly as she thought of the Winchester Inn. It was a stark contrast with its antiques, colorful wallpaper, and constant busyness.

The office was quiet. The thick windows blocked out the traffic noises from the streets below. Lia took in a deep breath, embracing the first moment of silence she had since she received the phone call from Mike about the inn. She relished the few moments alone before she had to deal with Elizabeth's grating existence.

Sitting in her desk chair, familiarity washed over her. The muscles she hadn't realized she'd been tensing relaxed.

That's all it was. I was unsettled. Now I'm back home, and things feel right again. I just needed a minute to get back into the swing of things.

The visit to Boston would be short-lived and the flight to Fraser Hills was only a few hours away. The drastic change back and forth was a lot to process, but she tried to ground herself in this feeling. Boston was home. Being in her element—one she felt comfortable in, one that she was good at—would help her recenter herself before she got thrown into the chaos of the inn again.

All those people depending on her. All those questions. All those hopes and fears.

"Cordelia," Talia called through her desk phone intercom.

She hit a button to respond. "Yes?"

"Melody will see you now."

"Thank you."

Lia pulled out her compact mirror and checked her makeup, touching up her lipstick and fluffing her travel-endured hair. Melody's appearance was always pristine, bordering on unnaturally perfect. Even if she had long travel days or sleepless nights, the woman still looked like a goddess. Lia often wondered how Melody never had bags under her eyes. Hell, she was fairly sure she didn't even bloat when she was PMSing.

Melody would have a field day if she saw how Lia was living the last few days with her jeans, sweaters, and natural locks. Then again, it was also hard to picture Melody in her quaint hometown. There were none of those four-diamond hotels, Michelin-Starred restaurants, or luxury brands she was accustomed to. Fraser Hills would be like *Man vs. Wild* for her.

Lia wondered if Melody's perception of her would change if she knew where she'd been raised. The elite liked to deal with those in similar standing. Lia was far from it. Good thing she'd never see it.

She smoothed her shirt as she stood and grabbed a notebook and pen. Melody would want status updates on Elizabeth's event and would likely have a few suggestions for Lia to consider.

"Consider" being the code word for "you better do this."

Countless times throughout the last few months, Melody mentioned that Elizabeth Sinclair had been a family friend of the Kensie's ever since Melody was an infant. Although Kensie Affairs offered world-class event planning services for all their clients, Elizabeth was an extra special exception. Melody told Lia she'd be "hands off" so Lia could prove she could handle the next phase in her career. But in some sneaky way, Melody had continued butting in on the event planning from the beginning, making remarks and subliminal recommendations. There were times when Lia wondered if she was cut out for this business. Her original ideas for the event were becoming a distant memory as Melody's suggestions overrode her own.

If the event was a success, would it be because of her own creativity and ingenuity or because of Melody's influence?

Lia knocked on the door to Melody's office. Through the glass, she could see Melody hanging up the phone and gesturing for Lia to enter with one of her delicate manicured fingers.

"Take a seat," she directed as Lia entered the room. She sat in one of the high-end fabric chairs in front of the powerhouse desk.

Melody folded her hands and leaned forward slightly. "Let's talk about the Sinclair event, shall we?"

Leave it to her to get straight to business. No questions about how Lia's parents were recovering. No small talk. Nothing. Again, everything about Melody was about complete efficiency. "Absolutely."

"I understand you had to change the caterer."

"Yes. Elizabeth and I are going to do a tasting at the new one today."

"Is this caterer from the list I gave you?"

"No." Lia inwardly cringed, waiting for Melody's reaction.

She raised an eyebrow. "You found another caterer on this short of notice for an event of that scale?" She pinched her lips in disapproval.

"It's a caterer I've used at previous events. They'll be able to serve food worthy of the crowd." *Not that anyone would touch it.* "I've brought them a lot of business throughout the years, so they squeezed us in as a favor."

"Does this favor affect quality?"

"Absolutely not. I'm certain Elizabeth will be pleased."

Melody didn't appear convinced. "If you say so." Her words were coated with doubt. "What else do you have scheduled for today?"

"For Elizabeth's event, we'll finalize seating arrangements, stop by the florist to select centerpieces for the tables, and sign off on the songs the quartet will perform. I also have a few quick meetings with my other clients."

"The flowers should be elegant and seasonal without being so on the nose." She pointed a finger at Lia. "Don't even think about poinsettias anywhere."

Lia made a mental note to scrap that idea. "Got it."

"Did you select a singer?"

"A singer?" Confusion raised her voice.

"Yes. You don't expect this crowd to dance to some elevator music, do you? You'll need a singer to liven things up. There'll be a younger crowd, and they'll be looking for it. The happier people are, the more booze they'll drink. The more drinks they have, the more money will flow for the fundraiser."

"Elizabeth didn't say she wanted a singer."

Melody waved a dismissive hand. "You have to give clients things they didn't know they wanted. Trust me, it will be much better."

Lia made a note, heat flaming under her collar. "I'm concerned about finding someone for an event in three weeks."

Melody turned to her computer, tapped a few buttons, and clicked the mouse. Lia's phone buzzed. "I sent you contact information for someone I highly recommend. Just tell her it's at my request, and she'll make it work."

"Great," Lia responded through clenched teeth. "Anything else?"

"This is a good start. I expect you to stop by the office after your day with Elizabeth and report back."

Lia hadn't planned on coming back to the office. Doing the calculations in her head, she realized she'd be cutting it close making it to the airport if she still stopped by her apartment. "Okay," was all she could say. She was on thin ice for staying longer in Fraser Hills than she originally planned, so she had agreed to do whatever Melody asked to keep her faith in her.

Melody turned back to her computer without so much as a word of dismissal. Lia had become invisible again as if she hadn't been sitting there having a conversation barely three seconds ago.

Had Melody always been this way? Was she acting out because Lia would be gone longer than expected?

No. Lia was just being sensitive. Being in North Carolina the last few days must have made her soft.

A lot was riding on this event. Not just her career, but also the reputation of Kensie Affairs. They'd be getting in front of a lot of big spenders who could convert into new clients. Melody was probably anxious about that, but since she never showed weakness, it was coming off as cold. That's all.

Are you going to sit on your rocking chair with your job when you're eighty?

Her mother's words popped into her head as Lia made her way back to her office. It wasn't like her mother to be combative. Maybe the pain medication was making her irritable.

Even so, the words dug deep. Her mother didn't have the slightest idea of what it took to get where she was today and accomplish all she had. Maybe Lia's job wasn't the same as having someone to come home to or family, but her job was going to be the thing that ensured she had a porch to put that damn rocking chair on when she was old and gray. Whether she was rocking alone or with a significant other, she'd be taken care of.

The pep in her step turned into a half-hearted slog. She grabbed her laptop, purse, and phone and hailed a taxi, making her way to Somerville where she was scheduled to meet Elizabeth for the tasting. Lia got out of the cab onto a quiet street off Union Square and entered the storefront of the caterer.

A cheery young girl led her to the private tasting area. The space was intimate and elegantly decorated, creating a relaxing atmosphere. Lia hoped it would put Elizabeth, a woman who was not easily impressed, in a positive mood before it started.

A moment later, Elizabeth appeared. She held her large Louis Vuitton purse tightly with a gloved hand against her matching tweed jacket and skirt like she was about to get robbed. Her platinum-white hair was cut in a straight, smooth bob that ended right below her chin, and her wrinkles had been smoothed, likely thanks to consistent Botox injections. She looked like she was made for politics, but Lia suspected her status in Boston society was attributed to the way she carried herself and her appearance.

"Elizabeth. It's so nice to see you again." Lia offered to take her coat.

Elizabeth's stony expression stayed put. "Yes, well. I was hoping to have these details sorted already." She handed her purse to Lia like she was her personal servant and took a seat.

"I apologize, but I can assure you this caterer is just as good."

The older woman seemed unconvinced.

The owner, a polished Italian man in his early forties, entered the room. "Ladies." He greeted them with a charming smile and an accent that still held a hint from his early days in Italy. He gave Lia a kiss on each cheek. "Good to see you again."

"Likewise, Enzo."

"It's a pleasure to have you here with us today." He pointed to a menu next to each of their plates. "Here you will find details of what we'll be presenting in just a moment. I'll be available to answer any of your questions about what we've prepared. You are sure to be delighted," he finished with a flourish.

She had met the owner several times throughout the years and always enjoyed his company. She turned to see Elizabeth's reaction only to find her seemingly unamused. Still.

Was her face permanently like that? Lia could have sworn not a single muscle had moved. *Maybe it was a fresh round of Botox.*

He clapped his hands. "Okay. Time for the first serving. Appetizers."

A waiter entered the room, holding two small plates with six different appetizers ranging from light and vegetarian to savory and rich, all of which looked and smelled delectable. Lia's eyes widened in appreciation. She recognized a few from events with Enzo in the past, but there were several new ones on the plate as well. She couldn't wait to try them.

"We have options that will address any dietary restrictions your guests have," he told them.

Elizabeth took delicate bites as Enzo talked about the ingredients used and the taste profile of each. Lia loved every single one of them—even the one with goat cheese, which she despised. Elizabeth said very few words, kept her pinched expression, and seemed to ice out Enzo no matter how upbeat both he and Lia were throughout the entire tasting. He was full of life the whole time, and by the way he spoke about the dishes, his passion for food was apparent.

The only positive thing to come out of the day was Elizabeth signing off on several selections of food. But beyond that, the other meetings with the florist and the band went the same way. She barely spoke, and what she did say was critical, every interaction tenser than the last.

It grated on Lia's nerves. Everyone went above and beyond to adjust their schedules to meet with Elizabeth last minute—Lia included—and the woman acted as if she was the one being put out. Not a simple thank you. No words of appreciation or encouragement.

This all feels wrong. Why couldn't she be more like the people of Fraser Hills? Even one simple, kind smile would have made a difference.

Lia tried to ignore the quiet voice nagging at her from the back of her mind and pressed on.

After parting ways with Elizabeth and a quick stop at the office to give Melody an update, Lia made her way back home later that evening, swearing her jaw might fall off from forcing a smile all day. It had been a rough one, maybe the most trying day she had in the last few months, but her spirit brightened as she entered the historic building in Back Bay where her apartment was located.

As she climbed the three flights of stairs to her one bedroom flat, her mood improved. Even though she would only be there for a few moments, the sensation of being home and in her own space was all-consuming. She wished she had more time to take a shower in her shower and lounge around in her living room, but time was ticking, and she had to make it back to Logan International Airport. The hour she had there would have to do.

The positive vibes disappeared when Lia unlocked the door and swung it open. Her shoulders sunk. The oasis of solitude she longed for seemed bland and sterile. Similar to her office, she lived a mostly minimalist life, choosing simple decor that added a bit of color and texture without overwhelming the space. She liked when houses looked staged. It seemed cleaner and simpler to her.

Made for easy dusting too.

Now thinking about it, the staging made the apartment she loved for the last four years appear unlived in. Aside from very minuscule effects, like the one photo hanging on the fridge and her favorite slippers sitting by the couch, nothing about the place screamed, "This is Cordelia Winchester's home."

She flicked on more lights as she made her way through the apartment and sorted her stack of mail. A few bills. Some junk mail. A couple of credit card offers. Nothing personal in there.

She thought back to the mail she received the last few days at the Winchester Inn and how her mother gushed over the Christmas cards coming from friends, family, and previous guests. Somehow, Mariam found room between all the photos placed around the lobby to display the cards as they came in. It was a bit cluttered but added a feel of love and personality there.

Lia tossed the junk mail into the trash and slipped the bills into her purse. Walking to her bedroom, she opened the door to the poor excuse for a walk-in closet and pulled a few items from the hangers and shelves before shutting it again.

As she entered the bathroom, she stopped short at the mirror and frowned. The travel really wore on her. Her eyes seemed to have lost their ambitious sparkle, and the fine lines of aging on her forehead were more pronounced. No wonder Melody had that disapproving expression when Lia came back to the office later that day. She couldn't hide those dark circles.

Her phone alarm beeped, warning her she had to get moving. Grabbing a few toiletries from the bathroom, she placed the items into her nearly empty carry-on she brought with her and hightailed it out of there, giving one last look at her apartment before turning off the lights and locking the door.

On her flight back to North Carolina, the knots tying up her stomach all day seemed to release.

She landed at the Asheville Regional Airport around nine that night and took the quiet roads back to Fraser Hills. She smiled at the cheerful Christmas tree in the town's center as she made the roundabout to the inn. She was exhausted and a little worse for the wear after the day she'd had, but she couldn't deny the joy she felt in the small mountain town.

Lia pulled into the drive, grabbed her bags, and made her way up the porch of her cabin. She put the key in the door, and it swung open. Logan stood on the other side with the boyish grin she was coming to love, startling her. She dropped her carry-on and her hand flew to her heart.

"Sorry to surprise you. Mike said he was having some issues with one of the windows. I was hoping to get it fixed before you got back from your trip."

Seeing him there, standing in the doorway of her cabin, with the warmth radiating from the fireplace inside…something clicked for her.

Today made her realize she was stuck in the in-between. Her past in Fraser Hills. Her future in Boston. And as she saw Logan there, the overwhelming sense of being present filled her. She'd spent so long trying to move on from her old life, forging a new path for herself, that focusing on the here and now was always overlooked.

But not now. Not here.

Logan stopped her right in her tracks and made her take notice. And for once in her life, she wanted to stay in that exact moment.

Chapter Eleven

Maybe it was the way the cabin's dim light illuminated her face with a warm glow. Maybe it was how her eyes focused so intently on him or how white puffs of air floated from her slightly parted lips.

Maybe it was because she looked vulnerable. Raw.

Logan was positive the woman standing before him was different. He didn't know why or if something had happened while she was in Boston, but something about her in that moment had him reaching for her, abandoning all logic.

She's leaving. I'm not looking to start something. She's my bosses' daughter.

Every reason reminding him this was a bad idea left his mind. None of that mattered.

The overwhelming need to hold her was all-consuming. He couldn't stop himself even if he tried.

Resting his hands on her hips, he drew her to him. A surprised sound escaped her, but the way her body effortlessly gave in to his touch made it clear she felt something too.

He peered into those brown eyes, like warm melting caramel in the light, and saw a flash of…something. Relief? Longing?

He couldn't be sure. All he knew was he had to have her. Wanted to be closer to her.

Cupping her face with one hand, he stroked the soft skin of her cheek and tentatively leaned down, giving her the opportunity to push him away if she needed to.

But she didn't.

She stayed rooted there, flush against his body, her gaze locked on his as his lips moved closer to her perfect mouth. Just centimeters away, her eyes fluttered closed and she tilted her face toward him.

Lia's mouth parted as his lips touched hers. Soft, full lips returned his kiss. She wrapped her arms around his neck and held him tighter, overwhelming his senses. Her soft body pressed against him. The scent of her floral perfume. The taste of her sweet mouth. It was intoxicating.

What had been a polite first kiss edged toward something more passionate. Logan's heart thundered wildly in his chest as their tongues explored one another.

She let out a soft moan—a sound he was instantly addicted to—as she dug her fingers into his hair.

Legs getting weak, he pushed her against the door frame to keep them both steady and groaned when her teeth nipped lightly at his bottom lip before capturing his mouth again.

This kiss was explosive. Unlike anything he ever experienced in his life.

And he had some great experiences, but something about this was undeniably different.

A gust of frigid mountain air whipped around them, and Lia shivered, breaking the spell. Pressing his forehead against hers, they held each other close as they caught their breath and warmed up. He placed a gentle kiss in her hair.

The pressure of her fingers on his back made it seem as if she was trying to hold him tighter or keep him exactly where he was.

So he stayed.

They stood in the doorway of the cabin wrapped in each other's arms for a few more moments, not uttering a single word.

They didn't have to.

The last few days had been leading up to this. Now that it was here, he wasn't sure what to make of it. However, there was one thing he was certain of: he wasn't ready to let her go.

~ * ~

Logan could barely sleep that night. The kiss made his wildest fantasies pale in comparison and left him wanting more.

It was clear there was chemistry between them, but he'd never have predicted *that*.

One kiss, and she ruined him for all other women. He felt both alive and a bit shattered.

After Christmas, she'd be gone again. Logan was off relationships at this point, especially ones that had no future. Despite it all, he still found himself eager to get out of bed and see her at the inn that morning.

He was a glutton for punishment.

It was still early, but Lia would be there already. Logan walked down the hall quietly as if not to disturb the peacefulness of the early morning, and heard her speaking softly on the phone.

"Yes, I understand." She paused. "Absolutely. Everything is

taken care of." Another pause. "I'll handle the change. Okay. I'll call later. Bye."

He stopped in his tracks before he came into view. Something about the call put him on edge. Her tone, although completely professional, held a hint of defeat. Not at all the same lively voice she had while calling out directions for the inn's event a couple of nights ago.

Did it have to do with the way she looked last night? The vulnerability in her eyes gutted him, bringing out his primal need to protect and care for her.

"It will be okay. You've got this," Lia murmured. "Deep breaths."

He turned the corner and found her behind the reception desk, eyes closed while she inhaled long, steady breaths.

"Everything okay?" he asked.

Startled, her eyes popped open, and she jumped, hand to her chest. "Jesus. You scared me." She dropped her hand, and her shoulders relaxed.

"Twice in less than twelve hours." He rubbed the back of his neck with his hand. "I overheard a bit of your conversation when I was coming in. You sounded stressed."

Her lips lifted in a self-deprecating smile. "That's my normal state of being these days."

"You need to give yourself a break."

"I don't need a break. I need more time in the day."

He let out a frustrated breath. Would he ever be able to talk sense into this woman? Her determination and work ethic were admirable, but there was a point where it would get to be too much. She was on the verge of a burnout. He'd been there himself. It didn't do the person or the people they're supporting any good.

"You can afford a couple hours to decompress. You'd be much better off taking that time than running yourself into the ground and being down for the count for much longer."

She leaned her elbows on the reception counter and propped her chin on her hands. "And what do you propose I do?"

He mirrored her stance, his face now only inches from hers. It took all of him to not kiss the soft lips he'd been craving since last night. "You can take a real break for starters."

"What does one do on a 'real break,' Mr. MacDermot?" She batted her lashes and twirled one of her curls around her index finger.

"You. Me. Dinner. Tonight."

"Like a…"

"Date. Yes."

Conflict flashed across her face, her eyebrows drawing together. "Listen, I know things are...complicated."

She nodded.

"I'm not sure what all of this between us means, but to put things simply, I like spending time with you."

I want you.

A genuine smile formed, the one that made the little dimple on her cheek appear. The one he was starting to love. His insides fluttered. She was stunning.

"You make a compelling case. Would six be okay? Things tend to get quieter in the evening hours so I think I could get Mom or Dad to cover. I'm sure they'd be eager to get out of the cabin."

"Sounds perfect." He straightened. "But caring for your mental health wasn't the only reason I'm here. I have some good news."

"I could use some good news."

"We'll be done with the roof and room repairs today. I'll get Donnelly in as soon as possible to sign off."

She let out a sigh, this time a happy one. "Thank God. There's been a lot of interest after I started posting those photos and videos. I hate having to turn people away. It would be great to have that block of rooms available."

"I'll do whatever I can to get Donnelly here sooner."

"Thank you. I don't know what I'd do without you."

The sincerity in her tone warmed his heart. "Anything to get you to smile like that. I'll see you tonight," he said with a wink, excited by the prospect of being with her again.

~ * ~

Lia pulled out the clothes she gathered from Boston and laid them on her bed, eyeing them critically. All the pieces were elegant and tasteful, but none of them were right for tonight. A memory of Logan flashed through her mind. The rugged man could make worn boots and blue jeans look like a million bucks. Even though he looked absolutely dashing the night of the inn event, she would take him in his work attire any day.

She'd probably take him anyway, truthfully.

Kissing him last night transported her back to the anticipation and exhilaration of young love. For a long time, she didn't think she could feel that way again. And then it happened. As soon as his hands were on her hips, she was done for.

That kiss. Oh Lord, did that man know how to kiss.

The whole evening took her by surprise, one she was curious to explore. It was uncharted territory, bound to end in heartache in a few weeks, but something about Logan made her want to uncover the possibilities despite the inevitable ending.

Being around him tapped into some hidden part of herself, one she hadn't seen in a long while. One that got trapped behind those walls she erected so many years ago.

The starling part about it wasn't that a man she just met found ways through her tough exterior, but her willingness to let him in. She had her reasons to be closed off to people, but that resolve slipped every moment she was near him.

He was good for her in that way.

Going back to the closet, she selected jeans, boots, a lace cami, and a cardigan. Much more casual than the outfits she brought back from Boston and fitting for a night out in Fraser Hills.

She freshened up, changed, and spritzed her favorite perfume. Then she headed out the door and found Logan sitting on her porch.

"Hey, you," she said as she locked the door.

"Hey. I got here a few minutes early, but I didn't want to rush you."

"That was thoughtful, but it was fine to knock. I wouldn't want you to freeze to death before you showed me how a proper 'break' is done."

He laughed and stood, offering his hand. "I hope you're ready for this. It's going to be a big night out."

Lia took his hand, loving how large and protective it seemed when his fingers wrapped around hers. "Did you print an itinerary for tonight's adventures?" She smirked.

"All out of ink. I'll be happy to dictate it to you. First, we'll take a stroll down the main street and stop at the infamous Christmas markets."

"You mean the ones we just started this year?"

"Nonetheless, the Wednesday and Friday Christmas markets are quickly becoming a can't-miss shopping experience during Fraser Hills' Countdown to Christmas."

"Countdown to Christmas?"

"It's just a little something I whipped up." He puffed out his chest with pride and winked.

"All jokes aside, I actually really like it." She nodded. "Maybe you're a marketing genius after all."

"Thank you. I expect a fair percentage of royalties."

She shoved him playfully with her hip. "All right. And after this shopping experience?"

"We'll make our way to The Lodge for small plates and cocktails. I know the bigwig there. She'll have a special table reserved for us by the fireplace and she'll whip up signature cocktails made especially for us."

"This bigwig wouldn't happen to be Sarah, would it?"

He grinned, his eyes twinkling. "I wouldn't want to name drop."

Lia squeezed his hand, his humor putting her in a significantly better mood. "And after this exclusive dinner?"

"I'm going to walk you back home and kiss you goodnight." His voice went low and raspy.

A shiver of delight ran down her spine. "A man of confidence, I see."

"A selfish man. Once I knew how amazing a kiss with you could be, I could only hope to have that experience again."

Her cheeks heated. "Me too."

As they walked the fifteen minutes down the main strip, she found she enjoyed the balance of companionable silence and conversation, especially with the cozy scene surrounding them. The trees lining the median and sidewalks were adorned with white twinkle lights, making the flurries that were currently falling sparkle like diamonds as they floated around them.

She took a deep breath of crisp, clean mountain air and the stress that had accompanied her back from Boston lessened. Maybe Logan was right about needing a break. She couldn't remember the last time she strolled just for the sake of strolling. It was nice.

They came to the town center, where the large Christmas tree stood as a colorful beacon, welcoming everyone to the festivities. Stalls lined the center with various sellers from Fraser Hills and neighboring towns.

They browsed the offerings, ranging from handcrafted toys to jewelry, stationery, candles, artisanal food, artwork, and more.

Logan purchased a few small items for his nieces, sister, and parents while Lia was drawn to a beautiful antique sapphire ring. She picked it up and the light caused the blue stone to twinkle like the ocean during a cloudless summer afternoon.

"That's pretty," he said.

"It's my birthstone."

"A September baby. It all makes sense now."

She laughed. "Don't tell me you're into zodiac and astrology."

He nodded his head at the ring. "Why don't you get it?"

"I don't wear a lot of jewelry on my hands. And this is far too beautiful. I don't trust myself not to lose it." She placed the ring back on the velvet display holder and gave it one last wistful look before turning her attention to a couple of stalls down. "Now *that's* something I can trust myself with...mostly." She grabbed his hand and dragged him along.

Standing in front of a churro stall, she all but drooled over the scent of fried dough, sugar, and spices.

"Churros? What's with the churros? I remember them at the tree lighting."

"Apparently one of the first people who stayed at the Winchester Manor was from Spain. His contribution to the first Christmas meal at the house was churros. But not just any churros. They were Christmas churros."

He raised his brows. "Now you're just making things up."

She put her hand to her chest. "Cross my heart."

His lips lifted in a smile, and his eyes crinkled. "I find these Fraser Hills' traditions unexpectedly fun."

"Wait until you try them." She turned to the vendor, selected three different options, and paid. Turning back to him, she held one up to his mouth. "Try it."

He looked at her when he took a bite, the heat in his eyes making her heart flutter. She watched his lips move and imagined them on hers again.

After he swallowed, he asked, "What was that? It was incredible."

She cleared her throat to rid herself of the X-rated images floating through her mind. "That's the gingerbread churro. I also got the churro with mint chocolate in the center and a nutmeg cinnamon churro with hazelnut chocolate dipping sauce."

"You don't mess around."

"This girl knows her desserts." She pointed to herself. Taking a bite, she let out a soft moan. "I haven't had these in forever. I forgot how amazing they were."

He tried the mint and made a noise of appreciation. "I might not need a kiss after all. This is enough to satisfy a man's deepest cravings."

She nudged him with an elbow. "Don't you dare hold out on me."

He gave a hearty laugh, one she found infectious. "I wouldn't dream of it. Now that you've gotten your sugar fix, are you ready for dinner or did you spoil it?"

"Don't worry. I came ready with an appetite."

He slipped his hand back into hers like it was the most natural thing in the world. Like he'd held her hands a million times before.

Truthfully, the whole evening felt that way, which was a welcome surprise. As they approached The Lodge, overwhelming nostalgia filled Lia. It was as if muscle memory reminded her of how life once was and how easily she could fall back into it.

Logan held the door open for her, and the warmth from the roaring fire thawed her frozen skin. She unwrapped her scarf and took off her gloves as Sarah appeared out of nowhere.

"Hi," she greeted them with more enthusiasm than usual. "Right this way, ma'am."

Lia laughed. "You're such a weirdo."

Sarah stuck out her tongue and led them to a private table near the fireplace. Logan took her coat like a gentleman and got her settled before Sarah came back with two menus.

"Today's specials, specifically for you."

Lia scanned the list. Mulled cider sangria. Pimento cheese and biscuits. Spicy fried chicken with creamy aged gouda mac and cheese. Gingerbread patty cakes with mascarpone filling.

She looked up in awe. "These are all my favorites."

Sarah grinned. "I remembered."

"But it's been so long."

"Friends don't forget those kinds of details. Plus, when's the last time you had some of these Southern classics?"

"Too long."

"And now we're here to change that." Sarah winked at Logan and disappeared.

Leaning in, Lia bit her bottom lip, all kinds of gooey and warm inside. "Is this your doing?"

"I had some help." His smile reached his beautiful steel-blue eyes, only making her want to melt more.

"This town seems quite taken with you."

"More like they're taken with you. They were one hundred percent on board when I mentioned taking you out. Said they wanted to put a little Southern back into your soul."

She rolled her eyes. "They've tried to get me to come back for years. I thought they gave up."

His grin faltered, his lips forming a thin line. "I'm sure they'd be thrilled to have you back, but I think they'd be just as happy if you embraced where you came from. Maybe take a bit of who you were back to Boston or be more willing to visit."

She focused on smoothing the napkin on her lap. "Who I was wouldn't survive in Boston. I had to adapt."

"Boston could benefit from having more people like you to

breathe some life into it."

"Life? Have you been to the city? That place is nonstop. Always on the go."

He cocked his head. "That's different, and you know it."

"I know. I know."

"But...," he continued, "it could be said the town is benefiting from what you're bringing from Boston."

The statement filled her with pride. "It only works because the people here are willing to put in the effort. They care. They're passionate about this town."

He studied her as he leaned back in his chair. "One could say you are too."

She held his gaze before answering, the words she kept to herself for so long rolling off the tip of her tongue. "I am. Always have been even though I left." It was freeing to finally admit that to someone.

What was it about this man that made her open up?

"Then why so hesitant to come back more frequently?"

"The truth is, I love Fraser Hills. There was nothing wrong with being here. Even just walking with you tonight reminded me how special it is. How calm it makes me. And being in the markets and a part of all the events made me rediscover what I enjoyed about this town during the Christmas season."

Shaking his head, Logan opened and closed his mouth. She waited for him to say something. Anything.

If he was confused, she couldn't blame him. Everything she said and did over the last few years screamed she wanted nothing to do with her hometown. But that wasn't it at all. Not by a long shot.

Sarah dropped off their drinks, giving her another moment to collect her thoughts. She took a sip of her sangria, contemplating how she would explain it in a way that didn't make her seem ungrateful.

"When I was in high school, my friends talked about their college plans. Their plans for life. They discussed what they wanted to study, what careers they envisioned for themselves." She spun the straw in her drink. "For me, they always said how lucky I was to have everything mapped out. The Winchester Inn was passed down from generation to generation. Since I was a young child, my parents showed me the ins and outs of working there and the important traditions. They were grooming me for my future here.

"I remember one year had been pretty rough, like a mini version of what's happening now. The weather was warm that year, which meant less tourism. My parents didn't know, but I overheard them arguing—they never argue, by the way—about low reservations and what they'd do if they couldn't pay the bills. The Winchester Inn was their whole world. They put everything into it. If they lost it, where would they be?"

Logan was fixated on her, his gaze never leaving hers. His attention encouraged her to continue. "I decided to go to school someplace else because I needed a backup plan if things didn't work out with the inn. I wanted to make sure my knowledge and skills would be practical in a world where the Winchester Inn might not exist. I wanted to diversify. I couldn't put my all into something that might not be there for me once I was old enough to take it on."

"I can understand that," he said, empathy filling his voice. "We had similar situations on my family's ranch in Texas. I know how stressful and scary it can be if your livelihood is at stake."

She nodded. "By the time I graduated college, we were going through a recession. Travel was down, and my parents weren't in a good spot whether they told me or not. So I stayed in Boston and worked hard to get real-world experience. Things steadied out, and my parents seemed to have gotten everything under control. They said they missed me but encouraged me to build my career. And I did. I've had a lot of success I'm proud of. I know Boston is not Fraser Hills, but now I'm too far into my career to walk away."

The biscuits with pimento cheese came out, giving her another welcome break from the heavy conversation. She tried not have a *When Sally Met Harry* moment as she took a bite of the fluffy, buttermilk goodness. How had she lived this long without them?

"Can I ask you something?" he asked after polishing off his own biscuit.

"Sure."

"Why did you look so heartbroken when you came home last night?"

Her stomach dropped as she considered the reasons for her sadness. She wasn't ready to admit it to herself, let alone to him. But talking to him was cathartic, so why stop now?

"It's hard to see the positives of Boston after being back here," she started, but then paused to collect her words. "It's probably why I try to limit my visits. There are so many differences. This most recent trip hit a little harder."

"So why don't you come back to Fraser Hills if your heart isn't in Boston?"

"My life is in Boston."

"Home is where the heart is. I think one could argue that it's not really your 'life' if you aren't all in."

She sighed. "It's not that simple."

"It's not that hard either."

She pierced him with a glare, telepathically willing him to see her side of things. Not everyone could be like him and uproot their life at this age.

As if sensing her unease, he switched the subject. Bless him. "Anyway, I forgot to tell you Donnelly will be coming tomorrow to sign off on construction." She tensed. "Why are you so wary of Donnelly? Or I guess of anyone or anything for that matter? You seem skeptical."

"It must be my Boston conditioning," she half-joked.

God, this man is hitting all the tough subjects tonight.

"Lia, I want to know you. Understand you."

Her heart fluttered at his earnest tone. His sincere look of concern only made it harder for her to sidestep the conversation.

She let out another exaggerated sigh. "You're not going easy on me tonight."

A boyish grin crossed his face, his lips rising higher on one side. "Your breaks aren't a common practice, so I'm trying to cram in as much as I can."

"Fine." She slathered pimento cheese on the last bite of her biscuit and stuffed it into her mouth, buying some time. "But you can't tell anyone."

He held up his pinky. "I promise."

She made a face but linked her pinky with his. "You're just a big kid."

"Nothing wrong with that. At least I'm having fun."

"I suppose you're right." They released pinkies, and she took a deep breath. "I haven't told anyone, but there's a specific reason why I work so hard and why I'm so distrustful."

"I'm on the edge of my seat."

She glared at him again. "Anyway, before I was so rudely interrupted." She gave a small smile so he knew she was joking, but it turned into a cringe as the memories flashed back. "My first real job after college was at a marketing agency in the city. I worked with the field marketing team that set up events to enable our sales team. My senior manager said I had a lot of potential. Said he could see me moving up quickly.

"I worked hard. Long hours. Weekends. I came up with new ideas. I really pulled my weight and proved I was ready for the next step after a year and a half. Well, I didn't realize the promotion was more of a quid pro quo situation."

Logan's expression turned lethal. "Did someone do something to you?" His voice was low and serious.

She placed her hand on his to calm him. "He didn't force himself on me if that's what you're asking. There were some comments and an inappropriate touch or two. I was young. I didn't know how to handle it."

"So what happened?" Logan's protective nature both surprised and flattered her.

It's nice someone has my back for once.

"I told him I wanted to get the promotion based on merit, not what I could do for him personally. He accepted that at the time, but his advances and comments didn't subside. After about a month, I told HR what happened and quit on the spot. I didn't have a backup plan, which was stupid, but I couldn't stomach it any longer."

"That's when you found Kensie Affairs?"

"Not quite. There's more."

"It gets worse?"

"Cliché worthy. The day I quit, I got back to my apartment early to find my roommate and boyfriend having sex. Basically, in the matter of an hour, I lost my job, my friend, my boyfriend, and my apartment. I was pretty much at a loss and struggled for another three months before I got the job with Melody."

He ran a hand down his face, a stunned expression crossing it. "Okay. Well, I guess I understand now. I'm sorry that happened to you."

She shrugged. "Everyone has experiences like this. It's what shapes us."

"How come you didn't tell your parents?"

"Because they'd convince me to come back home. I was at my lowest. If they just said the word, I would have been back in Fraser Hills in a heartbeat. That would have completely gone against the whole reason why I went to Boston in the first place. Me coming back here wasn't going to help anyone in the long run."

He regarded her as if he was seeing her in a new light. She squirmed under the scrutiny, feeling oddly naked as she let her admission hang between them.

"You're an amazing woman, Cordelia Winchester."

Her eyebrows shot up. "My humiliating failures impress you?"

"No, the way you handled them and still turned out to be the caring, passionate woman you are is what impresses me."

For a moment, the burden of that time in her life seemed lighter. She was lighter, less on edge. More willing. Open to the possibility of him.

Even though she was still leaving.

After she shared that low point in her past, Logan eased up on the questions. She learned more about him and his life growing up on a ranch in Texas, how he fell in love with building and woodworking, and all the exciting things he worked on in Charleston. His face lit up as he talked about the historical discoveries he came across while restoring the old buildings in and around the Southern city by the sea.

He shared more about his family and nieces, and she could see he genuinely cared for them all. He shared his love of the outdoors, and how when his uncle approached him about the opportunity at the Winchester, he all but jumped at the chance to be in the mountains with the endless beauty of the woods and lakes. And, most of all, the opportunity to enjoy seasons that weren't only hot and extremely hot.

"I went away for a bit to get my MBA," he told her. "I knew if I needed to take over my family's ranch one day, I'd have to understand the business side of things. Ranching is tough work, and the finances can be tricky. Not to mention, I've seen too many people hurt themselves on the job and have nothing to fall back on."

"That's smart. You covered your bases."

He nodded. "Yup. The thing is, I never was one to enjoy crunching numbers. I'd rather be outdoors, working with my hands. There's something special about being able to see your work in such a tangible way. I hope it's a long, long time before I'm stuck behind a desk."

He talked about how he fell in love with the girl next door, another rancher's daughter. And how he followed her to Charleston to start their future. Lia asked him what happened, and he simply told her it didn't work out, and they left it at that.

It had been a long time since she'd enjoyed a conversation this much. She forgot what it was like to discover new things about a person she was interested in. As their discussion carried on throughout the rest of their meal, she found there was so much about Logan worth admiring and liking.

As they made their way back to the inn after dinner, the snow fell steadily in thick, lightweight flakes, swirling around them like magic. The Christmas market was quieting down, and many of the vendors were closing shop.

"What's with the grin?" Logan asked as they walked at a leisurely pace, arm in arm.

"I love when it snows. Everything goes so quiet and still. Did you make this happen too as part of showing me a 'perfect break'?"

"Of course. I had to pull out all the stops."

She squeezed his arm and laughed. "Thank you, Logan. I had a really nice time."

"It's not over yet. I still haven't gotten you to your front door." A devilish grin filled his face.

"Something to look forward to." A shiver of anticipation ran through her.

In the distance, bells jingled, reminding her of her favorite Christmas event. "You hear that sound?"

"Mmhmm."

"Whenever I hear those specific chimes, it brings me back to when I was a kid here. On Christmas Eve, we would have a parade that led everyone to the inn for a community dinner. When I was younger, there was a reindeer-drawn sleigh that Santa—also known as my father—would ride on."

His eyebrows shot up. "Reindeer? Around here? How?"

"Dad knows a guy." Lia shrugged. "Apparently, they'd bring them down from a farm in Michigan for the season."

"Wow. Your family was really committed to making the sleigh seem authentic."

"When it comes to Christmas, they don't cut corners, that's for sure." She got lost in her thoughts. "That sleigh was so beautiful. It was crafted for the very first Christmas of Fraser Hills and the generations before my parents were able to preserve it over the years. The craftsmanship was extraordinary. As someone who restored all those historic buildings in Charleston, you would have appreciated it."

"What happened to it?"

She shook her head. "I don't remember the details, but it got damaged during one of the parades when I was twelve. I guess the damage was so severe we would have had to bring in an expert to repair it. Didn't have anyone local to do it and it would have been expensive. In the end, it was easier to modernize the parade with floats. That was the last year I saw it."

"That's a shame."

She sighed. "Yeah. The sleigh with Santa was the last part of the parade. It was the symbol of Christmas. We could all finally relax after a month full of events and enjoy each other's company. Take a breath and know the next morning we would be quietly spending time with our families." She laughed to herself. "After dinner, we'd ride the sleigh around the town, always singing *Jingle Bells* at the top of our lungs."

"That's a nice memory."

"Yeah. It is."

~ * ~

Logan knew spending time with Lia would be amazing, but he wasn't prepared for this. Learning more about her tonight and seeing her walls come down had taken him by surprise and then pulled him in deeper. Her tough exterior was worth breaking through. What he found on the inside was a beautiful, big-hearted woman with so much more to her than he initially realized.

He felt alive for the first time since Jolene.

He pushed the memory out of his head. This was no time to focus on his hang-ups caused by her heartbreak. Right now, he had Lia on his arm, and they were making their way up to her cabin, his heart thudding like a teen picking up his date for prom.

How did the simple thought of knowing he was going to kiss her have his insides all tangled up? What would happen if it went beyond that?

They made it to her front door, the sexual tension thick between them. Logan released her so she could fish out her keys. Her hands shook as she unlocked the door, and he wondered if it was from the cold or from the anticipation of what was to come. After she successfully turned the lock, he wasted no time spinning her around to capture her lips with his.

He wrapped his arm around her waist and cradled the back of her neck with his hand, pressing their bodies firmly together as he took what he'd been waiting for the entire night.

She responded, running her hands through his hair, scratching his scalp lightly with her fingernails, and giving him a whole other feel-good sensation. The world around them faded as the kiss deepened. If last night's kiss was incredible, this was entirely different. Rather than the vulnerable state she was in yesterday, tonight she was open. Bold.

Responsive.

He ran his hand up the back of her shirt, his fingers tracing her bare skin. She sucked in a breath, a shiver coursing through her body.

A *woof* from Logan's cabin broke them apart and left them panting hard.

He smiled, planting small kisses on her forehead and cheeks before dropping a last lingering one on her lips. "Sounds like Willow's calling for me."

They looked over to find the shaggy-headed dog staring back at them with teddy bear eyes through the side window.

"Probably jealous she has to share her dad."

He laughed. "Maybe so. We've been a duo for a while." Willow barked a few more times. "I better go."

"Where'd you get her by the way?"

"Found her at a work site. Stuck in a ditch under a willow tree, hence the name. She was barely eight weeks old. We've been thick as thieves ever since."

Things were still good with him and Jolene at the time. As soon he'd seen the golden retriever mutt, with her crooked smile and soulful eyes, he couldn't wait to bring her to Charleston and start their family. He'd waited a few weeks to see if anyone claimed her and another couple to get her shots and a clean bill of health from the vet. But in those mere weeks, Jolene had decided she didn't have room in her life for a dog.

Or for him.

Lia grabbed his coat and tugged him to her, kissing him once more and bringing him back to the present. "Thank you for tonight."

"I'm always happy to give you a much-needed break. You tell me when you're ready for another."

"Absolutely."

"Goodnight, Lia."

"Night."

As she disappeared into her cabin, Logan pulled his cellphone from his pocket and dialed Mike's number.

"Yo," he answered.

"Hey, Mike. I need a favor."

"What's up, man?"

"Do you remember that old sleigh your dad used to ride in the Christmas parade years ago?"

"Sure do."

"Where is it?"

"It's covered in one of the property's storage sheds. It hasn't seen the light of day in almost twenty years. Why?"

"I want to restore it."

Mike laughed so loudly Logan had to hold the phone away.

"What?" His tone was sharp.

"There's only one reason why you'd want to go through the trouble of restoring that old thing. Lia."

"It just seemed like an important part of this town's traditions." He attempted to sound nonchalant. "Lia mentioned you guys had a hard time finding someone to fix it up, and I happen to be someone with those particular skills."

Mike, still trying to contain his laughter, asked, "So it has nothing to do with catching feelings for my sister?"

"No," he lied. "We're just friends."

"Sure. Whatever you say, man. I'll show you where it is tomorrow."

"Thanks."

Logan disconnected the call, a new rush of excitement coursing through him. Maybe Lia wouldn't be sticking around after Christmas, but he was determined to give her a memory worth holding onto when she went back to Boston.

Chapter Twelve

Thoughts of her recent visit to Boston were a distant memory as Lia made her way to the inn the next morning. The break with Logan was precisely what she needed. Of course, she had a million emails from Melody and Elizabeth. Plus, there were several messages on the inn's answering machine and in the inbox when Lia returned. However, it didn't stress her as much as it usually would have.

Rather than fretting over her growing to-do list, her mind wandered back to that kiss. That toe-curling, mind-melting, wonderful kiss.

Fanning herself, she wondered if he was as skilled in other areas. It had been awhile since she'd been intimate with a man, but she'd been too busy with work to care.

Logan made her care. A lot.

She pushed sexy thoughts of him aside as she spent the first hour of the day going through the overflowing inboxes. Melody had a few more "suggestions" for Elizabeth's event, and the inn had several requests for last-minute reservations. She prayed the inspection with Donnelly later that morning would go smoothly so she could get those rooms booked.

Wariness crept up her spine. Giving him the benefit of the doubt was hard to consider, despite Logan's faith in the man. Logan and Jim worked laboriously to get the roof and rooms repaired quickly, to code, and under budget. She had the unsettling feeling all that hard work would be for nothing if Donnelly did what he always did—made things harder for Fraser Hills.

No. Think of what Logan said.

As much as she didn't want to admit it, he had a point. She'd held on to this anger and distrust for so long it was hard to see things for what they were. Maybe Donnelly was a smarmy guy who was hard to be around, but that didn't mean he'd flex his inspector power and take advantage of the situation. Would he?

Mike breezed through the front door. "Hey. Mom and Dad are

in the car waiting for you." He tossed her the keys.

"You sure you got all this while I take them for their check-up? I made some changes."

"I'm twenty-eight, Lia. I know how a computer, phone, and email work. If I can manage the tree farm, I think I can handle the front desk. I'll try not to destroy the inn in the hour you're gone."

She rolled her eyes and pointed at him. "Call me if you need me."

He jumped up and took a seat on the reservation desk, grabbing an apple from the fruit bowl. He took a large, crunching bite. "Okay. But I won't," he said around a full mouth.

"Can you maybe be a little professional for the guests?"

He looked around. "Do you see one? News flash. It's seven in the morning. Most people like to sleep in on vacation."

She glared at him. "I'll be back soon."

"Byeeeee."

Lia slipped on her coat, grabbed her purse, and left the inn. The smell of snow lingered in the air, and a light dusting covered the ground, likely to melt away once the sun peeked out from the thick gray clouds. She walked down the stairs and got into the driver's seat.

"Morning, honey," her mother greeted from the passenger side.

"Morning, Mom."

"How was your night out with Logan?" Her father wagged his eyebrows.

"It was just a friendly meal. Nothing more."

"Not from what I saw at your cabin last night," her mother gushed like she had a big fat secret.

Lia's mouth dropped. "Mom! Were you spying on us?"

She waved a hand. "Of course not. I heard Willow barking and went to see what all the racket was about." Her face lit up as she leaned closer. "Are you two an item now?"

Lia sighed as she drove around the circular drive and made her way into town. "No. It's nothing. In three weeks, I'm leaving. It can't be anything."

"Plans change." Her father mimicked the words Logan said to her the night before.

She eyed him in the rearview mirror. His normal joking manner had turned serious. "But my plans won't." His shoulders slumped as he broke their eye contact, causing her an instant pang of guilt. "I love being here and being with you. You know that, right?"

"I suppose."

Her mom lifted her gaze to the rearview mirror and shot her dad a look. "Of course. We just miss you."

"And I miss you too. But my life is in Massachusetts now. I have a great job, and I'm likely to get that promotion. I love my apartment. I have a full life."

Why did her words feel like a lie? They never had before. Even to her own ears, it sounded unbelievable. Lonely.

"The point is, I can't just drop all of that and move back for a man I met basically a week ago." *Even if he's kind, generous, and an amazing kisser.* "That's a mistake a naive girl would make. You can't give up everything you worked toward for something or someone you barely know."

Both her parents remained quiet, something they did when they disagreed but didn't want to say. "What?" she pressed, agitation lacing her voice.

"Nothing, honey. We're glad you're happy."

"I'm very happy." The words felt meaningless. A week ago, she would have believed them. But now, something had changed. She didn't want to acknowledge what that meant.

Lia couldn't give up her stability for a fantasy. Couldn't change her life for uncertain possibilities. It was reckless and went against her meticulously detailed plan. She had to stay the course. No detours.

She pulled into the parking lot behind the town doctor's building. Dr. George Evans was another staple of Fraser Hills, a man who never seemed to change. He was Lia's doctor as a baby, and even thirty years later, the man looked to be frozen in his sixties.

He was just as she remembered. Dark gray hair streaked with platinum white. His thick, white eyebrows were animated while he spoke. He was a kind man with an impeccable bedside manner. How he stayed the same all these years was a mystery.

"Miss Winchester." His Southern drawl was thick. "It's a delight to see you again. I'm sorry I missed the event at the Winchester, but the tree lighting was marvelous. Well done."

"Thank you, Dr. Evans."

"Ron, Mariam," he acknowledged her parents. "Great to see you out and about."

"Thanks, George. I only wish this happened any other time of the year," her father complained.

"Ah, yes. I reckon it's a tough time for you folks to be on the mend, but your daughter is handlin' things quite well."

Mariam beamed. "Apple doesn't fall far from the tree."

"I'll say. And that boy of yours has the tree farm runnin' like a well-oiled machine."

Her dad sat up taller and lifted his chin. "I'd like to think I trained him well."

Dr. Evans chuckled. "That you did. Let's get you into the examination room and see how you're both healin', shall we?"

"I'll be out here," Lia said as the doctor pushed her dad's wheelchair into the back, and her mother followed.

Lia spent the half hour checking and responding to Melody's calls and emails, which only put her in a sour mood.

Dr. Evans poked his head into the waiting area. "Lia, would you mind comin' back?"

"Sure." She stuffed her phone into her purse and followed him to examination room one. Taking a seat, she placed a hand on her mother's knee to stop it from bouncing.

"Let's have it, Doc," her father prodded.

The doctor placed two X-rays on a viewing board and lit them up. He first focused on Mariam's wrist. "From my perspective, your wrist fracture wasn't as bad as we thought and is healin' quite nicely. You shouldn't need the splint in another week, from what I can tell."

"Will I be able to bake and cook again?"

"I don't see why not."

Her mother let out a relieved breath. "Thank you, George."

"My pleasure." He turned back to the board and put up Dad's X-rays. "Now, Ron, your lung is lookin' mighty fine, but your rib will need another month or so to heal. You could ease your way out of the wheelchair but don't push it."

"I understand."

Dr. Evans leaned against the counter opposite where they were sitting and folded his hands in front of him, his face turning more serious. "Now I'm gonna have to level with y'all. Although things are mendin', this will be a long road to recovery for you."

"How do you mean?" Lia asked.

"Well, it's no secret your parents are gettin' older and age plays a large factor in the healin' process. A lung and wrist might look good on an X-ray, but that doesn't tell the full story, you see. These bones will be weaker, more fragile. The wrist and the rib could break more easily if there's another incident. But even if that isn't the case, the strength won't be there anymore. It's more likely these areas will have inflammation, pain, discomfort. Some of that may subside in time, but at this age, I don't see that bein' the case."

"What are you saying?"

"It means, Lia, that your parents have to adjust their lives accordingly. They can't be pushin' themselves the way they have. If they start experiencing discomfort or pain, they need to give themselves a break." He turned to face her parents. "This is a lifestyle change, you understand?"

They both answered with small nods.

"Mariam, although you can cook again, you might not be able to do it as often, or as much. Or if you plan on cookin', you best be findin' someone to handle all that cleanin'. You can't do both."

"I see." Her words sounded sad.

"And, Ron. You gotta get comfortable with Mike handlin' the tree farm goin' forward. I don't want to see you hikin' along, choppin', and luggin' those trees."

"It's going to be a lot for Mike to handle on his own," her father argued.

Dr. Evans held up a hand to stop the protest. "Mike has grown up to be a capable young man. He will be fine. It might just mean hirin' some part-time help."

Her mother knee bounced up and down. "We don't have the means to hire help on the tree farm or for someone to clean the inn regularly. We're making just enough to get by."

The doctor gave a sympathetic smile and nodded. "I see. But you also can't afford to hurt yourselves again. You might not bounce back next time."

Lia studied her parents, seeing them in a new light. When had their hair gone white? Were those crow's feet always so pronounced around their eyes? Come to think of it, didn't her mother seem a bit smaller since the last time she was here? Lia assumed it was her high heels making her mother seem shorter, but as she studied the woman closer, she seemed to have shrunk.

Her father's round cheeks appeared to have sagged slightly. Even his voice didn't sound as strong as it used to. Was it the pain from his lung or was his age affecting it?

Of course she knew her parents would get older. But, for whatever reason, she didn't believe the time would be so soon. If they couldn't take care of the inn or the tree farm, and couldn't afford to hire help, how would that impact their business? Mike couldn't handle it all on his own. He already said he was struggling at the farm, especially since good help was hard to find right now. Although he and Bee had been steadily dating, Lia doubted she'd give up her successful restaurant to help manage the inn and keep the Winchester tradition alive.

"Thank you, Doctor," was all she could muster as they left.

She helped her parents into the car, and they drove back to the inn in silence. Lia processed the doctor's diagnosis and what that meant for her parents' already shaky future. This had to be crushing for them.

After helping them settle in their cabin, she went back to the reception area, her heart heavy. She'd have to let Mike know what was going on, but first, she needed to figure out possible solutions to bring to the table. Having an action plan may make the news less daunting.

As she circled around to the reception area, she found Mike chatting with a man who'd been renting one of the rooms for the last week with his wife. From what she learned, this was their first time in Fraser Hills. They were newly empty nesters and were considering a buying a second home in the quiet, mountain town.

The front door opened, and an older gentleman who looked vaguely familiar walked to the desk. Assessing his outfit, she realized he was the same postman from years before.

"Miss Lia." His bushy eyebrows rose in delight. "I heard you were back. I wanted to come sooner, but you didn't have any mail."

She found it odd that the Winchester wouldn't have had mail in the last week. She squinted at him, trying to remember his name. "Mr. Sawyer?"

He saluted. "At your service."

"Wow. It's been so long."

He shared a big grin that was missing a few teeth. "Sure has, but it's always nice to see a familiar face." He inspected her for a moment. "My, you sure have changed. Beautiful, as always."

She waved him off with a smile and laugh. "Thank you, Mr. Sawyer."

"No need for thanks. It's simply the truth." He dug into his mailbag and pulled out a wad of mail. "Here you go, Miss Lia. I better get to my rounds. Lots of mail for the holiday season. I'll see you tomorrow."

"See you tomorrow." She waved goodbye. Flipping through the mail, she frowned. "Almost none of this is ours," she said to Mike.

"Oh, yeah. That's normal. Amber has a bunch of our mail. She's going to swing by in a bit to drop it off."

"Normal?"

He shook his head and let out an exaggerated breath. "Tim isn't as young as he used to be. Sometimes he forgets and gets it wrong."

"Why is he still working if no one gets their mail properly?"

Mike shrugged. "He's a nice guy. Says working keeps him sharp, so we don't want to take that from him. We all know we might need to pass the mail to the right people, but we're happy to do it if it means he's staying healthy."

"I swear, this town sometimes," she mumbled as she separated out the mail that needed to go to different people. She'd have to make her rounds later.

As she busied herself, Logan and Donnelly came down the stairs, discussing the recent updates to the roof and rooms.

"Ah, Lia. Just who I wanted to see." Donnelly sneered. He wore an ill-fitted suit in an unflattering brown, and his comb-over had become thinner, covering less of his bald head no matter how hard he tried. "Logan and I were just reviewing the work he's done."

Lia smiled through gritted teeth. She wasn't sure if it was his mere presence or his obnoxious voice made her instantly tense. "Donnelly, nice to see you again. How did the inspection go?"

"A woman who gets straight to business. I like it." He gave another cringe-worthy smile. "The roof and room repairs are all up to code. No action needed there. However, after further investigation, I'm concerned about the electrical."

She narrowed her eyes. "What about it?"

"When was the last time your wiring was updated?"

"I'm not sure. I'll have to ask my parents."

"Please do."

"What's the problem?"

"Well, it's clear the Winchester Inn hasn't had updates in some time if the roof was any indication. I did a quick scan of the electrical in the repaired rooms, and I have a feeling the whole place will have to be rewired. I'll need to get an electrician out here to be certain."

She exhaled slowly, trying her hardest not to snap. "Why wasn't this identified when you first came to see the damage? We could have taken care of this in tandem."

Logan shot her a look, silently begging her to keep her temper in check.

"The stability of the roof was the most important thing," Donnelly said. "But if the wiring is severely outdated, the whole place will need to be redone immediately." He pointed to the Christmas lights and tree in the lobby. "Especially with the strain you're putting on the system with these lights. I'm surprised you haven't blown fuses or set this place on fire."

The guest Mike was speaking to whipped his head in their direction. "Well, hold on now. Are you saying this place is at risk?"

"It's a possible hazard, yes," Donnelly said.

The man shook his head and pointed a finger at Lia. "This is outrageous. It was one thing to suffer through the roof construction. I was expecting one of the weeks we were here to be hassle-free. Now a possible rewiring is needed? How am I supposed to have a relaxing vacation with all this madness? My wife and I are leaving." He stormed up the stairs.

"Wait!" she called out, but it fell on deaf ears. She turned back to Donnelly, anger surging through her. "If you were a professional, you would know not to share that information in front of guests."

He shrugged, unphased by the man's outburst or Lia's frustration. "I think your guests have a right to know if their room will catch aflame if they plug in one too many things. Don't you?"

She got in Donnelly's face. "You always had it out for us. You want us to fail."

Logan pulled her back.

Donnelly held up his hands. "Whoa. Where are you pulling that from? You Fraser Hillers sure are sore, aren't you? I want what's best for the inn. I thought you would too."

Logan tucked Lia to his side, holding her as if he were a thunder jacket trying to calm her nerves. "We understand. Can you get an electrician out here today?" he asked.

"Most likely. I'll give you a call." He looked at Lia and did a fake hat tip. "Always a pleasure." With that, he left the inn. The raging man, his wife, and their luggage followed soon after.

Lia put her face in her hands. "This is a total disaster." A ding on the computer alerted her of a new message. She checked the screen and clicked a few buttons. "Great. That guy just gave us a shitty review." She read further. "He's claiming faulty wires and that 'the inn is a death trap waiting to happen.' This is going to ruin any progress we're making, even if the electrical isn't an issue like Donnelly said."

"We'll get it figured out." Logan's soothing, even tone didn't help calm her.

"Now you understand why I don't trust him? He's a rat."

He frowned. "He was just telling you about a potentially dangerous issue. Wouldn't you prefer to find out up front than have the place burn down?"

Mike made a noise. From the corner of her eye, Lia saw him shake his head at Logan.

She glared at Logan, showing him exactly how she felt about the situation. "Get the electrician sorted." She tossed the mail on the counter and crossed her arms.

He stared at her, likely taken aback by her rude behavior. When she didn't apologize or say anything else, he said, "I'll figure this out." He left without another word.

Mike let out a low whistle. "Way to go, sis."

She ran a hand through her curly hair. "Not the time. We have bigger issues to discuss."

She walked to the loveseat and gestured for Mike to follow. Once they were both settled, she rested her elbows on her knees and wrung her hands.

Worry flashed across his face. "What's going on?"

"It's Mom and Dad." Lia dove into the prognosis from the doctor.

"I see," he said after she finished and scratched his head. "I'm not surprised though."

"That's all you have to say?" she asked, frustration making her snap.

"Yeah. Mom and Dad are getting older. Even before the accident, their health was taking a turn. They're tired but kept pushing themselves. This accident might be a blessing in disguise. They wouldn't willingly take a step down to give themselves a break. Although it's not great, it's forcing them to finally do that."

"How are we going to support the inn if they can't do what they used to do?"

"I've already been thinking this through."

Unsure, she hesitated then asked, "You have?"

"Um, yeah. Earth to Lia. What do you think goes on here? Things aren't how they were twelve years ago when you left. I'm not a sixteen-year-old kid anymore."

"But—"

He held up a hand, his tone becoming more serious. "I've been picking up the slack. I get it. You think I goof off, work part-time, and freeload off Mom and Dad, but I've stepped up over the years. Do you even realize I managed all the lumber sales even before Dad got hurt? I don't just do the tree farm around the holidays. I handle that whole side of the business."

"I didn't—"

"And—" he cut her off again, "when I'm not dealing with that, I also help around the inn. When Mom is busy cooking or cleaning, I work the front desk and phones. She doesn't move as fast as she used to."

"I see." Her shoulders slumped.

Mike's nostrils flared. "Do you, Lia? You've done a damn good job avoiding all of this for years." He laughed, the sound of it harsh and unhappy. "You, Mom, and Dad are the most stubborn people I know. You won't come back home and barely check in. I'm lucky if you even answer my calls. Mom and Dad won't tell you the truth about what's going on because they don't want to bother you. If it weren't for me making the freaking effort to call, no one would know what the hell was going on. It feels like I'm the only one who cares about keeping this family together."

She reached for his hand, but he stood, shaking her off. "Mike."

"No. I'm tired. I'm tired of trying so hard. I'm tired of you thinking I can't hold my own and support our family and the inn. And I'm tired of you swooping in and everyone thinking you're the savior when all of us have been here working our asses off this whole time."

She stared at him, seeing him for the man he grew into rather than the kid brother who had been a pain growing up. The kid brother who seemed to skate through life without any responsibility.

She'd been wrong.

"I had no idea." Lia felt the color drain from her face.

"Of course you didn't. Pick up the damn phone once in a while. Book a trip home." He ran a hand down his face. "The thing that pisses me off the most is at the end of the month, you'll go back to your life in Boston, feeling like you did your part and forget about all the rest of us who are working to save this community and legacy."

"That's not true."

"Save it." He stormed off.

God, how many people would she piss off today? This was a disaster. As she rubbed her temples to ease her tension headache, she wondered how the day could get any worse.

Amber tapped her on the shoulder, startling her. "Hey, buddy. You okay?"

"Yeah, yeah. Just a rough start to the day."

"I hear you. I like to get out to the mountains on days like that. Fresh powder and clean air really clears the head."

Lia tried to smile. "I can imagine."

"Anyway, just stopping in on my way to work to drop these off." She handed Lia a large pile of mail.

"Good Lord. How long have you been receiving our stuff?"

"For years." She rolled her eyes, no doubt thinking about the town's elderly postman. "But this pile is just from the last few days."

"Wow. That seems like an unusual amount." She opened the first envelope and scanned it. "Hmm. Good thing you dropped by. This is an application for the gingerbread house competition tomorrow."

"Oh yeah. I love that competition. A good challenge gets me goin'."

Lia opened the next few, and her heart sank. She frantically opened the remainder of the pile. "Oh my God."

Amber tilted her head as she peeked at the mail. "What?"

Lia held up a stack of papers. "All of these are for the competition."

Her friend looked confused. "So?"

"So this is way more than what we planned for. Lovie's bakery isn't going to be big enough to house all these displays."

"Huh."

"I gotta call Lovie and get this figured out."

~ * ~

It was all hands on deck yet again at the Winchester Inn. With the influx of competitors—thanks to the calendar of events and marketing campaigns—the bakery was far too small to house the displays. Lia, Lovie, and a handful of others spent the afternoon contacting the contestants about the location change and setting up the dining area.

Lovie brought festive tablecloths and placed them on the tables. She added garland with holly, battery-powered tea lights, and sparkling ornaments to give the tables a little extra pizazz. A few hours later, they appraised the setup and agreed they were in good shape for tomorrow.

"Thank you so much, Lia. This is one of my favorite competitions. I would have felt awful if I had to turn people away." Lovie grabbed her hand and gave it a quick squeeze.

"It's no problem. We have the space. I'm just glad we found out about the submissions in time."

Lovie wrapped her in a tight hug. "You're a sweet girl. I should get home and rest up. Tomorrow's going to be a long day for me."

"Of course. Good night, Lovie."

It was an unexpectedly crazy day, but she was thankful for the distraction. Lia was having a hard time coming to terms with what the doctor said and Mike's outburst. Regardless, she shouldn't have snapped at Logan earlier. After the incident, she saw him for only a few minutes again when the electrician came through to inspect the wires, but it wasn't long enough to apologize.

Her stomach twisted in knots, worried about what the verdict would be. They were bound to come back at any moment with the news. News that could potentially be the end of the Winchester if the cost was too steep.

She was busy handling her Boston work when Logan came into the lobby. His body was tense. Her heart dropped, wondering if the expression on his face was because of something the electrician said.

"Hi," she said, biting her lip, hoping he wasn't angry with her.

"Hi," he responded when he approached the desk, his face unreadable.

"Listen, I want to say I'm sorry. I shouldn't have taken out my crappy day on you."

His smile seemed forced. "You're not the first woman to bark orders at me." His face softened. "Don't forget how we first met."

She winced. "I backslid. As a woman trying to establish a growing career in Boston, showing weakness can't happen. You have to have a strong, authoritative voice. Otherwise, you'll get crushed."

"We're not in Boston, Lia."

"I know," she admitted, unable to meet his eyes. "I shouldn't have spoken to you like that."

In the time she'd been here, Logan had been nothing but warm and lighthearted. Even when she was a complete bitch when they first met, he was unperturbed. In fact, he almost seemed amused by it.

But things were different now. *They* were different. What she said and how she said it to him mattered. It was clear as day on his face.

He took her chin with his finger and tilted her face up to look at him. "I know you've had to be a certain person in the years you've lived in the North. I understand it's hard to drop that facade. But I also know that's not you. This is a safe place. You can be yourself here. And your voice will always matter to me, even if it's a whisper."

Her heart thundered against her chest as appreciation filled her. How was it he could say words that made it so easy to trust? To believe.

It wasn't the words, but in his actions and how he treated her. "I don't deserve your kindness."

His smile was genuine. "You're just going to have to accept it." He pulled away and ran a hand through his hair. "Lia," he said, growing serious. "People have flaws. I'm not perfect. You're not perfect. Hell, this situation between us isn't perfect. But there's enough good here from what I can see, despite all that. I hope you will too when my less than favorable qualities come out. The thing is, we only have a few short weeks together. I want to make it worthwhile."

She circled the desk and wrapped her arms around him, placing a soft kiss on his lips. "Me too."

"And in a few weeks, when you're back in Boston, you'll have plenty of time to use that demanding, authoritative voice you love so much." He squeezed her against him so she couldn't thwack him for his smartass remark. He kissed the top of her head. "For such an impatient person, I'm surprised you haven't forced the electrician's news out of me yet."

She snuggled against him. "That should show you how high up on the totem pole my apology was. Do you have any idea how hard it was not to ask you about that first?"

"I'm so honored."

"Well?" She shook him playfully, earning her a deep laugh from Logan that vibrated in his chest.

"Everything's okay. We don't need to rewire."

Her body relaxed. "Thank God." She released him and sat down on the loveseat. "I wasn't sure what we'd do if we had to eat that cost. I honestly don't think we could afford it, not with what the doctor said today."

He sat next to her and took her hands. "What's going on?"

"My parents' health isn't too hot. He said there will be some limitations after they're healed. We need to hire help around here going forward." She focused on their hands, his thumb rubbing her palm in soothing circles. "It's been weighing on me all day."

"It makes sense why you were so on edge earlier."

"Yeah. Mike had some choice words with me about it too afterward." She sighed. "The inn doesn't have the funds for any hiring, but I've been crunching numbers. If I get this promotion next month, my raise could afford an entry-level part-timer. Maybe full-time if I tap into my savings, but that's not going to be a constant source of income, so I'm not sure how that would work."

"Your savings?"

"Yeah. When you're a workaholic like me, you don't find much time to spend money on things like trips, nice dinners, or anything non-work related. I've built quite a nice nest egg over the last five years."

"Lia, that's offering so much. What if things don't work out? Your savings is your safety net."

"If I knew my parents hurt themselves further or lost the inn because they didn't have the help and I didn't do everything I could, I would never forgive myself." She raised her chin. "I *have* to do this. I'm *going* to do this."

He admiration shined in his eyes. "You're one determined woman."

"Let's just hope it's enough."

Chapter Thirteen

"What do you think you're doing?"

Lia's mom jumped at the sound of her voice, spilling a bowl of chopped strawberries in the process. Her hand flew to her chest. "You frightened me!"

"The sun has barely risen the day after your doctor's appointment, and you're already in the kitchen." She eyed her mother's arm. "Where's your splint?"

"You heard Dr. Evans. I don't need it." She stuck out her tongue and got back to chopping fruit. "Clean that up, will you?" She nodded her head at the strawberry catastrophe on the floor.

"He also said you shouldn't push it." Lia bent and scooped up the mess. "What's that smell?"

"Oh, just some stuff for breakfast. The usual." Her mom was acting strangely aloof.

Lia sniffed again. "No. That's not it. Is that...gingerbread?"

Her mother tucked her head down, trying to hide a grin. "Well…"

"Mama!"

"Oh boy, you must be mad. You haven't called me 'Mama' in years. Did I hear a little Southern twang again?" Lia simply made a face to show she wasn't amused. "Tonight's the gingerbread competition, and we're hosting it here. How ridiculous would it be if we didn't have our annual Winchester Gingerbread Inn?"

Lia bit her lip. "I forgot about that."

"You've been busy, honey."

Lia discarded the strawberries in the trash and took a seat on the stool by the kitchen island. "I know. I've been slipping up. I forgot to put a cap on the attendees for the tree decorating and the gingerbread competition. Both events had me scrambling. It's not like me to screw up like that. Twice. That's a rookie mistake."

Mariam poured two mugs of coffee and slid one over. "Your mistake is our gain. So many people are coming to town and making us their new Christmas tradition. So what if we have to make some adjustments to fit them all? The more the merrier."

Lia shrugged a shoulder, her lips forming a tight line. "Yeah, well. I won't get the same reaction if I screw up something for Elizabeth Sinclair's event. I spent three hours last night double- and triple-checking things. After I set attendee limits on the Fraser Hills events, of course."

"Do I smell gingerbread?" her dad sing-songed as he entered the kitchen.

"Where's your wheelchair?" Lia scolded.

"I'll survive a couple of hours without it. Couldn't have it blocking up the kitchen when we build our house."

She shook her head. Both her parents were diving right in after their chat with the doctor, even though he had told them to take it easy. They were never the type to take things slow though. These last few weeks must have been torture.

Guess that's where I get my workaholic genes from.

"Sorry I'm late," Mike said as he breezed through the kitchen. "Then again, I never was much help."

"If you spent more time building the house rather than eating it, you might not be half bad," her father said.

"Guilty," he replied while grabbing M&Ms from one of the dishes.

Mariam slapped at his hand. "That's for the gingerbread house."

"Seems like you told everyone about doing this except me." Lia tried to keep the disappointment out of her voice.

"Didn't think I'd have to tell you. You're always here before us."

Logan strolled in. "Morning, everyone."

Lia straightened at his unexpected, but very welcome presence. "Are you here for the gingerbread house too?"

"Sure am. Your mom said she could use my construction expertise."

Her mom's eyes twinkled, guilty with conspiracy.

"I'm sure she did." Despite her flat tone, Lia was excited to have Logan there. They hadn't had much time together since their dinner date the other night, and she was aching to be near him. Sure, her whole family was there to witness it, but she'd take it.

"Okay, y'all." Mariam clapped her hands, earning everyone's attention. "We have all the fixin's for the house." She pointed to the counter behind her. "There, you'll find the main structures. To the left are the garnishes and frosting. Questions?"

"Let's get going." Mike licked his lips as he checked out the garnishing.

"Hands off the supplies," she warned.

The next hour was a frenzy, all of them circled around the island, working together to make the base of the inn. Logan offered insight on how to make the structure sturdier so they could build it taller. Apparently, her mom and dad wanted this year's house to be bigger and better.

Edible glitter and frosting covered them. Chocolate sauce was spilled haphazardly on the island. They all kept running into each other. Arguments erupted over how the roof should be designed and how to decorate the front. Chocolate candy? Candy canes? Gumdrops? They all had their own ideas, claiming theirs was the best choice.

As they added the final touches and took a step back to admire their masterpiece, that feeling of nostalgia filled Lia again. She glanced at Logan. His work clothes were now covered with glitter and there was a bit of frosting on his cheek. A rugged man with a bit of domestication. She smiled.

He put his arm around her shoulders and pulled her closer. His intoxicating woodsy smell was mixed with the sweet sugar, driving her nuts.

"Well," her father finally said. "It's got to be the ugliest dang thing I've ever seen."

The kitchen erupted with laughter.

"I guess it's a good thing we're not in the running for the competition," Mike said as he ate leftover gingerbread scraps.

"It might be ugly, but it's *our* ugly little gingerbread house." Her mother was always the optimist.

"Thanks for helping," Lia whispered to Logan as her family fussed over how they were going to get it to the dining area.

He chuckled. The deep rumble in his chest was something she was coming to love. "Not sure I did so good. I think I got it structurally sound, but I couldn't offer much in the looks department."

"Don't worry. It always turns out ugly."

Logan grinned and kissed the top of her head when no one was paying attention. "I'm glad I got to spend time with you. I liked being part of this tradition."

"Me too." She held his gaze, wishing they could play hooky and spend quality time together. The days were ticking by, and she knew this would be another night they wouldn't have a chance for one-on-one time.

And she desperately wanted to be alone with him.

She'd been finding it impossible to get him out of her head, even during her busiest and most stressed times. A conversation or special moment would come back to her, each time making her stomach flip and her desire to see him that much greater.

Kissing him was no longer enough.

The thought of being with him was borderline obsessive. Yet, she kinda liked it. All the giddiness and anticipation.

Her toes curled and her cheeks flushed.

"I've got a few work orders to deal with, so I better get going." He squeezed Lia tighter as if he was unwilling to let her go, completely oblivious to the fact that she was two seconds from throwing him on the island and having her way with him.

"I should too. I'll see you at the competition?"

"Absolutely." He winked and went off to do his thing.

Her mom shimmied up beside her and smiled.

"What?" Lia demanded, squinting at her mother. She was on to her scheming.

"Oh, nothing." She feigned innocence. "Have a good day, dear," she called out as she disappeared with a tray of freshly made pastries for the morning rush.

The day already started off great. Yesterday was rough, but spending time with her family and Logan, doing something as simple as building a gingerbread house, made her realize the importance of enjoying the small pleasures in life. There were always going to be challenges and bad days, but giving herself a break like this put things in perspective.

Both her parents were healing. They may not be as strong as they used to be, but they were still capable. With that perspective, the task of finding her parents help wasn't as daunting.

Maybe Logan was on to something with the whole "taking a break" suggestion.

Leaving the kitchen, Lia bit her lip to suppress a laugh when she found her mother and father in the dining area standing near the horrible gingerbread house, speaking to a handful of guests with unabashed pride. She shook her head with a smile. They didn't care about being the best, they just wanted to have fun and spend time with their family.

She used to think that sentiment was shortsighted but now it felt different. Maybe her parents didn't have it wrong all these years. Rather than busting their butts and making sacrifices to build the Winchester into something it wasn't, they stayed true to the traditions and embraced the here and now.

Her father kissed her mom on the cheek. She looked back at him lovingly. What would it be like to have someone there for her who was solid? Stable. Her rock. Someone who would still love and cherish her even in her worst times?

Your job isn't going to help you through hard times or be there when you're old and gray.

Her mother's words rang in her ears again. The same words Lia had argued with her about only a few days prior. She watched her parents, together now for nearly forty years. Even after all that time, they acted like newlyweds. Maybe her mom was right.

Lia had filled that void with her job. Would she still feel so passionate about moving up and taking on more responsibilities—filling her every waking moment—if she had someone like her mother has to come home to each night?

Logan's face flashed in her mind, causing her to pause.

He'd been a surprise to her, but as she spent more time with him, she realized she had been unconsciously reevaluating her priorities. He got her thinking about their possibilities, even though there was no future for them after Christmas. There couldn't be. They both knew it.

But there was no harm in fantasizing, was there?

~ * ~

Logan entered through the back door of the inn later that evening. These last couple of weeks gave him the sense of community he was longing for. In Texas, there was the ranching community, of course. But with acres upon acres between each family, and a tiny, out-of-the-way downtown area where people sometimes gathered—if they weren't exhausted from a long day of manual labor—the community aspect was severely lacking.

It was also no wonder why he and Jolene ended up together. With the minimal options for socializing during post-college years, what else was there?

He hoped to find that sense of community when he followed Jolene to Charleston. He had read all the articles about Charleston and had seen the numerous awards they won for being the best and friendliest city. Its rich history, strong tourism, vibrant downtown, and accessible beaches made it seem like the world would be at his fingertips.

He had big plans for them. Dreamed of long days on a boat and nights filled with amazing food and cocktails, shared with friends they'd undoubtedly make in the growing city.

However, things don't always go as expected.

Charleston had seemed like a large place when he first arrived, but the city soon closed in on him. It'd been hard to avoid seeing her or meeting people who knew of her. He needed space to deal with her betrayal. Soon, he found himself becoming a recluse, trying to stay out of her way and rid himself of those constant reminders. Those were three lonely years.

In the few months he had been in Fraser Hills, he discovered what he'd hoped to in Charleston. Mostly a spectator at first, he took it all in. The town was small, only around four thousand people. But living in the valley kept them close together, building bonds Logan was never able to as a rancher. It was just recently, with the flurry of Christmas activity and the arrival of Lia Winchester, that Logan went from spectator to an active member of this tight-knit town.

It was exactly what he'd been always searching for.

Yet, he wondered if the feeling of inclusion had more to do with Lia than finally finding his place. Would he still feel this way when she was gone?

The thought escaped his mind as soon as he stepped into the lobby of the Winchester Inn. Inside, the place smelled of ginger, cloves, sugar, and mulled spices. Daniel, Walt, and Savannah were playing modern Christmas songs while people flowed through the front doors to the dining room where so many different houses were on display. He followed the masses and laughed at the horrible gingerbread house they made earlier that morning sitting proudly in the lobby.

They should all keep their day jobs.

Following the line of traffic, he walked by the displays. He noticed some new faces—probably out-of-towners—mixed with Fraser Hillers. They greeted him, showing off their designs like Vanna White, trying to win his vote.

"Is that a sushi restaurant?" Lia asked from behind him when she approached Bee and Sarah's display.

"Yup," Bee answered with a smug grin.

Sarah rolled her eyes. "I wanted to do a cabin, but she hijacked the whole thing."

"Oh, honey." Lia looked at Bee with mock concern. "Have you talked to someone about your sushi obsession?"

Bee glared. "I'll have you know that making these details took great skill."

Lia bent closer to inspect it. "Is that the sushi place we used to go to in high school?"

"Not exactly, but it definitely gave me the inspiration."

Lia laughed. "Well, this doesn't scream Christmas to me, but I have to give you credit for sticking to what you love."

"If that were the case, she'd have a masterpiece of me." Mike came over and kissed Bee on the cheek.

"Masterpiece? That would be a stretch," Lia joked.

Logan enjoyed the easy banter between family and old friends. Even though he didn't grow up with them and share their memories, he was comfortable around them.

"Hi, you," Lia finally said to him after her sparring match of playful insults with Mike.

"Hey, beautiful."

Logan took in her dark, curly hair and bright, brown eyes that sparkled in the light. She'd been embracing the more casual side of mountain life lately, which he appreciated. She could make jeans, boots, and a sweater look damn good.

"See anything you like?"

"I do." His voice was low as his gaze trailed her body up and down.

What would he do for a moment alone with her? Anything.

He'd been craving it since their night at The Lodge. She opened up to him and let him see behind the curtain. It helped him understand a bit more of who she was, and he liked it.

He liked it a lot.

Her cheeks turned pink as she grinned. "I meant the gingerbread houses. You have to fill out your vote before eight." She waved a card in front of him.

He gave her one more smoldering look, his ego getting a nice boost when she started fanning herself with the cards as she practically panted, her eyes dilating and her lips parting. He wanted gather her into his arms and capture that mouth with long, lazy, hot kisses. But he knew he couldn't just yet.

But later? Maybe.

She bit her bottom lip and sucked in a breath. As if remembering they were in a room full of people, she straightened and shook her head. "I better make my rounds." Shoving a card into his hand, she sauntered off.

Lia spent the next hour busy with the contestants and guests. The woman was pulled in all kinds of directions, so much so that any normal person would have been overwhelmed. But not Lia. She handled it with grace and ease, a warm smile on her face as she interacted with each person.

Although he gave her space to keep the event running smoothly, they occasionally stole glances. Their eyes would lock, and all he could see was her. Everything else faded away. Each time they shared a moment, his chest squeezed.

God, he had it bad.

This was a dangerous road to go down. To allow his feelings to run deeper than what was right for a relationship with a fast-approaching expiration date was only going to make things harder for him. But, damn it, he couldn't help but hope those beautiful eyes of hers would find his again. He needed the event to wrap up soon so he could finally have time with her.

"Ladies and gentlemen. Boys and girls." Ron stood at the front of the room with a jolly smile, the apples of his cheeks red, contrasting with the bright white of his beard and hair. His health was improving, bringing life back to his face. Seeing him with the decorative backdrop helped Logan understand why he was the perfect Santa. He was the spitting image.

"Thank you for joining us for the annual gingerbread competition and welcome to our newcomers." He held up an envelope. "Now, the moment you've all been waiting for. Drumroll please."

Mike mimicked a drumroll with his mouth from the back of the crowd as he hugged Bee against him.

Ron opened the official-looking envelope. "And the winner is Sheriff Riggs Perez for his replica of the town center."

Upon hearing his name, the older man's face lit up with a dopey smile. How Riggs landed the role of town sheriff was beyond Logan. He was a nice guy, but definitely not suited for the high stakes of law enforcement. He was a skittish man. A mama's boy. And one who loved the attention of those around him. Logan had gotten stuck one too many times listening to the stories Riggs embellished to get a laugh or to wow his audience. He would be milking this win for months to come.

"Thanks again for joining us tonight," Ron said after a photo op with Riggs. "And remember, caroling will start in just a few moments. Step out onto the front porch to be a part of the magic. You'll sing Christmas favorites around town, ending at Lovie's for complimentary hot chocolate. It's not to be missed!"

Logan found an opportunity to slip behind Lia. His fingers grazed hers lightly, careful not to attract watchful eyes. "Caroling, huh?" he whispered in her ear. He loved how his touch caused goosebumps to rise on her skin.

"Mmhmm. Thinking of getting out there?" Her voice was melodic and soothing.

He gave a low laugh. "I may be talented in some areas, but singing isn't one of them."

"And what other talents do you have that I haven't had the pleasure of experiencing?" There was a flirty tone in her quiet voice.

He gripped her fingers as his pulse raced. That simple question made him consider all the many talents he ached to share with her.

"You're playing with fire, Miss Winchester."

She squeezed his hand back. "Sometimes I don't mind living on the edge."

"Lia, honey," Mariam called out from across the room. "Can you come help me?"

He chewed his bottom lip and let go of Lia's hand, somewhat grateful Mariam had called her away. Logan took a deep breath. He was losing his cool, but he was also happy knowing she was just as affected by those sexy glances all night as he was. His need for her had grown stronger in that simple interaction. If he thought he couldn't wait to get her alone before, he was damn near desperate now.

"Logan, come here." Lia gestured as she peered out the front door, excitement making her eyes light up. "You're going to miss it!"

Logan met her at the door as *Noel* filled the still night air. Slipping outside, he stood next to Lia as a group of thirty people, ranging from children to the elderly, held candles and sang their hearts out.

"They're pretty good," he said

From the corner of his eye, he studied her, loving the way she appeared so happy and at peace while listening to the song and quietly singing along. It made him question why she would ever want to leave Fraser Hills and wonder how hard it was for her to stay away. Judging by what she told him about her time in Boston, he could imagine how difficult it was for her to not come back to a place where things seemed easy, pure, and right.

As the candlelight danced in her honey-brown eyes, he concluded she was the most beautiful person he had ever seen. He wanted to reach for her, hold her, and make her feel wanted. Loved.

Loved.

He swallowed. He couldn't deny there were things to love about Lia. Her determination. Her intelligence. The way her one cheek dimpled when she was purely happy, which seemed to happen a lot more lately. How, as much as she tried to keep her distance from Fraser Hills, she was fighting tooth and nail to make things work. All those little things she did when she thought no one was watching.

But he was watching. He saw. And he loved it all. Even her stubborn tendencies.

Did that mean he was falling for her?

When the song ended, her eyes misted, and she clapped so hard he could have sworn her hands would be bruised tomorrow.

Yup. He was falling for her.

Damn it, Logan. What were you thinking?

For once, he wasn't. He'd spent so long living a shell of a life when he was in Charleston, he didn't realize what would happen if he finally opened himself up again. Now here he was, falling for a woman who would be gone too soon.

And there was nothing he could do about it.

"Wasn't that amazing?" she asked, bringing him back to the present. The group walked down the circular drive toward downtown, filling the air with another Christmas carol.

"The best."

"I wish I could go with them, but there's so much to do around here."

"Maybe you'll have some time. I'll be joining the clean-up crew."

"You are?" Her eyebrows lifted in delight.

"Your dad wasn't feeling too great, so I offered."

"Might not be the most ideal way to spend time with you, but I'll take it."

He gave Lia a quick kiss. "I second that."

They walked hand in hand to the dining hall, enjoying their private moment before they had to help Lovie and Mariam. But as soon as they made it there, her hand slipped away.

"Emmett?" Her steps faltered for a second as she walked toward a polished, professional-looking man.

His blond hair was expertly cut and pushed back from his face. His suit was tailored to perfection. Emmett shot Lia an appreciative smile, full of straight white teeth, and wrapped her in a tight embrace when she met him, lingering for a moment.

A moment longer than Logan liked.

He was instantly on edge. Where had he heard that name before? Clearly they knew each other, yet Logan hadn't seen this guy around town. When Emmett looked at Lia as if he were coming home, as if it were the most familiar and natural thing in the world, Logan's muscles instantly tensed.

"I'm so glad I had time to make it back here," Emmett said as he released her.

"Lovie said you were here for business." Lia stepped out of Emmett's arms, but still stuck close.

"Yeah. It ran longer than I expected, but I'm here now." He grabbed both of her hands and assessed her. "How is it you've become even more gorgeous?"

Then it hit him. The first day Logan and Lia had gone to town, they'd stopped at Lovie's bakery. She went on and on about her son being back and how much she wished Lia and him would get together again.

Emmett. Lia's ex. The one people hoped she'd end up with.

Logan watched them reconnect as he practically faded into the background, completely forgotten. The casual way they talked to each other. The way he made her laugh.

Without warning, Logan became the outsider again.

"Mom's been keeping me up to date on what's going on with the town and the Winchester," Emmett said. "I have a few ideas on how I can help. Want to grab dinner tomorrow, and we can discuss?"

Lia paused for a moment. Logan prayed she'd say no. He prayed she'd turn to him and make an introduction. To make it clear there was something there between Logan and her.

Maybe they hadn't defined it yet. Maybe they hadn't talked about it. But the simple acknowledgement of his presence would have calmed his racing thoughts at least.

"Sure. That would be nice."

"Just like old times." Emmett hugged her again and said goodnight.

It was as if history was repeating itself. The woman he cared for turning her attention to another man. A wealthy, sophisticated man who could offer her the world and never leave her wanting. Able to fix all her problems.

Someone Logan could never be.

Whatever future he had with Lia slipped away.

Chapter Fourteen

To say she was confused would be an understatement. As Lia mindlessly got ready for dinner with Emmett the following evening, she wondered what happened the night before. It seemed like she and Logan were getting closer. She had planned to invite him over when they finished cleaning up after the gingerbread event. Maybe put herself out there and take things beyond those fiery kisses.

But in a matter of minutes, something changed with him.

He'd become quiet and withdrawn as they cleaned up. Before Lia could even ask him over for a nightcap, he said goodnight and left for his own cabin.

Talk about a one-eighty.

She wrote it off as him being tired, but when she noticed the strange behavior was still present today, she knew something was up. He'd made himself scarce, aside from picking up the work orders and prioritizing what needed to be done. She hoped to run into him after work when he took Willow for her evening walk, but they were nowhere to be seen.

What the hell happened?

Before she could dissect it any further, a knock sounded at her door. Emmett was always punctual, even as a child. She checked herself one last time, smoothing a stray strand of her sleek, straightened hair.

She looked like her old Boston self. A person who no longer felt like her at all.

Grabbing her clutch and coat, she opened the door to find Emmett standing patiently outside. He'd always been a stunning man, even during the awkward, gangly adolescent years. As he became more successful, he found a way to look the part. Any woman would feel lucky to be seen with him, but Lia's mind kept traveling back to Logan. The rugged, casual man who had her turned inside out.

Emmett pecked her on the cheek. "Gorgeous as always. Ready to go?"

"Thanks." Her cheeks heated under his appreciative stare.

"Yes."

He held out his arm, and she looped hers through it, glancing at Logan's cabin from the corner of her eye. There was no movement or lights on.

Where was he?

Emmett opened the passenger side door of his rented Porsche—which was highly impractical for the fickle winter weather—and she slid in before he closed it again. Always the gentleman.

"I hope you don't mind a bit of a drive. I made reservations at a wonderful French restaurant in western Asheville."

"It sounds lovely," she murmured, then realized her preoccupied thoughts made her seem rude. She tried her hardest to snap out of it and stay engaged for the next few hours. "So, Emmett, your mother says you've been doing quite well in New York?"

He pulled onto I-40 with smooth precision, likely used to handling expensive sports cars like this. "Yeah. It's been an adventure. Things were touch and go when I first made the move during the recession. I thought my career in finance would be over before it even started, but I pulled through."

"I wouldn't say a highly trusted investment banker at one of the world's top financial institutions is simply 'pulling through.'"

He laughed at that. A pleasant sound, but not the same as Logan's deep rumble—the kind of laugh that seemed like it was coming from the depths of his soul.

"I guess when you put it that way, I've done really well for myself. My work has been recognized on a bunch of lists in the *New Yorker, Time Magazine,* and so on. I've got a great apartment overlooking Central Park. I also get to travel all over the world to see clients."

"Wow. I'm so proud of you, Emmett. You really made something of yourself, not that I ever doubted it."

"You should be proud of yourself, too. I always believed you'd do something remarkable." He sent her a lingering sidelong glance and smiled. "You know, you'll always be the girl who got away."

Lia raised her eyebrows. "I would hardly call me the 'girl who got away.' You switched schools and left Boston to pursue your finance degree in New York."

"I wanted you to come with me." His playful tone took on something slightly more serious.

She shifted in her seat. "And it was a great offer. Romantic even. I just had something to prove to myself. You understand?"

"Absolutely. It was ridiculous to even ask that of you." He

grinned, relieving the tension. "We were only sophomores. What we had was good while it lasted. Right?"

"It was." Her time with Emmett was perfect for that period in her life. Sadly, it was one of her last real relationships aside from the jerk who cheated on her with her friend.

Life with him was easy. They had been good friends while they lived in Fraser Hills, and it was nice knowing someone when she moved to Boston. Although they were at different schools, they made it a point to meet each other regularly and explore all the city had to offer. By the end of freshman year, their friendship had transformed into something more.

The awkward early stages of dating were nonexistent thanks to growing up together, letting them fall into a hassle-free relationship. It was fine but lacked all the passion and fire she believed she wanted. Like what she felt now when she was with Logan.

Emmett was never able to pull her away from the world inside her head the way Logan did. He had something better to offer than what was in her imagination. It was both exciting and terrifying.

Moments later, they stopped at the valet in front of a cute restaurant with large windows and small tables outside. Lia imagined stumbling upon this if she wandered along one of Paris's charming streets. For a moment, she forgot she was in a mountain town in North Carolina. Even the inside was stunning, with the dim lighting coming from rustic chandeliers and the sound of Ella Fitzgerald singing overhead. It was classy in an unpretentious way.

As they sat enjoying their *aperitifs*, Lia asked, "What did you have in mind when you said you wanted to talk about the Winchester Inn and the town?"

"Ah, you were always a woman who got down to business." He laughed and relaxed into his chair. "Usually my clients want me to wine and dine them before we talk money."

She rolled her eyes playfully. "It's been great catching up, Emmett."

"You've never been someone who beat around the bush." His eyes twinkled with amusement. "I'm surprised you lasted as long as you did before saying something." He smiled and leaned forward, folding his hands on the tabletop. "I'll give it to you straight. My mother shared the rundown on what's going on with the town. I know some of those issues have to do with things the town can't control, like weather affecting the lumber trade and tourism."

"Correct."

"But I also know the inn is struggling too."

She twisted the stem of her glass between her index finger and thumb. "Yeah. I just found that out myself. The roof repairs made it worse, and now there's going to be even more strain." She told him about what Dr. Evans said and how she planned to use her savings to hire someone until they found a better solution.

Emmett took her hand from across the table and looked at her deeply. The intimacy of it made Lia squirm. "Although it's noble of you to do that, I wouldn't recommend it."

"It's my family. Our legacy."

The one I desperately tried to fight becoming my legacy. Now, my absence might be the reason we have no legacy at all.

He rubbed the top of her hand with his thumb. She stiffened in her chair. "I understand. However, what if there isn't a viable solution down the line? Your family will lose their livelihood, and you'll go down with them if you dump all your liquid assets into the inn. Do you own your apartment?"

"No. I rent."

"Another reason why you shouldn't do it. If it all goes to hell, you wouldn't have that to fall back on either."

"What else can I do, Emmett?" Lia pushed down the lump in her throat. She couldn't leave her family in this state without trying to help. She stared blankly at their hands on the table, feeling wrong for letting him touch her like that, even if it was friendly.

"I want to make an investment. Be a silent partner of sorts."

Her gaze shot back up to meet his. "You want to buy the Winchester Inn?" She pulled her hand back slowly. "It's only ever been owned by the Winchester family. Giving it to someone else would change tradition."

"Lia," he said in a soothing tone, "that's not what I'm proposing. I'm offering to invest money to keep things running. A cash infusion, if you will, to generate more business and give the town and the inn the boost they need to get back on track. Your family would still be majority owners. I'm not trying to take anything from you or your family. I may not be in Fraser Hills anymore, but it's still my home and my mother's home. Just like you, I want to do anything to keep that town afloat."

"I see."

He cocked his head and studied her. "Tell me you'll think about it?"

"I will." She nodded but uncertainty weaved its way through her body, tightening her chest.

"Very good." He raised his glass to cheers. "Enough business talk. I also want to share some other news with you."

She took a sip of her drink as she waited for him to continue, trying to focus on the conversation and not the anxieties running through her mind.

"I took a new role at the company which requires me to build new offices and teams."

"That's wonderful. Congratulations."

"It is. Thank you. My first assignment will be in Boston. I'll be living there full time for about a year come January."

She almost did a spit take. "What?"

"Yeah. I'm moving back. Temporarily, at least. But it also offers the opportunity to make that my home base once the project is done. If I so chose."

"Wow. Just wow." She blinked, completely thrown off guard. No wonder Lovie was talking about how good a couple they would be. She must have known he was moving back to Boston.

He took Lia's hand again. "I know it's been some time, but I've always considered you a good friend. I'm hoping we could spend more time together once I get settled. Maybe see if there's still something between us after all these years?" He sounded hopeful.

She bit her lip and assessed him. A mere two weeks ago, this would have been the type of guy she would have hoped to be with. Business savvy, professional, kind, generous, handsome. A companion. But now...well, after Logan, things were different.

"Yeah, that would be good," she finally uttered, but her stomach twisted. Two weeks in Fraser Hills couldn't have changed her that much. Once she got back to Boston and back in sync with her life, things would return to normal.

Once she had to move on from Logan, she needed to think about her future. Her real future. One that no longer had Logan MacDermot in it.

Her heart cracked.

~ * ~

Logan was pissed. Maybe he wasn't being fair to Lia, giving her the cold shoulder today, but he couldn't help it. All he could see was Emmett and her together and how easily Logan seemed to be forgotten.

Would it be that easy for her to forget him once she left?

Last night brought up old memories. Barely healed wounds. He shook his head, angry for putting himself out there and in that position again. It was one thing to get burned because she was leaving town. It was another to know she'd chosen the pretty, rich boy on top of it. Logan was just the stand-in until the man she really wanted showed up to sweep her off her feet.

Just like Jolene.

Logan liked to consider himself a confident, yet humble man. He knew who he was and what he had to offer. But when it came to situations like this, where he had to compete with someone who had the means to give Lia the world, he'd always fall short.

He sat in the old storage barn that night, working out his frustrations on the forgotten sleigh, convincing himself he was restoring it for the town and not to win over Lia's heart.

To show her he was worth it.

He didn't like the possessiveness he was feeling, like he was some sort of Neanderthal with no control over his emotions. After all, Lia was her own person. If she chose to play the field, she could do so.

However, call him old fashioned, but when he shared intimate moments with a woman, he focused on them exclusively. He hoped Lia would have approached it the same way.

Their time together was limited as it was. He didn't want to share her.

He shook his head, the internal war raging on.

No, he wouldn't fight for her heart, giving his all just to lose.

He needed to keep his distance. Maybe it was for the best he found this out now before he got in too deep.

Yesterday, he'd believed they were on the verge of something that would be hard to recover from. He was falling for Lia. He thought she felt the same.

What a crock of shit.

He'd planned on finding a way to get her alone after the competition. To try to explore what was causing this heat between them. To understand what this undeniable connection meant. If they did, he'd get pulled in even further. The thing was, he'd been willing to risk it.

All that mattered was her.

He shoved his hand through his hair and stretched his neck. He'd been working on the sleigh for hours and was starting to feel stiff and sore. Deciding to call it a night, he cleaned up his tools and threw a cover over the sleigh. Just as he was about to leave the barn, a car crunched along the snow and gravel toward the cabins.

He froze, hidden in the shadows of the barn.

Emmett got out of the car and opened the passenger door, offering a hand to Lia. Logan tried not to lose his temper when Emmett didn't release her hand as they walked back to her cabin. Logan couldn't make out what they were saying, but their conversation looked cozy and too intimate for his liking.

They paused at the front door, and Logan's throat constricted.

He couldn't breathe as he waited for what came next. Would she put him out of his damn misery already?

Emmett leaned in, his face only inches from Lia's.

Logan twisted away and stormed back into the barn before he could watch any more.

He was infuriated. Fuming.

And he couldn't do a damn thing about it.

Chapter Fifteen

Avoiding Lia wasn't easy. Still angry with himself, Logan tackled specific work orders that forced him to be away from the main lobby.

Away from her.

He'd run into her briefly that morning and almost gave in when she didn't bother to hide the confusion and hurt in her eyes. Putting distance between them was a monumental task. Those brown eyes, full of unspoken feelings, were going to be the death of him.

I'm a fucking bastard.

It wasn't right for him to leave her in the dark, but did she deserve an explanation? One second she was kissing him and the next she was casting him aside for someone else. Someone who would fit better in her life in the city.

Maybe he'd tell her the truth when he could speak rationally. Emotionally-fueled conversations weren't in either of their best interests. Even if she was moving on to someone else, they still had to be around each other for another couple of weeks. There was no point in making it harder than it needed to be.

His raging feelings were torture, sucker-punching him. He wasn't sure he could stomach working with Lia through the end of the season. How did he let his heart this far off its leash? It was so far gone, it was impossible to reel back in.

Despite his heartache, Logan managed to get through the rest of the day without seeing her. He took a different path while walking Willow to avoid the off chance of running into her.

He couldn't believe her transformation. Back to those fancy clothes, high heels, and sleek hair. He wasn't sure why, but seeing her like that made him feel like he was losing her before he'd planned to. It was as if the past two weeks had been a vacation from her real life, with him just a fling in the process.

Although she looked just as beautiful in her professional clothes as she did in her casual mountain wear, the change reminded him how different they were.

And how temporary this was for her.

The sun had set hours ago, and the cold air seeped into the poorly lit barn. He blew into his hands, trying to warm them, while he considered what to take on next regarding the sleigh—the only thing that pulled his mind away from Lia.

Somewhat.

He stared at the sleigh, with its intricate details and impressive craftsmanship. It was unlike anything he had seen in his life, as if the sleigh were the original from the North Pole itself. What had initially been a restoration project meant to make Lia happy had turned into something else entirely. This sleigh was far too precious to be forgotten. It was the symbol of Fraser Hills. He wanted to bring it back to its glory days. For whatever reason, he believed fixing the sleigh would reignite the magic of the struggling town, giving them back something they'd lost.

Logan spent hours in the barn, carefully assessing the state of the sleigh and the right way to restore it, while also making it stronger for years to come. His eyes grew blurry and heavy, convincing him it was time to call it a night. He only hoped his exhaustion would be enough to put him to sleep. He couldn't take another night of tossing and turning, wondering if Lia had invited Emmett back to her cabin.

Throwing a cover over the sleigh, Logan cut the lights and locked the barn behind him. Making his way back to the cabin, the weariness caused by back-to-back days working at the inn and his new side project weighed on him.

Suddenly, a scream came from Lia's cabin. Adrenaline coursed through his veins as he raced from the barn. He made it to her front door at breakneck speed, barreling through it without so much as a knock. He scanned the living room, his panic rising when she was nowhere to be found.

"Lia!" He rushed down the hall to search for her. "Lia, damn it. Answer me!"

"Here." Her faint voice sounded from the bedroom.

He followed it, finding her pressed against the far wall, her face pale. She wrapped her arms around her body.

"What's wrong? Are you okay?"

Logan stepped in, a wave of protectiveness filling him, and reached for her, checking for any signs she was hurt. His eyes roved over her body, hidden by a loose-fitting T-shirt from college, oversized PJ pants, and colorful fluffy socks. He pushed back a strand of her hair that had fallen loose from her messy bun, his gaze reaching her face again.

Their eyes locked. He couldn't breathe.

"I-I'm okay," she finally said, pointing to the desk across the room. "There was a spider."

"A spider?"

"Yeah. It dropped from the ceiling, right in the middle of what I was working on."

"A spider," he repeated, taking a step back. "You screamed like that because of a spider?"

She crossed her arms and glared at him. "It was huge and startled me. I'm scared of spiders."

Logan walked to the desk, finding the spider—barely anything compared to the monsters he'd seen in Texas—and scooped it in his hands, making her cringe. He walked to the front door and let it free before returning and leaning against the door jamb of her room, trying to create the distance that had been breached just a moment earlier.

"Anything else? Do you want me to check under the bed for the boogeyman?"

She took a seat on the bed, her glare turning cold. "Ha. Ha. Very funny. What do you care anyway?" Her shoulders tensed to her ears as she turned away from him. "You've done everything you could to avoid me the last two days."

There was that hurt again. Although Lia tried to sound tough and indifferent, he could hear the fringes of confusion.

How he had acted mattered to her. But why?

He couldn't stand knowing she could barely look at him and he'd been the one to make her feel that way. Running a hand down his face, Logan let out a breath. There was no point in avoiding this conversation any longer. She wanted answers, and it wasn't right to keep them from her, especially now it was clear it was bothering her.

"I saw you. And Emmett," he admitted.

Her eyebrows furrowed. "Me and Emmett? I don't get it."

"Last night. After your dinner." When realization didn't dawn on her like he thought it would, he added, "I saw him kiss you."

She balked. "He didn't kiss me. Unless you consider a kiss on the cheek something to write home about."

Now it was his turn to feel unsure. "On the cheek? But he leaned in..." And then it hit him. His vantage point from the barn mainly showed Emmett's back. From where Logan was standing, it could have easily looked like it was something more.

"Yeah. On the cheek." She sounded annoyed and had every right to be.

"I just..." He rubbed the back of his neck. God, he was an idiot.

"I remember Lovie saying you guys belonged together the day we went to her bakery. Remember that?"

"Yeah. She always says that. Even when we were barely out of the womb."

"And then I saw how you two were at the competition. I guess all of that made me jump to conclusions. I thought you were getting back together." His gaze darted down to the floor and then back up at her from under his thick eyelashes. "It's been…"

"Confusing?" she finished for him.

He pushed away from the door and took a seat on the corner of the bed, considering what to say next. "I wasn't planning on feeling how I do for you. Then I saw you with him and how perfect you two were together…"

She took his hand, forcing him to look at her. "I want you, Logan." She sucked in a deep breath. "This isn't what I planned for either."

"It's insane."

"Totally insane." The hurt in her eyes was now replaced with something else he couldn't quite name. "But I can't help myself when it comes to you." She laughed, but it wasn't a happy sound. "Of course, the first guy to come along in a long, long time is someone I can't be with."

"Our time is limited."

She smiled sadly and nodded. "It is. And I have no idea what to do about it."

"The woman who always has a plan is finally planless?" His not-quite-a-joke was quiet, but they both heard.

"I guess we all have our moments."

Logan shifted on the bed to face her. "Since I'm being honest about my stupidity, I think it's probably beneficial to explain the reasoning behind it. After all, I owe you after what you shared with me the night at The Lodge."

Her eyes widened. "Oh?"

"Honestly, I was jealous as hell thinking about you with Emmett. Clearly. The situation brought back bad memories of my ex, Jolene."

"What happened?"

"She lived at the ranch that backed up to ours, so we knew each other all our lives. Kinda like you and Emmett." He rubbed his hands down his pants to get rid of the sweat that coated them. "Anyway, after college, we spent more time together. I offered her dad a hand when he was short-staffed from time to time. She was always around. Eventually we started dating, and things became serious.

"A year into it, she got accepted into grad school in Charleston.

We decided our relationship was ready for the next step, so she went to live at the dorms, and a few months later I'd follow her. We'd move in together off campus when I got there."

"Why the gap? Why didn't you go right away?"

"I wanted to do things right. I had to make sure my family had the right skilled hand to replace me, and I was saving up for a ring. I was going to propose to her when I got there, so we were respectful of her father. He was a religious man and preferred for us to be married before we moved in, but he was more lenient with me since he'd known me all my life. He just wanted me to make some sort of promise to her.

"A few weeks before I was set to go there, I got delayed. I found Willow, and I wanted to get her cleared before we traveled. Jolene missed her dogs back home, so I thought it would be a nice surprise. A new start to our family."

"All this buildup makes me think you crashed and burned."

"You're right. In the four months we were apart, we only saw each other once. I had to save money, so I could only visit Jolene when she first moved. She was busy with school and couldn't make the trip back." He pinched the bridge of his nose as he remembered it all. "When I got there…"

Lia squeezed his hand, encouraging him to go on.

"I don't know why she couldn't have told me before I uprooted my life." He shook his head, the old resentment coming back. "When I got there, I found out she had fallen for someone else. A guy from Charleston with deep roots. Old money. So, there I stood in her dorm—a puppy in my arms and a ring in my luggage—thinking I'd get a warm welcome. Instead, I learned she'd traded up."

"Don't you dare say that, Logan. How could you think this guy was better than you?"

"Money. Jolene wasn't exactly bred for manual labor. You'd think she'd have it in her soul, being a rancher's daughter and all. Nope. She was a Southern belle, and the new guy made it her reality."

"Money isn't everything."

"For some people, it apparently is." Taking in a deep breath, he continued, "I was stuck there. I had just put down a deposit on a small house rental in the suburbs. I accepted a job. I no longer had a job at the ranch since I essentially replaced myself. I had no choice. I had to see things through. Charleston seemed like a big town at first, but I soon realized how small it was when I constantly ran into her and her boyfriend…fiancé," he corrected. "They got engaged a few months later."

"Logan, I'm sorry. I had no idea."

"She was the first girl I loved. After that, I made a deal with myself. I said the next woman I fell for, I wouldn't be competing for her heart. If it came down to it, I'd walk away. I refuse to go through that again."

"Is that why you shut me out this week?"

He nodded. "I thought I had moved past all that, but you're the first woman I really saw myself with again." He gave an acid laugh. "The one who's leaving. Go figure. Then I saw you and Emmett."

"And you assumed I was 'trading up' to a guy with money," she finished for him.

Logan said nothing as he sat there, reeling from the emotional baggage he just unpacked. "I shouldn't have assumed," he said finally. "I just didn't want to be blindsided like that again. I figured I'd save myself by walking away."

"To set the record straight, I make my own money. Emmett did offer to help the Winchester Inn as a silent investor of sorts."

"And?"

"And I'm going to tell him no. He gave me great advice, and maybe I should consider it before I put myself in a hole. Regardless, I couldn't take his money. I worked so hard and have earned enough money that can help my family. I'm not going to give away my family's legacy at the first sign of trouble, especially since I still have the option to support them on my own."

"You're really something else." His voice filled with admiration.

"Did it work?"

"Did what work?"

"Trying to distance yourself from me."

"Not even close." He shrugged. "It's dangerous having these feelings for you, Lia. I can't make sense of them, and I can't turn them off. If I give in, they'll get stronger, and you leaving in two weeks will feel like shit. I was trying to avoid all of that."

She slid closer to him and wrapped her arms around his neck, pulling his head against her chest. Stroking his hair, as if she knew his admission was tough on him, she said, "I know. I swore to myself that nothing and no one was going to make me stay. I was going to get in, do what needed to be done, and go back to Boston."

He straightened and looked at her. "Are you saying you're considering staying?"

"It gets harder every day to say I'm going to stick to my plan." Her shoulders sagged. "Being here, and being with you, it all feels amazing. But I don't see how I can walk away from what I worked for. I spent years trying to get where I am now. Plus, my family might need to rely on my income until we sort out everything. I'm their lifeline."

Logan cupped her face, stroking her jaw lightly with his thumb. "Plans change, Lia," he reminded her again.

She leaned into his touch and let out a breath as if considering what she'd gain if she gave it all up. She kissed him gently on the mouth, making all his heartbreak melt away.

He wanted her. Needed her.

It was time for a new plan to show Lia she belonged in Fraser Hills, with him, whether she was ready to accept it yet or not.

Watching her walk away wasn't an option. He'd do everything he could to make her want to stay.

Chapter Sixteen

Relief washed over Lia after she and Logan cleared the air. Although their relationship was a train wreck waiting to happen, it was easier to ignore that tiny detail now they were on the same page. No more beating around the bush. No more guessing where they stood. They had twelve days left. Right now, it was just the two of them in their little bubble of bliss.

Logan had stayed a while longer last night, and although they mainly lounged around with a couple of bourbons by the fire, she preferred it more than the dinner with Emmett. Sure, the food and wine had been exquisite and the restaurant itself was beautiful, but a simple night in with Logan outshined that.

Oh, and Willow too. Logan had run to his cabin to grab her when they heard her pathetic whines. The dog came barreling into Lia's cabin when he brought her back. Sixty pounds of pure joy nearly mowed Lia to the ground.

She wouldn't have had it any other way.

With Logan, she remembered what it was like to be herself. It had been so long; she'd started to forget. Sharing each other's secrets, trials, and tribulations was cathartic in a way. They didn't have to pretend to have it all together, and being accepted for exactly who she was, messy mistakes and all, felt good.

Unlike today.

Lia would have loved to get lost in those good memories from last night and stay there, but the real world had a tendency of breaking into their party-of-two cocoon. No sooner had Logan left than Melody had called her, explaining Elizabeth was having second thoughts about the layout of the event.

The same layout Lia had been tirelessly working to put together and had already confirmed the setup and materials needed for it. It was impossible to make changes this time of year, as most companies and vendors were strapped with the sheer amount of holiday parties. Lia only prayed she could smooth things over with Elizabeth. Unfortunately, it couldn't be done via phone.

Another early morning flight to Boston allowed her to meet Elizabeth at the State Room in downtown before noon.

The State Room was a wonderful place to host the fundraiser, with its clean lines, open space, and two-story floor-to-ceiling windows overlooking Faneuil Hall and the Christmas market. Lia gazed at the massive Christmas tree below and the tourists milling about, getting gifts for the holidays. If this location was good enough for the former president's birthday party, then it should be good enough for Elizabeth.

But knowing that woman, it still wouldn't be up to her standards.

Lia was wary when Elizabeth entered the room in that stiff way she did, always with an expression of suspicion and disapproval. The polished woman did a slow walk around the massive space, stopping every so often to cluck her tongue with unspoken criticism.

Each cluck grated on Lia's nerves.

"Miss Kensie said you had concerns. How can I address them?" Lia finally offered after one too many disapproving noises.

"This layout won't work."

Lia plastered on the smile she reserved specifically for difficult clients. The one that challenged her facial muscles, leaving her sore by the end of the day. "If you'll take a seat over here, we can look at the designs together. Again." She mumbled the last part under her breath.

She led Elizabeth to a small table near the bar area and smoothed the mockups of the event space. Elizabeth dusted off imaginary dirt from the chair before taking a seat and putting on a pair of glasses.

"These are the same designs we looked at in the summer?" There was a glint of distrust in her eyes. Lifting one design, she held it away and inspected it thoroughly. She grabbed the remaining mockups, her face looking more constipated with each one. Finally, she placed the last ones down, removed her glasses with a huff, and folded her hands on the table while staring Lia down. "This won't do, Cordelia."

"You were pleased with them when you signed off in September. And again in late October."

"I don't believe I would have signed off on this. It won't work. Anyone with half a brain could see that."

Lia flushed with frustration. "I could—" she started, about to say she could forward the numerous email chains between them all with Elizabeth's approvals, but Lia bit her tongue.

Melody would have her head if she back talked a client. At Kensie events, they did everything they could to be accommodating. These clients paid an exorbitant amount of money and expected white-glove treatment, no matter how ridiculous their requests could be. "I'll

157

see what I can adjust," she said instead. "What aren't you happy with, Mrs. Sinclair?"

Satisfaction crossed the older woman's face as if she successfully asserted she was the alpha in this relationship and that Lia conceded she was in the wrong.

Elizabeth waved a hand over the designs. "I'm not impressed by the theme."

"What specifically?"

"The colors, some of the decor, the flower arrangements around the space." She let out a big sigh as if exhausted thinking about all the changes. Not that she'd be the one who needed to actually make them. "I'm sure I'll need to review the song list again while we're at it."

Lia's blood boiled. It took months to coordinate with the vendors. Now they were less than two weeks out, and she wanted to change nearly everything.

An internal panic attack came on, but Lia kept her expression collected and her voice as steady as possible. "Okay…so you want us to swap out the colors for something else, change the plants, and potentially get a new song list. Is that a safe assumption?"

Elizabeth gave a curt nod. "Yes."

"Elizabeth, to be frank, this might not be doable. The song list wouldn't be too hard, but judging by how big this event is and the materials needed to be preordered for it, I'm concerned about timing."

The woman looked down her nose, minimizing Lia to nothing with a simple stare. "Melody won't be pleased to hear this."

Lia's skin burned under the restrictive collar of her fitted blazer, furious Elizabeth would dangle Melody's approval over her head. This could cost her the promotion. Melody would think the issue was because Lia half-assed it from Fraser Hills, when truthfully, Elizabeth was asking for a miracle.

A miracle she didn't even think Melody could pull off. "I'll make calls today and figure something out."

"Yes. You do that. I suggest you come up well before the event to ensure it's all taken care of."

Lia's frustration reverted to panic. "Yes, Mrs. Sinclair. I'll do that."

Why does the thought of coming back make me feel like I'm suffocating?

"I expect to hear your progress by tomorrow morning." The woman stood, indicating she was done with the conversation.

"You will."

Once Elizabeth was out of sight, Lia placed her head in her hands and tried not to sob. This was a disaster, and she had no idea if she could fix it.

~ * ~

Rather than go into the office, Lia went to her apartment, thinking it would be easier to get this event under control without Melody there to hound her on every little detail. Her feet were like lead as she walked up the stairs to her landing. She greeted her neighbor who passed by her on his way out. Despite being the only two people in the hall, mere feet from each other, the man locked his door and walked by her without so much as a glance.

It was funny how she used to love that about Boston. The fact no one bugged her. Now it seemed cold and unfeeling.

She let out an ironic laugh. Fraser Hills, a town full of busybodies, with people constantly in your business, felt better than the lack of connection she had in Boston. No wonder it was hard for her to build relationships here—friendships and lovers alike—no one gave a shit enough to say hi.

She pushed through the front door and dropped her purse on the tiny entranceway's side table. Walking to the large window in the main living space, she took a moment to compose herself and figure out who she needed to call first. She imagined how these conversations would go. Her vendors were likely to laugh at her or hang up.

How was she going to pull this off?

What's worse, she'd agreed to come back early for the setup. Although she already knew she'd miss the Christmas Eve parade and dinner at the Winchester Inn since she had to run Elizabeth's fundraiser that same day, Lia hoped to spend at least a little more time there to watch it be set up.

She just wanted every moment she could get, especially since this might be the last time they celebrated these traditions, the ones she'd known her whole life. If her family lost the inn or the town went under, who could say what next year would bring?

The thought depressed her almost as much as it shocked her. It had been a couple of years since she'd been home for Christmas, but for whatever reason, things were different this time.

She looked out her window at the buildings lining the streets. Although it was winter, would it kill someone to put out some festive flower boxes to break up all the brick, stone, and concrete? And what about decorations? Boston had a mixed community of religions, but even folks who celebrated Hanukkah in her hometown put up their decor to represent that. People were proud of who they were and loved to share their traditions with others.

But here in Boston, there were no stringed lights. No festive wreaths. Even the Salvation Army Santas were sparse.

Pausing, Lia realized she was judging all these lackluster, joyless homes when she could have said the same about herself. Wasn't she the one working on Thanksgiving? Didn't she cut holidays short with her family—if she even made it down there—to get back to work? She thought about her apartment's decorations over the years and how they became fewer and fewer. Last year, she at least bought a tiny Charlie Brown tree. Granted, it sat in the corner, undecorated, and died soon after she got it because she'd been so busy and forgotten to water it. Aside from the tree, that had been the extent of her Christmas decor.

How did things get so turned around?

The buzz and energy of the city that had once inspired Lia now just sounded like grating noise. She gazed out the window a moment longer, wishing the buildings were replaced with the tree-lined mountains from her home and wanting the city street sounds to be replaced with the quietness of small-town life. Being in her sterile apartment made her realize how lonely she had been all these years. Maybe it wasn't the job that kept her busy every waking moment, but the need for the job to fill an unfulfilled life.

For years, she'd told herself all those people from Fraser Hills and their expectations had smothered her. Now? Maybe not so much.

A memory of what Logan said to her the night before filled her mind. Her heart fluttered in her chest knowing he wanted her too. It was complicated, but realizing she wasn't in it alone brought her a sense of peace. And excitement. And lust. And God knows what else.

Her phone pinged with a text from Melody asking her what happened with Elizabeth. The rush of warm and fuzzies vanished in an instant. Lia sighed and responded to the message, letting Melody know it was being taken care of.

That was her cue to start making those dreaded phone calls. Her vendors were going to think she was crazy. She wouldn't blame them if they wanted to cut ties with her after this. Hopefully all the business she brought their way in the past would make them a little more lenient.

Yeah right.

The next three hours were spent on calls, formulating ideas, playing phone tag, and generally ripping her hair out. As expected, it wasn't easy. Thankfully, no one threatened to tear up their contract, and no one had outright hung up on her.

She had small, quick wins, but the event rental company was going to be the tough one to swing. Her account representative had gone silent for a solid minute after Lia explained the situation. For a moment, she thought the line was dead.

"You understand what you're asking, right?" Ruth questioned in her thick, no-nonsense Boston accent.

"I know. I know. And you know I don't usually make this kind of change request, especially so late in the game."

"You're asking me if I have new inventory for table covers, chair covers, and linens in high-demand colors, days before an event, during the busiest time of the year," the woman stated.

Lia clicked her pen anxiously. "Yes."

"It sounds impossible."

"But is it actually impossible?"

"I'll have to make some calls and check our systems." Ruth couldn't hide her annoyance. "Give me until tomorrow."

Lia let out the breath she was holding. "Thank you so much," she said.

"Don't thank me yet," Ruth warned before hanging up.

Maybe it wasn't a definite solution, but it wasn't a no yet. That was enough for Lia to hold on to.

But that hope was short-lived.

Her cellphone rang. Melody's contact information flashed across the screen. Lia's stomach clenched as she hit the button to answer.

"Cordelia," Melody said, her sharp tone even more terse than usual. "I just got off the phone with Elizabeth Sinclair. I had to spend the last thirty minutes talking her down."

"Why would you need to talk her down? I said I'd take care of it."

"Apparently, she doesn't believe you're competent enough to do so. I tried to be accommodating with your family situation in North Carolina. You've been a star here, and I figured I could trust you to take on this *very* important client. However, now I'm having second thoughts."

Tears stung Lia's eyes. She'd worked her ass off for months on this event. Sure, she had her family to deal with, but she made every effort to be there for Elizabeth. How could Melody be saying this?

Lia took a cleansing breath, trying to find her inner Cordelia. The tough, career-driven woman who could handle anything, even people like Melody and Elizabeth.

She needed to be that woman again if she were to survive this event and keep her job.

Take the emotion out of it and get shit done.

"Melody," she said, hiding the irritation and disappointment in her voice. "Elizabeth told me today she wanted to change a core chunk of the event. I'm doing whatever I can to make that work, but I assure you the issues Elizabeth brought up have nothing to do with my lack of trying or the fact I'm not local this month."

"Elizabeth is a smart woman. I assume she would have made these decisions before now. Have you not been listening to her requests?"

"Of course I have." She wanted to scream but chose to stick to the facts. Melody couldn't deny a paper trail, could she? "I have sign-offs on everything. I have no idea why she decided to throw this curveball now."

"Whatever the story is, it needs to be fixed. I wanted to be hands-off on this account, but that approach clearly wasn't right for you. From now on, I'll be keeping a closer eye on what's going on." Melody sniffed, sounding put out as if this were any different from her usual micromanagement. "I was relying on you to handle this. I've been taking on a lot more, and I need someone I can depend on. This doesn't instill a lot of confidence, Cordelia."

The air escaped Lia as if she'd been punched in the gut. "I understand." Her voice was flat.

"Please send me the notes from today. I'll be following up with our vendors."

"I've already talked to them." Once again, the urge to scream was tempting.

"If you did it skillfully, you wouldn't be waiting on answers, you'd have them. I'll take care of this mess."

"Melody, please—" she tried to reason with her, but was cut off.

"Cordelia. The notes. Now." She hung up.

Lia stared at the phone in shock. Even if she had stayed in Boston and hadn't gone to Fraser Hills, she had a hunch this would all be the same. After she had some distance, she found a new perspective regarding Melody Kensie.

She was an unappreciative bitch.

Lia had always admired the woman, thinking her strength and ambition were the reasons Kensie Affairs skyrocketed in less than a decade. She was impressive, with many spotlight pieces featuring her throughout the years. Lia felt lucky when she'd been hired and had done everything she could to be mentored by Melody so she could be just like her.

Now she was left wondering why.

There was no doubt Melody was successful, but what other redeeming qualities did she possess? And how had Lia missed it all these years?

Probably because Melody hung that carrot in front of her. Whenever Lia thought she might break from the stress, suddenly there was a promotion to keep her motivated. The cycle continued to the point where she was working often, taking the brunt of the ill-mannered clients, and an even worse boss. Each promotion brought her closer to the goal of being like Melody.

But at what cost?

Lia shook her head. It was just a bad day, that was all. The pressure and lack of sleep were affecting her. Between that and the stark contrast of Boston compared to Fraser Hills, it was no wonder she was acting overly sensitive.

That must be it. Whatever doubts she was having about Kensie Affairs had nothing to do with the possibility it was wrong for her. It couldn't be. Not after everything she'd endured to get to this point in her career. She'd just fallen into the safe haven of Fraser Hills, her family, her friends, and Logan. It was hard not to want to sink further into that simple, uncomplicated world.

But, throughout her adult life, she'd always taken the hard road to prove she could handle anything. On her own. This was just another test. Working at Kensie Affairs was a relentless uphill battle, but she'd proven herself time and time again. She became stronger. More independent. More capable.

It was understandable that she was feeling a little burnt out and underappreciated. Although the inn was also hard work, with a lot of challenges to overcome, it was like a vacation compared to what she dealt with in Boston.

She'd gotten sucked into the Christmas cheer, the warm embrace from her mother, the constant words of affirmation, and the smile from a man who drove her crazy. And she loved the people's willingness to come together as a team and pitch in so she wasn't taking on the burden alone like always.

It wasn't real life though. It wasn't her real life, anyway.

Not anymore.

Worn down and a bit sorry for herself, Lia remembered what was at stake. All she wanted was that damn promotion to prove everything she'd done—everything she'd given up—was worth it.

It's just a rough patch. Suck it up. You haven't come all this way to give up now.

She couldn't. Wouldn't.

Chapter Seventeen

"Hi, Mom," Lia said as she entered the inn's kitchen early the next morning.

Mariam looked up from the cookies she was decorating and smiled. "Hi, honey. How was your trip to Boston?"

She poured herself a cup of coffee, the tension headache from the day before still wearing on her. "It was…tricky but nothing I couldn't handle."

"Of course. You always can."

"What are these for?" Lia took a seat and watched as her mom's steady hand added special details to each cookie. Her holiday desserts were always a work of art. Lia almost didn't want to eat them. Almost.

"For the guests. Savannah will also bring some to the homeless shelter."

"That's kind of you."

She frowned and waved it off. "It's nothing. I wish I could have done more for our guests and our community. With the accident, some things fell through the cracks." She swapped the piping bag of green frosting for one with red, now adding ornaments to the trees. "But I'm happy to report I'm getting stronger every day."

Lia regarded her mother with concern. Still in "Boston efficiency mode," she wanted to tackle the issue of the inn. They needed to if they had any shot of making this work. However, seeing her mom so happy in her element gave her pause.

"Mom, we need to talk about how we're going to manage the inn going forward and how we can take some of the responsibilities off yours and Dad's plates."

"Let's not think about that now. Can we just have this moment together? It's been too long since it was just me and you decorating cookies. I don't want to ruin it with talk about the future."

Lia bit her bottom lip. Her mom, always the optimist, had a hint of sadness in her voice. Hearing it gutted Lia. How could she push the issue any further right now? "You're right."

A small smile played on Mariam's lips. "All right then." She pointed the piping bag in the direction of the counter. "Can you grab the gold glitter star sprinkles and put them at the top of the trees I'm finishing?"

"Yes, Mama."

Her mother laughed. "There's my little Southern girl again. I'm glad your trip to Boston didn't take it out of you."

For the next hour, Mariam and Lia worked together to decorate the cookies. They made snowmen, trees, ornaments, mittens, reindeer, and more. Being in the kitchen, away from her cellphone and the front desk, was just what Lia needed. With each stroke of the frosting, the tension from the day before lessened. She felt more like the Lia from these last few weeks and less like the robot from yesterday.

Her mom was right. Sometimes it was better to focus on the special moments rather than the future, at least for now.

Lia put aside her finished cookies and studied her mother, hesitant about what she wanted to ask. "Mom?"

"Hmm?" Mariam continued to pipe the frosting without looking up.

"How did you know this was the life you wanted?" Lia's voice was quiet.

Her mom glanced at her from the corner of her eye. When she noticed Lia's serious expression, she put down the frosting and pushed a stray lock of hair behind Lia's ear. "What's going on, honey?"

"The Winchester Inn has been part of our family for forever. When you and Dad got together, you knew you'd have to take this on when you got married. What made you sure it was right for you? Did you have other dreams for your life?"

"Ah, I see what's going on." She gave an understanding nod, took Lia's hands gently, and sat on the stool next to her. "I'll admit, it was a scary thought knowing that in choosing to love your father meant I had a future planned out for me. I suspect it was scary for you too when it came to college and your future." Lia nodded, a tinge of guilt nagging at her. "I understand."

"You do?"

"Of course. Things might have been different in my time—you certainly have a lot more opportunity than I did—but I still had choices. I could have chosen a different path."

"But you didn't because you loved Dad?"

"That was part of it, not all of it. In my soul, I was certain Fraser Hills was my place. And before you say it's because it's the only place I've ever been, I'll have you know I've seen other places too," she said proudly. "Maybe not to the extent you have, but I've left the Fraser Hills borders from time to time. Nothing ever felt right to me like being here did, in this town, surrounded by a community of wonderful—albeit sometimes exhausting—people. This was a place where I had history, and your father's family had even more history. To think I could be part of preserving and celebrating that history mattered to me. That in choosing that path, I'd be doing something purposeful."

"Do you still believe that all these years later?"

Mariam put a hand to her heart. "That conviction is even stronger now. Working at the inn has had its challenges over the years, including what we're going through today. There have been times when I wondered how life could be different. What it would be like if we walked away from this legacy. But nothing I could ever dream of came close to how I feel about here, despite the hard times."

"And how do you feel?"

"Like I belong. Like I'm doing something that makes a difference." Mariam got up and moved the finished cookies to a clear spot on the counter. She shook her head. "Of course, I'm not saving the world," she said with her back still turned to Lia. "What we do here isn't helping starving children in Africa or creating world peace, but I believe in my heart that what we do here is still important." She turned around, her eyes glistening. "We created a safe place people could call 'home.' We're keeping traditions alive. In a world that's constantly changing, having these traditions is grounding. People can count on it when they can't rely on anything else. For some, this is all they've known. For others, this is a safe haven they were lucky to discover. That's enough for me."

Lia was speechless as she processed her mother's passionate speech. Was what she was doing in Boston purposeful? Did it speak to her the way Fraser Hills and the inn spoke to her mother? Lia had felt important all those years, making the big, splashy events happen for the Boston elite. She was proud of the glitzy, glamorous, and large-scale affairs she put together. She was even happier when the event was for a good cause, like Elizabeth's event, which she was busting her ass for.

Yet it wasn't the same as what her mother explained. Her job—although a big part of her adult life—now seemed like a fleeting accomplishment. Once the event was done, it was forgotten about. On to the next. Each one different and new. She was constantly challenging herself to think innovatively and creatively, always looking for new ways to outdo herself.

When all was said and done, did it matter to anyone? Did attendees make lasting memories at the events? Did they look forward to it? Or was it just another "thing" to attend in the sea of things to do. See and be seen.

Helping with the Christmas events these last few weeks gave Lia a glimpse into what her mother meant. It was a celebration of community. A way for Fraser Hillers to share timeless traditions with their new generation of family, friends, and loved ones. It gave newcomers a chance to discover something to add to their own holiday traditions. It was memorable. A keepsake, like the ornaments hanging on the tree in the lobby from years gone by.

Lia thought about when she found her ornament hanging there from when she was a kid, and the memories it brought back to her from the day she made it. She remembered Logan making his first ornament and the joy he got from hanging it on the tree, knowing someone—maybe even himself—would discover it in the future.

That was, if Fraser Hills and the Winchester Inn could survive. What would happen to all those cherished memories and traditions if they didn't?

Her heart broke at the thought. She now understood why the townspeople were doing everything they could to support her ideas. They'd do anything to keep the place they loved intact.

How could she not have seen how special it was? Her mother said this was enough for her. Why had Lia been so desperate to reach for more? She'd pushed and pushed. Pushed forward in her career. Pushed Fraser Hills to the back of her mind.

Pushed her family away.

And for what?

"Lia." Her mom's eyebrows wrinkled with worry. "Don't forget that we're proud of what you've made of yourself. Life can throw you for a loop, and sometimes decisions aren't cut and dry, but you need to do what's right for you. No one else."

Lia offered a weak smile and nodded before walking to the lobby, her stomach in knots and heart aching.

~ * ~

"Something's wrong with Lia." Logan hoisted another tree off Mike's truck.

"Let's put this in the barn. The snow isn't going to let up any time soon."

Mike grabbed one end of the tree and worked with Logan to lug it into an empty spot in the barn where it was nice and dry. They took a beat to watch the snow come down in thick, fluffy flakes. It had been snowing for over an hour and was accumulating fast. The weather forecaster said it was only a mild storm, but Logan hoped it was enough to drive people to the nearby slopes.

The town could use the skiers passing through.

Mike punched Logan lightly in the arm, pulling him from his thoughts. "What's wrong with Lia now?"

"I stopped by the inn to see how much firewood we'd need to replenish, and she seemed out of it."

They trudged through the snow to grab the next tree. "How?"

Logan brushed snowflakes from his hair. "I don't know. Lost? She was in rough shape when she came back from Boston the last time, but this time was different. She was more withdrawn."

"I checked out that sleigh you're working on. Coming out nice." His wolfish smile told Logan he knew the real motivation behind the project. "I hope you aren't trying to convince her to stay." This time his words were more serious.

Logan grunted as he picked up a smaller tree on his own. "Uh huh."

"I mean it. She doesn't take well to people telling her what to do. She's always been like that. Determined. Independent. Stubborn as hell. Even as a kid. It only got worse when she moved to Boston. She started taking herself way too seriously." Mike rolled his eyes.

"So I've learned."

"She's got a lot weighing on her, between the inn, my parents, and whatever bullshit Melody's dishing out." Mike said her name with disgust. "But, honestly, there are moments when Lia seems better than she's been in a long time. I can almost see my old sis in there somewhere." He threw another tree onto the pile.

Logan cringed when he realized how much wood he had to chop. "She said the inn was at capacity and was trending to be that way for the rest of the month." Which meant a lot more wood for the rooms and a lot more service calls.

"Yeah. Mom told me."

"I thought that would have made Lia happy. It's what she's after, right? But there was no excitement at all when she told me. She was like a zombie."

Mike shrugged and grabbed the last tree. "I don't know, man."

"I just want to see her happy," he said, more to himself than to Mike.

"I have an idea." Mike casually leaned an elbow on the truck bed.

Logan looked at him with suspicion. "What?"

"There was one thing Lia loved to do every Christmas." He laughed a little. "Actually, it was a tradition she came up with all on her own. Hasn't been done since she left." Mike eyed Logan up and down.

"What?" He crossed his arms over his chest.

"Before you do anything, it's time you got some real winter clothes. You're not going to survive the season dressed like that."

Logan compared his lighter jacket, jeans, and work boots to Mike's snow boots, snow pants, waterproof thermal jacket, and thick hat and gloves. He shrugged.

"Have you ever owned winter gear? What about skiing or trips?"

"Never had time. Rancher's life," he explained. "There wasn't a whole lot of money rolling in for those kinds of luxuries. Plus, it didn't snow in Texas or Charleston, except for that freak snowstorm they had this past January." Charleston was shut down for a week, and he had been just as well prepared as the rest of the suckers of the South.

"Well, you live in the mountains now. If we get snow like we normally do, you're not going to stand a chance." He gave another sly smile. "Plus, you'll need quality stuff if you're going to pull off what I'm about to tell you."

~ * ~

A few hours into chopping firewood had Logan realizing Mike was right. Despite how hard Logan was working and the fact he was sheltered in the barn, the cold seeped into his bones. His fingers burned. Each whack with the axe sent pain shooting up his arms.

Taking a break, he put the axe aside then headed into town. Mike gave him a great idea on how to lift Lia's spirits, and he wouldn't take no for an answer. He just needed to get supplies to make it work and some warmer clothes while he was at it.

Driving into town, he found a parking spot in front of Mountain Range Sports and went in, stopping at the door to stomp out his boots from the quickly accumulating snow. Despite the lack of visibility, people were still out and about, which was a good sign. Maybe skiers were passing through after all.

"Hey, Logan. What brings you in?" Amber greeted him as he entered the sports outfitters. She scrutinized his outfit the same way Mike did. "Seems like you need winter gear." She darted off before Logan could even respond.

It was like a movie montage with the way Amber kept loading him with stuff to try on. With each "fashion show," she'd examine him critically, giving him approvals or swapping things out for something more fitting. It was tough to swallow the price tag for all his purchases, but Amber assured him he had everything he needed to survive winter in the mountains for years to come.

On the way back to the inn, Logan was awash with a mixture of pure excitement and anticipation. He was practically vibrating with energy. The dark cloud that had forced him to hide within himself after Jolene dissipated. Now, he had the urge to put himself out there and for a woman who wouldn't be around long enough to see what could happen between them.

But he didn't care.

All he cared about was seeing that dimple on the apple of her cheek. He wanted to be the reason she had the uninhibited smile and be someone she remembered years in the future, the memory of him still bringing that smile to her face.

He pulled around the circular drive and threw his truck into park. Walking up the steps and through the double doors, he was relieved to find Lia behind the reception desk. She was so engrossed in whatever she was doing, a crease crinkling her forehead, she didn't notice he was coming until he was right in front of her with the beautiful bouquet in hand he picked up from Kathleen's flower shop during his trip downtown.

Lia peered around the large arrangement to find him brimming with a large grin. "Hi," she said, her tone still downcast, but now filled with some curiosity. She inspected the flowers, the serious expression on her face softening a fraction. "Are those for me?"

"Yes, ma'am."

Her body relaxed, a beautiful smile spreading across her face. "Bringing out the cowboy charm too I see. If I didn't know any better, I'd think you were buttering me up for a favor." She took the flowers from him, inhaled their fragrance, and let out a happy breath.

"No favors, unless it's asking too much to steal you away for an hour."

"She'll go," Mariam called out from the dining room where she was cleaning after the lunch rush.

They both laughed. "I guess that settles it," Lia said. "Are you going to tell me what you need me for or is it a mystery?"

"It's a surprise. Just make sure you dress warm. I'll meet you at your cabin at three."

She bit her bottom lip, the grin still there. "Okay."

He dipped his head as if tipping a Stetson and made his way back to his truck with a spring in his step.

~ * ~

Lia's doom and gloom emotions from her Boston trip were slightly less oppressive as she swapped her shoes for winter boots and slipped on her jacket and scarf. The generous flowers and Logan's mysterious rendezvous invitation were just what she needed to pass the time while she waited to hear from her vendors. Rather than worrying herself into a blubbering mess, she got to spend the afternoon with a man who filled her with warmth. He knew how to get her out of her head and pay attention to what was in front of her, which was no easy feat.

What would she do without him around once she went back to Boston? Who would be there for her when Melody or her clients were driving her to the looney bin?

A solid knock sounded at the cabin door. Swinging the door open, Lia found Logan and Willow. The pup was wriggling next to him, her face filled with joy. Lia took in his new ensemble and nodded. "Looks like someone went shopping finally. You got the good stuff too."

"Amber helped me out today."

"Good. You'll need it if you're working outside all winter." She zipped her jacket, locked the door, and slipped on her gloves. "So, what's on the agenda?"

"You're not going to get it out of me that easy." He led them away from the cabins.

Willow whizzed by them, springing through the half foot of snow like a bunny. Logan threw a snowball into the air, and she jumped up, catching it with ease. The snow exploded in her mouth. After the thrill of catching it wore off, she looked around, confused, as if wondering where her "ball" had gone.

"I take it she hasn't seen snow?" Lia laughed.

"She saw it once in Charleston. She was still figuring it out by the time it melted away."

"She seems to really like it."

He tossed another snowball. Willow darted after it. "Yeah. We both do."

Lia admired the outline of the mountains in the distance, hidden by clouds that were still dropping a steady stream of light snow. There was so much about Fraser Hills worth liking. It was a picturesque place filled with natural beauty. She hoped Logan would enjoy discovering all it had to offer.

They walked for a few minutes to the entrance of the county park trails. "We're going hiking?"

"Kind of."

She shook her head. He would be a tough one to crack. Rather than worry about what he had planned, she regarded the trail, lined with evergreens now layered with fresh snow. Everything was perfectly undisturbed. Pristine. Had the first Cordelia Winchester found it as enchanting as Lia did at this moment?

"Will you at least tell me what's in that backpack you're lugging around? We aren't pitching a tent out here, are we?" she questioned as they continued down the path deeper into the woods.

He stopped and examined the tree-lined path. Willow took advantage of the break and rolled in the snow, getting clumps of it stuck in her fur. "I guess this is as good a time as any."

He slipped the pack off his shoulders and dropped it on to the ground. He unclipped the top and unzipped the main pouch, pulling out multiple strings of lights.

She tilted her head. "What's this?"

"Solar string lights." He continued to take the lights out of the pack, followed by a colorful array of ornaments.

Realization dawned on her. Her heart clenched in her chest, and appreciative tears misted her eyes.

Overwhelmed with emotion, Lia reached out to draw Logan closer and kissed him hard on the lips, putting every ounce of feeling behind it. He reacted, gripping her hips, and hoisting her up so she could wrap her legs around his waist. He kissed her feverishly, angling her head so he could access her mouth deeper.

Holy hotness.

Cold air rushed along her skin as his hands caressed her back and explored her body. She wished the bulkiness of their jackets wasn't between them so she could touch the hard planes of his chest pressed against her.

After yesterday, she could use a bit of his strength and stability.

He kissed her face, moving his mouth along her jawline, making his way down an area of exposed neck peeking out from her scarf, leaving a trail of fire on her skin. She moaned, her body involuntarily grinding against him. The sensation of his warm breath on her chilled skin drove her wild.

It wasn't like her to act so primal, especially in public, but the gesture of this hike had brought it out in her. Her feelings for Logan had gotten clearer. Although the situation wasn't ideal, she was done fighting it.

Lia was falling for him.

He broke their kiss and rested his forehead against hers. Their breathing was labored, humming from sexual anticipation and want. Electricity coursed through her veins. She could fall apart in his arms right here, and they hadn't even taken off their clothes.

Yet.

Logan kissed her lightly. "Lia," he whispered against her mouth.

She pulled away, dazed from his kisses, and stared deeply into those beautiful blue-gray eyes she loved. "How did you know about this?"

"Mike told me."

"Why?"

"Because I couldn't stand seeing you so defeated today. I had to do something."

She held his gaze, the overwhelming emotions raging inside her. His thoughtfulness took her by surprise. "You're amazing."

He simply smiled and put her down, clearing his throat and adjusting himself. "So, tell me exactly what this is all about."

"I grew up on Christmas, obviously. We always had these fantastic traditions that were passed down from generation to generation. I loved being a part of that and seeing the community come together for these grand gatherings, but I wanted something of my own. Something that could be happily unexpected. A subtle way to bring Christmas someplace else.

"Every year, I would head down to the park—along this very trail, actually—and find a few trees to decorate. I loved knowing someone hiking down these paths would come across those trees. I wanted them to feel like it was decorated just for them. It would be a special moment, without all the pomp and circumstance."

She picked up the lights, her eyes going wide with delight. "But I never had *these*. This will be a game changer."

Logan yanked out solar-powered tree toppers from his pack. "And these?"

She took the star and angel from him. "This is going to make it better than it's ever been."

They spent the next hour decorating a few random trees along the trail. Logan talked more about his life as a rancher and how it helped him discover his love for building and how he could bring new life to things that would otherwise be forgotten. Lia shared more stories about life in Fraser Hills, including funny stories about the townspeople he was starting to get to know better.

The time they spent together was meaningful to her, even if they were merely decorating trees in honor of a silly idea she had when she was a kid. It meant more to her than he would ever realize.

She wanted to believe her happiness wasn't because it was like taking a vacation from her real life, but rather because she remembered what made this town so special. She considered herself lucky to have grown up in a place like this and was glad to make new memories to add to her favorites.

A nagging idea started turning over in the back of her mind, interrupting her positive thoughts. She froze, trying to pinpoint what was making her uncomfortable during an otherwise lovely afternoon with Logan.

Then it hit her like a ton of bricks: the notion of being the next Melody disgusted her. She didn't want that life anymore.

She wanted this one.

Taking a step away from her incessant phone filled with calls and emails reminding her that no matter how hard Lia tried, she'd never be good enough in Melody's eyes, led her to this realization. Being here removed the fog clouding her brain and judgment.

Maybe she'd been coming to that slow realization over the last few weeks, but it had gotten buried by her never-ending to-do list worries. Or perhaps she had subconsciously recognized it some time ago, but it had become too hard to break momentum she'd built following in Melody's footsteps. Staying the course had been easier.

Now that she's come to terms with it, she didn't know what to make of it.

"You okay?" Logan asked when he noticed her pause, an ornament dangling from her fingers.

Was she?

She blinked, repressing her unexpected revelation back into the recesses of her mind. "Yeah," Lia said, hanging the ornament on an undecorated tree limb. "It's starting to get dark. We should head back."

They packed up what was left and took a moment to appreciate their work. There, among the white-lined firs, was a hidden wonderland. The snow—now falling lightly—floated around the trees. The lights sparkled, making the colorful ornaments shine. She appreciated how the solar lights made a world of difference and dared anyone not to feel joy if they stumbled upon this.

At that moment, she promised herself that thoughts of Melody wouldn't ruin her joy either.

She'd figure it out. Just not right now.

~ * ~

Lia finished up at the inn, humming an upbeat Christmas song as she completed the last of her tasks. Even the stress caused by Elizabeth and Melody or her nagging thought from earlier couldn't shake her happiness from the way the rest of her day had gone.

After their tree-decorating extravaganza, Logan offered to cook her dinner later that evening. She popped by her cabin to freshen up and made her way over.

She couldn't stop thinking about him all afternoon—not that it was significantly different than how things had been lately—but something about today made things shift. Again.

He put her needs first and made an effort to give her something meaningful. The memories they were creating together were ones she'd never forget.

Thinking about it made her miss him already. In nine days, she'd be back on a plane to Boston, and all of this would end.

They had tonight though. She planned to make the most of it.

Her breath caught in her throat when he answered the door, knees going weak at the sight of him. He was wearing casual jeans and a tight Henley that showed off his broad, muscular body. He flung a dish towel over his shoulder. A slow, sexy smile spread across his lips and made her toes curl.

Willow pushed past him and danced at Lia's feet with her goofy, crooked smile. "Well hello to you, girl." She kissed the dog on the head.

"Spoiled dog."

Lia rose to her toes, grabbing his shoulder for balance, and placed a kiss firmly on his mouth. "Is that better?"

He licked his lips as if he were savoring her taste. "I could work with that." He led her into his cabin, taking her coat and hanging it by the rack near the front door. "Dinner will be ready soon." He went to the kitchen and held up two bottles of wine. "Red? White?"

"Red, please."

Pouring her a glass, he brought it to the living room and encouraged her to take a seat on the couch in front of the roaring fire.

"You sure you don't want some help?"

"Sit back and relax. I got this."

"If you insist." She sipped her wine and pet Willow, who nestled next to her. The sound of the crackling wood in the fireplace put her at ease. She was lost in thought as she watched the orange, yellow, and blue light dance along the logs, enjoying the warmth from the fire and Willow, who was happily sleeping on her lap.

Her apartment in Boston had never felt like this. Hell, she didn't even think it had ever smelled like whatever it was Logan was cooking. Most of her meals were eaten out, ordered in, or microwavable. Her mother would have a stroke if she found out Lia never took time to cook a proper meal, let alone bake anything. Aside from working in the Winchester Inn kitchen, she honestly couldn't remember the last time she'd baked.

Suddenly, Logan was in front of her, drawing her from her thoughts. He held out his hand and helped her up. "Dinner's ready, milady."

"It smells amazing. What is it?"

"Chicken piccata with angel hair pasta."

"I didn't realize Texan ranchers mastered Italian fare. Aren't you all Tex-Mex and steak?"

He laughed. Pulling a chair out for her at his small four-seater dining table, he said, "We took turns cooking throughout the week at my family's ranch. We all worked hard, even my mama, so it was only fair for us to give each other a break. If it were up to my dad, we probably would eat steak for breakfast, lunch, and dinner. That's his specialty. Steak and beans. Steak and eggs. Steak sandwiches. He's a simple man."

Logan placed the plates on the table and took a seat. "My mom and sister were decent cooks. I wouldn't say they hold a candle to Mariam, but they at least tried to add some variety to our meals. I took it upon myself to learn how to cook. Going out to a restaurant wasn't common where I lived, so if I wanted a good meal, it was up to me to make it."

Lia regarded the beautiful presentation on her plate. "Seems like you took that seriously. This looks and smells amazing."

"Hopefully it tastes just as good." He picked up his fork. "Dig in."

She took a bite and moaned. "This could compete with the North End in Boston. Those Italians are straight off the boat. My God, you are a man of many talents. I would kill to have you cook for me every day."

She paused, stunned by the words that slipped from her lips and how much she wished they'd come true. If Lia stayed in Fraser Hills, he would gladly have done that for her. Of that, she was certain.

Picking up her wineglass, she took a sip and cleared her throat. "Thank you for today, Logan. Between the excursion in the park and now this. You've outdone yourself. I don't deserve this."

"Of course you do. You deserve everything." He took her hand from across the table and kissed her inner wrist.

Her heart raced. This man. He was a dream.

The calmness and clarity she got being in his presence was becoming addictive. It was like all the angry, overwhelming noise in her head went quiet. The churning in her body forcing her to keep pushing forward to the point of exhaustion all these years had gone still.

With Logan, she could breathe.

Compelled, she got up from her seat and straddled his lap, surprising him with the sudden shift. Sitting down slowly, she ran her hands through his hair and kissed him. But this time, her kiss let him know she didn't want it to end at just that. She wanted him. All of him.

But you're leaving.

She shook her head, trying to forget all the reasons why sex with Logan would complicate things.

If she felt this good around him before sex, how likely was it she'd be able to walk away at the end of the month without her heart completely breaking in two?

Crossing that line and being intimate with him was dangerous. There was no happy ending for them.

By the way he responded, devouring her mouth, gripping her hips, and pulling her against him, he wanted her just as badly. That reaction alone made her push aside all her conflicting feelings.

Right now, there was only one thing on her mind: getting him naked.

Logan pushed away from the table, holding her as he stood. She wrapped her legs around his waist, their lips still locked together. Carrying her to the bedroom, he kissed her with an intensity that went straight to her soul. She tugged at his shirt, breaking their kiss only to pull it over his head. The warmth from his skin and the hard muscles of his back, shoulders, and chest drove her insane. She wanted to be pressed against him with no barriers.

As if sharing the same thought, he tore her sweater off and expertly unlatched her bra, tossing it aside in a millisecond. She moaned when her skin slid against his as he kissed her neck and shoulder. A shuddering breath escaped her lips when he dipped his head and took one of her nipples in his mouth.

He placed Lia carefully on the bed and leaned over her, kissing a trail from the swell of her breasts, down her stomach, and to her hips. He stopped at the waist of her jeans.

"Is this what you want, Lia?" The desire in his voice was raw and real, making her own need unbearable.

"Don't you dare stop," she managed, clutching at his hands, and encouraging him to continue by placing them on the button of her pants. She could barely contain herself. If she didn't have him now, she would lose it. "I want you, Logan."

Without the need for further convincing, he undid her button and zipper and slid her pants off, stripping her down to her black lace panties. The cool air against her warm skin was electrifying. The anticipation was killing her.

He got to his knees, dragging her panties down her legs, leaving a path of kisses in their wake. He'd occasionally nibble lightly, and the unexpected sensation of his teeth between the soft kisses drove her wild. Finally, he removed her last piece of clothing and spread her legs, putting his mouth to her core.

Lia felt exposed. It had been a while since she'd been with someone, and normally the first time was a fumbling mess of nerves and a bit of awkwardness. But when it came to Logan, she wanted to give him everything. Wanted him to enjoy her.

She almost came at the first brush of his tongue against her bundle of nerves.

Slowly, methodically, he stroked her with his tongue, adding pressure and speed as he brought her closer to the edge. She gripped the sheets, arching her back, and yelled out when he twisted his fingers inside of her. The added friction made her eyes roll into the back in of her head. Logan used his free hand to hold her hips in place, making her take every stroke of pleasure.

He consumed her, and something about his insatiable need to taste her turned her on like nothing else.

Thoughtful and sweet in the streets, and a sex god in the sheets. He's fucking perfect.

"Logan." She moaned, her orgasm starting to build. She wanted to give in, but she wanted him far more. "Logan," she said again, grabbing his hair to get his attention. "I want you. Now."

He jumped to his feet like a man on a mission and ripped off his jeans and boxers. She sucked in a harsh breath when she saw the length of him, ready for her. Sliding further up on the bed, she opened her legs wider for him. Beckoning him.

The look on his face would be burned in her mind forever.

He sucked in a ragged breath. "You're beautiful."

Slipping on a condom, he climbed into bed, and placed his body between her legs. She hooked her heels around his hips, eager to feel him, and ran her hands along the warm tense muscles of his back.

Underneath his massive hard body, she seemed so small. So delicate.

Though, the hunger dancing in his eyes made her feel anything but innocent.

He positioned himself and took a beat to hold her gaze as he gradually entered her. The sensation of him filling her up inch by inch almost took her over the edge right then, but she held on just a little longer, wanting him fully before she let go.

He moved inside of her slowly at first, and Lia could see his restraint was as much of a challenge for him as it was for her. The sexual tension that had been building since day one was more than either of them could handle.

They wanted it to last. Ride it out until they made these last few weeks of torture worth it.

"Let go," she encouraged him, moving her hips in sync with his.

He leaned down, kissing her mouth as he thrust deeper and faster into her. She wrapped her arms around his neck, pulling him to her as her pleasure built once again. Finally, she exploded. She moaned his name against his mouth.

He bit her bottom lip and showered her with kisses, continuing to move his hips, allowing her to ride out the most intense orgasm she'd ever had in her life. As she came down from her first orgasm, he slipped a hand between them, his thumb gliding back and forth along her sensitive spot so she could come for him again.

When he was satisfied with her near instant response, he gripped her hips for better leverage, and moved harder. Even deeper.

She saw stars. Maybe heaven.

He tensed and let out a low groan as he came.

Panting, he leaned on his arm and gathered her against him. Their legs tangled with one another as they kissed and caught their breath. He traced his hands down her back, now slick with sweat, and gave her ass a playful squeeze. She let out a small laugh as she ran her hands along the scruff on his chin.

"Okay. Now you've outdone yourself," she finally said when her breathing had steadied.

He kissed her collarbone. "The night's still young." His voice was a rumbling in her ear.

Logan was right. Soon after, he showed her just how much he wanted her again. This time, leisurely. He savored every inch of her, slowly igniting that fire between them over and over. He clutched her hands as he moved inside her, worshiping every inch of her body. What was first an act of relieving the sexual tension had now turned into something more intimate. More personal. More powerful.

Something Lia didn't think she'd ever be able to come back from.

She had fallen in love with him.

Chapter Eighteen

The next morning, Lia silently slid from the bed and crept to Logan's bedroom window to peek at the breathtaking landscape outside. The sun had barely risen, but it provided enough light to see that the snow had accumulated a few more inches overnight.

The rustling of a comforter sounded behind her. Logan's voice, rough from sleep, called out, "It's early. Come back to bed."

Despite being up most of the night exploring each other's bodies, she was surprisingly energized. She slipped under the covers, and he wrapped his strong arms around her bare skin, holding her against his warm body. He placed lazy kisses on her temple and face, his eyes still closed.

"What are you thinking?" he asked between kisses.

"That it looks like we have about a foot of snow out there."

"Mmm." He let out a tired groan. "Means I have a lot of clean up to do."

"It also means there's going to be ski traffic. We could get a spike in tourism as they pass through."

"That's good." His voice was faint as he buried his face in the crook of her neck.

"I have an idea."

"Hmm?"

"Logan, are you even awake?"

"Mmm." His grunt was slightly louder this time.

Lia sighed. "I think we should do a pop-up today."

He gripped her thigh. "I like the sound of that." He nipped her neck, the stubble from his chin scraping against her skin.

She laughed. "Not that kind of pop-up."

He squeezed her again. "What did you have in mind?"

"With all this snow, we should have a snowball fight. Make it a competition. I'll see if some of the local stores and restaurants can offer prizes. We can capitalize on the fact people will be in the area anyway. Maybe do it closer to dinnertime so they'll stop by when they're done with the slopes. Come for the competition, stay for dinner."

"Sounds great." His response had gone quiet. On the verge of falling asleep again, he snuggled her tighter, causing Willow to stir at the foot of the bed with a huff. "Go back to sleep. Too early for your big ideas."

Normally, Lia had a hard time staying still once an idea struck her, but being wrapped in his arms with Willow sleeping soundly at her feet, she found her eyelids heavy from exhaustion.

Is this what content feels like? she wondered as she drifted back to sleep.

~ * ~

Lia was a woman on a mission and had outdone herself again. Logan admired her ability to rally and throw together another great event despite the fact he had kept her up most of the night. She had called the townspeople about her idea and secured prizes to entice visitors to come. She'd even managed to launch a quick online campaign that had driven a ton of ski traffic to the quaint town. Logan had no idea how she pulled it off in just a few hours, but she did, as usual.

She was always full of surprises.

Last night especially.

That woman. His eyes nearly rolled into the back of his head at the memories. He couldn't wait to get her alone again.

But first, he'd have to wait for the event to be over.

The snowball fight at the Winchester Inn was teeming with activity, generating an impressive crowd. Mariam and Ron moved around in a flurry to offer treats to spectators and act as the tourism board, sharing insights into where people could eat or shop.

The small snowstorm was just what Fraser Hills needed, and Lia's idea to do the pop-up was brilliant. The crowd's energy was palpable, breathing new life into the tiny mountain town. Thankfully, the temperatures stayed low so the snow didn't melt away, making conditions favorable for Lia's idea to work.

"Got time for dinner?" Logan asked once the snowball fight had died down and the visitors ventured around downtown.

Lia waved to the last of the crowd and turned to him with a bright smile. "Why, Logan, are you asking me out on a date?"

"Only the finest dining, little lady," he drawled and winked.

Laughing, she checked her watch. "I'd say so. Mom and Dad need me back at the inn around eight. We have a couple of hours for dinner. Is that okay with you?"

"Perfect."

Logan took Lia's hand and led her to the main strip downtown.

Walking by the newly designed town square, they paused to take it all in. Jim, with his usual genius, had taken advantage of the cold weather to create a small ice-skating rink. With all the extra space by the center's Christmas tree and gazebo, it was the perfect addition to create a real-life Norman Rockwell feel. The vision of people skating along the main street added more charm than all the decorations combined. It was picture perfect.

Logan smiled as happy skaters of all ages passed them by. "Lia, what you did today…wow. Just wow."

She peered at him from under long her lashes and blushed. "It was nothing. Just being an opportunist. Trying to make the most of what we've got to get this town turned around."

"It's not nothing." He squeezed her hand and pointed to the people circling the rink. "Look at those faces. That's pure, genuine happiness. You made the day for a lot of people. This is a memory they're going to take with them, and hopefully create the kind of nostalgia they want to relive over and over. It's the same look I saw on your parents' faces. Even yours."

Her beautiful honey-brown eyes filled with pride. "It was good. Like old times."

Logan barked out a laugh when her growling stomach broke the trance between them.

"Glad you're hungry." They continued walking down Fraser Hills Road, and made a left onto Evergreen, stopping in front of the fifties-style diner.

"Hmm. A fancy dinner of hot dogs? I'm the luckiest girl in the world," Lia teased.

"I know it's not one of your swanky Boston restaurants, but I also know you haven't tried one of Jeff's gourmet hot dogs."

Lia made a face. "I'm still not sure I get the whole concept. You finally got a chance to try them?"

"Yup, and trust me on this. The names and the descriptions sound nuts, but it's worth it."

They walked into the diner and the hostess, a woman in her late sixties with a beehive hairstyle and horn-rimmed glasses, sat them at a corner booth. Logan slid in behind Lia, wrapped an arm around her shoulders, and opened a menu.

"Wow. This is a long list. I never thought grumpy Jeff had it in him to come up with so many."

Logan thought of the gruff man who never said much and grinned. "People can surprise you." A waitress took their orders of hot dogs, fries, and chocolate milkshakes.

"We're like a couple of teens on a date in the olden days."

"If that were the case, we would have shared a milkshake." He wagged his eyebrows.

"Oh, scandalous," she teased and eyed his arm nestled around her. "Pretty bold for that time. You completely bypassed the hand-holding phase. It takes a while to work up to this."

"And what about what we did last night?" he whispered and nipped her ear, causing her cheeks to flush and her full, kissable lips to part as she exhaled. "Were you okay bypassing the hand-holding stage then?"

Her lips twitched. "Without a doubt."

Logan enjoyed their time at the diner, and he liked how effortless it was to be with her. He would have loved to take her out to an upscale dinner and shower her with the things she was probably used to in Boston, but being there, in the quaint town diner, eating messy hot dogs and feeding each other french fries was perfect. This simple moment made it easy for him to picture them, years from now, enjoying each other's companionship.

He tried not to let the reality of knowing there would be no "years from now" for them ruin this night. There was only now and only this. Somehow, he'd have to be okay with that and appreciate it while it lasted.

After dinner, Logan walked her to the inn's front door and dropped a quick kiss on her lips, with only moments to spare before her meeting with her family. As she turned back to blow him a kiss, he realized she had crept into his heart.

He was in love with Lia Winchester.

~ * ~

Lia practically floated into the inn. Logan was more than anything she could ever imagine. Down-to-earth, funny, thoughtful, strong, caring, and sexy as hell. She cherished the moments with him and vowed to make the most of these last few days they had together.

All her happiness came crashing down when she entered the kitchen. The grim expressions on her mom and dad's faces made her stomach drop. Mike walked in a minute after her, looking just as confused as she felt.

"What's going on?" The hair on the back of her neck rose, hinting at impending doom.

"Sit down, honey," her mom instructed as her dad set a cup of chai tea in front of her.

Lia slowly sat on a stool next to Mike and wrapped her hands around the warm mug, trying to ease the coldness coursing through her veins.

Her mother, always one to find a silver lining, looked downright depressed.

Lia's cellphone rang, and Melody's name flashed on the screen. She hit ignore. Melody would have to wait.

"Kids, your mother and I went to visit the accountant today," her father started.

"We took into consideration what Dr. Evans had told us during our last visit," Mariam added. "Although it's been great working again, it's clear to us we aren't as spry as we used to be. The baking and cooking take a lot out of me now. I'm not sure how I'd be able to tend to the front desk and do the cleaning, too. Your father feels the same way about the tree farm."

Her dad, tight-lipped, stared at both of his children. "We talked about the option of hiring a manager part time. Or even a cleaning service." He shook his head. "With the cost of that, plus recouping the cost of repairing the roof, it's not possible. Our insurance didn't cover enough, and we were left paying for the section of the roof Donnelly required us to update out of pocket. Although we have a nice retirement fund, that will dry up quickly if we tap into it. We'd be left with nothing to live off of if we used it."

All the air was sucked from Lia's lungs. "I thought this winter was going well. The inn is at capacity. We're bringing in new tourism. Weather's good."

Her mother nodded. "It's been a great December so far, and we're thankful for all you've done to make it successful. However, one good month isn't enough to make up for the setbacks we've had the last couple of years. We need consistent tourism throughout the year to afford help. We get a bit during the other seasons, but not nearly enough to make it work."

"I have money saved up. I can help you hire someone." She rose from her chair, frantic. Helpless.

"Enough to hire someone for a year, but then what? We'll be in the same spot, and you'll be suffering, too," her dad countered.

Mike spoke. "The tree farm's doing well. We've got new contracts coming in for lumber."

"That's great, son. But those contracts aren't large enough to pay for the labor we need to manage that and the inn."

Lia remembered the offer she rejected. "I can talk to Emmett and tell him we're interested in his investment."

Ron shook his head again. "That won't do. If someone invests in the inn, they could change the way the business is run."

"He said he wouldn't do that."

"You're a savvy businesswoman, Lia. You know the realities of these situations. How we've been running things isn't turning enough profit. It would be hard for an investor to give us money and then let us keep doing the thing that failed." He looked dejected. "I couldn't stomach having someone tell me how to run my family's legacy. Not after all these years."

"What are our options then?" Mike asked.

Regret filled her parents' faces. Taking Mariam's hand, Ron delivered the blow. "We'll be selling the Winchester Inn after the new year."

Lia and Mike yelled out objections.

"Are you out of your mind?" Mike argued.

"You can't do that!" Lia shrieked.

Her dad held up his hands, trying to calm them so he could get in a word. "It's the only way. We wouldn't do this if we had any other option."

Stunned, Lia flopped into her seat. "But we tried so hard."

"And we succeeded, in a sense. However, we didn't plan on a tree falling through our roof and having our health suffer because of it. This was out of our control, honey." Her mom tried to soothe the defeat they were all feeling, but her wavering voice made it harder to hear.

"What about the tree farm?" Mike asked.

"We'll add contingencies for the buyer. The tree farm will stay intact, and you'll continue to run it." Lia's dad gave her a pointed stare. "Logan will be offered a three-year contract. After the contract, the buyer can decide if they want to keep him on."

"And the inn?"

"The inn is a historic building, so there will be regulations, but the seller could make changes. They may not keep it as an inn. Could even name it something different."

"Stripping our history from it?" Lia's blood boiled. "So, if there's no more inn, how will that affect the town's economy?"

The question went unanswered because they all knew what it meant. Without a place for tourists to stay, there wouldn't be much for people to do. Fraser Hills would become a pass-through town if they were lucky. The heart of their town, the Winchester Inn, wouldn't be there to help them. There would be nothing left to keep the community together.

"How can you be okay with this? To watch generations of Winchesters be wiped away?" she pressed.

"Lia, honey. This is the hardest decision we've ever had to make.

Do you know how much this pains us? To feel like we failed our family's legacy?"

Lia stared at them, speechless, then walked away. All the hope she had for saving the Winchester Inn had been ripped away from her in an instant.

Chapter Nineteen

All Lia wanted to do was to race to Logan's cabin and feel his strength and steadiness as she cried in his arms. She wanted Willow there, nudging for pets and comforting her with her fuzzy body. But she promised her parents she wouldn't say a word. They wanted to share the news after the holidays on their own terms. So rather than be with the man who grounded her, Lia spent the evening alone in her cabin, crying to herself.

Just as she likely would when she returned to Boston, in her apartment that now seemed cold and empty, like her life there felt in general.

She couldn't sleep that night. Her failure floated through her head in cycles. All the effort she'd put in after years of ignoring her family and their needs. How her last-ditch attempt to save the inn wasn't enough. Nothing she had done in Fraser Hills had made a difference. Nothing she ever did for snooty clients like Elizabeth Sinclair made a mark.

After all these years of trying to find her purpose in the world, Lia saw the truth. She simply wasn't enough.

Hopeless and broken, she struggled to get out of bed early the next morning. The news of losing the Winchester Inn was like a piece of her was being ripped away, and nothing she'd ever do would replace it. As hesitant as she had been to come back home, it was important to her that the community and the inn had remained the same. Sure, there were a few minor changes as it moved forward with the times, but the traditions and the people were still there, just as they once were.

There was comfort in that. She always knew she could go home. She could count on it.

And now?

If the inn was no longer there and the traditions of the Winchester family were lost, what would become of Fraser Hills? What of its people? Would they leave for more prosperous towns? Would the townspeople lose their source of income and have to board up their shops? And her parents, where would they go? Would the new owners let them keep their cabin or would they be pushed out along with the memories of the inn?

Her heart ached at the thought of her parents looking for a home. Or worse, being put into one of those soulless retirement homes before their time.

Going through the motions of getting ready, she let her curly hair hang in its natural state, applying the bare minimum of mascara and lip balm. She slipped on her Fraser Hills uniform of jeans, boots, and a sweater before making her way to the inn's reception desk. She didn't bother stopping in the kitchen for her usual coffee. Her stomach couldn't handle that right now, not with how much it had been turning over since her parents had shared the news.

She could only imagine what her parents must be going through. They had put up a strong, brave front last night, but how does a person accept letting go of something they'd put their all into?

The inn was their life. Now it was over.

Although Lia had put her all into her career too, she had the inn there as a backup. A safety net. Her parents didn't even have that.

I guess neither do I anymore.

She mindlessly answered emails, work requests, and social media comments. Each response was hollow as she forced herself to put a positive spin on something that wouldn't exist soon. At least, not in the way that made this place special.

The front door swung open, but Lia didn't bother to acknowledge it. She hadn't mustered up the energy to paste a fake smile on her face to welcome her guests.

"Excuse me, miss," a woman's voice called out as she approached.

A familiar woman's voice.

The sound of high heels moving along the wooden floors and the scent of expensive perfume reached Lia before the woman did.

No.

Lia's head shot up to confirm her worst fear. Melody froze and squinted, as if trying to process that yes, the woman at the front desk was, in fact, Cordelia Winchester.

"Oh," Melody said in half surprise, half disgust. "I didn't recognize you." She straightened, recovering from her initial shock.

She was pissed, that was evident in the way her gaze pierced Lia and how her lips formed a tight line. She stared at Lia a moment longer, a tactic she likely used to make the other person sweat so she'd get the upper hand.

"Do you know how many times I called and emailed you yesterday, Cordelia?" Lia flinched at Melody's harsh tone. "We have pressing issues to address for the Sinclair party, and you've become unresponsive." Melody placed her large, designer purse on the desk, nearly knocking over the flowers from Logan.

"I'm sorry, Melody. I had a family situation come up."

Melody crossed her arms and looked down her nose with disapproval. "Do you think I have the time to check on my employees, let alone book a flight to find out what they're doing? This is the busiest time of year for us. I don't have the luxury of babysitting you."

Her eyes scanned Lia's computer and noticed the Winchester Inn event page. Melody scowled. "What's this?" Lia didn't miss the accusation in her voice.

"It's an event for the town and the inn."

Melody lifted her delicate wrist to look at her watch. "It's nearly nine in the morning. As far as I'm concerned, you're on my time."

When wasn't I on her time?

Lia rose from her seat, planting her hands on the desk. She gripped the edge, trying to control her temper. "Melody, you agreed to allow me to come here and help my family in their time of need."

"Yes. As I recall, you were helping them recover from an accident." She pointed her manicured nail at the computer. "Not managing their events. Are you billing them for this?"

"No!"

"Then I expect you to be fully focused on Kensie Affairs. Do you understand?" She took her phone out of her purse. "You have five minutes to pull yourself together. I expect to see you at the cafe in town to tackle this Sinclair problem. I didn't come all this way for nothing."

Snatching up her purse, she strode out of the Winchester. Her spine was ramrod straight, showing Lia exactly how furious she was.

Lia froze in stunned silence. How dare Melody come here and speak to her like that? Yes, Lia wasn't as available as expected yesterday, but had she not made herself available every other time, including the back and forth trips to Boston?

She sucked in deep breaths, reminding herself she worked too hard to do something foolish. She was on the verge of telling Melody to shove it and that Elizabeth Sinclair had enough fortune to donate to the charity she was fundraising for without the lavish party. But, of course, Lia couldn't. She was a professional, and she never left her work unfinished.

With her safety net now cut away, she really couldn't afford to lose her job.

At her cabin, she quickly changed into more professional attire, smoothed her hair and placed it in a knot at her neck, and added a touch more makeup. It was the best she could do to get to the Shaky Page, a cafe and bookstore located on the main strip, on time.

With moments to spare, she parked her rental car a few storefronts down on Fraser Hills Road. The town was still buzzing from the recent snow, and she was happy to see more people were out exploring.

Not that it made a difference anymore.

She walked into the cafe, grabbed a latte from Savannah at the counter, then sat opposite Melody. Melody barked orders into her phone and hung up, finally addressing Lia's presence. "I'm glad you made yourself somewhat presentable." She peered around the cafe with judgment. "I swear, Cordelia. I knew you were from a small town, but I didn't realize how backwoods it was."

"It's not backwoods, Melody." Lia seethed on the inside. "These people are dressed appropriately for the weather." She regarded Melody's pencil skirt, heels, and blouse.

"Yes, well. I suppose none of them have real jobs here anyway." She pulled out her tablet and spun it in Lia's direction. "Do you see these messages from Elizabeth? She's not pleased. If she wasn't a family friend, she would have dropped us."

"I told Elizabeth I was taking care of things. My event rental contact had to see what inventory they had on such short notice. She said she'd get back to me by close of business today."

"If—and that's a big if at this point—you're going to be working with clients of this status, you should know that waiting is unacceptable. You should have been at your vendor that same day, getting a solution sorted immediately and informing the client. You make your vendors work for you. You don't let them dictate your event."

"I've worked with these vendors for years. They've bent over backward for me before. I wasn't going to ruin the relationship."

Melody shook her head, her perfect hair not moving out of place. "There are plenty of other vendors out there, and they're all clamoring to do business with us. If you lose a vendor, so be it. If it means getting our client what they need when they need it, then you do whatever needs to be done. Got it?"

The sentiment left a bitter taste in Lia's mouth. She wanted to be surprised and believe this nasty way that Melody did business—and generally treated people—was something new. But if she was honest, this wasn't the first time Melody had spoken like that. Although Lia did all she could to be fair to her company, clients, and vendors, Melody had more than once forced her to test her ethics.

Oblivious to Lia's internal struggle, Melody placed a call to the event rental company. She put the phone on speaker, ignoring the glares from the people at the tables surrounding them.

"This is Ruth." Lia's contact answered on the fourth ring.

"Ruth, hi. This is Melody Kensie," she said in the voice reserved to instill dominance. "I'm here with Cordelia Winchester. She got me up to speed on the Sinclair event."

"Yeah." Ruth practically grunted in the phone, clearly not caring for Melody's tone.

"I understand we've been waiting a couple of days for a response from your team. Is that correct?"

"Listen, Melody. I told Cordelia the same thing I'm gonna tell ya. It's a busy time of year for us, and the request is a tall order for this late in the game." She paused, and the sound of shuffling paper came through the phone. "Okay. Looks like my guys got back to me earlier today. There's a note here saying they don't have enough linens available in that color."

"That simply won't do."

"Well, if ya'd let me finish, I'd tell ya we have another option, but it's gonna cost ya."

"We're listening."

"We have some white linens available. I can have my guys dye them the color requested, but that means you're no longer renting. You're buyin'."

"How much does that run?"

"For the amount you need? Close to ten grand, give or take."

"And they'll be dyed and delivered to the venue in time for set up," Melody stated rather than asked.

"Yeah. I just need the money upfront."

"Great. I'll have Cordelia follow up with your finance department today."

"Okay." Ruth sniffed.

"We'll be in touch."

Melody hung up the phone and folded her hands on the table. Her look of satisfaction was quickly replaced when she glared at Lia. "Cordelia," she fumed. "This is called taking initiative."

"Ruth just found out this morning—"

She held up a hand, cutting her off. "You heard those papers she shuffled. That message would have been lost in the mix. I've met Ruth. She's not made for admin work. That notice might have been missed for days and then where would we be? Hmm? Elizabeth's event would have been a disaster."

"It wouldn't have been a disaster," Lia mumbled.

Melody pursed her lips. "If she didn't get what she specified, then yes, Cordelia, it would have been a disaster." She paused, the silence only increasing the tension. "Are you sure you're up for this promotion? It's not like you to fumble so badly. Although you've had distractions," she said as waved her hand limply around to indicate Fraser Hills, "life happens for all of us, and I need to be assured I can count on you to provide the superior experience our clients expect and deserve from us. Our clients come first. Always."

Eight long years Lia had worked for Melody, and all she'd have to show for it was another promotion. It was everything Lia had worked for, and yet, it seemed pointless now.

"Yes." Her response sounded empty. Just like her.

She didn't have it in her to put on the brave face of the driven, professional woman who had served her well in Boston for the last decade. And, truthfully, she didn't want to. She knew it in her heart now that she didn't *want* to be that woman anymore.

After growing up in a place like Fraser Hills—full of warm, caring, and open people—how had she become that person anyway? More importantly, why would she ever think the persona she took on was better than who she'd been?

Oh. Yeah. Because only the type of person I was in Boston could survive the likes of Melody Kensie and her unappreciative clients.

As Melody droned on and on in her condescending tone about the importance of their clients and how Lia needed to do better, she had every urge to tell the woman to shut up. Melody insulted where she grew up. She made it seem like her family was second-class citizens. Lia was told her work was slacking, despite the long nights and frequent trips to Boston. Melody came all this way, and not a single kind word was uttered from her lips.

It was almost laughable, really. All this time, Lia portrayed strength and determination. She made it a point to never be taken advantage of or to be treated like a doormat. Yet there Melody was, doing just that. In fact, that was all she had ever done. She took Lia's strength and crushed it. Every single time. How could Lia have missed it?

Anger. Sadness. Defeat. All of it swirled inside her, making her gut clench. She wanted to scream. She wanted to cry. She wanted to storm out of there. Mostly, she wanted to tell Melody she and her company weren't better than Lia and her family. Instead, her body and mind shut down, going into self-preservation mode.

Everything that happened this month, especially the last twenty-four hours, had taken a toll on her. She had hit her threshold of stress, disappointment, and self-loathing. Now, her body decided to go numb to all of it.

What's the point of all this anyway? It's meaningless.

She'd spent so long putting her career and Melody's reputation first that she'd neglected the things and people who actually mattered. Now it was too late. Those things would be a distant memory soon.

"Do you understand?" Melody asked, bringing her back to the conversation.

Lia blinked, her voice flat as she said, "Yes." She rose stiffly from her seat before Melody indicated the conversation was over, a big no-no typically. "I'm sorry you had to come all this way to clean up my mess." She sounded like a robot and wondered if Melody caught the lack of sincerity.

"It was very inconvenient." Melody put her tablet into her purse, stood, then dusted off the imaginary crumbs from the food she didn't eat. "I'll need you back in Boston by the twenty-second. With how this event is going, I want you to oversee every tiny detail to make sure it goes off without a hitch."

"I wasn't supposed to be back until the twenty-third."

Melody just glared at Lia, ending the discussion. "I will see you on or before the twenty-second."

~ * ~

Logan hadn't seen Lia much that day. Mariam mentioned Lia's boss had shown up, which only meant trouble as far as he was concerned. How could Lia be so blind? Every time she talked about Boston and her job, her whole demeanor changed. Her fresh face lost its youthful sparkle. Her shoulders sagged like the weight of the world was resting on them. Her voice was emotionless like she was reciting a dry monologue from someone else's life.

Lia was stubborn as hell though. You couldn't tell her what to do. You just had to stand back and trust she'd come to a conclusion on her own. He only hoped she'd see what was in front of her before it was too late.

He had planned to stop by her cabin after work to check on her, but her responses to his texts were short and delayed. Despite the warm glow shining from her living room windows and the welcoming smoke billowing from the fireplace, he knew she didn't want company. Not even his. He had to give her the space she needed.

Logan busied himself with the sleigh to distract himself from the urge to pound on Lia's door and kiss her worries away. After several hours, he saw hints of the final product. He looked at the faded picture

Mike had given him and confirmed it was coming along beautifully.

Stretching and yawning, Logan called it a night. Throwing the cover over the sleigh and locking up the barn, he strolled to the cabins and stopped in his tracks. Lia stumbled out of her front door and slumped onto the rocking chair, slugging a healthy gulp from a bottle of wine. She hiccupped and took another sip.

He wasn't sure if he should be amused or concerned. "Hey there, stranger." He nodded at the bottle as he approached. "Everything okay?"

"Define okay." She didn't outright slur, but she probably was well on her way there.

"As in are you drinking that bottle to celebrate or forget?"

"How could I ever forget that my life is shit?" She took another sip.

He walked up the steps and threw his jacket over her shoulders. "You're going to freeze to death out here. Where's your coat?"

She shrugged and pointed a wobbly finger at the house. "Somewhere."

"Let's get you inside."

"I need air."

"You need water."

He helped her up and pried the bottle from her hand as she took another swig. Once inside, he placed her on the couch while he got her a large glass of water and ordered her to drink. "Let's start at the beginning," he encouraged as he took a seat next to her.

"The beginning. Oh, the beginning. Where do I even start?"

She sighed, misery making her eyes puffy and red. Logan wanted to wrap her in his arms and promise he'd shield her from all the things making her so sad. But with her being the strong woman she was, it wasn't the right move. Not until she asked for it. So, he opted to hold her hand, tracing his finger back and forth to soothe her.

"Logan, what am I doing?" She leaned her head on the back of the couch, her eyes misting over.

"What do you mean?"

"Every decision in my life has been wrong. I thought I was doing the right thing, but in the end, I'm left with nothing."

He shifted in his seat, wiping away a stray tear that escaped her eyes. "Tell me."

"Being here…" She let out another breath. "Being here opened my eyes. I've become so de…de. Ugh. What's the freaking word?" she said with exasperation. "Desensitized. There we go. That's it. I've sheltered myself, got thick skin, and kept my eye on the prize. So much so I stopped realizing what was right and wrong. What was kind and fair.

Validation came from how quickly I scaled my career.

"You know how hard it is to actually get a position in the field you went to school for in the economy we graduated in? Most of my friends are doing something completely random because there were no jobs thanks to the recession. But not me. Oh no. I was the success story," she spat out with mirth. "Small-town girl makes it in the big city. Builds a career with the esteemed Melody Kensie, working among the rich and elite. And she did it all on her own." She gave a dry laugh. "She did it alone." The last part was quiet and sad.

"What happened today?"

"I think the correct question would be, 'What happened yesterday?'" She hiccupped. Holding her breath, she tried to stop them unsuccessfully. She exhaled. "Yesterday I learned not only am I a useless failure, but also my stupidity caused my family to lose everything important to them."

The hair on his neck rose, and his skin prickled. "What?"

Her drunkenness was coming on fast. She put a finger to her lips, missing them the first couple of times. "Shhh. I'm not supposed to tell you, but my parents need to give up the Winchester Inn."

He gently took her face in his hands, trying to get her to focus. "What do you mean?"

"I mean, I failed. Whatever I did here was for nothing. They can't afford to keep up with it anymore. After Christmas, it's going on the market, and that's it for the inn. And my family. And all our memories. And everything that ever frickin' mattered." Sobs escaped her lips. "If I had just stayed. If I'd just come home sooner. If only I'd known what was happening."

A loose strand of her hair stuck to the wet trail of tears on her cheek. He pushed it away. "Hey." He forced her to look at him. "Listen to me. Your family and this town are proud of what you did for us. You can't live in a world of 'what ifs.' I did that with Jolene. It's a miserable existence. All you can do is deal with what is. Have you truly done everything you could to help them?"

"I thought so."

"Then that's all they could hope for. It's out of your hands now."

She took a deep, shuddering breath. "I'd hoped maybe one day there could have been the chance to come back home." She sobbed. "But I'll no longer have a home."

"Fraser Hills will always be your home."

She shook her head. "It's not the same, and you know it. What's worse is I can't even enjoy my final Christmas here. Not only do I have to miss Christmas Eve, but Melody is making me come back sooner. I leave in a week." She looked deep into his eyes. "I'm not ready to say goodbye. Not to the Winchester Inn and not to you."

She pressed her lips against his, giving him a heartbreaking, heartfelt kiss. He wrapped his arms around her, partially to console her, and partially to position himself to receive her hard kisses, fueled by her raw emotion, more fully.

"I don't want you to leave either." His voice was hoarse against her mouth. "Why don't you stay?" he nearly begged. "I want you here, Lia. With me. There has to be another way."

"It's done, Logan. We're out of options." She pulled away to examine his face, and he saw his own heartbreak reflected in her eyes. "I hate that I met you only to lose you. You've become everything to me, but I can't keep you, and it kills me."

She placed her forehead on his shoulder, her warm tears trailing down the crook of his neck. He could do nothing but hold her. It took everything in him not to break alongside her.

Chapter Twenty

The weight of an arm resting across Lia's middle held her tightly against the firm body behind her. She cracked open an eye. Her bedroom was still dark, but hints of morning light peeked through the window.

Her head pounded, mostly from the wine, but also from the tears last night she'd been convinced would never stop flowing. It wasn't like her to fall apart so completely. Throughout the past decade, she had learned to keep herself emotionally detached. It did her good when it came to business, but she should have known all those repressed feelings would come back to haunt her eventually.

Logan, in his slumber, kissed her shoulder before falling back to sleep. His quiet snores somehow comforted her as the anxiety of the day before came rushing back.

Lia had done her best to create distance between her and Fraser Hills, making a point not to slide back into what was expected of her. Now, even if she wanted, there would be nothing left for her to come back to. After Christmas, the place she worked so hard to get away from would be gone from her forever.

Maybe she hadn't wanted the pressure of taking on the family legacy, but she didn't want to be relieved of that expectation like this.

The only place left for her was Boston, a place that suddenly felt like a prison.

She grabbed the cup of water Logan had kindly left for her on the nightstand, the movement causing him to stir.

"Hi," he said in that just-woke-up deep voice of his.

"Hi." She winced as pain shot through her head. She took a sip of water, both grateful and nauseous because of it.

He reached for her, turning her to face him, and pushed back one of her knotted curls while searching her face. "How are you?"

"I'm so embarrassed."

He shushed her. "There's nothing to be embarrassed about. Even the strongest people have a weak moment. You're human." A small smile graced his lips. "Whether you like it or not."

Lia rested back in the bed, curling up against his bare chest, enjoying the warmth of his skin against hers. "I shouldn't have told you about the inn. My parents wanted to tell you. I'm sure they would have said it in a much less doom-and-gloom way." She sighed. "They're going to make sure you're taken care of for a few years. This is your home now, and they'll do their best to keep you here."

"I appreciate that." He kissed her forehead and hugged her tight. "But it's not me I'm worried about."

"Hmm?"

"I think there's more to your pain than losing the inn. Why are you going to back to Boston?"

Logan's direct question startled her. Not because his serious tone was unusual for him, but because she was starting to see the truth and wasn't ready to admit it.

She pushed away slightly, trying to create a little distance and buy some time. "Because I have a job to do."

"You can do event planning anywhere, Lia." He clearly didn't believe her reasoning. "Why somewhere so far away from the people you love? Do you remember telling me how alone you were up there?"

"No," she said sheepishly, feeling foolish to have borne her deepest secrets to him.

"From what I gathered, you don't seem happy."

"What should I do? Completely uproot my life? Start over? I'm too old for that now, and I have too much to give up—" She stopped herself, realizing Logan had just done that exact thing a few months ago. If she offended him, he didn't show it.

"Things you don't seem to want anymore. Think of the possibility of what you can gain."

"I can't give up my future for possibilities. I need a sure thing." She let out a humorless laugh. "Then again, my parents thought they had a sure thing with the inn, and now they'll be left with nothing. What do we really have to count on these days?"

Lia wrapped herself in her comforter and got out of bed, gathering their strewn clothes across the bedroom floor. Logan sat up and grabbed her wrist, forcing her to stop and meet his eyes.

"Your family. Your friends." He looked at her meaningfully. "The people you love."

Her heart skipped a beat. Could Logan tell she had fallen for him? If so, did he feel the same?

"It's complicated." She slipped her shirt over her head.

"Stop dodging, Lia. We need to talk about this."

There was no use putting up her walls anymore and denying the reality of the situation. Lia had avoided saying the words out loud because it would make them real, but the sooner they came to terms with it, the sooner they could accept it.

Lia let out a breath and sat next to him on the edge of the bed. "With my family losing the inn, they'll rely on me. It might kill me to continue working for Melody, but it's a stable salary my family might need after the sale is final. They'll be homeless. They won't have a source of income. I don't even know if they have enough retirement money saved because they thought they'd have the inn forever. If they need to tap into the nest-egg I saved over the years, I can't deplete it by quitting my job with no backup. And even if I did quit because I found a new high-paying job to support them and myself, it likely won't be anywhere near here. It'll be in big cities. New York. San Francisco. Chicago." She bit her bottom lip. "I don't want to let them down again. This is the way it has to be, for now, at least."

"I'm not ready to give up so easily. I don't buy into what you said last night."

"What?" Parts of last night were fuzzy. It had been an emotional rollercoaster, and the wine binge didn't help.

"That we're out of options. There has to be another way to make this work."

Her shoulders slumped. "I just don't think there's a Christmas miracle for us. I'm sorry."

Their conversation ended in a stalemate, Logan still hopeful and Lia knowing it was impossible. He went back to his cabin soon after to get ready for the day, leaving Lia with way too much to consider with the state her head was in.

She got into the shower, trying to rid herself of her foggy brain, and somehow found the smile she needed to face the day, fake or not.

She went through the motions at the inn, greeting guests as cheerily as she could, managing reservations for months her family wouldn't be there, putting out more social media posts about the upcoming events this week.

It all felt like a sick joke. She was finally back home, starting to make a difference, and in a few weeks, it would have been for nothing.

After the work at the inn, Logan invited her over to watch a movie, promising not to bring up their discussion from the morning. For tonight, at least.

As much as Lia wanted to stew alone, snuggling up with Logan and Willow was too hard to pass up. With only a few days left to spend with him, she didn't want to miss out on a single moment, no matter how much harder it would make it when she left.

Logan handed her a glass of wine and set his beer down on the coffee table while he grabbed the remote. He flicked on the TV and started the movie *The Holiday*.

She looked at him with amusement as he sat down.

"What?" he asked and took a swig of his beer.

"I didn't take you for much of a rom-com kinda guy. You're sweet, don't get me wrong, but your natural ruggedness and passion for manual labor make it seem like you'd be more into action."

He shrugged and wrapped his arm around her shoulders. "I appreciate a good rom-com. Plus, my sister loves this movie. I figured it might put you in a better mood. Get you in the Christmas spirit. I'll try not to get jealous if you gush over Jude Law."

Her grin fell. It was hard to get into the Christmas spirit when she'd be spending it alone in her unfestive apartment, probably eating cold leftovers from Elizabeth's event.

Ho. Ho. Ho.

God, she was acting like the Grinch. Logan was trying so hard to make her happy, and all she could think about was what things would be like when she was gone. She should be enjoying the here and now. The feel of his strong arm pulling her against him. Willow curled up on the other side of her, making small barks in her sleep. The crackling fire. An upbeat holiday classic on the TV. The twinkling string lights. The smell of fresh Fraser firs.

What more could she want?

Nothing.

The answer surprised her. After years of constantly striving for more, always reaching for the next big thing, she never believed she could be content. She didn't think she had it in her. What's more, she actively pushed herself to avoid being content. That's what she thought her family had done and why they'd stayed in their same old lives without ever questioning it.

The fact they never challenged themselves was something horrible. She remembered pitying them for never wanting to see all the world had to offer.

Only now she realized it didn't matter what the world could offer them because they had everything they could ever want right here in Fraser Hills.

At that moment, sitting with Logan in the cozy cabin, doing nothing but enjoying each other's company, she finally understood. The emotion bubbling inside her made her the happiest she'd ever been, while also equally as miserable because she knew how short-lived it would be.

But she had it. Right now. It was tangible.

Maybe they didn't see eye to eye on her reason for going back to Boston, but they could agree on one thing: their want for one another.

She glanced at Logan and loved how relaxed he looked, a beer in one hand, a slight smile on his otherwise neutral face. He was everything she could hope for in a man, and she was lucky enough to have found him.

Shifting in her seat, she lifted her leg to straddle him, making him jump slightly by the unexpected movement, but shock quickly turned into raw desire. She slipped the beer from his hand and placed it on the coffee table. The second it was safely down, he pulled her toward him and caught her mouth in a scorching kiss.

His instant arousal against her made her feel like the sexiest woman alive. They kissed in a frenzy, demanding and rough, as he gripped her hips, pushing her down against the hard length of him.

She moved back and forth, needing the friction of him. Needing everything of him. Wanting him closer.

No matter how hard she grinded against him or how tightly his hands held her, it wasn't enough. Ravenous, she pulled at his clothes.

Logan flipped her onto the couch, causing Willow to scurry off to her bed. Within seconds, he had Lia naked. She was overwhelmed by the sight of him, his bare, muscular chest leaning over her. The way his triceps flexed as he held himself up while slipping on a condom.

Before she could even think, he was moving inside her, slowly at first. He kissed her deeply, his hand cupping her face as he moved in long, purposeful strokes. Her heart raced as her hands held onto his broad back, savoring the smoothness of his skin.

Never in her life had she felt the way she did now. She wanted to lose control and, at the same time, wanted it to last forever.

But the pressure built and the need for sweet release had taken over. Logan's tempo picked up, bringing them both over the edge. She cried out his name, and he let out a deep groan into her hair.

Carefully rolling off her, he held her while they caught their breath, occasionally placing soft kisses on her bare skin.

"Lia." His voice was rough from exertion. "I love you. I'm *in* love with you. You need to know that. I probably fell for you the second I saw you lying in the mud."

Her breath caught in her throat. Her heart pounded like a jackhammer. "I love you too, Logan. So damn much," she admitted breathlessly.

He smiled, his eyes glimmering in the low light of the cabin. He kissed her again, the only kiss two people could share after they'd admitted something so intimate. So important.

"I want you to stay." It was barely a whisper, but his words resounded loudly in her mind.

And at that moment, there was nothing more in the world she wanted than to do just that.

Chapter Twenty-One

Lia's heart ached, both from knowing Logan loved her and the devastation that she couldn't give him the answer he wanted.

He asked her to stay and the word "yes" had tried to force its way out of her mouth. She practically clamped her lips shut to keep it from escaping. Since that night, there had been a lump in her throat. When Lia spoke, she had a constant need to push it down to find her voice. Her chest tightened with every word.

The task of keeping up appearances was even harder when she was about to fall apart.

She'd dealt with extreme stress before, but this was an entirely different beast. It took everything in her to pull in a steady breath. To keep pushing through everyday life was a monumental task.

Occasionally, Lia would catch both her parents giving her a look as if they wanted to step in and help her make sense of it all. However, in their typical fashion, they let their daughter embrace life's experiences without interfering.

Both the good and the heartbreaking.

The next few days went by in a blur. Now that the ramainder of the town's events had been organized and the inn was at capacity, there was nothing more for her to do. She spent the rest of her time in Fraser Hills finalizing the changes for Elizabeth's event, and hanging out with Logan and Willow. She cherished the quiet nights with them, the walks through the forests, and the more private moments between her and Logan.

They'd enjoyed themselves during the snowman and ice sculpture competition, finding the creative ways people had designed theirs to be funny, delightful, and outright beautiful. They had a blast during the sled race, where they'd spun out on ice halfway down and lost so significantly all they could do was laugh. They'd admired the Festival of Lights and how the displays danced with the Christmas songs being broadcast on the local radio station.

He hadn't pressed her on what he asked her a few nights before, but she could tell it was always on his mind. He was holding on to the hope she'd see she belonged there and would finally tell him she wanted to stay.

The thing was, she knew she belonged there. There was no doubt in her mind. It simply wasn't an option anymore.

It nearly crushed her to see his face when he watched her pack her bags. In the morning, she'd board a flight to Boston for good. All they had was tonight.

She moved through her cabin, grabbing things along the way, while Logan sat at the kitchen table, staring down at his tumbler of whiskey. His face was grim as he took a sip, occasionally peering up as Lia stuffed another item into her suitcase.

The silence was deafening, the tension in the air so thick it was suffocating.

He was entirely unexpected, and despite all the reasons why they shouldn't have fallen for each other, there they were. She'd never met a man who seemed to know her so well. He was a rock when she needed the support, but he also got out of her way and let her do what she needed to do. He showed her kindness and compassion and made her feel like she was perfect the way she was. That she didn't need to be anything more if she didn't want to be.

Living a life that made her constantly push herself to be more, she hadn't realized how important it was to believe she was enough. That realization alone made Lia want to let out a breath she'd been holding for more than a decade. In Logan's eyes, she was more than enough, and she should be damn proud of it.

She shook away her nerves and walked slowly from her bedroom, now finding Logan standing at the kitchen counter with his back to her. His empty tumbler sat next to the whiskey bottle, but rather than pouring another, he stood frozen with his hands pressed on the countertop, his head hanging down.

"Logan." She reached for him, lightly touching his shoulder to make him face her.

He lifted his hand, pushing the hair from her face. "Lia. Please. Stay with me." His face was filled with anguish.

A lump rose in her throat and her eyes burned. This was unbearable. "I can't. You know I can't."

She wrapped her arms around his torso and hugged him close. He rested his head on top of hers, burying his face in her hair and occasionally kissing her forehead.

Lia wasn't sure how long they stayed like that. All that mattered was holding him, trying to find a way to make to make time stop.

He didn't say another word and somehow that crushed her more. His silence made her believe he'd finally accepted she was leaving and there was nothing they could do about it. Guilt seeped in when she recognized how hard it must be for him to have no say in the matter.

After some time, his hands slid down her back and reached for hers, leading her to the bedroom, love and despair flashing in his eyes with each step. He dropped his head down to meet her lips, his kiss slow and tender. She savored the feel of his lips and each flick of his tongue against hers.

Lia's emotions tormented her, bouncing between wanting to cry in his arms and wanting to make tonight something worth remembering.

Not that she could forget a man like Logan MacDermot. Ever.

He planted hot open-mouthed kisses along her jaw and neck as he slipped her shirt gently from her body and then pulled off his own. He ran his hands along her skin and his gaze trailed the movement as if to burn the memory of her in his mind. She felt beautiful to be seen like this. Wanted like this.

Loved like this.

Logan kissed her shoulders and unhooked her bra, dipping lower to her bare breasts and swirling his tongue around her pink buds. She arched, giving him more access that he gladly took.

Moving his fingers along her back, he kneaded it every so often. Shivers ran down her spine, and at the same time, she was on fire. His lips made their way back to hers, and she dug her fingers in his hair to hold him there, kissing him with everything she had.

Maybe she didn't have the right words to ease his heartache, but she'd show him how much he'd grown to mean to her instead. Here. On their last night together.

She might be leaving Fraser Hills, but her heart would stay behind in his care. He needed to know that.

Her pulse thundered in her ears as he pulled the rest of their clothes off and got her into bed, draping the sheets over them. He gathered her into his arms, their legs tangling together, and continued to kiss her with more passion and heat. Everything in her hummed with awareness. His fingers were so close to where she wanted them.

"Lia." His voice was a rough whisper against her mouth as he positioned himself between her legs. "I love you."

He thrust himself into her, making her gasp with the delicious sensation, a mix of friction and pleasure. She was addicted to how he filled her.

He moved slowly. Deliberately. Deeply. A combination of hurt, lust, heartbreak, anger, and love were there every time their bodies came together.

How could they make this moment last forever? She wasn't ready to give him up.

Why can't things be different?

She wrapped her legs around his waist to guide him, taking in every inch of him. "I love you too," she said between pants as he brought her to the brink.

He called out her name, a pained guttural sound. She cupped his face, capturing his mouth as they crested together and came down.

Logan rested on top of her, their bodies slick with sweat, his hair falling across his forehead. She looked into his eyes, wanting to get lost in them and live there.

By how he looked at her now, she knew no one would ever come close to loving her like he did.

She also knew she'd never come close to loving another man like she did him.

And yet, she still had to go.

Chapter Twenty-Two

Overnight, fresh snow had fallen, giving the perfect amount of powder leading up to the big Christmas Eve parade and dinner at the inn. The event would be as it should, with the breathtaking backdrop of snow-covered mountains. It would be a wonderful last Christmas at the inn before everything changed.

And Lia would miss it.

Wrapping her body in the sheets, she stared out the window at the brilliant white that stretched on forever.

Untouched. Simply beautiful.

She wondered if it had snowed in Boston yet. She cringed at the thought of the piles of dirty snow that would line the streets and the angry drivers frustrated with the lack of parking. People would bump into one another with the limited sidewalk space.

Nothing would ever compare to the way the endless snow led up to the tree-lined mountains in Fraser Hills. Nothing could ever replace the way she felt when she looked at the inn blanketed in white, the windows bright with warm light, and the smoke billowing from the chimney.

Logan came behind her and held her, placing a soft kiss on her shoulder and neck. She leaned into him and let out a calm breath. The alarm on her phone buzzed, crashing through their moment, and alerted her it was time to get ready for the airport.

She cursed at her phone, angry that it forced her to face reality.

In a few hours, she'd be gone.

Reluctantly, Lia left his embrace, took a shower, and finished packing while Logan took care of Willow. An hour later, he was helping her load her bags into his truck.

"Are you sure about this?" she asked, emotionally wrought after saying a long, tearful goodbye to her family.

"Yes. I'll take your rental to the closest place later today." He planted a kiss on her lips. "I want to spend every last minute I can with you."

There was a tightness in his voice when he spoke, and Lia wondered if he was fighting the urge to ask her to stay again. If he did, she didn't know if she'd have it in her to say no.

She took one last lingering look at the inn before slipping into the passenger seat.

Next time she'd see it, it could be completely different. A pang shot through her heart.

They barely spoke during the forty-five-minute drive to the Asheville Regional Airport. For most of the way, Logan held on to Lia's hand, gently rubbing his thumb against her palm and kissing it occasionally. He inhaled deeply while he did, as if trying to remember her scent. She could feel him giving her sidelong glances here and there, probably waiting for her to yell, "Stop the car!"

But she never did.

Before they were ready, they pulled into the short-term parking lot. Logan grabbed her bags from the truck bed, and they walked slower than usual through the doors that led to departures. This would be as far as he could go with her.

Lia's stomach twisted.

This couldn't be real. This couldn't be it.

All night she tried to picture her life without him in it. Wrong. It was completely and utterly wrong. How could one person make such an impact in only a month's time, so much so she couldn't imagine what life would be like without him?

Coming home to her apartment, working long hours at Kensie Affairs—all those days enjoying her "independence" were now a distant memory. It was a lifetime ago. She took in the man in front of her—how his jaw muscle ticked under his scruff, the way one piece of hair fell across his forehead, and how his steel-blue eyes saw into her soul.

Meeting him had changed her life. Now she had to find the strength to let him go.

Logan dropped her bags to the floor and wrapped her in his arms, crushing his lips against hers. "Lia. Please. Stay," he pleaded, giving her one last chance to change her mind.

She couldn't.

The inn was done for, and she couldn't risk staying and losing her job.

Everything about this was wrong. The searing pain in her heart was unbearable, but if she was going to survive, she had to put her walls back up. It was the only way, no matter how awful it would be to do it. She had to be cruel to be kind. Logan couldn't keep torturing himself with this insane hope that things would work out.

They wouldn't. The sooner he realized that the sooner he could heal and move on.

And forget her.

Her heart cracked.

"You knew what this was," she said the words in the cold, calculated way she learned from Melody.

He cursed under his breath and shook his head before piercing her with his frustrated stare. "You're just scared, Lia. Stop acting out of fear and pushing me away. Be honest about what you want—"

"This was only supposed to be a temporary thing. I was always going to leave, Logan. Nothing was going to change that. Not even you."

He released her and took a step back. The simple statement gutted him. It was clear as day on his face. Lia felt horrible saying it, making Logan believe she didn't care. That she was over this. Over them.

That whatever between them was just a fling. A quick stop in fantasy land she'd be fine without.

Even worse, she hated herself for doing it. Especially knowing he moved to Fraser Hills explicitly to start over after the failure with Jolene.

And Lia had gone and ruined that.

Maybe they were still early enough in their relationship this could be a clean break. Maybe his love for her wasn't as heart-wrenching as hers was for him. Maybe with a little time and separation, she'd become a fading memory and he'd find that new beginning he was desperate to have.

Yeah, right.

He gripped her shoulders and stooped down to eye level, his stare working hard to get past her newly erected walls. "Things *did* changed Lia. You can't deny it." He straightened and let her go again. She instantly felt alone without his touch. "But I'm not going to be the man who stands in the way of what you want. If you still believe you need to go and aren't willing to find an alternative to stay and make this work, then go."

Even though he didn't say it, this must have been how it was with Jolene. He had given his all, put his heart on the line, and made his intentions clear.

And he got burned for it. Again.

That only made Lia's guilt a million times worse. "I'm sorry," she choked out, her eyes misting, her cool demeanor slipping. With that simple phrase, she saw him break right before her eyes.

She would be a damned liar if she didn't admit part of her had shattered too.

He gave her one long last look, the rims of his eyes turning red. "I hope you get everything you want," he said so quietly she almost didn't hear him.

Turning, he walked away from her without so much as a backward glance. Everything in her body screamed at her to run after him and jump into his arms. To tell him she wanted to stay and that they'd figure it out.

But she stayed rooted in place as he disappeared into the crowd of people bustling back and forth. He walked out of the airport and out of her life, taking a piece of her with him.

~ * ~

Lia slowly made her way up the stairs to her apartment, full grocery bags in one hand and a small tree in the other. She had walked into her place an hour earlier and promptly left, restless the second she entered. Rather than let the overwhelming sensation of a million knives stabbing her repeatedly overtake her—like it had the whole plane ride—she thought an old routine would help ease the pain.

Every step she took ached. Every single moment hurt.

Lia unlocked the door and deposited the bags on the counter, placing the pre-decorated Christmas tree near the unusable fireplace, which was more of a statement piece than a tool for warmth. She went back to the bags, dug through to find the cheap stocking and hung it from the mantle. Taking a step back to inspect her work, she couldn't deny how depressing the whole of it was.

There was no point trying to recreate the real thing. Nothing would come close to it.

She unloaded the groceries, changed into comfortable clothes, and poured herself a glass of wine. She booted up her laptop and tried not to let the sadness of leaving Logan weave its way into her mind. The look he gave her before he walked away would haunt her dreams.

Her mom and dad checked in to make sure she got back safe and told her how they wished she could have spent Christmas at home. She hadn't corrected her parents by reminding them she was home now. In Boston.

Technically.

After her time in Fraser Hills, it would always be home to her.

In her heart, Boston no longer was.

Lia was tempted to ask them about Logan but decided not to. She didn't want to drag them into her mess, especially since he was still their employee. At least for the time being.

She spent the next hour going through her emails and planning the next two days. It was going to be absolute madness preparing for

Elizabeth's fundraiser. Lia prayed the busyness would keep her mind from wandering back to Fraser Hills and all she left behind.

Unlikely, she decided as she crawled into her empty bed later that night and cried herself to sleep.

~ * ~

Logan had been slaving away at the sleigh for hours now, working on the final details until his muscles ached, his fingers bled, and his eyes burned. He was punishing himself. He needed some way to release all the anger when *another* woman he loved choose something other than him.

Then he pushed himself further when he realized the fallout with Jolene didn't even come close to how it felt when he walked away from Lia earlier that day.

It was like all the air had been sucked from his lungs and someone kicked the crap out of him.

No. It worse than that.

He understood why Lia believed she had to leave. It was a tough situation for all of them, and she had worked hard to get where she was in her life.

Even if she hated it.

He didn't want to discredit that. It was never about that. What he wanted to know was that she'd at least consider staying as an option. That the thought of being with him, and her family, and this quirky, lovable town he now considered home was enough to give her pause.

There had to be other ways to support her family if they needed it, but she wouldn't even entertain the thought. She was set on Boston.

She gave up without a fight.

What happened to the determined woman who always found a way to solve problems?

He stayed in the barn for as long as he could, far away from his phone so he wasn't tempted to call her. All he wanted was to hear her voice, to have her whisper that she loved him one last time. It damn near broke him to turn away from her at the airport the way he did without telling her himself, but she had put up her walls again when she tried to write them off as a temporary arrangement. Deep down he knew she didn't mean it and that this was just as hard for her as it was for him, but that didn't stop the sting from those words.

The way she said it made him feel like nothing. However, her eyes betrayed her.

He meant what he said though. If this was what she wanted, he wasn't going to stand in her way, no matter how much it killed him. No matter how wrong she was. Calling her would just prolong the pain. It was best to let it go so they could move on. There was no need to drag this out, especially since she was dead set they had no future together. He wasn't going to waste his breath trying to convince her otherwise. What would be the point? Her mind was made up, and if there was one undeniable thing about Lia, it's that she was stubborn as hell.

He stood, his joints popping in the process, and appraised his work. The sleigh was nearly complete, aside from a few minor details. Overall, it had been brought back to its original glory. It was a beautiful piece of work, but seeing it cleaned up with fresh paint made him appreciate how gorgeous it truly was.

No wonder Lia had loved it so much as a child. Logan's heart ached when he realized she wouldn't be around to see it.

He shook his head. This wasn't about her. Sure, she had been a large part of it, but he wanted to give back to the community that welcomed him with open arms and showed him he belonged. He wanted to give something special to the Winchesters, a kind family with big hearts, especially now that the inn might no longer be theirs. This was a small token of gratitude he could offer them for providing his uncle a wonderful life and showing Logan the same when he took over.

Despite how sore his muscles were and how physically drained he was, he bent again to finish the remaining work. Anything was better than going back to his cabin and seeing Willow's pathetic face looking for Lia.

And it was a hell of a lot better than knowing he'd be lying awake tonight, alone in his bed, wondering what he could have done to make her stay.

Chapter Twenty-Three

On Christmas Eve, Logan and Jim found an open parking spot on the corner of Fraser Hills Road and Evergreen Avenue, securing prime real estate for the parade. Logan zipped his jacket and noted the faint smell of snow in the air. It was funny how after only a few months of living here, he could sense when the snow was on the cusp of falling.

Smiling faces surrounded him, children laughing with glee, likely thrilled to know they'd be waking up to a white Christmas tomorrow. He'd never experienced it himself, and even as a grown man in his thirties, he was excited by the prospect. It was one small thing to make an otherwise shitty few days seem okay.

"The crowd's going to go berserk when they see the sleigh. A lot of us townies remember it from way back when. You did great work on the restoration." Jim sipped his coffee, appreciation filling his features.

Logan stuffed his hands into his pockets. Willow had stolen his gloves and hidden them somewhere in the cabin, and now the cold air stung his fingers. "I hope so. I'm glad the snow stuck around so they didn't need to use the wheels. Looks more authentic this way."

In the distance, Christmas music played. The crowd farther down the street erupted into enthusiastic cheers, some singing along to the music. Sure enough, the first float was Daniel, Walt, and Savannah playing upbeat Christmas music to get the parade going.

Lia would have loved the energy here.

He frowned.

Lia was gone. He needed to remember that. Or, better yet, forget her altogether.

Young children from the Boy and Girl Scouts followed the float singing *Rudolph the Red-Nosed Reindeer,* all dressed up as reindeer, elves, and angels. They performed simple dance moves, which were often out of sync, but adorable all the same. This was followed by the Fraser Hills Elementary School band playing more holiday music with their brass and drums.

After the elementary school passed, another float from the local high school drove by, decked out with a winter wonderland theme. A few sugar plum fairies danced to music from *The Nutcracker*, and boys dressed as nutcrackers tossed out mini candy canes to the crowd. A manger scene from the Fraser Hills Church followed the dancing fairies, trailed by the animal society with their dogs dressed in jingling bells and festive sweaters.

A roar of excitement erupted down the road.

"Here comes your sleigh's debut," Jim yelled over the noise.

More music sounded in the distance. Logan could tell it was holiday themed, but was a song he'd never heard before. As the float got closer, he could make out the beat and some of the words and knew it wasn't a popular song, which was surprising. The music was cheery, the lyrics were fun, and everyone danced around to it. How it wasn't a Christmas favorite all over the radio was shocking.

Daniel's band floated by a second time, setting the stage for the finale. Eight larger-than-life reindeer followed the float at a steady pace, pulling the sleigh Logan had rebuilt. Audible gasps came from the children around him when the sleigh came into view. Tears glistened in some adults' eyes who talked excitedly, sharing old memories about the last time they'd seen the sleigh. Mr. and Mrs. Claus waved at the crowd.

He had to give it to Ron and Mariam. They looked like they could be the real deal. Ron's ruddy cheeks peeked out from a long, flowing white beard. His Santa suit seemed to be made of quality material and fit the look and feel of the original sleigh from the 1800s. Mariam's usual warm, motherly persona was elevated with her short, white curly wig and red and white dress.

Every face in the crowd filled with pure joy. Logan swelled with pride when he saw how important it was to the town, and was glad he was able to bring this historic icon back to its rightful place.

After the Santa sleigh made its run, people dispersed. Some headed home to have Christmas Eve dinner with their loved ones, but many went to the Winchester Inn to meet Santa and partake in the community dinner. Mariam had set up a buffet-style meal, its aroma making Logan's mouth water. Daniel's band was once again playing in the lobby—the whole experience undeniably perfect.

On his way to the buffet, Logan stopped short when he noticed a camera crew walk up the steps to the porch.

A woman with unmovable, perfect hair, presumably a reporter, approached him. "Excuse me, sir. Do you know where I can find Mariam Winchester?"

"Over here, dear," Mariam called out from the lobby.

The woman gave Logan a quick smile before heading toward Mariam. "Hi. My name is Catherine Mercado, and I'm with Asheville News 4. We've heard a lot of chatter about your little town and wanted to do a feature on the Christmas events and the inn. We got some great footage already."

Mariam's hand went to her chest in delighted surprise. "Oh my! Really?"

Daniel's band switched over to a new song, another one Logan didn't recognize. The reporter's head craned in their direction. "I'd like to feature the band too." She gestured for her cameraman to get footage of the musicians while she went over the specifics of her segment.

"This will give good exposure to your town for upcoming years and the season. We can showcase all the town has to offer for those searching for a ski retreat in the surrounding mountains."

Mariam had called Ron over at this point. They were holding each other, smiling, and nodding with interest.

"Our writers can take this content and add you to some of our lists."

"Lists?" Mariam asked.

"Yes. Something like, *Best Small Towns to Visit for Christmas* or *Quaint Inns for a Romantic Winter Getaway*."

Mariam and Ron's mouths dropped. Bewildered, Ron held out his hand to shake the reporter's. "Absolutely. Whatever you need."

Logan's heart raced. This was precisely the type of exposure the town and inn needed to help save them. The kind of exposure Lia worked so hard for. Maybe enough revenue would come in that Ron and Mariam wouldn't have to sell.

His fingers itched to reach for his phone to call Lia and tell her she did it. That everything had paid off.

But he couldn't. She wasn't his to call anymore. As much as it pained him, he'd have to leave it to her parents to share the good news.

Deep down, he hoped it would make her want to come back. He knew it was a long shot and he was setting himself up for a letdown, but it was Christmas after all. He was praying for a miracle.

~ * ~

Lia turned her ringer off and dropped her phone into her clutch. She'd spent the last two days getting the venue ready for tonight's event, a monumental task with the last-minute changes and Elizabeth's excessive disapproval. Their relationship had been tense, and to get back in the good graces of both Elizabeth and her boss, Lia needed to be fully focused on tonight.

She sighed. Her mother had called her this morning to wish her a Merry Christmas Eve. Lia wondered how the parade had gone and tried not to feel depressed thinking about the party she was missing.

And Logan.

Lia ached to hear his voice, but she couldn't bring herself to do that to him. It wouldn't be right for her to keep stringing him along. She needed to move on just as much as he did.

Their timing just wasn't right.

She sat in the back seat of the cab as the city flew by in streaks of gray, white, and beige. Light flurries fell from the sky and disappeared as they touched the ground. People were bundled up as they walked down the city streets.

"Is this good?" the cabbie asked from the front seat as he pulled up to the corner of State Street and Congress Street.

"This is fine."

She paid and grabbed her clutch, slipping out of the cab and onto the city sidewalk. Her forest-green gown blew against her legs as a blast of wind whipped between the buildings. Determined to get out of the cold, she beelined it to the doors of the skyscraper that housed the State Room.

Once inside, she took the elevators to the top floor and strode into the now beautifully decorated venue. The space was lit only by candles, creating an intimate mood. Flowers scattered throughout the first floor provided a pleasant, relaxing fragrance. The decor and tables had rich color, providing comfortable seating where people could sit back and mingle. Overall, it was opulent but cozy.

Not at all like the cozy feel of the inn. This screamed money and status. Those who would be attending tonight were some of the wealthiest in the Northeast. Elizabeth's fundraiser was bound to get a massive cash injection.

Lia walked over to the floor-to-ceiling windows and peered out to the city below. The light snowflakes swirled around, blurring her view of the Christmas tree in Faneuil Hall. It was gorgeous, but not quite the same as the tree that sat in the center of her hometown.

She felt a pang, and hollowness spread through her chest.

Homesickness.

She hadn't been homesick since she first left for college. Her stomach sank and made her wonder if she'd made the right decision.

No, she scolded. *There was no decision to make. The inn is done for. There wasn't an option to choose.*

But somehow, she didn't believe it.

"There you are." Melody's voice sounded behind her, her expensive high heels clacking against the wood floors. "I have a few adjustments for you before the guests arrive."

Lia fought the urge to roll her eyes. Melody was still micromanaging, even up until the last minute. Lia had done everything she needed to do to get the event ready. She couldn't think of what else was left.

Melody stared at the table centerpieces and made a sour face. "I'll say, the florist you chose doesn't have great taste."

"That was a last-minute change from Elizabeth. The florist did the best they could with what they had." Lia held up a hand to stop Melody from interrupting. "Yes. I called everywhere in Boston and beyond. No one could accommodate her changes."

Melody cocked her head and attempted to reestablish her position of power. "I'm sure that's not true."

"It is. Apparently, it's pretty tough finding these kinds of flowers in the dead of winter. You know, because things aren't growing." Lia snapped her mouth closed, shocked by her snarky comment. Never in her life would she ever speak to Melody that way, and by the way Melody was glaring at her, there was a reason for it.

"Cordelia. Do we have a problem here?" She gave a steely stare.

She pasted on her best fake smile. "No. Sorry."

"That's what I thought." Melody dangled a list from her long fingers, expecting Lia to make a move to grab it. "Now, take this and get it done before the guests get here. We have one hour before Elizabeth shows up. Everything needs to be perfect."

Lia took the list, and Melody walked away, not even offering to explain the changes or to help tag team. As Lia scanned the list, she realized not only were the changes ridiculous, but she'd also be working her ass off to try to get them done in time. Knowing Elizabeth, she'd be early.

Lia got to work, her styled hair starting to sag due to the sweat from the effort. Her feet were rubbed raw from walking back and forth in her heels, and she had to safety pin a small tear in her gown when it got caught on one of the tables. She got it all done in record time, but when she checked her appearance in the bathroom mirror before everyone was set to arrive, she was horrified.

Her skin was flushed, and her perfume was practically nonexistent. Her hair drooped, and her mascara and eyeliner had melted slightly under her eyes. She cleaned herself up, but with every swipe of her mascara wand and every spritz of hairspray, her stomach dropped further and further. Her insides clenched. She wanted to cry.

She didn't want this life, but she was stuck.

"Cordelia," Melody called into the bathroom. "Elizabeth's here.

Wrap it up and get out here as soon as possible."

Lia touched up the last of her makeup, resolved that she wasn't looking her best, and tried to smile, preparing for her meeting with Elizabeth and Melody. It fell flat. She didn't have it in her to pretend anymore. It all felt pointless.

After being in Fraser Hills, Lia had changed and she didn't know why she thought she could go back to this life afterward. Every second she tried to fit into who she used to be while in Boston was killing her. She was suffocating, like the real her was trapped in this shell of a person she wore for the benefit of her boss.

But what could she do?

"Cordelia!" Melody whisper-yelled into the bathroom, making Lia realize she had zoned out.

"Coming." She grabbed her clutch, held her head high, and walked out of the bathroom, ready to face the firing squad.

As expected, she found Elizabeth with her usual pinched face. "Elizabeth," Lia greeted. "Merry Christmas. I hope you find everything to your liking."

Elizabeth pursed her lips, and Melody's eyes shot daggers at Lia. "It's not what I envisioned," Elizabeth started while surveying the space, running her hands along the linens, and inspecting the flowers. "I suppose this is the best I could expect," she said in a condescending tone. "Given the circumstances."

Melody stepped in, placing a hand on Elizabeth's overly padded shoulder. "Elizabeth, I can assure you this isn't the high standard of quality Kensie Affairs is accustomed to providing our esteemed clients like yourself. I apologize you didn't get what you wanted. I stepped in when I realized what was going on, but it was fairly late at that point."

Melody continued, throwing Lia under the bus, and then reversing to run her back over. Lia was fuming. She'd bent over backward for Melody, and this was how she was treated?

However, it was this treatment that finally pushed her to the brink. Now, she was feeling brave. "Melody, a word?"

Melody didn't look pleased with the request or with Lia at all, but Lia couldn't care less. She had enough. After being in Fraser Hills, she deserved so much more than this.

She led Melody to a private area near the coat check and looked directly into her eyes. "Melody, after this event, I'm done."

"What do you mean you're done?" she asked, utterly confused.

"I mean I'm resigning."

A hand went to Melody's pearls, and her face turned cold with calculated anger. "Resigning?"

"Yes."

Quitting now would make things complicated if her parents ended up needing her help, but the thought no longer scared her as much. Thinking of her hometown and the way every single person rallied to support her made her believe they'd be there too if her family struggled.

They've always been there, for her family and each other. Even if they didn't have much to offer, they were willing to give back in some form or another. With their big-hearted determination, they could find a way to turn things around. She knew it in her gut.

Logan was right. There was always another way. Maybe the answer wasn't as clearly defined as she'd be comfortable with, but she had faith they'd figure it out. Together.

She just wished she'd realized that before she stepped on the plane to Boston.

"I have to say, I'm disappointed, Cordelia."

Lia lifted her chin with a new sense of clarity and confidence. "That's the point. You're *always* disappointed. You've pushed me so hard these years to grow, and I've learned a lot because of it, but it was never good enough. Was it?"

"I expect excellence. Everyone can benefit from stretching themselves."

"There's a way to develop your employees without belittling them, micromanaging them, or taking over their lives."

"People come to us because they expect a certain experience. We always need to be available for them. That was abundantly clear from when you first joined the company, so it shouldn't be a surprise to you."

"Maybe so, but things change." She said, echoing the words Logan and her father said to her repeatedly this month. "Do you realize every time I pitch an idea you shoot it down or completely dominate it so it's no longer my own?"

"I've been successful in this industry for years. I have knowledge to share."

"Then share the knowledge and let me run with it. Don't just take it from me." It was empowering to air her grievances. "You might be great at the event management side of things, but you don't know how to treat your employees."

"Why I never," Melody shrieked, offended. "You know what you are? Ungrateful."

"I'm not trying to be hurtful, Melody. I appreciate all you've done for me, but I'm trying to share this now so you can be better for the next person who takes my place. You did say we can all benefit from striving to be better, didn't you?" She threw Melody's words back in her face.

Melody stood there, shell-shocked. Lia bet no one had ever spoken to her like that.

"I'll do everything I can to make sure this event goes well," Lia assured her. "But once the stroke of midnight sounds, I'm officially done."

~ * ~

She might have made a huge mistake, but regardless, everything in her was relieved, the burden weighing on her had been lifted. True to her word, the fundraiser went beautifully regardless of Melody and Elizabeth's constant nitpicks. What used to bring Lia down no longer mattered. Melody had made sure she did her best to make Lia miserable those last few hours, but the thought of what came next got her through the night with a smile on her face.

After the event, she rushed back to her apartment. Her phone had died during the evening, so she was forced to hail a taxi. The snow continued to swirl around, now sticking firmly to the concrete, and forcing the driver to go at a snail's pace to avoid slick spots. After an eternity, she catapulted out of the back seat and up the stairs to her place as quickly as her dress and heels allowed.

Running around her apartment like a lunatic, Lia pulled out every available suitcase she could find and stuffed it with as many things as she could. Her heart was racing. Getting to the airport was her only focus.

She was going back to Fraser Hills.

She no longer had a job. Didn't have a backup plan. And probably wouldn't find work once she got there. Melody would undoubtedly reject her request for a referral, especially after how Lia had resigned, but she'd figure it out. All that mattered was getting back home.

Home.

Her phone was still dead, making it hard to catch a ride to Logan International Airport. She nearly froze to death in her dress—which she didn't bother to change out of after the event—as she waited for an available taxi that was willing to take her and all her luggage.

"Lady, hate to tell ya, most of those flights are grounded. There's a snowstorm blowin' up from the south," the driver told her. "You're better off waiting it out at home."

"I don't care. I want to be there for the first flight out."

He shrugged. "Whateva ya say."

Once again, she was stuck in the slowest moving taxi in existence. Her knee bounced up and down impatiently. She wished her phone worked so she could call her parents and tell them she was coming home for good.

And to tell Logan the same.

She was an idiot. Lia could have saved herself a lot of heartache if she'd just stayed when Logan had asked her to.

She was a stubborn, stubborn woman.

They finally pulled up to the airport, which was nearly deserted. She grabbed her suitcases, juggling them all and almost falling over, and threw them on a cart.

"I'd like the first ticket to Asheville, North Carolina," she practically demanded when she reached the ticket counter. She couldn't help it. Her nerves were frayed.

The woman looked at her like she was crazy. "Ma'am, all flights south are grounded at this time."

"When's the next flight out?"

"None to Asheville for a couple of days. The regional airport is shut down due to the storm down there."

Lia tapped her finger on the counter and bit her lip. "What about Charlotte?" Charlotte's airport was much larger and had the resources to keep the runways clear. She silently prayed they'd been prepared for the snow. It was a hike to get from there to Fraser Hills, but it would at least get her close enough.

The woman tapped loudly on the keyboard and made a few clicks with the mouse. "Earliest flight I can get you is at five tomorrow morning."

"Great! I'll take it." Lia was a little too enthusiastic, practically throwing her credit card at the woman.

She frowned. "That's if the flights are moving again tomorrow morning. There's no guarantee at this point."

"I don't care." She pushed her credit card further into the woman's face to make her point.

Annoyed, the woman snatched the card from Lia's hand, made the reservation, and handed her the ticket. Lia checked her bags and moved as quickly as she could through TSA, even though she knew she had another few hours to wait, which was torture.

She grabbed food—or what could be considered food—from the only open kiosk and found a space where she could plug in her phone. Checking the time, she realized it was far too late for her to call her parents. They'd be exhausted after the parade and dinner. Maybe Logan would be awake?

When she had enough power, she called him immediately. Her heart sank when it rang twice before going to voicemail, indicating that he was ignoring her call.

"Call me, please," she texted him.

She waited. And waited. And waited.

Clutching her phone, she willed him to call her. As she boarded the plane hours later and there was still no response, she worried she had ruined any chance she had.

Chapter Twenty-Four

Lia was reluctant when she pulled into the driveway leading to the cabins. She landed after seven that morning and had a three-hour drive to Fraser Hills. She thought she would have heard from Logan by now. He wasn't a cruel man. She couldn't imagine him ignoring her straight out. Yet, when she cut the engine in front of his cabin and realized he still hadn't called, she wondered if she was too late.

She could hear Willow barking her head off inside. Lia found it strange his lights were still off even though it was mid-morning. Perhaps since it was a holiday, he decided to take it easy. Or maybe he had gone to see family.

Or maybe he had company. Someone who actually planned to stick around.

She shook her head at the idea. Their goodbye at the airport may have been rough, but she couldn't deny how real things were between them, and Lia couldn't see him running into the arms of another woman as a rebound only three days later. It wasn't like him. She only prayed he'd be happy to see her.

Wading through the fresh snow still in her high heels and gown from the night before, the snow latched on to the material, weighing her down and making each step a struggle. Logan would think she was ridiculous dressed like that, but she didn't care. All she could think about was seeing him again.

Raising a fist to the door, she found the courage to knock. The sound of her knuckles hitting the wooden door seemed to echo on forever as if the cabin was empty and he was just a figment of her imagination.

But Willow's frantic barks and the sound of her toenails tapping across the wood floors let Lia know that the past month with this man wasn't some sweet dream.

She had to make things right.

Time stretched on since the moment she first knocked. She was getting antsy. No movement—aside from Willow—had made itself known in the cabin. Defeated, she turned away.

I was too late.

The door creaked open. "Lia?" His sleep-laced voice was a rough whisper.

She turned to see Logan in the doorway, his bedhead tossed haphazardly around, and his eyes wide with confusion and happiness.

At that moment, she appreciated how unguarded he was. She almost collapsed with relief seeing that the love for her was still there in his eyes.

Before she could even apologize, he reached out and tugged her to him. He put his forehead against hers and breathed in. "Are you really here?" His voice cracked with emotion.

"Yes."

Logan raised her face to his and kissed her with a raw passion.

"You left me," he said between long, hard kisses.

"I was wrong," she breathed as his mouth moved to her throat.

"It killed me." His voice rumbled against her collarbone.

She lifted his head and looked into his steel-blue eyes, full of hope and longing. "It was the biggest mistake of my life, Logan. I love you. I love Fraser Hills. I love the inn. I belong here."

He smiled and let out a deep laugh before hugging her tightly. "We've all known that, Lia. We just wanted you to see it." He kissed her cheek. "I guess I should be glad you figured it out sooner rather than later. It's been hell without you."

"So, does this mean you forgive me?"

"I'd do anything as long as it meant I could have you."

He took her hand and led her into the cabin where an ecstatic Willow danced and rubbed her wriggling body against Lia for pets.

"She missed me." Lia laughed.

"We all did. Did you hear the news?" She took a seat next to him on the couch, and he gently took off her heels, wrapping her in a blanket. "Although you're a gorgeous sight for sore eyes, your outfit isn't exactly made for the mountains."

She swatted and grinned. "I was a little eager to get back here."

"A little?"

"Okay. A lot. Now, what's this about news?" she asked.

"Fraser Hills has become a national sensation."

Her eyebrows furrowed. "What?"

He covered his mouth with his hand and blinked rapidly, speechless. Logan shook his head. "You mean your parents really didn't tell you?"

"I had a missed call from them, but they didn't leave a voicemail. It was too late to call them by the time I saw it."

He grabbed her hands, and a large smile spread across his face, his eyes going bright. "You did it, Lia. Everything you did this month caught the attention of an Asheville reporter. She came here to do a segment on us for the local news. It was such a hit, it was picked up on national news, too."

"National?" she squealed, tears filling her eyes.

He nodded. "She said something about being added to lists. And some music producer approached Daniel, Savannah, and Walt for their original songs. There's a video of them from the parade that's going viral on social media."

"Really?" She smiled, thinking of how Daniel had worked so hard for a music career, one he never truly found in New York. Maybe he'd found it now.

"Yes. You put Fraser Hills on the map. With that exposure, the town and the inn could potentially bring in enough money to stay afloat and more."

She couldn't stop the tears streaming from her eyes. It was all so surreal. Logan captured them with his thumbs. "Shhh, honey," he cooed. "This is a good thing."

She took a deep breath, trying to process the unexpected news. "I know. They're happy tears." She paused, processing the turn of events. "I came back to take over the inn."

He pulled back and grabbed her shoulders as if to hold himself up. "What?"

"I quit my job, finished the event, and came straight here." She reached up and touched his face. "Where I belong."

"You did that without knowing any of this? You took that risk?"

She nodded.

He pushed a hand through his hair. "What are you saying?" he asked, his voice shaking with disbelief.

"I'm saying I let go of what I thought was important and realized what really is. It's being here in Fraser Hills, the inn, my family, and you."

"But you worked so hard for your promotion. It had meaning to you."

She laughed. "Are you trying to talk me out of this decision?"

"No, ma'am." He snapped his mouth shut.

She kissed his lips softly, feeling the tension in his body melt away. He put his hands over hers and squeezed. "I thought the promotion and the money that came with it was the next step, especially with what my family was facing. I thought that's all I had to work and live for. But after being here and seeing how I can make an impact, I realized all my hard work in Boston wasn't just about that specific promotion. It wasn't going to go to waste if I walked away. The skills and knowledge I built were for something greater."

He sucked in a breath, and she grinned.

"I saw what I was capable of without someone like Melody pushing me around," she continued. "I decided I wanted to try to make it work here. I have enough saved to at least try. I could put my all into managing the inn for at least a year to see if I can turn things around. I'm not ready to give up without a fight. Plus, I had another idea."

His eyebrows lifted with interest. "What's that?"

"Christmas has been Fraser Hills' sweet spot. It will always be. It's the history here, after all. But we now see what happens if a few seasons aren't as strong. Why not safeguard the success of the town and think about what we can do for the other seasons?"

He leaned back and searched her face. "Are you saying what I think you're saying?"

"Yeah. I'm going to do my damnedest to make Fraser Hills a year-round destination. This is my home...*our* home," she corrected. "I'll do whatever I can to save it."

When a sincere expression of admiration crossed his features, her heart swelled. How could she have ever considered leaving this man? Just being around him brought her a sense of peaceful hope, making her believe she could accomplish anything, and he'd be right there rooting for her every step of the way. The fear of losing him these last few days washed away. Now, looking into his eyes, she saw her future. A future that seemed even better than what she had originally planned.

"Lia," he whispered, his voice growing more serious. "It was the hardest thing to watch you walk away."

"I'm sorry—"

"But," he cut her off and kissed her palm, "you're the smartest, most determined woman I have ever met. If you were going to decide to come back, it had to be on your own terms. Not me, nor your parents, nor anyone else could tell you differently."

She bit her lip, appreciating the fact he seemed to know her so well. "Bold move," she teased.

"I said I'd do whatever I could to get you back here with me and I meant it. Even if it meant letting you go."

She wrapped her arms around his neck and slid her fingers through his hair. "I'm not going anywhere, Logan. I'm right where I need to be." She shrugged and smiled. "I guess I gave myself the best Christmas present this year."

His face lit up. "We're not done with Christmas presents yet."

He grabbed a jacket hanging by the door, threw it on, and tossed her a pair of snow boots. Taking her hand, he led her through the deep snow to the shed.

"Logan, what's gotten into you?" she laughed, not caring that her dress was no match for the freezing snow.

"You'll see." He pushed open the door and flicked on the lights.

When her eyes adjusted, she gasped. "The sleigh," she breathed out and slowly approached it. Every memory of Christmas as a child came flooding back as she ran her hand over the intricate details. She captured his gaze, tears misting her eyes. "It's beautiful. You did this?"

He nodded. "I knew how important it was to the town. And you."

"It's better than I remember. Thank you, Logan."

He pulled her to him, enveloping her in his warmth, and kissed her. "Merry Christmas, Lia."

Epilogue

Late November, the Following Year.

Logan watched from a distance as Lia stood at the back of the Winchester Inn, staring up at the same section of the roof that had collapsed a year before. She inspected it thoroughly, just as she had when she first arrived after the accident, but that's where the similarities ended.

Gone was the posh, distant, skeptical stranger from Boston who wanted nothing to do with the small mountain town. Now, the woman who stood before him with her wild hair and beaming smile was full of love and passion for her town, family, friends, and him.

True to her word, she gave it all up. As defiant as she was about making a name for herself in Boston, it didn't mean one destined path in life. She found her own legacy, building her career into something she could have only dreamed of. As her own boss for her events and marketing business, Lia put Fraser Hills on the map for every season.

Spring took advantage of hiking the nearby trails. Summer promoted the town festivals and watersports. Fall focused on camping. And, of course, Christmas was the big finale for the year.

They were just getting started with this year-round approach, and she had plenty of ideas on how she could make it better but, for the most part, it did the trick. The townspeople were always willing to help with the events—much to Lia's chagrin—but they added the special heart and quirks that made each moment memorable. To come here meant to have an experience that stayed with you.

To find a place where you belong.

The town had pulled out of a rough spot. They were no longer—at least for the time being—worried about going under. The Winchester Inn was able to remain in the Winchester family without the need for outside investors. Although Mariam and Ron had to adjust to being less hands-on, they were thrilled to have their children continue the legacy.

As the woman he was so desperately in love with stood in the same spot as where they first met, he was in disbelief. He came to Fraser Hills to start over, focused solely on finding a place to call home. Within a matter of months, he not only found somewhere he felt fully part of the community, but he found the love of his life.

A stubborn "city" woman who instantly distrusted him the second she met him.

Well, look how far they'd come.

"Christ!" she screamed as Willow came barreling in, knocking Lia to the ground.

Rather than fuming this time, she wrapped her arms around Willow's neck and showered her with kisses. Maybe it was because Willow was now her dog too or maybe it was because she wasn't sinking in the mud like she had the first time. Either way, his plan was well in motion.

"Who's a pretty girl?" Lia laughed as Willow licked her face.

Logan strolled up casually, just as he did the day they met, but this time his heart was pounding out of his chest. He was waiting as patiently as he could for her to notice what he had in store.

She froze when she did.

"Logan, what's this on Willow's neck?" she asked with a shaky voice, her eyes going wide. She adjusted to a sitting position and pulled a squirming Willow closer to inspect. Clutching the box dangling from Willow's collar, she gasped.

Logan got down on one knee and took the box from Lia's hand, opening it for her to see. She bit her bottom lip and her eyes glistened.

It was the sapphire ring she'd admired at the Christmas vendors on their first date.

"Cordelia Winchester," he said.

"Lia," she corrected, causing them both to laugh.

"Lia Winchester. You were the most unexpected gift of my life. At a time when I thought I needed no one, you opened my eyes to the possibility of what could be. You made me want to take a chance. You made me want to be a better man. I don't know what I did to be so lucky to have met you, but I promise I'll cherish you and do everything in my power to make you feel loved, worthy, and appreciated. Will you do me the greatest honor and be my wife?"

She hugged him, tears streaming down her face, and whispered, "Yes," over and over.

She pulled back, concern etched on her face. "Wait."

His heart dropped. "What?"

"There's a question I have to ask you now."

His eyebrows furrowed, confused by the change. "Anything."

"Logan MacDermot, if I agree to be your wife, do you agree to all the terms and conditions of what that means?"

He cocked his head. "To have and to hold? Death do us part? That sort of stuff?"

She smiled. "We Winchesters have a small addition to those vows."

"I'll do whatever you want if it means I can be with you for the rest of my life." He grinned.

"Okay. Logan MacDermot," she said again, "will you help me run the Winchester Inn, for better or worse, until we can pass it down to our children?"

"I do," he replied wholeheartedly and kissed her with everything he had.

Acknowledgement

To create a town with quirky and loveable characters was no easy feat. Thankfully, I'm surrounded by a ragtag group of quirky friends to be the inspiration for the residents of Fraser Hills. I want to thank the following people for allowing me to use their likeness (ridiculous qualities and all) to help me dream up a town I want to move to ASAP if it actually existed.

Thank you to Bridgette Clayton, Sarah Cornwall, Daniel Flores, Amber Foster, Kathleen Lucas, Klare O'Keefe, Tommy Nunis, Jim Sweeney, and Jeff Williams. You guys are nuts.

I also want to give a HUGE thank you to my agent, Jana Hanson from Metamorphosis Literary Agency. If it wasn't for your willingness to read my manuscript after the #KissPitch Twitter contest, this book might have never happened. Thank you for being an encouraging partner and for giving me this chance. I'm so glad I have you as my agent!

Another big thank you goes out to my editor, Jennifer Windrow and the whole Champagne Book Group crew for working with me to make this the best book it could be for my readers and for making the publishing process easier.

And lastly, I want to thank my family. I appreciate you always encouraging me to go after my dreams, for celebrating my big moments, and for being there through my tough times. Your support and belief in me gave me the courage to pursue my writing career, and I'll be forever thankful for that.

To my readers: I hope you fall in love with Fraser Hills. Enjoy!

About the Author

When Sofia Sawyer's fifth-grade teacher handed her a journal, encouraging her to keep writing, she vowed she always would. A lifelong storyteller, Sofia writes contemporary romances featuring independent women who take charge of their destinies.

Based in Charleston, S.C., she follows her wanderlust whenever she can to new and exciting places, often finding story ideas throughout her travels.

When she isn't reading, writing, or jet-setting across the globe, you can find Sofia playing with her dog, taking advantage of the amazing Charleston restaurant scene, hiking, or hanging at the beach.

Sofia loves to hear from her readers. You can find and connect with her at the links below.

Website/Blog: https://www.sofiasawyer.com/
Facebook: https://www.facebook.com/sofiasawyerwriter/
Instagram: https://www.instagram.com/sofiasawyerwriter/
Pinterest: https://www.pinterest.com/sofiasawyerwriter/
Twitter: https://twitter.com/sofia_sawyer

~ * ~

Thank you for taking the time to read *Saving the Winchester Inn* and hope you enjoyed reading it as much as we loved bringing it to you. If you enjoyed the story, please tell your friends, and leave a review. Reviews support authors and ensure they continue to bring readers books to love and enjoy.

DURING A MAGICAL HOLIDAY SEASON, EMMA AND ANDREW KEEP FINDING THEMSELVES SNOWED IN TOGETHER, AS THEY FACE THEIR PASTS AND FALL IN LOVE.

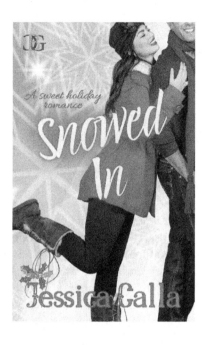

TURN THE PAGE
FOR A LOOK INSIDE!

Chapter One

Emma Ballard hated snow. Cursing her shoe choice—leather designer boots clearly not made for mid-Atlantic winters—she stomped her feet on the frozen sidewalk under the overhang outside of the Portuguese restaurant in Newark, New Jersey. As she rocked to stay warm, she wrapped her gray wool coat, a Ballard original, a little tighter around her chest, pulled a cap from her oversized bag, and cursed all things winter.

Despite her hatred of the white flakes falling around her, the bitter air cooled her cheeks, still warm from the heat and activity of Russell Westingman's retirement party. Thanksgiving had just passed, and it was early in the season, but the weather people had been predicting a snowy winter, starting with the storm today.

Emma had insisted on keeping the party as scheduled. As CEO of Ballard Industries, she wanted to send Russell out in style, and the five-course luncheon, complete with a band and open bar, seemed to do the trick. If only Mother Nature had agreed with her plans.

She should have left earlier, but after the party cleared out, she and Russell polished off a pitcher of Sangria. With her belly full and her head spinning from the alcohol, Emma had listened to Russell's stories about her father, making a conscious effort not to let her tears fall. Russell missed Daniel "Danny Boy" Ballard, almost as much as she did.

She had known Russell all her life, since her father started Ballard Industries with a flagship store thirty years earlier, and Russell had been his first administrative hire. Later, while her father focused on building the global brand and business, Russell "kept the home fires burning," working out of the Jersey branch and focusing on human resources, office management, and technology. Their competition—Ann Taylor, Dress Barn, the Gap—had tried to lure him away, but he'd been loyal to "Danny Boy" and BI from day one.

When they finally said their goodbyes, Russell thanked Emma for the party, gushed over his generous retirement package, and cried reading the card she'd written for him. His shoes would be hard to fill.

Shoes.

She stomped her feet again, but her toes had officially become numb. They'd received word earlier that the trains to Manhattan were cancelled due to the storm. Emma debated staying in a hotel for the night.

But holding onto one last thread of hope that she could get home to the city, she willed herself to be patient, and waited for the car she'd summoned.

After adjusting her wool cap over her ears, she pulled out her phone and opened her email, figuring she'd give the car another ten minutes before high-tailing it to the nearest Hilton. Snowflakes dropped onto the device as she texted the Assistant CEO, Rhonda Lewis, that she was still in Jersey. She brushed the annoying flakes off her phone as she typed, hating the snow even more.

"Ms. Ballard!" a man's voice called from the street.

"Thank God," Emma murmured, shoving her phone back into her bag. Another minute waiting, and the frostbite would have set in.

A gray, Honda something-or-other idled at the curb, while the man attached to the voice waved from the driver's seat. "Everything okay, ma'am?"

"Fine now." She walked a few careful steps toward the car. The man exited the vehicle and met her on the icy sidewalk, offering an arm to steady her. He was tall, but so was she, and she grabbed his forearm and leaned on him for support. "You can get me back to New York in this mess?"

The man quirked an eyebrow, glancing down at her with green eyes. The snowflakes gathered on his blond, unruly hair—hair that was overdue for a cut. "Oh, um." Looking across the street and then up to the sky, he finally focused on her. "I don't think so."

Her shoulders slumped. Dumb weather. She'd never make it back to the city. "Then why did you answer the call to pick me up?"

"Call?" His broad shoulders, covered in a navy dress coat, shook with his nervous laugh. "Oh, I'm not your driver. I... I work for BI. I was at Russell's party."

Her breath caught, and she groaned, embarrassed. "I'm so sorry." She hadn't noticed him inside and certainly didn't know every one of the company's fifteen-thousand employees, or even the few hundred that worked in the New Jersey branch. Still, she made excuses. "I'm a little out of it. Drank too much and I'm tired. My feet..." She stopped talking. She shouldn't be complaining to an employee, especially a stranger.

"What's wrong with your feet?" He peered down to the ground.

"They're cold." She stomped them with the hope of feeling her toes again. No luck.

Shaking his head, he pointed. "Makes sense. You're not wearing proper footwear for a snowstorm."

Ah, a know-it-all. "Aware, thanks."

"Why didn't you bring your snow boots?" He lifted his foot to show her his perfectly outdoorsy, warm and dry looking footwear. "I did."

Who *was* this guy? "Good for you. But I don't have snow boots. I don't make it a habit to be out in this awful weather."

"Not a fan of winter?"

"Not at all." She scooted back under the overhang of the restaurant before she froze to death or started babbling. Either outcome was possible. "How can I help you, Mr.…?"

He held out a gloved hand. "Mooney. Andrew Mooney. IT supervisor, Jersey branch."

She shook it, the warm wool scratching her cold, uncovered palm.

"Nice to officially meet you, Ms. Ballard."

Emma smiled as she racked her brain for prior interactions with Andrew Mooney. "You can call me Emma." In her five years as CEO, she hadn't come across Andrew. That full smile. The angled jawline. Those bright green eyes. Had she met him, she would have certainly remembered.

"Okay, Emma. As much as I'm enjoying holding your hand—"

"Oh!" Her hand was still encased in his. She pulled it away as if it was set on fire.

"—we should probably not be standing in the snow on the streets of Newark. My company policy only allows for a few sick days a year, and I'm already tapped out." He let his jaw drop, feigning shock. "Did I say that out loud?"

Smirking, she wondered how many sick days employees actually received. Her Human Resources Department handled those things, and HR was Russell's end of the business. Now that he was gone, she'd have to learn that side of the company too. "You're fired," Emma barked, pointing at his chest.

The guy gasped. "For realsies?"

She tried to maintain her fake scowl but couldn't stop the grin from forming. "No, for fakesies, I guess."

His cheeks turned a cute shade of pink. "Sorry. I have little girls at home, and that's one of their favorite questions. 'For realsies?'"

Girls at home. A wave of disappointment rushed over Emma upon learning that he had a family. Not for his sake, but for her own. Their short exchange was the most non-business-related conversation she'd had with a man her age in a long time. Maybe she was even flirting? It'd been so long, she wasn't sure anymore.

"Do you mind if I start using that in my meetings? Like, when someone says something inappropriate or completely off the wall, I'll smirk at them like this," she scrunched her face, "and ask, are you for realsies?"

He nodded. "Great technique. Now if you want to add the palm in the air and the hip jut, you'd be exactly like my girls."

She tried again, following his directions. "Like this?"

"Perfect," he said, his gaze dancing. "You're a natural."

"Imagine that." She adjusted her bag on her shoulder. "Well, I hate to do this in the middle of our training here, but I kind of need to find a hotel since it doesn't look like I'll be getting home tonight."

He held his palm to the sky and caught some snowflakes in his glove, studying them like they were magical. "Oh right. That's why I stopped originally, to help you, but then I got distracted by your shoes and stuff."

The way he peered down at her, like a complete gentleman helping a damsel in distress, made her pulse race. But she wasn't a damsel in distress, she was his boss, and she was competent enough to deal with a weather inconvenience. "That's okay, Mr. Mooney. I appreciate the offer of assistance, but I'll be fine."

"Call me Andrew." He tilted his head. "Why don't you at least come wait out the storm at my place?"

She squinted at him.

"That came out weird, didn't it?" he asked, copying her expression. "I mean, you can meet my family, have a meal. I'll show you my company ID if you're worried I'm some wacko kidnapper or something."

"Funny, I didn't think that until you mentioned it." Would she go home with this man? He was a stranger, sure, but he worked for her company and was willing to help. He had a houseful of girls too, apparently. Seemed sincere. She thought for a second. "How about this? I'll ask you a company question, and if you answer it right, I'll believe you work for BI and take you up on your generous offer."

"For realsies?" He rubbed his chin. "Okay, shoot."

"What's the name of the chef from the lunch café in the Jersey branch who ran off with the V.P. of Sales?" Everyone at BI knew this story. The tale was corporate legend.

"Millicent," he answered without hesitation. "Personally, I think she could have done better."

Emma stifled her laugh before it escaped. He wasn't wrong.

"Did I pass?" Andrew asked.

"You did. Still going to text a picture of your license plate to Rhonda, though."

He drew his hands to his chest, feigning pain. "Ouch. But smart. I'll pose next to the car if you want."

"Perfect." She dug her phone out of her bag and waved him toward the Honda.

With a huff, he leaped the two steps and leaned against the snow-covered trunk, crossing his boots at the ankle, and extending his long arms to the side. "My chariot. And my regards to Ms. Lewis."

After she tapped her phone to take the picture, he jumped back to her side, offering his arm. She held on, wobbling her way over the sidewalk, into the street, to the passenger side. He opened the door for her, and she sat in the warm car, texting Rhonda the photo while he scraped the snow that had accumulated off the windshield.

Emma: Know this guy?
Rhonda: Andrew Mooney. NJ office. Something with IT?
Emma: He's giving me a ride. Thoughts?
Rhonda: Neutral. If you go missing, I'll know where to look.
Emma: Great.

By the time he sat in the driver's seat, she'd defrosted and dried off a bit. "Thank you for helping me, Andrew Mooney."

He put the car into drive and glanced at her in the passenger seat. "It's an honor, Boss Lady."

Smiling at the nickname, she had no idea where they were going, but she didn't care. Despite Rhonda's neutrality, Emma's instincts told her she was safe with Andrew. Best of all, in the heat of the little car, she could feel her toes again.

Andrew pulled the Accord onto the streets, which thankfully were plowed, and pointed them toward his home, mentally reviewing his factual knowledge of Emma Ballard.

He knew as much about the woman sitting next to him as she seemed to know about him. Very little. Emma Ballard. CEO. Former model. Hired over five years ago when her father died, which would make her his boss's boss's boss. Considered a reluctant CEO, he'd heard she was a good businesswoman, tolerated by the Board of Directors as a legacy to her father but mostly as a placeholder until the Board could usher her out for a more suitable candidate of their choice. Smart. Neutral about employee issues. She didn't bother the staff; they didn't bother her.

He glanced at her in the passenger seat and added to his fact base. Beautiful. Brunette. Long, thick hair. Brown, mysterious eyes with full lashes, perfect for catching snowflakes.

At Russell's retirement party—Russell being his boss's boss—

she'd glided around the room, somehow avoiding attention but at the same time lighting up the place. He vaguely recalled seeing her on the cover of magazines, but had a hard time reconciling the supermodel with the CEO. That afternoon was the first time he'd seen her in person.

That afternoon was also the first time he'd had a woman in his car since Hayley.

When the silence between them became awkward, for him at least, Andrew cleared his throat. "So, Emma. Any big plans for the holidays?"

"Not really. Just working. How about you?" Her friendly tone invited the conversation.

"Hanging with my girls. They already made their lists for Santa."

"Already? But Christmas is still a month away."

He smiled. "They insisted the elves need the lists now to start making toys."

"Smart. How old are they?"

"Six."

She paused then said, "Both of them?"

"Yep. They're twins."

"The Realsie Twins?"

He liked the nickname. "You got it."

"How fun. You and your wife must have a blast with them."

Andrew gulped and glanced at her. "Oh, I'm not married."

"I'm sorry." She groaned. "I'm an idiot. You wear a ring, but I shouldn't have assumed…"

"My wife passed away." He hoped she'd leave it at that. Andrew had loved his wife more than the world but hated talking about her out loud. Even after six years, when he heard the sadness in people's reactions to her death, a vise gripped his heart.

"I'm so sorry," Emma said quietly. "For you and your girls."

She didn't ask any follow-up questions, which he appreciated. "What about you? Any kids?" He knew the answers to these questions from the company gossip hounds, but figured they'd make do for conversational purposes.

"Not married. No kids."

Andrew couldn't imagine a life so free. He had loved his wife, and loved his girls more than anything, but between work and them, he didn't have time for much else. Thankfully, his father lived next door and helped out more than he should so Andrew could do things, like attend the retirement party for Russell. "What do you do besides work?"

Emma shifted in the passenger seat. "Not much. I mean,

sometimes I sew."

"You do?" He hoped the shock in his voice was indecipherable. "What do you make?"

She twisted her hands in her lap. "I love to stitch. I've been making a lot of scarves lately. It's my new obsession."

"Really?" He tapped his fingers on the steering wheel. "Wasn't your mom a clothing designer? I vaguely remember something in our company's history."

"She was." When he peeked at her, her eyes lit up. "She created the first designs my father sold for BI."

"Such an amazing story. I'm proud to work for the company." He smiled and gave a curt nod.

"That's a nice thing to say."

They drove in silence for a few more blocks. Traffic slowed as the sun set and the roads iced up. "Only a few more minutes, and we should be there." He tapped the wheel.

"What about you?" she asked. "What do you do besides work and parenting?"

Andrew pressed his lips together, unsure whether or not to confide in the fancy pants boss lady sitting beside him. He glanced her way. She may look fancy, but she didn't act fancy, and he could probably trust her with personal information. "Promise not to laugh?"

"I'd never," she insisted.

"I like theater."

She gasped. "Me too! Are you an actor?"

"I was, in another life. I still love Broadway. Musical theater is my passion. I've memorized every song in *Heatherby*."

She reached across the console, grasping his upper arm. "Wasn't that a wonderful play? I loved it so much."

He flinched, surprised at the feel of her touch on his body. "I never saw it. I don't have much time to get to the theater with the girls' schedule. It's expensive too."

Placing her hands back in her lap, she nodded. "That's true. Well, I hope someday you get to see it. *Heatherby* is...," she sighed, "...absolutely indescribable."

He smiled. "I bet." He pulled up to the duplex, his tires crunching over the snow in the driveway he already dreaded shoveling. "This side is me. The other side is my dad. He's babysitting tonight so I could attend the party. Want to come in and meet everyone?"

"Sure," she said. "Beats being home alone."

If it weren't for the sadness underlying her tone, he may have taken that as an insult. Instead, it almost made him feel sorry for her. As if he should be feeling sorry for a rich lady, his boss, while he struggled to make ends meet.

Andrew helped Emma over the slick driveway, and then opened the door to his home, the feeling of relief washing over him. He always loved walking through that doorway. Whatever happened on the outside always faded away as his girls ran to give him hugs and tell him about their days.

That evening was no exception. The soft lights and the crackle of the fire had created an orange glow through the house, and a smell of winter and Christmas wafted toward him.

Devon and Bella darted into the room, screaming, "Daddy!" but then stopped short when they saw Emma.

"Devon, Bella," he said, in his best "dad" tone, "this is Daddy's boss, Ms. Ballard."

"Hi, Ms. Ballard," Devon said.

His father hobbled over to join them, extending a hand to Emma. "Jeffrey Mooney, Andrew's father. Nice to meet you, ma'am."

Emma shook his outstretched hand. "Please, call me Emma. I'm sorry to intrude on your evening."

The girls circled Emma as she spoke, inspecting her like she was a great mystery they had to solve.

She addressed them directly, obviously not intimidated by their scrutinizing glares. "Your dad was kind enough to offer me shelter from the storm. I hope that's okay with all of you."

Bella stopped in front of Emma, crossing her arms. "You're my dad's boss?"

Emma nodded.

"She's more like my boss's boss's boss," Andrew added. "And I expect you all to be polite and respectful."

"Yeah, yeah," Bella said, waving an arm around. She turned back to Emma. "Why can't he have more days off?"

"Bella!" he yelled, then looked at Emma. "I'm sorry—"

"It's a fair question." She pressed her lips together and side-eyed him, clearly trying not to laugh. She turned her attention back to Bella. "What would you do if he did?"

Devon joined her sister, striking the same pose. "Go to the zoo. I like elephants."

Emma exaggerated a gasp. "I like them too. I got to see some when I was on a safari in Africa."

"For realsies?" Bella asked.

Andrew's heart clenched at her sweet tone. Even though the girls' schedules were just as busy as his own, he had to find a way to spend more time with them, outside of carting them around to their various activities. He made a mental note to research season passes for the zoo.

Without missing a beat, Emma jutted a hip and lifted her chin, in the pose he had coached her on. "For realsies." She winked at Andrew. "How about this. Since you've all been so nice to me, I'll do my best to get your dad more days off, okay?"

Bella flashed Emma a thumbs up. "And you have to tell us about your safari."

"Deal." Emma offered Bella a hand, and Bella shook it.

Amused, he shot a grin over the girls' heads to his father. Jeffrey raised his brows and nodded toward Emma, clearly impressed.

When Devon waved her down to eye level, Emma squatted before her. "You have a nice nose," Devon said, reaching out to touch it.

"Devon!" Andrew barked. "Leave Ms. Ballard—"

"Emma." Emma smiled and stood up. "Ms. Ballard makes me sound old and official."

Official maybe. Old? Not so much. He vaguely remembered reading that she was thirty-something. He threw his stern dad look at Devon. "Leave *Miss* Emma, alone please. Can you let her take her coat off and get comfortable?"

His father shooed the girls into the living room and directed his attention to their house guest. "How about a cup of coffee, Emma?"

"That sounds perfect," she answered, as she slid her coat off over her arms. "You'll join me?"

Andrew wasn't sure if she was talking to his dad or him, but they both jammed their fists into their front pockets and answered in unison. "Sure."

Something about Emma Ballard had turned the Mooney men to mush.

Chapter Two

Emma woke to the sound of whispers from the other side of the bedroom door. Confused, she glanced around and remembered that she was in Andrew Mooney's house.

"Why is she in your room, Daddy?" the little voice whisper-shouted.

She smiled at the girl's attempt to be quiet. The clock on the nightstand read six-fifteen, and sat next to a picture of a woman, presumably Andrew's wife, on their wedding day. She was beautiful—smiling, beaming, in a long, lace-covered, A-line gown. Emma wondered how she died. How this family had survived without her.

"Because she was tired, and the blizzard would have made it hard to get her home." Clearly, that was Andrew's whisper voice.

"But where does she live?"

"In New York City. I think. Quiet. We don't want to wake her."

"Like Eloise?" the little voice sang.

"Huh?"

"You know, the book? She lives in New York City too."

"I thought Madeline was from New York?" he asked.

"No, Madeline lives in Paris."

"Oh, that's right. Come on. Let's get moving. Go get Devon, and we'll have breakfast."

"But I need my library book. I left it in there."

Emma sat up, focusing as she scanned the room. Books covered the dresser, mostly adult sci-fi, except for the one pink book.

"You'll get it later," Andrew's tone was hushed but stern.

With a long stretch, Emma dragged herself out of bed and grabbed the book with the illustrated elephant on the cover. She looked down at her attire—a long, black, men's T-shirt with a spaceship on it, and a pair of flannel pajama bottoms rolled up at the ankles. She barely remembered changing out of her party clothes the night before, after Andrew convinced her to stay the night.

She shuffled to the door and opened it, as the two stunned faces turned to her. "Good morning. I think this is yours." She held the book out to Bella.

"Thank you," Bella said, as she grabbed the book. Then, in a flash, she stuck her tongue out at her dad and ran down the stairs.

"Hey, you. Watch that attitude." Andrew's loud, deep "dad"

voice couldn't scare a fly, as he called after Bella.

Emma took the opportunity to check him out. He was showered, shaved, his messy hair tamed with gel. He wore the typical IT outfit of khakis and a button down. "These kids," he muttered, turning back to her. "Sorry. It's only a little after six, but that's like noon around here. We didn't mean to wake you."

"Please. It's your house. There's no need to apologize."

"Did you sleep okay?" he asked.

She crossed her arms over the ridiculous shirt, as his eyes did a quick sweep of her. The combination of his warm gaze and the smell of bacon wafting up the stairs woke every wonderful nerve inside her body. "Perfect." She made a show of sniffing the air around them. "That smells fabulous."

"Breakfast is our favorite meal." He pointed down the hallway. "Two doors down is the bathroom. Why don't you get cleaned up and meet us downstairs?" His gaze darted back to hers. "Not that you're dirty."

She raised an eyebrow as he shifted before her.

"But, you know, women do things in the morning in the bathroom I guess. I mean, what they do I'll never know, but you'll figure it out. I think what I'm trying to say is, you look great, but, if you need…"

He huffed as she poked his arm, hoping to put him out of his misery. "Andrew. Stop. It's fine. Yes, I'd love to have a minute in the bathroom."

Clearly embarrassed, he shook his head. His blush was cute. She couldn't remember the last time she'd made a man so uncomfortable, at least outside of the board room.

"Anyhoo," he continued, rocking back on his heels, "we'll eat and then I'll drive you wherever you need to go. The roads are plowed, and the world keeps spinning so… Does that sound good?"

"I'd be grateful, but I don't want to put you out. I can call a car." Emma already dreaded the ride back in this weather. Andrew Mooney's house was so warm and bacon-y, she didn't want to leave.

"It's no problem. You may have to write me a late note for my boss though."

"Who *is* your boss?" she asked, realizing the topic of work hadn't come up at all the night before. Mostly, they'd discussed elephants, nail polish, and television shows. "I'm not exactly clear on where you sit in the company flow chart."

His laugh indicated he'd relaxed a bit. "I have three employees I supervise, so I'm sort of low-middle management. I report to Stuart, who used to report to Russell."

"Stu Borowski? Oh, no problem. I'll text him right now." She knew Stu well and would probably promote him to Russ's now-vacant position.

Andrew held up a hand. "Maybe that's not the best idea. Don't want the rumor mill to get started."

She raised her eyebrows. "Good point. You'd probably be embarrassed that I'm squatting in your house…"

"I don't mean for me, for you. They'll say you're slumming with the IT guy. It would be scandalous." He sputtered out an awkward chuckle.

With a tilt of her head, she grinned. "You've been a perfect gentleman. But whatever you want me to tell Stu, I'll respect that."

"Thanks." He ran a hand over his head, but with the gel it only made his hair stick out at weird angles. "I'm really annoying, huh? How about I go downstairs? You take your time, help yourself to what you need, and meet us down there for breakfast. Deal?"

Anticipating bacon, she nodded curtly. "Deal. And you're not annoying."

"Glad to hear that." He walked toward the staircase.

"Andrew?" she called.

He turned to face her.

"Thank you for letting me have your room last night."

He smiled a warm grin, his eyes crinkling in the corners. "You're welcome, Boss Lady."

A few hours later, after Andrew dropped her off at home and she had a much-needed shower and outfit change, Emma made her way to BI headquarters. She spent a minute to appreciate her office view overlooking Midtown Manhattan. The snow-lined streets were busy with business people weaving around the holiday influx of tourists who'd taken over the area. She hated snow, but she especially hated snow when it painted her city that dingy-gray color.

The people rushing around in business coats reminded her that she had to send an email to Stu. She opened her inbox and composed a new message, copying Andrew. Seeing his name pop up in the company mailbox made her heart race. He really did work there. She wondered for how long.

She sent a simple message to Stu, explaining that Andrew had "assisted her with business that morning" and thanking him for excusing his lateness. Then, she called Rhonda's office, opposite hers in the executive suite, and asked her to stop by when she had the chance.

Born in Trinidad, Rhonda Lewis had started working for Emma's father at the flagship Ballard store in Brooklyn the month after she arrived in New York, shortly after her sixteenth birthday. She'd worked her way up through the corporation as she pursued her business degree and eventually her MBA. Twenty years from the exact date of her hiring, Daniel Ballard asked Rhonda to be the Assistant CEO, the position she still held. Besides Emma's late father and Russ, nobody knew more about Ballard Industries than Rhonda.

Knowing that Mr. Ballard wanted Emma to learn the business, Rhonda didn't object when Emma was named CEO after his death. Instead, Rhonda had taken Emma under her wing. *Your father gave me a chance when I started out. It's only right he should do the same for his daughter. I respect that man and his wishes more than I care about which office I sit in,* she'd said. As much as Rhonda tried to teach Emma the art of people skills over the past five years, Rhonda was the expert on sensing the tone of the company's staff. The employees often approached her with issues, feeling more comfortable with her than with Emma. Rhonda also knew how to get information on employees, and Emma needed her help.

After a quick knock, Rhonda poked her head into the office. "Hey, Emma. What's up?"

She cleared her throat. Rhonda had known her since she was a child and would be able to sense the curiosity in Emma's voice if she wasn't careful. "Could you find me a personnel file on the down low?" Her cheeks warmed as she shuffled papers on her desk in an effort to appear disinterested.

"Sure. What's the name?"

Emma folded her hands on her desk, sitting up taller and meeting Rhonda's gaze. "Andrew Mooney. The guy from the Jersey branch."

Rhonda lifted her chin, squinting at Emma. "From the party? Did he give you a hard time? If HR needs to get involved—"

"Oh no, not at all," Emma interrupted. "He helped get me home, and I felt terrible that I didn't know who he was, that's all."

"That's all?" Rhonda asked, quirking a brow and studying Emma.

"Yes." *And I want to know more about him,* Emma didn't admit to Rhonda.

"I'll have it to you in an hour." Rhonda smiled and closed the door as she left.

Later, when Rhonda emailed the file on Andrew Mooney, Emma clicked on it but deleted it before reading anything. He'd been nice to her, and she wouldn't abuse her position by stalking him through his company history.

She spun in her chair and then picked up her phone. Thinking of Andrew, she made a few calls, cashed in a few favors, and spent more than a few dollars.

No, she wouldn't stalk him. She'd be direct. She had no idea how it would play out, but one thing was certain—she hadn't felt so alive at Ballard Industries in her five years.

A courier delivered the letter after work as Andrew returned home with pizza for dinner. He didn't get a chance to open it until the girls were fed, bathed, and in bed.

His jaw dropped as he read the handwritten note.

Andrew,

I can't thank you enough for helping me last night and for the hospitality your family showed me during the snow storm. I'll never forget your generosity, your bacon, or your beautiful girls' advice on life (secret girl stuff!). I came across these Heatherby *tickets and remembered how much you wanted to see it. It's late notice, I know, but I've set up a car to pick you up and bring you to the city if you are able to go. Please take a guest, maybe your father. I'd love to babysit the girls. They are welcome at my place, or I'd be happy to watch them at your place if you think they'd be more comfortable there.*

I hope you enjoy the play as much as I did. Talk soon.
Emma.

She'd signed the note and scribbled her phone number on the bottom.

The first thing he did, the first thing he always did when life threw him a curveball, was call his father.

Jeffrey hobbled into the kitchen before Andrew had a chance to put down his phone. He grumbled a greeting, then went straight for the leftover pizza, tossing a piece onto a paper plate. "What's this about a letter?"

Andrew shoved the card and the tickets toward his father. As Jeffrey scanned the card, Andrew paced the kitchen. He'd read the thank you note from Emma twice and barely recovered from the shock at the feel of the *Heatherby* tickets between his fingers. "Do you believe this? Is this even real?"

"Nice penmanship." His father held the tickets to the overhead light, as if he were an expert on counterfeiting. "They look real to me."

"Not the tickets, the...the...sentiment."

Jeffrey handed the card and its contents to Andrew and grabbed his slice of pizza. "I think it's appropriate for her to send a thank you to her employee who helped her out. You gave up your room and drove her into that horrid city in the ice and snow. She's a classy lady, with a good upbringing—"

"She's a corporate viper." He tossed the card onto the counter.

"A damn pretty one—"

"Dad! You can't say things like that. It's not the sixties."

Jeffrey scowled and pointed the tip of the pizza slice at his son. "If I think a woman is pretty, I sure as heck can say so."

Andrew rolled his eyes, brewing a cup of coffee as his father bit into the cold slice. After Jeffrey finished, he stood next to Andrew, who focused on the coffee streaming into his "World's Best Dad" mug. He reached for Andrew's shoulder. "I think maybe your...jitters...toward Emma come from a different place than you think."

"A different place?" He felt like the twins snapping at his own father like that. All he needed was to put a hand on his hip and stick out his chin. "So it's not because she doesn't care about her job? It's not because she has no clue how to run a company?"

Jeffrey growled and turned away. "You know that's not true. The woman has an MBA, and the company's doing fine. The stock has held since she took over for her father. Listen, son, it's been six years since Hayley—"

Andrew held up a hand to stop his father's words, words he didn't want to hear because they hurt his heart. "This has nothing to do with Hayley." He picked up the note and tickets and waved them at his father. "It's not like she wants to date me, Dad. She wants me to take you."

Jeffrey huffed. "So then why are you so upset?"

Andrew peeked at the envelope. He didn't know why he was upset. Maybe because he'd never have been able to score *Heatherby* tickets on his own, and all Emma Ballard had to do was bat an eyelash and they fall from the sky. Maybe because she'd assumed he'd leave his girls with her, a practical stranger, while he gallivanted around the city. Or, maybe it was because, like his father had said, she was gorgeous, and had been sweet and nice to him during her stay in his home.

Emma Ballard scared him. Not so much as his boss's, boss's, boss, but because she was likable. He didn't want to like her.

"I should have never stopped to help her yesterday. I should have left her to her own devices."

Jeffrey grunted in disapproval. "That is not how you were raised.

Don't you lose your manners because you're out of your comfort zone, young man."

Young man. His father hadn't called him that since he was a teenager. The whole situation with Emma was completely out of his comfort zone. "I'm sorry."

Jeffrey snatched the note and pulled out the tickets again, studying them. "Friday night. I'll be around to watch the girls."

Andrew furrowed his brow. "I'll call Mrs. Fletcher to watch them. You're coming with me, remember?"

His dad laughed. "Oh heck no. I hate that city, and you know I can't sit through that musical stuff. I fall asleep, and my hip gets sore." Jeffrey hated Broadway, a bone of contention between him and Andrew for years. It didn't help that he'd had hip surgery after his time in the Army, which made it difficult for him to sit for long periods without stiffening up. "I'd rather have a movie marathon with Dev and Bells."

Andrew sighed. "Well, who am I supposed to take?"

His father held up the card, tapping his thumb over Emma's signature.

"Are you insane?" He grabbed the card from his chuckling father's grasp. "She's my boss, Dad. And she doesn't want to go. She said she'd seen it already, and the card says to take you."

"Of course it does. A classy lady like Ms. Ballard wouldn't invite herself out with a man she barely knows, especially one who works for her."

"Exactly."

"But I bet if you asked her, she'd say yes."

"Well, I'm not asking." Andrew huffed again, proving to himself that he was his daughters' father. He sounded just like them. He glanced sideways at his father. "And what makes you think so?"

Jeffrey shrugged. "Just a feeling. The way she looked at you like she needed a friend. The way she poked around the house after breakfast, picking up the picture of you on the mantel, like it was the most fascinating thing ever."

"Oh please," Andrew sang, feeling his cheeks heat. He hadn't noticed any of that. Did Emma really look at the picture of him with his prize-winning tuna catch? "You make her sound like a schoolgirl with a crush. She's an ex-model, a spoiled princess turned CEO of a major corporation. She's a vi—"

"A viper," Jeffrey finished. "Yeah, right. She really seemed viper-ish and spoiled when she let Devon paint her fingernails orange last night."

Andrew ignored his father's sarcasm, taking a minute to think while he cleared the table and crushed the pizza boxes for recycling. Sure, Emma had seemed nice, sweet. But he'd heard stories about her tearing things up in the board room. Stories about how the Board constantly challenged her and tried to force her out, and how she'd never been able to move her agenda. She wasn't strong enough to fight for the company, but that didn't mean she hadn't tried. At least from what he heard through the gossip that filtered from headquarters to the Jersey branch.

Jeffrey stood next to him, leaning his bad hip against the counter. "It's a play. You don't have to marry her. Heck, you don't even have to talk to each other. It would be a common courtesy to ask the person who got the tickets if they wanted to accompany you. Just like you do when Uncle Sal gets you Yankee tickets."

Andrew scowled. Why did his father have to be so smart? He glared at Jeffrey, then sputtered out, "Fine. I'll think about it."

Out Now!

What's next on your reading list?

Champagne Book Group promises to bring to readers fiction at its finest.

Discover your next
fine read!
http://www.champagnebooks.com/

We are delighted to invite you to receive exclusive rewards. Join our Facebook group for VIP savings, bonus content, early access to new ideas we've cooked up, learn about special events for our readers, and sneak peeks at our fabulous titles.

Join now.
https://www.facebook.com/groups/ChampagneBookClub/

Made in the USA
Monee, IL
29 December 2020